ANZULLA
ACCORDING TO ISH

NEW BEGINNINGS M/M SERIES BOOK THREE, CROSSOVER TO CHILDREN OF ANZULLA

KASHEL CHAR

KASHEL CHAR

Title: Anzulla: According to ISH - Children of Anzulla Prequel and New Beginnings M/M Series Book 3

Draft2Digital Electronic ISBN: 978-1-0688085-4-8

Draft2Digital Paperback ISBN: 978-1-998713-13-4

Publisher: Koda Calmz Publishing

Editor: Reresa Fornoff, Anita Ford

 Formatted with Vellum

APPRECIATION

Firstly, a BIG thank you to my mentor, Stefan Pride. Stefan, may you be blessed like Jabez. Without you, I never would have been able to start writing.

Secondly, to my two Alpha, Beta, and ARC readers. (My all-in-one team, spoils me with their thorough editing work.) Thank you to my editor, Anita. You are awesome!

Ida, thousands of thank yous for helping me write better, for your unfailing support and motivation to keep going and figure out all the shit. Thank you for checking in with me, and asking if I'm okay.

Teresa, thank you for helping me find those small details and for making me laugh while I read your comments. You helped me tremendously and I wish you all the success in your editing career.

Lastly, to my husband and daughter.

Thank you for listening to me going on and on about Ishtar and the storyline and allowing me the time to live my dream and finally finish my first trilogy.

CONTENTS

WARNING

DEAR READER/LISTENER

PETER MAY SMELL AND LOOK DELICIOUS, BUT HE IS as tart as pomegranate juice. You will either love or hate him. Ishtar loves him, so by association, I pinched my nose and swallowed him down while I grew to love him too.

The overarching story flows in one direction—in a circle—with no beginning or ending. Readers may loop in at any point.

I ADDED a timeline at the end of the book for readers who want to figure out what the fuck had happened and when in chronological order. It contains spoilers and is hidden to avoid revealing too much.

. . .

MY STORIES EXPLORE the possibility of ancient civilizations being visited by advanced beings from Atlantis, who shared their knowledge of tools, agriculture, and architecture. They simultaneously speculate how Atlantis came into existence but disappeared from the ocean floor.

Is time travel possible in the real world? I don't know. But in my quest to write a time-traveling sci-fi fantasy novel, I researched theories surrounding time, speed of light, electromagnetism, and sound energy.

I AM NOT A SCIENTIST, but some who have studied, who are smart, who are educated, and who are true scientists say time does not exist. Others just as educated, say time is duration, an outward motion of matter called dilation, and that it is not an illusion. Therefore, time is relative motion as counted or measured by each observer's clock and space is the illusion, for it is nothing more than relative time between events as seen by each observer.

MATTER IS what we see in each of our futures, but mass is the connective tissue centered moment to moment within our past. Our consciousnesses keep up with the speed of light, which gives each of us the illusion of a static state called the present, but only with math can you make time stand still, then you are only representing a moment of time. How long was the duration before the motion that started our universe and how long will the duration go on after? How could we call or know it other than as an infinite time?

You may argue the measurement of time is just a human thing we constructed to make sense of time itself. If nothing travels faster than light, it is based on a law of physics that nothing is infinite and non-existent.

What if it is not infinite and not in a line, but a loop, or uncountable loops? No beginning and no end, *according to Ish*. Irrespective of what new physics we learn, an eternal universe is logically unpalatable. We could have never gotten to the present point if time went back infinitely, because for us to arrive at this present point, an infinite amount of time should have passed. There simply cannot be an infinite series of events. There has to be an event that caused the whole thing to get going.

ANZULLA, According to ISH, is fantastical, yet imaginable and hopefully, with a little persuasion, believable. In my imagination, time travel happens when Ish rides the magnetic lines of force, as if Earth and the universe exist inside some kind of bubble, loop, or circle. I imagine electromagnetism as a source of light while sound waves are propagated but at the speed of light. The sound waves would have to exceed the sound wave barrier which creates electric charges like sparks of lightning connected by the lines of force in space, which loops by propelling the electromagnetism, and so on.

I hope you enjoy traveling with Ish and Peter.
Love to all creatures,
Kashel Char.
Source: physicsforums.com

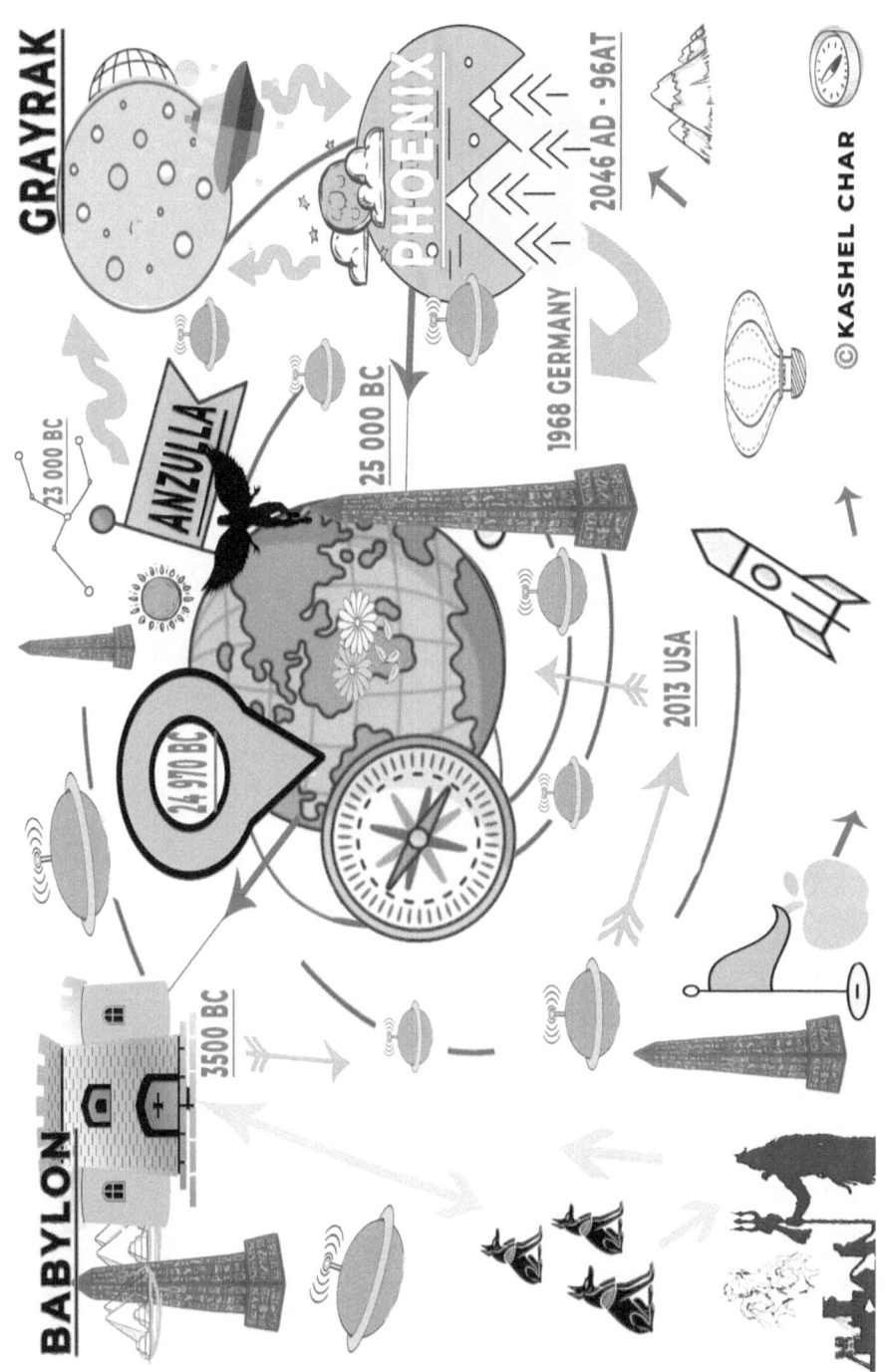

INTRODUCTION

Deep inside the secure, underwater domes of Phoenix, a group of scientists and soldiers survived three waves of global catastrophes.

The first cataclysm was the Doomsday of 2046 A.D., marking the conclusion of the final World War.

It became clear that the World Health Protected Species Society (WHPSS) had been secretly enlisted by the Disciples of Anunnaki, a clandestine global society, to engineer a genetically superior human race under the guise of environmental projects to launch genetic research initiatives across every continent, and even on the moon.

Experimentation and dabbling with DNA has led to the creation of biological weapons engineered within Environment Project Three. This laboratory was in an underground facility in South Africa. The same science project produced Eryn and his Brawl brothers.

They were artificially conceived and did not have the

same prominent DNA markers. His family was a psycho-pathic cannibalistic frog-man, and multiple toxic amphib-ian-like monsters that had escaped the underground complex, and released neurotoxin spores that spread like the Black Death from Africa to Europe, then across the globe, eradicating all humans within weeks.

Phoenix, yet another research facility called Environment Project One, sequestered two thousand male scientists and soldiers who had escaped the neurotoxic pandemic.

Thanks to the quick thinking of their leader, General Brad McCormick, who had ordered a lockdown and asked Connor, the second in command, to hastily take control of orbiting satellites to download all recorded human history for safekeeping. Thus, saving the last of mankind from the deadly and highly contagious neurotoxic infection by being confined for three years inside the glass-domed city of Phoenix.

Having used the downloaded information, they founded Phoenix University to train citizens in essential professions like engineering, architecture, medicine, and food production, all vital for maintaining their advanced city.

Central to their society was Lasitor, a sophisticated AI that not only archived downloaded history but also aided residents with everyday activities.

Meanwhile, Dr. Peter von Leutzendorf, without the knowledge of his lab partner, Dr. Mika Romanov, continued to refine the DNA splicing method initially used in the underground South African lab. This pioneering technique of fertilizing cryogenically frozen human donor eggs with the Romanov sperm and Anunnaki DNA, using artificial wombs, culminated in the birth of the first twins in Phoenix, Cian and Ivan Romanov.

Their birth marked the Year of the Twins (A.T.) when the second wave of natural catastrophes plunged the Earth into a global winter.

For two decades, Peter von Leautzendorf played God. More boys were born, but only with human DNA. He kept his connection to the Disciples of the Anunnaki and the knowledge of the Anunnaki gene sequencing a secret.

The population of Phoenix thrived and continued to prioritize scientific advancement and research. The birth of children necessitated the establishment of a school for their education and development.

Additionally, Dr. Peter von Leutzendorf's life-extension research led to the creation of the Eden Bean, also known as the Peter Pan Cap. This implantable slow-release capsule prevented aging while speeding up healing.

The Phoenician population, although all male, underwent a rapid transformation into a new human race with advanced intelligence and prolonged life spans.

Twenty-one years after Ivan and Cian were born, they were abducted by Eryn's flesh-eating Brawl brother and held captive in the abandoned underground laboratory.

Eryn, like Cian and Ivan, was a genetically manipulated specimen with extraordinary abilities. He sided with the humans and killed his amphibious family to free the abducted young men.

Cian and Ivan were enhanced human children, products of human and Anunnaki gene splicing, while Eryn's birth resulted from the splicing of amphibian, human, and Anunnaki genes.

Following the third wave of natural disasters, these three superhumans saved Phoenix by encapsulating it in a protective barrier. As the ice melted and the Earth flooded, Phoenix, cradling the highly sophisticated and advanced human race, was thriving at the bottom of the Earth's ocean.

Despite initially being drawn to each other, these three gifted hybrids broke their throuple after their first mating revealed that Ivan and Eryn were fated mates. This left Cian living a solitary life with a strong, inexplicable pull towards the moon and an obsession with spaceflight and defense.

During their first lunar reconnaissance mission, Eryn brought Ishtar, a secretive stranger who seemed to know much more than he was willing to reveal, on board their Spacecar.

All the while, on the moon, a third group of Disciple scientists called the Zelk, tasked by the WHPSS to study the merging of humans with machines, lost control of a rogue, splinter group of Zelk who built a lunar factory to create more of their kind using body parts harvested from living humans corralled in Grayrak City.

This human settlement on the moon, led by Barkor, was rescued by commandeering the Zelk warship Horizon. Cian's pull toward the moon was explained when Barkor was found to be his fated mate.

Ishtar assisted with the moon evacuation, but his

knowledge of time manipulation and his Anunnaki heritage led to him being suspected of being in league with the Disciples of Anunnaki. He was taken into custody for interrogation by the leadership of Phoenix.

Under the new group of lunar refugee residents, the long-awaited female residents had arrived and moved in.

The changes to Earth's history, and many secrets like those of the Disciples, the existence of their tablets, and a special apple, describing the techniques and mathematical calculations of Anunnaki gene splicing, brought on the Phoenician inquisition of Ishtar.

This is Ishtar's story.

CHAPTER I
GU, LEADER OF
THE SAN PEOPLE

MY NAME IS GU, THE SAN ARE MY PEOPLE.

United we guard, the sacred mountain deep in the jungle.

Engraved in limestone,
a story of two Gods.
Uncountable sun turns, never wanting a throne.

DESCENDING FROM SKIES, the Gods blessed generations.

Many moon and sun turns later,
my father and elders,
gave the Blue Demon God,
things that don't matter.

ISHTAR, a sad and solitary One, stories passed from father to son.

Shaping our beliefs and our way of life, seeking a mate and not a wife.

Legends of the Gods became real.

No more stories, but bodies we see and feel.

Lonely and seeking, He came down from his chair,

the one in the sky, to us down here.

Desperately seeking the arms of his lover,

not my sister or my mother.

BUT, Gods need company from others.

Heavy drinking, lots of food, and blood from my brothers.

Afterward, we pretended to search,

"Here He is," and "There He is, Demon God."

Lots of laughs and lots of fun,

never helping Him find his special one.

UNTIL HE'D GOTTEN tired and went back home.

One day I asked myself if we are a blessed people,

if we were the friends of the Demon God of the mountain,

why couldn't anyone see how wrong it was?

To pretend, while He became more than just a friend.

I QUESTIONED the rituals of our ancestors.

Ceremony, of my father's fathers.

Pretending, disappointing,

not only Him, but ourselves.
So very depressing.
So, I took Him to my furs.
My mighty cock, blood, and seed,
is what He preferred.
Not a young warrior of eighteen sun turns,
but a mate, his Kuku is what He deserves.

OUR DEMON GOD *was very-very miserable.*
I went to the top of the mountain.
to plead his case to the Gods in the stars.

BULGING *my fists around my obsidian weapons, I yelled,*
"Hey, you lazy, self-righteous, Old Ones.
Help your Baby Gods, and children, down here below the
mountain.
Send us Ishtar's lover. Bring us His mate, his Kuku!"
The Ancient Ones opened the skies, then sent the snake
to bring us
the Birdman God with the white hair, to trick us.

SOMETIMES GODS SPOKE, *but most of the time they*
ignored us.
We waited for Ishtar, but he'd forgotten us.
Many sun turns later, strange things started to happen.
I guess it's because the sun turns for Gods and not for us
under the mountain.

ANZULLA

Kuku and San bickered like children.
Always getting into trouble and never helping.
That was to be expected,
Baby Gods sit in the sky and never lift a finger.

I WENT BACK to the top of the mountain
to have another word with the Gods in the stars.
"Hey, you lazy, stupid, Old Ones.
You did half a job! You sent one, but not the other!
I demand you make this right. It's unfair!
Send down the Blue Demon God,
so He can save us from his Kuku, down here."

THE FLAMES of the village firepit were still burning,
when the snake in the sky was seen returning.

CHAPTER 2
I SLAYED MY FATHER

"*Good day, Ishtar.*

Did you know timekeeping devices date back to when ancient civilizations first observed astronomical bodies as they moved across the sky? Timekeeping has evolved from liquid-filled water clocks to mechanical clocks and pendulums. Sundials and water clocks were first used thousands of years ago in ancient Egypt, later by the Babylonians, then the Greeks, and then the Chinese.

Did you also know that time is ticking, and as much as I would like to say, move at your own pace and take as much time as you need, the reality is there is no bloody time for your needs or desires.

Good luck!"

ISHTAR

2000 B.C.
Rome

SWEAT DROPS BEADED on my forehead, rolling down my temples, and dripping from the tip of my nose. I gazed down at Platonius, hissing through my teeth. "Yesss, suck it harder!" A jolt of pleasure rushed through me to tighten around my balls—I was greedy, I wanted precise timing, his finger, that extra trigger, to blow harder, to unload.

"Gods yes. Keep your eyes open," I grunted my order. "I want you to see how I'm enjoying fucking your skilled, pretty mouth." I shuddered and exhaled, staving off my orgasm. I wasn't ready to come, not yet. He was sliding a hand up between my legs, and I urged him to plunge his finger faster and deeper inside my hole. My best orgasms are those with something up my ass. "Yes, push it in, I'm about to shoot." I clenched my jaw. My unused fangs itched for a bite, but this was a quick goodbye and I'm not staying another night.

Widening my stance, I gave him better access, while I balanced on my elbows against the cold wall. He sat on his heels, one hand around the base of my pulsating organ, while the other... "Yes, oh my dear Fates, work it in— work it harder—work it faster."

Blazing scarabs, that stunning pale Roman face, my dark blue cock pistoned—machined—into it. Sending his wild red curly hair flopping all over the place. Obediently, he kept his gaze on me. Staring up at me with dark enthralled eyes. His lips stretched papyrus thin around my wide girth.

"Hmmm-hmmm, hmmm," he hummed around my cock. I'm not fucking pulling out to have a conversation, so I scanned his thoughts, *like this, is this what you want?*

"Hmmm, yes, dammit!"

The corners of his eyes stretched into pleased smile lines. Tears spilled from them and down his rosy cheeks, mixing with spit and snot and his sadness.

I know you will miss me, I will miss you too, but to make it easier for you, I will erase myself from your memory.

"Yes, keep doing that, deeper, push deeper. Ah, yes. Yes, that's the spot. Oh, fuck, that feels—so good!" I fisted his red curls with one hand as I worked my cock down his throat. Closing my eyes I exhaled a thunderous cry of ecstasy as my whole body snapped straight. "Fuck, yes, here it comes-s-s-s!" Jolting and balancing, my seed projectiled into his muzzling throat. My body buzzed as I repeatedly discharged, violently. Thrusting, every last drop into his stomach—until, until, until, until all pleasurable shocks vanished.

I opened my eyes—trembling, sweating, and sated. He'd swallowed every drop I gave him, like always. "The Fates blessed you with a damn magnificent mouth and mind, Platonius," I said and stooped down to kiss him.

"You taste sweet. The best I've ever tasted and I'm happy to have it all inside me, as a farewell gift. It should satisfy my hunger until you visit me again," he said, wiping his mouth with the back of his hand.

Time to say farewells. "Thank you," I said and pulled

him back up to his feet. I pointed to the bronze tablet he had so carefully stamped for me. "For your exquisite mouth and your brilliance. It's timeless—a gift that never rusts. My father will like it, he will listen to us."

"Again, it's my honor, and you're welcome. Anything to help you," Platonius replied while aiding me by pulling up my trousers and tucking my limp sensitive cock back into its place. He exuded mixed emotions of love, of regret, and of composed anger. "Have a safe trip. Remember, I love you. I love you even more for trusting me with your secrets." He waited...

Tears brimmed, unspilled. He gulped, broke his stare, and repositioned himself.

My eyes flicked up and down and left and right.

Where to look, where to look, where the fuck should I look? I smiled and sighed. Ignoring the outline of his hardness visible against his tunic, and his eyes. I had fucked him good earlier today, I shouldn't feel guilty for leaving him hard and wanting.

He knew I was fond of him. I've never said *I love you*. Not to him or anyone.

I will say it when I recognize and feel it.

I thumbed the lever up. The door swished open. Announcing the unspoken okay-that-was-fun, and see-you-never-again.

"One last hug?" he asked, hugging me anyway.

"May the Fates bless you, Platonius." He was considerably shorter, so I just kissed his messy scrunched hair and patted his back.

"Yes, and you. May Athena grant you a hero's

courage." Platonius spun around, his eyes red and leaking, face flushed, and firing anger and disappointment at me. I delved into his mind, erasing all memories of me. I always cloaked my true appearance to humans. But I wanted him to forget me, to live his life and never miss me.

As soon as he stepped off the third and final step, I flicked the lever down, activating the stairs to retract and the door to slide close.

"Perfect." Hastily, I gave a couple of long strides across the small cargo area to the cockpit with two seats. I rubbed my Anubis's head where she was sleeping in the passenger chair. I started up the ship's navigator. "Lasitor, time to go home. Please jump before Platonius snaps out of his trance and sees us."

"Where and when shall we land?" my onboard guide asked, ever friendly and helpful as the ship started up and the seat vibrated beneath me.

"Two days after we left. My time. Babylon, 3500 B.C. I promised Titus to meet up with them before they reached the valley outside the city's borders. And good news, we transcribed your mathematical calculations." I lifted the tablet as if Lasitor had eyes and showed him the copper plate wrapped in purple silk.

"Those will ensure your bloodline lives on."

"Yes, if I present this to Apsu, surely he will reconsider and meet our demands."

"Ishtar, he will refuse. He won't understand the calculations," Lasitor added in a low tone.

"I hope not. Now hurry, before Platonius sees us. Please park us on the palace grounds."

. . .

3500 B.C.
Babylon
Earth

Thwop! I popped my constricting golden helmet off and threw the heavy thing aside. It *clunked* behind me as I leaped and soared over the flames. My arms up, a sword in each hand, I landed in a crouch, ready to block and strike. I inhaled, I breathed, I focused, and I sighed—shaking and loosening my freed braids.

"The Fates blessed us. We've got him cornered now," Titus shrilled from across the blazing flames and went into a coughing fit. He was smothering himself with that wet cloth wrapped around his head and *not* breathing easier. It looked and sounded like a matter of minutes before they succumbed to the smoke and flames and exhaustion. Titus and the remaining three soldiers are human, and I am not. Only four men and I are still alive—trapping and hunting.

We had trapped and were now hunting my father, King Apsu, the patriarch of the Anunnaki—an animal—evil and forgotten by the Fates. Killer of thousands. From suckling babies to soldiers.

The noisy humans were becoming a distraction. For days, we've battled by attacking and retreating.

Over and over and over.

We've been weakening him, and now he's caged in the throne room. All of us are at our last—wounded, and the Fates willing, winning.

"Get out of here. Humans retreat!" I ordered Titus, not

taking my eyes off the shadow moving behind the wall of flames.

"No, I'm not leaving you!"

"I need silence."

"We fight to the end with you."

"Titus, it is time. Take the men and leave us! Do as I ask. Guard the children. Make sure my nieces and nephews find safety. Go now." I prayed Titus, my Igigi, and Generalissimo, the great overseer of my fallen army, would flee unharmed with the children to the northern mountains, across the seas to the land where, if I die today, my father won't find them. I'd given the gift of longer life to Titus by sharing a few drops of my blood with him. He is stronger and faster than the average human and will live hundreds of years longer. He walks in daylight, and he doesn't need blood like Anunnaki to survive. "This is my fight now. Go!"

"Are you sure, my lord?" Titus dragged his sword behind him and heaved air into his lungs. He was near collapsing. They all were. "Yes, thank you. Now go!" I gave a slight nod as I lifted my swords, ready to continue the hunt. "Leave!" My voice was stern, loaded with compulsion and command.

They obeyed. *Doob-doop-doop-doop-tip-tip-tip-tip*, their clattering feet disappeared behind me. "May the Fates shield you!" Titus's voice faded.

I couldn't afford to take notice and lose sight of the shadow beyond the black smoke. My father was impossibly fast.

I squinted through the blinding smoke. Nausea curled

in my belly as the putrid stench of burning bodies bittered my dry tongue. I licked my cracked, bleeding lips and swallowed the salty mixture of blood and sweat down my scorched throat. My swords were heavy, but steady in my hands. I gave a determined snarl as I cat-footed ahead. A warning that I was close and coming for him.

I was not unafraid, but I was ready to end him.

The plan was to bribe Apsu to abdicate, but he was already on a rampage when I arrived. Already busy destroying the palace and moving to wipe out Babylon.

Wiping away all life.

Genociding. Massacring. Slaughtering.

Playing God as he did in Anzulla.

I am fighting, not only to save myself but also to free my people from the chains that have bound them by sweat and blood to this monster, this thing of evil.

With every blow of his sword, I struck back with pure disdain and loathing. His dark hunger for power made him treat me like worthless spawn—a child not even worthy of being sacrificed.

Soundlessly, a flash of light and shadow flew right at me. *Thwack!*

I stepped back—my movements, fluid and hard as water.

I lifted my arms again. And with my left sword blocking, I sliced off his left kneecap with my right hand. Various shades of red arced up between us, and I reveled in my successful counterattack. I savagely hacked away at his vulnerable areas, determined to chop off every bit by calculated bit until he was nothing but a heap of bones, cartilage, and stumps. His regenerative abilities had slowed, and his strength was wavering. I was hyper-focused and brutally determined to end him.

His blood dripped from my face and blades. I smiled, knowing I was giving back all the pain I had gotten from him all my life. He growled at me—foul, flagitious, and furious.

Profound hatred flamed and kept me alert. I veered back, fought back, pushed back, and attacked using my uniquely fused fighting style. A style I had crafted from techniques I had learned from the best warriors, stretching from Egypt to Japan. The fluid movements of the Samurai mixed with the powerful strikes of Tahtib created a deadly combination. I accurately jabbed and blocked. My body was fatigued, but mentally I soared, as this shit was thera-peutic. I was resolving the internal struggles I had carried within me for hundreds of years. Every slice of his skin, every flying kneecap, chopped elbow, or missing hand, mirrored every single painful wound on my body and heart. Every scar he had given me—I carved out of him.

His eyes flashed a dull green sheen. A visible sign he was weakening. He knew I saw it when I saw a flash of something I had never seen before in his eyes. Fear.

He stumbled forward and clumsily rammed his sword to impale me. I blocked him. He attempted to hack my right leg, and I countered. My size and reach allowed only the sword tip to penetrate his side, below the ribcage. He grunted and pulled back. Doubt in himself grew evident in his eyes, and I anticipated his next move. With his arms raised, he swung his sword wide and ill-coordinated to behead me. With a quick move, I disarmed him by flipping his sword out of his hand. It clattered to the ground. He gasped and stepped away, saying nothing. Grappling for a piece of roof beam, he threw it at me. I ducked and lunged forward to drive my blades deep into his lower right chest. Cracking and snapping, I hit a rib bone. Egyptians' swords were meant for chopping, not thrusting. I turned my blade hard and jerked it out. Blood gushed out of him. He stood heaving breaths, shoulders hunched over. The puncture to his lower lung would leave him temporarily unguarded and breathless. I stepped forward to run my sword through his guts. But he straightened, hopped to the side, and laughed at me.

Was he toying with me? Was I underestimating him again? Did I send the men away too fast?

"To hell with you!" I yelled after him as he sprang into the air, executing a backward tumble-turn before disappearing behind a gigantic sculpture of my dead mother, currently engulfed in flames. My jaw clamped. I sniffed the air and snarled through my long incisors. A tsunami of rage drove me to end his catastrophic and destructive reign.

To kill a monster, I had to be the better monster. I sucked in hot air and blinked to ease the burning sensation.

Around me, Babylon was burning.

My brothers cowered, believing it was impossible to defeat him. One by one, they fell at his feet as he emasculated them. Not a single one of them had dared to stand up against him. And now, they were all dead, victims of their stupidity and cowardice.

"I'm coming for you, Father!" I shouted. I refuse to let this cycle continue. I'm going to wipe him from history. There will be no more cruel repetitions. It ends here, today, with me.

This is my birthplace. My timeline. I love it as much as I love and belong to these humans.

Smoldering pieces of palace walls crumbled into the ashes, reminding me we were inside a collapsing throne room. I ducked just in time as the overhead roof beams cracked and the light fixtures plunged around me. I jumped, avoiding burning roof tiles as they tumbled to the ground. Glass shards and jewels that once draped from chandeliers of candles cracked beneath my feet. I checked to see if anything else was coming at me from the growing, gaping hole in what once was a decorative high ceiling. Orange-red flames were dying as thick streaks of rain cut through the smoky night sky, blessedly dousing the surrounding fires.

I crouched, then stepped light-footed on the outer edges of my feet to maneuver without sound through the sludge.

I sought revenge for the injustices he had done to my siblings and my people.

Only my death, or his headless corpse, will make me stop fighting today.

My shredded pants were now a knee-length wrap-around that hung and constricted my hips like a woman's wet leather skirt. My limbs ached, and my arms and shoulders were numb. My body armor grew heavier as it soaked up the rain, sweat, and blood. I appreciated the rain that had just started, but I had to conserve my strength. I released the clamps on my shoulders, freeing myself from the burden of wet leather and pure gold inlays. It fell with a dull thud into the smoldering coals and the burning roof beams.

Beneath my boots, blood painted the blackened tiles with steamy dark red trails behind me. The once glittering marble would never shine again.

I slithered forward, the vision of his severed head my motivation.

My slashed knuckles and open gashes stung and bled rivulets of blood, no longer healing. I ignored the pain, flames, and suffocating smoke, clenching the swords in my fists tighter.

"You killed your mother...both of you failed me! She couldn't keep her mouth closed, always nagging me. 'Feed me, feed me, feed me. I love you, Apsu. Feed me.' You can't do the one job I gave you. Find us a new home. If you are my son, as your mother promised me, I am ashamed of you! Even with my blood running in your veins, you are useless. To me and your people. You filthy man lover!" He baited me in the Anunnaki tongue. I'd encased my heart in thick armor a long time ago. I wasn't reacting to those words anymore.

"You thought I was the weakest of my brothers," I shouted back at him. "Too young, too dumb, too soft, too kind, too slow, and too powerless to be your son. It doesn't matter how many wars I win or what gifts I bring. All you want is more offspring to suck them dry, to harvest their power for yourself. I bet you are regretting it now. You should have drained me of my power when you had the chance. I am not so weak now, am I, father? Apsu, bringer of pestilence and famine?" I said, and like a lion, I growled. "Your time has ended! You chose to fight. Your reign is an atrocity. You take, drain, and rape. I will be the last one standing. The only one you couldn't kill!"

I halted. Listening, feeling, sensing, and tasting the air. Every nerve in my body honed in as I slowly swept my gaze from side to side. Determination thumped through me—I refuse to let him live another day. If I died taking him with me, so be it. He had taken everything from me, slaughtering everyone I held dear without mercy.

There. His horns. He was still hiding behind the statue.

Our eyes met. His uncertain gaze betrayed his once terrifying presence. His dark Anunnaki features, the vile darkness that consumed him, was fading. I caught a flicker of realization—I was the hunter, the predator, the triumphant. The feeling pushed me to keep going and outsmart him.

Glass smashed. The sound of crushing shards beneath running feet drew my attention further to the opposite end of the hall. He snuck behind the toppled-over golden thrones of the king and queens of Babylon, Xerxes and my twin sisters, Ki and An. My heart constricted and pumped outrage. The once grand symbols of a powerful reign lay destroyed, and they are now dead. Blackened, melted, and misshapen.

I slowed my breathing and listened. He was moving again.

"Humans are useless. They are dumb, dirty animals.

You should know, you live with them," he snickered as if he thought he was upsetting me. "I admit it was a mistake to come here, to this place. We should go home to Anzulla and start over. I needed you. Your family needed you. Your failure to report back caused the death of us all. You ran away from your obligations to us. I will offer leniency one more time if you promise to take me to the timeline where I belong!"

Yeah, unsated, and all-powerful, I thought.

"This time, you can help me make it work!" he shouted. The evil in his voice cut through my bones and shredded my heart. Just a few days ago, I still believed there was a chance. That there was goodness deep down inside him. I can't believe I sought his favor and his approval.

But today, I ignored the hurtful, manipulative words and zoned in on the direction from which they came.

Ice-cold tremors inside my core radiated outward and made me shiver from head to toe. That draining feeling, that sucking, pulsating dark emotion was back. "That sneaky bastard," I whispered through pursed lips. *I should disperse him.* He is inside me, inside my mind. *I hate him.* Like a leech, he slurped at my energy. My unrelenting psyche throbbed like an old toothache, every heartbeat a heartache.

I stilled my mind and turned my focus inward, searching for that thing, that consuming, filthy thing. I wanted it out of me. I focused on expelling the unwanted connection. I imagined ripping it out. The finality of it is like an axe splitting a hair—a painful whine, much like an animal being kicked, resounded through the crackling flames. A smirk of triumph curled on my lips as I confirmed his location. My hands tightened into a death grip on my swords, my muscles primed, ready to pounce. I moved closer, preparing to strike with deadly precision.

"You set the precedent. It's kill or be killed. Your rule is discord in itself, you are the embarrassment. You wanted to be a God, a giver of life, and yet you steal the life sources of those you want to follow you. You're a fool, and you've doomed yourself. Who will pray to you if you kill them all? You caused your demise with your power-hungry corruption. Like a snake eating its tail. Big mistake," I taunted. My fingers twitched with anticipation as I prepared to deliver the final blow and end his shameful existence.

I baited him while moving back two steps behind the veil of time.

I counted twenty heartbeats.

The skies above brightened as the stars pulsed and flickered. Like lightning sparks, they illuminated the charred grounds beyond the palace.

A sign that I was freezing time.

I ran the sharp tips of my swords along the shattered marble, creating a cacophony of scraping sounds and fiery sparks that would surely distract him when I unfroze time. Then, stalking closer, I stood right in front of him, an arm's length away.

Positioning myself for the last strike, from the perfect killing position, I crossed my arms while raising my swords. Hyper-focused on killing him and setting the scales of right and wrong back into balance.

Standing ready to unleash my deadly vengeance, I waited.

I kept time by the beating of my heart. Everything around me moved as I unfroze time. The sound and sparks of my swords dragging broke the silence. His toes moved underneath the crystal and gold bead curtains, taking my bait.

I lifted the tip of my boot and held it in place over pieces of broken glass. Ready to slice and decapitate him with my sickle-shaped swords. I inhaled slowly and soundlessly, then willed and visualized the sight of his skull flying.

I crushed the glass under my boot.

His black, burned, shriveled toes moved as he planted them deeper into the ash. I waited. His foot lifted, accompanied by the start of a deafening, vicious battle cry. He crashed through the curtain. Running straight into my guillotine of blades. Dark brown blood spurted like a red fountain into the air as his head flipped up, tumbling with eyelids peeled wide open. I cut his cries short with finality as the air stopped flowing over his vocal cords. His body slammed into me, knocking me over with an indescribable force. My swords went flying to the sides as the momentum carried me. The raw destructive energy threw me back. The explosion of unleashed power spilling out of him flashed a blinding white light. It propelled and shot me further back with a second shock wave. The mystical forces escaped into the universe as it blasted and pulsated a third time. I was airborne, tumbling back ass up, my head hitting a hard surface. My vision blackened for a few seconds. I shook my head, bringing myself back from the clutches of unconsciousness.

"Fillet me sideways with a Katana!"

I lurched upright, gasping for air. Around me, crackles of an electric, otherworldly magic made the hairs on my arms stand on end. A last burst popped with a deafening lightning strike next to me. I sprang to my feet, ready to defend myself.

An empty sigh of silence drifted through the smoke. I was alive. Alive and alone. The haze of battle cleared. The demon king who terrorized men was slain.

One of my eyes was swollen and useless, and pain radiated through my skull like a Mongol gong being hammered. Using my forearm, I wiped at my eyes to clear the hazy, red, blurry vision. I swayed and swept my gaze over the scorched battleground. The soles of my boots were hot and melting, puffing up clouds of ash as I stomped and stumbled. I brushed my blood-soaked braids aside to see better. They clung to my neck, matted and heavy, as I swiveled my body to survey the devastation. I exhaled and held my breath, confirming and listening for any sign of life around me.

Pitter-patter, pitter-patter.

Drops of blood and rain plopped around my feet, dousing the smoldering orange coals. I should tend to my wounds—later, after I had confirmed that he was dead.

Like a half-slaughtered ox, I heaved and struggled to

get air into my lungs. "Hmmm," I grunted, pissed off at myself for needing to breathe.

Stormy winds and icy raindrops blasted through shattered window openings, lashing my skin and open wounds like needles. Instead of triumphant relief, utter loneliness washed over me just as my will to fight washed away with the rain. My arms were weak, my legs heavy. Swinging around from side to side through the rubble, the stench of burning flesh sickened me. I felt lost and hopeless, seeing only death through my one working eye.

Thick beads of sweat and blood continued to drip into my eyes and run down my face as I looked through the shattered windows to far below, beyond the ruined city, the only constant that remained was the endless crashing of waves against the cliffs below. My uncoordinated attempts to wipe it away were futile. I could no longer contain the despair that had been building inside me, it broke through the walls I'd built to keep it all inside.

It started with one drop, and then many, and then it all exploded, releasing eons of sadness as a rushing waterfall of tears. I fell to my knees, with my arms hanging at my sides, sobbing. I was all broken.

I did not know how much time passed as I grieved. A gentle voice flickered within me like a small flame, illuminating the darkness and breaking through my hopelessness and despair.

"Get up," it urged me.

Exhausted, I obeyed and found the will to live a little longer. I pushed myself up, nearly face-planting as I limped.

"Where is it? Where is your head?" I wanted confirmation that he was dead, done, and gone. I kicked through the sludge until a dull thud and fine *cling-clang* sound revealed the head. I scooped up the golden necklace, using the tip of my sword and swinging it like a pendulum. It called to me. *Tick-tick-tick-tick.*

I bowed to the head on the ground. "Thank you, now it's mine," I said, with a smile that was anything but genuine. I never knew the whole history behind him wearing the pendant. I assumed it was because he was the King of the Anunnaki. And now that I have slain him, it is mine—what does that make me?

I didn't want to know, and I didn't care.

I wouldn't—couldn't stay here. Leaving this place and never looking back was my only option. As soon as Titus caught up with Xerxes and his children, word of Apsu's death would reach them. They would then return, hoping I was going to take Apsu's place.

But the throne belongs to Xerxes. It's his rightful place.

It would be best for them to start fresh without me. *It's time for me to disappear and move on to give the rightful king a chance to rebuild their lives without my interference.*

One last time, I looked at Apsu's ugly face. Disdain crawled again in my belly and wrapped its tendrils around my spine, up into my neck. His large, pointy ears and goat-like horns bloody irked me.

"Xerxes will destroy all those terrifying statues of you. No one will remember you. You will be forgotten. It will be as if you never existed." My words rasped out with difficulty, made gruff by smoke and emotion. I turned, estimating the direction and distance his torso could have flown. "Tisk-tisk, you made a grand exit, didn't you?" With shoulders shaking, I chuckled cynically. "That *oh-shit-look* suits you."

Then, with my arms spread wide, I arched my back and let out a victorious howl that echoed into the sky, and across the land—a wail of triumph. "Fuuuuck you!"

CHAPTER 3
THE OBELISK

"GOOD DAY, IT'S NOW SIX A.M.—SOMEWHERE.

Did you know the speed of electromagnetic waves always equals the speed of light? Scientists once said that nothing travels faster than the speed of light and that the speed reduces when it is reflected in a mirror.

Did you also know it's because the Anunnaki gold was first discovered in the Middle East about 6000 B.C. that, according to Lasitor's new law, by replacing the silver with gold on the backside of my warp drive mirrors, the blues are being absorbed and the remaining colors are reflected? When the reflected stream of light crosses and joins an additional stream of light, the speed increases inside the hyper-condenser.

In other words, time travel is one hundred percent possible, because it pushes the machine beyond into nothingness. The trick is to reverse right out of there to the precise time intended by the driver, because the blue waves force the condenser to slow the reflected light—like a rubber band stretching to maximum and rebounding back to its original state.

To learn how to navigate properly, please, read the manual.

Safe travels."

ISHTAR
3500 B.C.
Babylon

I STUMBLED FORWARD, dragging myself, my pain, my exhaustion, and my swords.

I hobbled. Down and down and further down the winding path. Hissing and sucking air through my pursed lips. The steam rising from the healing waters ahead called out to me, a serene contrast amidst the chaos surrounding it.

Two more steps. I dropped my swords and ripped off my tattered clothes. My naked body *sloshed* into the dark waters, battered and gushing blood. My skin felt like a thousand needles were knitting it back together. I waded deeper. *Brrrr*, goosebumps covered my vibrating body as the heat enveloped me. Lips and jaw quivering, I cupped my hands and drank in the warm, magical fluid to quench my thirst before fully submerging. I lay back, feeling my muscles relaxing and repairing themselves. Each breath was a struggle, but I persevered, clinging onto that small ember of determination that drove me to keep going, to survive, and to fill my lungs again. My reasons for living were hazy, but I held onto them, nonetheless.

I stretched out my limbs and let myself float on the surface of the water, weightless like a piece of driftwood. The stars above twinkled as I felt a sense of peace washing over me, drowning out Babylon's destruction. Slowly, my breathing and heartbeat calmed, and I found a new sense of contentment in the moment. But with that contentment came a feeling of guilt and regret. I hadn't listened. I thought...I thought wrong. My naivety had caused the deaths of An and Ki. If I had only calculated my return time a few hours earlier, maybe they would still be alive.

If I attempted to travel back in time to warn them—no, I can't risk that—I might lose the battle if I had to fight him a second time.

Even after all I'd been through, all I'd lost, I still felt responsible for saving their mate, the rightful king of Babylon, and his children. That thought kindled a spark of hope within me. I knew they still had a future in Babylon. Titus would help Xerxes appoint his successor until his eldest son was ready. Xerxes needed Titus now, having survived the loss of both his life-mates.

Through chattering teeth, I whispered, "I'm sorry." A useless, weak apology to my deceased family. My eyes burned with tears. I allowed myself to wail.

Depleted in body and mind, but not hope, I closed my eyes. The swirling galaxies of lights faded away, and the soothing waters enveloped me, washing away my pain. When some of my strength returned, I loosened my braids and washed myself thoroughly. Then, I took a deep breath and gathered the willpower to leave before falling asleep in the water. Eventually, I made it back to the stairs of the pool, dragged myself up and out, tumbling onto the scorched grass with a heavy thud that knocked the wind out of me. At last, I gave up and surrendered to unconsciousness, ending the struggle to stay upright and awake.

MY EYES SNAPPED OPEN, my heart racing as I bolted upright. The images from my nightmare still lingered, slowly fading as the reality of my surroundings seeped in. The world was covered in a thin layer of ash, and for a second, I thought that it had snowed overnight. Except it wasn't cold or snowing—it was the aftermath of my father's rampage. Apsu had been an evil thing, hell-bent on destroying everything in sight.

The once vibrant palace grounds and gardens now resembled a desolate wasteland. All around were burned bodies, dismembered bodies—bodies of soldiers strewn about like discarded carcasses. I shuddered at the thought of the thousands of soldiers who fought and sacrificed themselves for our cause. For me.

Desperate to escape the guilt, chaos, and devastation, I hastily shoved my feet back into my melted boots, leaving my tattered clothes where they lay. I cringed at my golden Khopesh blades were stained with the blood of my enemy, the blood of my father. I washed them, washed the blood, the fury, and the anger away. I'd crafted them with my own hands, and they'd been a constant companion since my first battle, fighting at the side of the legendary king of the Egyptian Empire, Hor-Aha.

Bare except for the small tick-tick talisman around my neck, I stumbled back to my ship, where I had left it after visiting my dear friend and Greek scholar Platonius.

Memories of discovering the once beautiful city in turmoil assailed me. I relived the dread that filled me when I saw smoke rising in the distance—the palace burning. I had pushed open the door to the royal harem and was hit with the overwhelming stench of death and decay. My sisters. Their bodies were torn apart and scattered across the floor like trash amidst the flames. The smell of their blackened, decaying flesh and spilled blood was burned forever into my nostrils—an image and odor that would surely haunt me till the day I died.

The anger. The shock. It ignited the determination to avenge their deaths.

After countless years of meticulous planning, strategizing, and preparation, I almost failed, I thought. The bribe gift—no, it was as useless as their deaths.

Titus's forces were ready and mobilized beyond the city gates. The war I couldn't put off had arrived far sooner than expected. I should never have gone to visit Platonius. I barely got Xerxes and the children to safety.

My sisters were haunted by the memories of what our father did to Anzulla. They'd warned me about his descent into madness, but I hadn't acted quickly enough. If Titus and his army hadn't been ready, I would be dead.

Years ago, before I had shared my seed and blood with Titus, I had confided in him, trusting him with the warning of my sisters. At a young age, he possessed a sharp intellect and quick wit. Instead of reacting with wild frenzy, he remained calm and steadfast, refusing to charge into battle like a bloodthirsty berserker. He convinced me that we couldn't win this war with brute force alone. We needed strategy, cunning, and skill. Together, we found the most gifted, experienced, and intelligent humans to learn from, to train, and to help us become the most skilled sword-fighting warriors to battle my father. We began rigorous training under their expert guidance. As a master of war, Titus understood that our success hinged on more than strength and power. It required precision, tact, and strategic planning. In hindsight, I was grateful for his prudence and prowess. It was our diligent preparation and training that enabled us to ultimately defeat my father in combat and end his tyrannical reign. Not just in Babylon, but everywhere and for all.

It was now almost daybreak.

A light breeze was blowing the feather-light white ashes as my malformed boots hit the cobblestoned footpath, obscuring it and reminding me I had survived.

My thick, long cock swung from side to side as I climbed the steep stairs carved into the rock leading to the palace docking station. A glimmer of movement, of hope, caught my eye—humans and animals were scurrying about in what once had been a bustling city. My stomach twitched, reminding me I was hungry. I bristled at the thought of leaving without feeding. The healing waters I drank were sufficient to heal me, but my stomach was empty. I forced myself to turn and leave in search of a better future. To admit to Lasitor that he was right about Apsu and that my gift was never given. At least Apsu was dead.

When I reached the top, the sight that greeted me gutted me—the charred remains of my beloved Anubis. "No!" I roared. My fists bulged with renewed rage. I savagely kicked at the ground. Tears spilled from my eyes. My loyal Anubis, my faithful protector, was now reduced to nothing but a blackened pile of flesh and bone.

"Fates, damn it all!" I exclaimed, my cry a mix of overwhelming anger and grief. I stumbled forward, assessing my ship and the vacant platform. My golden, oval-shaped ship appeared undamaged. The top part still spun in one direction, while the bottom part spun in the opposite direction. In the middle, the open door waited with the extended three steps.

She, my Anubis, was outside. She'd died at the foot of my ship. Someone had tried to enter it, to steal or damage it. She'd guarded it. My swords *clanked* on the ground. I fell to my knees, with my arms hanging loosely at my sides. Confused objections bubbled out of my mouth as tears streamed down my cheeks. My friend had been loyal to the end. I loved her, and with her by my side, I felt loved. *I wish I had killed my father slowly.*

How many tears do I have left inside me?

With blurred vision, I turned away from my beloved Anubis and looked up at the intricate carvings on the ancient Anunnaki obelisk. Silently, it stood in the middle of the platform. Pointing towards the heavens, towards the Fates that ignore us.

As usual, they offered no answers. "Why did they have to die?" I yelled, my voice thundering into the distance. "You gave me the power to defeat him, but what is the purpose behind it all? I cannot make sense of this!" My body trembled with the frustrated confusion swirling inside me.

No one answered. Only the early morning birds' song urged me to hurry. The sun was rising.

My heart thumped against my ribcage like a war drum. I entered my ship, hastily put on some clothes, and threw my old, half-melted shoes out the door. I grabbed a tool that resembled a shovel and gathered what was left of my Anubis before bringing her to a special place near the sacred springs in my sister's garden.

"You never enjoyed getting off my ship, and even less so when I came home," I reprimanded her as if she could hear me. "Why didn't you wait on board like you always do? Why did you get out?"

After digging a deep enough hole, I gently placed her inside and covered her remains with soil. As I gazed at the mound of earth in front of me, I took a deep breath and let out a heavy sigh with bitterness in my heart.

I searched for something that could serve as a makeshift headstone. After finding a suitable marker, I carefully carved out the words: "Here lies Anubis, friend of Ishtar. In another life, may we journey together once again." After washing up, I hurried back to my ship before the blazing sun could scorch me.

"Lasitor!" I turned to my onboard electronic guide, desperation gripping my voice. "Do you think Anzulla could still hold survivors? Maybe a few Anunnaki escaped the destruction and created new lives there." The sight of humans earlier had sparked an idea in my mind. "Damn it!" I slammed my fist on the dashboard, flipping switches and shaking my head in annoyance. If anything had happened to my ship, it would have crushed me. "Come on," I pleaded. "Don't tell me the fire melted your wires."

Electric crackles, followed by a hum, filled the cabin for a few seconds before a familiar, upbeat voice greeted me. "*Hello, Ishtar, welcome back.*"

I couldn't help but smile as my mood lifted. I responded, "Hey there, my friend! I thought you had died, like my Anubis. I was afraid you'd left me stranded and alone. I would have ripped out and reconnected all your wires. It's good to hear your annoying voice again."

"It is I, Lasitor. I'm sorry about your Anubis, your pet friend. She had protected me as if I was a ball. She grew big and blocked the flames from reaching your ship. Luckily, you have me, your faithful companion, and I can't or won't ever leave you. I need you as much as you need me. Ha-ha-ha!" He laughed robotically. I had been traveling with my ally since I started my time machine.

I had been a young, lonely boy, tinkering with scraps and electronics. It kept me entertained and out of trouble from the politics and drama of the king's court while I built my time machine.

I shifted in my seat. "Alright, I'm eager to leave Babylon." I ran my long fingers over the buttons and knobs on the dashboard, adjusting the endpoint settings. "My father is not a threat anymore. I slew him and have his tick-tick thing. I'm now the Anunnaki patriarch."

"Congratulations, are you planning on staying here and taking his place?"

"No, I was wondering if you would take me to Anzulla. Now that I have the pendant, maybe you will take me there. Perhaps there is something left after all. Do you remember how to get there?" I asked. I wasn't sure if they came from a time and place on Earth, or somewhere else, because I never could find Anzulla, and Lasitor always said that I wasn't ready. "I want to see what my sisters' homeland looks like, find out if there were any survivors, and see what they have created, and if possible, stay there. I think I'm ready for the truth."

There was a long pause, and I knew he was calculating the correct answer by running through his memory files, as he had explained to me frequently when I got impatient with him not answering me immediately, so I waited.

"I can take you, though you might not enjoy it."

"I wouldn't know that unless you do. How else can I be sure if I don't see it myself?"

Lasitor went silent; my question hung unanswered for minutes. "Why not stay here or go to a place where you are needed? I assume General Titus helped you. Is he alive?"

"Oh yes, he is. I am sad to part ways with him, but he will guard Xerxes and the future kings and queens of Babylon.

"As you say. I do owe you a promise. Perhaps there is a bigger reason you fought so hard to save them—whether it was because of honoring those who died innocently before, like your family and friends, or maybe you are destined for greatness. Let me guide you toward your destiny," he said.

I agreed, "Maybe there's a happy place for me."

"There are many places, and I know the perfect time and place."

"Yes, my friend, regardless of whatever lies ahead, one thing remains certain—there is always a reason to keep moving forward, no matter how dark things might be in the past, especially with the Fates guiding me," I said as I glimpsed my reflection in the sapphire glass.

"Holy dung beetles!" I leaned closer to the wrap-around window, almost not recognizing the face that looked back at me. I frowned and blew out my cheeks. Poking and stretching them, making sure it was me. The complete reinvigoration of the palace pool astounded me. I haven't had any sustenance. No blood to drink. Before now, I had only used the pool once, before I left on my travels.

The eyes staring back at me were mine and wide with surprise. They glinted. My skin was as dark blue as the night sky, and I still had the irises I despised—yellow and black-ringed—like my dead father's.

I looked older but healthier, and a lot more dangerous. So dangerous, I was scaring myself. I turned my face from side to side and inspected it. My hair looked like a lion's mane. I rifled in the overhead cubby to find the jewelry I had removed before going into battle. I skillfully braided my wild black hair, also adding thin golden strings as I rolled it into manageable, thicker locks, and bound it all with a carved golden clasp. I lined my ears from the tips to the lobes with golden earrings, from small to larger hoops. Last, I put my rings on my fingers. Of course, they were also gold. My reflection smiled at me. Titus always liked the small hoop pierced through my nose septum, so I put that back on as well. My stomach clenched with longing for him, but I forced that to the back of my mind.

Ready to get away from here, I leaned forward and pushed the accelerator.

"Lasitor, I will take the chance to see how things have turned out after Apsu's death. Let's go see Anzulla, about fifty years after my family fled." I watched the ratchet wheels on the dashboard spinning backward.

"Guide me on my journey," I prayed to the Fates. Lasitor chuckled unemotionally.

I was beaming with pride for my trusty Lasitor and the quirky little ship that I had lovingly rebuilt and pieced together from the wreckage of the royal Anzulla spaceship that had crash-landed in the middle of Xerxes's kingdom. I wasn't born yet. But my siblings were. They told me the story of my father and mother walking out of the wreckage and into Xerxes's palace and sitting on his throne. There was nothing he could do. It was either a beheading or marrying my sisters, Princesses Ki and An. But the Fates had blessed Xerxes, he had taken one look at my sisters, and they all instantly fell in love. As the mate of not one but two princesses, he could keep his head on his body. With such an unorthodox beginning, it was no surprise that our family was able to bend laws and manipulate people to our will.

At least I had sent Titus after them. He would guard my nieces and nephews until his last breath. Mates couldn't survive long without each other. Xerxes would soon wither and pass away to be reunited with Ki and An.

"Lasitor, check the star map." The tick-tick around my neck felt warm against my skin as I closed my eyes. "Okay, take me to Anzulla!"

"As you say," Lasitor said, and I heard the gadgets and small gears inside my new tick-tick thing move. I didn't have time to figure it out. Without warning, the ship vibrated and gained altitude. My teeth rattled as we sped up faster than light.

"Ohhhhh, yes, here we go!" Stars became white lines, then melted away into one fine needle. "Oh yes, oh yes, oh yes!" Jumping was always an extraordinary experience. It was my favorite thing to do. I laughed, unable to hold it in. My voice was deep and jovial. My eyes pooled with tears. Whether from the happiness of being alive or the sadness of being utterly alone, I didn't know. But it felt good. I was free.

23 000 B.C.
Anzulla

Silence followed as the brightness disappeared.

A black void enveloped me. Relief stirred inside me. The ship slowed down, and we descended to a big orange-red orb. My gaze fixed on it, and I leaned forward in my chair.

"Dear Fates, is this Anzulla?" I stared open-mouthed at the deadness of the land.

"Yes, this is what was left after your family had departed," Lasitor confirmed.

A few minutes passed as we floated wordlessly, searching the barren world. In disbelief, I asked again, "Are you sure you have taken the correct route? Is this place exactly where your map showed?" I searched for something green and blue. For life. But all I saw was a desolate, dead planet—a big red rock. "Maybe you should fly closer?" I pushed the lever forward to the floor to glide closer to the surface. Dried-up rivers cut through bare mountains running into empty lakes filled with red-brown dust, birthing trails of dried-up streams and waterfalls that empty into the ocean with not a drop of water in sight. Spirals of black smoke escaped from between boulders and red-brown rocks that covered the entire surface and formed thick, dark clouds that hung over the valleys and hills.

"Lasitor, please check the star map to confirm this is Anzulla." I blinked rapidly to see better, to see something. I stupidly fisted a sleeve to polish the observation window and *clicked* my tongue when that didn't help.

"Ishtar, this is the time, exactly fifty years after your father had left it. Look into the sky. Look at the stars and the moon," he said, but I was too shocked and devastated to look up.

The horizon hanging over the surface was a sick

orange, red, and brown. I lowered the altitude for closer inspection. Nothing moved. There was not one living thing in sight. Nothing.

"What's that?" Something glinted through the layer of thick red-gray mist. Was that just a reflection? My heart shattered. Anzulla was a heap of smoke and rubble. If I hadn't stopped my father, this would have been my home. Thank the Fates I killed him.

I pulled the lever back, and with a jerk, the ship shot back up. We made another trip around the planet while I searched for movement, lights, or any sign that something was alive. The small light I spotted earlier was the only one in this forsaken place. My pendant stopped whirring like crazy and returned to its lazy tick-tick.

"Take me to that small light so I can stop and investigate." With a jolt, the ship landed right in front of a tall red-brown pillar.

"Will the air be breathable?" I wondered out loud.

"If it isn't, this would be a good place to die," my navigator said.

I ignored the sarcastic answer and opened the door. Gingerly, I exhaled and inhaled, sniffing and tasting the thin air. It smelled like dirt, dust, and smoke. Nothing acrid. I figured I wasn't dying yet. "I might as well exit the ship."

Desolation welcomed me. I scrunched my eyes as a whirlwind sandblasted my skin. I hunched my back and shaded my face with the lapels and hood of my jacket while searching for the source of the flickering light.

There! I pointed to a small hill of boulders.

There might be life after all. Maybe someone was sheltering themselves from the storm. Hope flared in my chest. Sword in hand, I climbed over the rubble. But as soon as I reached it, hope turned into disgust.

The wind blew my exclamation of howls away as I stumbled upon a startling sight. Instead of a pillar, it was the tip of an ancient Anunnaki obelisk emerging from the dusty ground. Using my sword, I brushed off the accumulated sand to reveal its golden surface, shining dimly, as there was almost no light coming from above. It must have reflected the searchlight of my ship. Upon closer inspection, I realized it was identical to the one erected in Babylon. Rubble had covered it until now, leaving only its tip visible. According to the Anunnaki belief, touching this obelisk would bring a divine message from the Fates. Some say that only those deemed worthy could touch it without facing instant death, like they did on Anzulla. Although my father was initially deemed worthy, he had received no messages. Since then, the Fates had been silent towards him, despite his constant pleading and demands for answers. They must have either stayed here on Anzulla or forsaken us entirely.

I fisted a jacket sleeve, polishing it. "Even the intricate carvings on its sides are identical," I said with a slow, disbelieving shake of my head and read the Anunnaki ciphers.

"Free my mind so I may serve not only in my dreams but by the blessings in my existence outside my narrow-minded trap."

I sighed. Far off to the left, I could make out the foundation of what I suspected was the old royal palace. I figured rubbing the obelisk engravings could only bring luck, *because shit like this couldn't get worse.*

"Tell me my next move, please." I sagged down, resting my back against it. In the distance, the hazy clouds of red sand dust shrouded my ship. After wallowing in deep defeatist and self-loathing thoughts, I began reciting the Anunnaki prayer, over and over. I banged my head against the obelisk, willing it to give me a reply. Miracles of miracles! I received an answer.

I jumped up as a boulder-crunching male voice, much like a giant troll waking up, said, *"Ishtar, your journey to save your bloodline begins here. You will leave this place and time."* Their voice was firm, deep, and distorted. The melodic cadence traveled up and down on the wind. Louder and softer, then softer and louder, "Go to Grayrak and wait."

I straightened up, tilting my head. "Say what now?"

"Stay occupied by watching, waiting, and learning. Don't alter anything. You can choose whom to assist, provided it isn't for your own benefit, and crucially, change nothing. Never for yourself. Only for others. This has to be a selfless undertaking, or else the darkness will latch onto you..." The voice trailed off.

I dusted my hands and backside. I waited. I cocked my head to one side and then the other. *Hmmm,* I placed my hands on my hips. I waited some more.

"Bloody damn hell! What? I don't have time for this. Talk! What about Grayrak? Is this a mission?"

"What did you say?" they asked—probably not understanding my colorful vocabulary. "Ishtar, don't mess with reality by moving things from one side to the other."

"Where's Grayrak? And why would you think I moved anything? How am I even supposed to move it?" I asked, but the voice remained silent. "I just don't understand!"

After a long pause, the voice replied, "We can discuss relocating essential items at a later time."

"Are you coming with me?" I shouted into the howling wind. "Who are you?"

"We are the force turning the cogs of your time. You killed the manifestation of evil. Your father broke that which was perfect, and his selfishness seeped out like the pus from an infected wound."

Fists clenched, I closed my eyes in resentment just thinking about him. "My father?" I asked, my voice barely above a whisper.

"He was on the verge of destroying everything we had worked so hard to build. Ishtar, this dangerous threat in Grayrak carries the same evil as your father. You destroyed the head of the monster, but to eliminate the darkness from all time, you will have to do it again."

Now I was certain the voice came from the obelisk.

With the sleeve of my shirt, I wiped at it, searching for the speaker.

"Why me? Why don't you do it?"

"I am. You are the weapon."

"Is the Loursveto growing in this Grayrak? Is this a place I can call home?" I asked because the Loursveto plant produces a flower, which is crucial for my kind's survival. It provides us with magical nourishment and physical vitality. Human blood was never meant to be our staple food. The Anunnaki had survived thousands of years by biting and drinking the life-giving water stored inside its fruit. That, and the blood of our mate. We can survive for a very long time on human food and Loursveto juice, but preferably not on blood alone.

"It's not your home, and no, the Loursveto can't grow there."

"But what will I eat and drink? Are there humans?" I asked, knowing I couldn't survive without their blood.

The obelisk emitted an eerie glow. "There will be humans. You may feed on their blood but never kill them. Never like Apsu." The voice resonated loud and commanding. I reached out to touch the obelisk. An electric surge coursed through me, sending shivers down my spine.

"Dear Fates! Are you the Fates?" Gasping, I inhaled, filling my lungs with tons of questions. "I'm your servant." Respectfully, I bent at the hips toward the obelisk. "So, I'm not allowed to kill them or ask them to kill themselves?" I asked and checked again, in case the Fates demanded it. I was not about to follow a voice blindly if they expected me to murder humans as if it were a sport or entertainment.

"None of that. That is precisely the reason you have been chosen for this task. Use your gifts to do good—while enjoying their blood and bodies."

I frowned. "But that's what I've been doing," I hissed and opened my mouth like an idiot to the obelisk— shaming myself for the disrespect—my long incisors slipped out, just thinking about feeding. I was ravenous.

"Just like your ancestors sucked the Loursveto's stem for its juice, you will too one day. Never reveal your true nature except to the ones who are like you."

"Ones like me? Will I meet more Anunnaki in this place called—what again?" This was turning out to be exciting. "I will gladly go if there are more of my kind."

"Grayrak. And yes, your kind will soon arrive. But your mission is to contain the darkness that lurks there. It's an old enemy of humans. It's a thing that hides inside the darkness. Like you saw hiding inside your father, it feeds off the malevolence, and it is multiplying. It is as old as time itself," they said.

I toed my boots against the foot of the obelisk and wondered what lay beneath me, while the weight of the world rested on my shoulders.

"So, like Anzulla or Babylon? Are you saying another Apsu awaits me? Am I to build another army?" I asked, already dreading it. I hated this darkness, this insidious force. *It wasn't defeated yet.*

"No, you don't need an army, as long as you stay with Lasitor on your time machine. It is yours. I will guide you. You have that time-keeping device around your neck. It's the key between here and there, and only you should use it. You don't need an army as long as you don't show your Anunnaki side to these humans, and until you see the ball-shaped ship."

I blinked wordlessly, shaking my head.

"Until then, you will have time to learn the modern human ways. Keep a watchful eye out for the round floating ship. It will look almost like yours, but not a gold machine. It can change colors. Make yourself known to the occupants and stay on that path at the same time."

"Can change colors? Who are these humans? Are they like chameleons? Where is Grayrak? What do you mean by modern humans?" I asked and got only chuckles for answers.

"Don't laugh at me," I said, upset and belittled.

"No, no chameleons," they said, still sounding amused. "You will understand when you see the ship. It's made of something like glass, but not glass like the window on your machine. I can't explain it better than that. But I warn you. Messing with the timeline means losing your home, me, and Anzulla forever. Destroying everything. Do you understand?"

"No, not a word." I threw my hands into the air, frustrated.

"You will, once you go. And no, you can't go back to Babylon if you've contemplated that. Go to Grayrak. It's on the moon."

"On the moon? In the future? How did the humans manage that?" I checked the tick-tick thing. Nothing made sense. Maybe this wasn't Anzulla. I searched the skies but couldn't see through the dark clouds surrounding me.

"When the humans arrive, you will understand. Remember the name Barkor. Search for him and watch the little one. He is special, like you. Protect him. Learn from the humans, and help them, but don't interfere or change anything. Not until your kin arrive. The less you help, the better, because you risk changing things in the future. Your machine is pre-programmed. It's just over twenty-five thousand years into the future."

"Holy scarabs! I was just with Platonius, counting the sun and moon cycles. How did they get to that number on the calendar?"

"You brought Platonius the gift of tracing time with the course of the sun. That was all because of you. By teaching him the lunar and solar cycles, time tracking remained precise. Your formula has been written and passed down through generations. Your father's destruction, the time of his reckoning, was what split his history into pieces. The discovery of the gardens your sisters created and the explosion of knowledge have led humans down some interesting paths. Paths you will find for yourself. You will soon see. It is all thanks to you." The voice cut in and out as the howling wind picked up speed. I was trying my best to see a face somewhere in the direction the voice came from. The cadence was familiar.

"Do I know you? I think I've heard your voice before," I said to what I thought were the Fates as I inspected the obelisk up close, deep in contemplation and trying to jog a memory by walking around it. In Babylon, it was so tall that I could never truly look at it from above.

I waited. No response.

I was worried they were getting annoyed because I had asked too many questions. I felt cold and hollow. Empty, like I was a bubble inside. I knew the feeling well enough. Time felt frozen, as if everything had come to a standstill in this place. I shivered. Those who died here haunted the land.

"Are you going to leave me in this desolate place?" I cupped my hands and shouted into the wind, hoping the voice hadn't already up and disappeared. As if on cue, the wind picked up. Billowing clouds of dust obscured my ship from view. I feared getting lost and not being able to find it. I should return to my ship, I thought, and turned to head back.

I could swear I heard the voice on the wind say, "Anzulla is not dead," but I could have imagined it as screeching winds surrounded me.

Gasping for clean, breathable air, I stumbled towards the open door of my ship. Dread surged through me as I realized I had forgotten to close it before venturing out onto the sandy terrain. I dragged myself inside and, with shaky hands, I slammed the button and flipped the lever to shut the door behind me, grateful for the safety of my machine.

Sputtering out chunks of dirt and grit from my mouth, I blew my nose and quickly stripped off my clothes, socks, and boots. It tickled like sand fleas, I itched, squirmed, brushed, and scrubbed myself violently. The stubborn, cursed grains seemed to have infiltrated even the tiniest crevices of my body. They clung to every pore, every hair down to my ballsack. After cleaning my body and putting on clean clothes, I swept the sand out the door, and back into the wind outside.

"Lasitor," I said after putting everything away and taking my seat at the controls. "Take me to Grayrak. Twenty-five thousand years into the future." I hoped to

find water to clean my butt crack once I arrived there.
"Let's go find some answers!"

CHAPTER 4
GRAYRAK TO PARADISE

"Good day, Ishtar.

I have no clue what time it is.

Did you know cryovolcanoes, also called ice volcanoes, may potentially form on icy moons and other planets? Just think of all that potential life pumping into space. Where there is water, there is life.

Unfortunately, I don't know what kind of life these humans are living, or if they know what they are doing here on the moon. Ice-spewing volcanoes or geysers are not something they will see soon. Nor will you see any water.

Happy hunting, have a good day!"

Ishtar
   2046 A.D.
   Grayrak
   Earth's Moon

. . .

As USUAL, on one of my worst days, I found myself intoxicated. I was not walking on sunshine, also, not in a straight line.

"Ishtar, go home! Bloody damn hell, you are drunk again." Barkor pushed me out of his tin-can house and shut the door in my face. "Go home, sleep it off, and come back when you are sober."

I turned on my heels, lifting my weighted moon boots high as I marched back to my hovel. "If that ball of shit—I mean, ship—doesn't arrive soon, I'm going to blow shit up!" I muttered to myself. I wasn't tired, I was restless. So, I climbed onto the roof of my time machine and crossed my legs and arms. The mixture of human blood and nasty drugs had intoxicated me beyond my usual rational thinking. I was all over the place with my thoughts.

I had slain my father, freeing my people, and now witnessed a forsaken human settlement on the moon of all places. A testament to the twisted beliefs of a cult group called the Disciples of the Anunnaki. I felt exiled and condemned by my actions or perhaps cursed by the sins of my father. My soul felt like it was rotting, and I was certain that the Fates had sent me here as punishment. My only purpose was to watch over Barkor, but even that felt like torture. I felt trapped in Grayrak, a level just below the final level of Sheol, a nasty reality where there's only clay to eat and bad water to drink.

Ugh! I shook my head, my braids swinging all around

me. I desperately needed to get the nasty taste of drugged blood out of my mouth.

Decades of years ago, maybe more—I can't say because again, we are on the moon, and the moon has two fucking seasons! Two! Winter and summer. No harvest and no floods. It's tidally locked with the blue planet. Sharing one sun. On the moon, one day is about six hundred and fifty hours long. Half of that is day, and the other half is night. The side facing the Earth is warmer, and the light is much brighter. On the opposite side, it is darker, but I can still see shades of colors in the grayness.

The first time, I had become desperate and unable to endure another second here. I had inadvertently, unintentionally, and with pure innocence stumbled upon a world where the air was filled with the scent of blooming flowers and the forests blushed with vibrant colors. Clean air, gentle breezes, and cheerful faces filled this city carved out of a mountain. It was heaven, a sanctuary from the horror-filled Grayrak, where the stench of unwashed humans polluted the air like the fourth Egyptian plague. It was also, I felt sure, hopefully, where I'd find my mate.

Since my return from this newly discovered place, with its jungle and its primitive people, memories and visions of a mysterious face haunt me day and night. These memories are disjointed and confusing, leaving me uncertain if they are from my past or glimpses of my future. My obsessive search for the man with the mind-numbingly beautiful face had both freed me and replaced, I had believed, my addiction to drug-tainted blood. Having not found him in all that time led me to my present, intoxicated self.

I looked up and growled. I must find the man this face belongs to!

For decades, my body knew where to go, even though my mind was still catching up. I wandered down dimly lit alleyways and steel-boxed houses in Grayrak, searching for a fix—for tainted blood—for humans smelling rancid with neediness mingled with the stench of misery. The most desperate for death. I would drag them into the shadows, strike their necks, and drink the bitter liquid from their veins. A sense of relief would wash over me, but it never lasted long. The hunger and longing for that euphoric high was a never-ending cycle, a vicious circle that could only be broken by leaving this place. I was lost among these humans. Their despair became my own, and yet, their pain only added to my twisted desires. Despite all my power and strength, I couldn't wipe away the overwhelming sadness, desperation, and loneliness that plagued them on this desolate moon.

But lately, something new and out of the norm has happened to me. I'm in pursuit of the man whose angelic face haunts my every thought. I can't shake off these visions and dreams of him. Water and lush forests always accompany it. I am charmed by a new obsession, trapped by a persistent yearning that refuses to release me. I know deep down that I am chasing a mere vision of a man, and now I cannot think of anything else but finding him.

Grayrak City needs a savior, but so do I. I almost shouted and felt my mind shift again.

"Ugh," I sighed. "What a shit show!" I spat my words with hands on my knees, back straight, closing my eyes for a brief second while I enjoyed the high.

When I first arrived on Grayrak, I made sure to hide my time machine behind a wall of building rubble in the southeast corner of Grayrak City, so it appeared from the front to be a small hill of gigantic boulders.

My hideout was a solitary haven, tucked away from the bustling human and Zelk commotion where I've observed them scurrying around like ants, constructing a towering structure that glinted silver in the sunlight. The sight always filled me with a strange mix of fascination and disgust. Sometimes, when I was feeling particularly hungry or restless, I would lend a helping hand. After all, the Fates had instructed me not to interfere with their affairs. But as time went on, my heart grew heavier, and my conscience was weighed down by the suffering I witnessed daily.

Just as I reached my breaking point the first time after arriving, before I drowned myself in mind-numbing chemicals—the urge to smash every blue silicone brick and scream at these delusional humans—a moment of pure rage and despair, pushed me to flee. By accident, I found an oasis for my soul, a sanctuary for my weary spirit.

I arrived there, thinking I'd jumped back in time to find Babylon, desperately seeking refuge from tainted blood. But instead, I found a jungle with positively happy, but primitive people who knew nothing of this advanced, chaotic world on the moon.

I've been there a few times. And I want to go again. I *need* to go again.

Grayrak is a burden that threatens to swallow me whole. I want to run back to that place where I suspect, for some weird, inexplicable reason, the stranger's face awaits me. This place offered me an escape from the constant reminders of human greed and destruction. I need to find my mate before I find myself totally addicted to the tainted, intoxicating blood here on Grayrak.

With every breath I take, this polluted air of Grayrak suffocates me. The stench inside their massive glass rotunda is a putrid combination of sweat, farts, hopelessness, and narcissism. As I sit here, forced to witness the depths of human depravity, I can't help but feel anger boiling within me. How low can these humans go? They are nothing but selfish beings, willing to do anything for eternal life, even if it means oppressing and destroying their kind. I feel trapped here, a helpless spectator to their self-inflicted torture and destruction. Every day, from the moment my eyes open until I am overtaken by exhaustion, I am subjected to the entertainment of watching these humans destroy themselves in pursuit of immortality. It sickens me to my core.

It's like watching one dung beetle pushing another dung beetle's dung all day. The struggles these men, women, and children endure just to stay alive are mind-numbing and tedious. I can't comprehend why they don't just throw themselves onto the nearest ship and flee back to Earth. Every day I ask rhetorically, only to arrive at the same bloody conclusion, "Because we are dumb as dung beetles."

While I stewed in my failure, I felt sure it wasn't totally mine, as the damn ship hadn't arrived yet. I slowly killed myself with tainted human blood. The Disciples had a sickening formula that promised happiness and eradicated all cravings for sustenance. The drug gave them the strength and endurance of ten men. They toiled for hours without pause, fueled by this vile concoction. Their blood intoxicated me, and today, to the point of drunkenness.

Meanwhile, the face in my dreams carried huge significance. Sometimes he smiled, other times I saw him looking down at me with love in his piercing blue eyes. The best times were when those eyes looked up at me.

I sat up straight, sucking air deep into my lungs, then closed my eyes. "The vision I see behind my closed eyelids makes me instantly hard," I whispered as I blew out a long breath, my body weaving side to side.

The deep blue of his eyes glinted like shards of glass, always drawing me in to look closer. When he narrowed his eyes with a hint of anger towards me, a strange, amused feeling tickled my insides. But when they held an intense gaze filled with love, I shivered. The silver specks and shifting shades of blue reminded me of sunlight dancing on undisturbed water, while a tumultuous storm of want and need for him rose within me. His beauty was painfully sharp and pure, radiating like the sun's scorching rays. I knew just looking at him in real life would be blinding, like staring directly into the heart of the sun. His hair was a rare white, like clouds painted against a pale blue desert sky. Touching and smelling him would make me forget where I was and who I was supposed to be.

And his hands—they were tender yet strong, reaching for me with a magnetic pull I couldn't resist. Though I didn't know him, I felt a nudge, a connection to him, as if we were meant to meet and he was the missing piece of my soul.

I wanted him. I was consumed by the burning desire to escape and find my elusive mystery man. It drove me to madness. He called out to me, beckoning me to find him before it was too late. Too late for what?

I was torn in so many directions, my jumbled thoughts so confusing. The Fates, the humans, my need for tainted blood, Barkor, the round translucent ship, the jungle, and my unnamed man in my memories.

"Scarabs!" I bellowed. How many variations of feeling like shit are there? According to my calculations, about one thousand two hundred and eighty-two. I've spent over seventy years twiddling my thumbs, counting, and waiting for a spherical spaceship that changes colors like a chameleon.

I was slowly losing my shit. Nope, wait, I guess it's my poop. Maybe the Fates were just pulling my leg this whole time. They were probably sitting back with a cup of wine, watching me make a fool of myself. Talk about leaving a load on your doorstep. "What a steaming pile of dung! Day after day, I sit here and watch Grizzly strut around like he owns the place." I slurred my words, gesturing wildly towards the Disciple compound. "Now those guys are full of bull plop." I squinted one eye to make sure I was pointing in the right direction.

"They couldn't give a crusty crab's ass about anyone else. Happy as pigs in mud, oops." I toppled over and smacked my face on the roof of my ship with a dull thud. I shook my head like a wounded warhorse to clear my vision.

"I'm going!" With a well-practiced move, I flung my legs over the side, gripping the doorframe to swing myself inside my time machine.

"I need to get out of here," I whined. "Same crap, different day. Or every other day, who knows?" I grumbled and tumbled into my seat. "Lasitor," I called and checked my tick-tick thing.

"Yes, Ishtar," he answered, sounding pissed off as usual.

"Take me to the waters. Take me to my lover."

"Which lover would that be?" he said with sarcasm in his tone.

He didn't approve of my impulsiveness. Ever since we'd time-jumped into the past and stumbled upon the jungle, my visions had come to me.

"Lasitor, I'm going there. It has become an escape to maintain a sense of sanity as much as for finding the man from my dreams."

"If you say so, but I wouldn't recommend growing attached."

"Even though Gugusan doesn't exactly resemble him, he still plays a vital role in satisfying my primal sexual urges and filling my stomach with healthy blood. Something you won't know anything about. You don't feel pleasure, and you don't get hungry. So we are going there, no matter how you see it," I said curtly. I was the captain. Having visited this time and place before, I knew my navigator had identified the exact coordinates. I strapped myself into my seat.

"Lasitor, initiate that pre-programmed sequence."

"Are you sure? Don't you think—"

"Of course I'm sure. Waiting for that chameleon ball ship to arrive is maddening. Take me to where I can breathe and think," I said and hoped this time I would meet the man with the beautiful face. If not, at least Gugusan and his people would welcome me. "Barkor seems to have it all under control. He doesn't need me. His flock needs a miracle, and I can't give it to them. The scientists are busy creating something, I assume, that will kill all of us. The Disciples think the Anunnaki is going to bring water to the moon. But the only Anunnaki I know that might do that are now dead."

My sisters could connect with nature and the life-giving elements to make plants grow. They didn't create the mystical pool guarded by Xerxes and his ancestors. Only the Anunnaki healed as fast as I. So that water wasn't as miraculous as the humans made it out to be. The garden was already there, and the tree next to the pool was thousands of years old. Its roots created a natural enclosure around the unending hot bubbling pond. So, no pool or water for the Grayrakians, even if I went back in time to ask them. All I could do was haul water with me from this paradise.

"These scientists who call themselves Disciples are sneaky and power-hungry. They are the source of all the darkness that lurks in this place," Lasitor said.

"I know. The only good thing here is Barkor," I replied.

Only a few days after my arrival, a sudden crash and explosion had rocked the quiet silence. A ship from Earth had plummeted to the surface, right at the entrance of Grayrak's scientist colony. The impact ripped its metal hull into pieces. I hurriedly made my way towards the wreckage, determined to help anyone in need. Amidst the chaos, a young mother, badly wounded, went into labor. I rushed to her side and was uncertain about what to do. Give me a sword and drop me in the middle of a battlefield—that day, I had never been so scared in my life.

With trembling hands and a pounding heart, I helped deliver her baby. She had succumbed to her wounds. He was a loud little thing with blue skin and purplish undertones. I knew that in my hands was the precious baby, the child the Fates had foretold back on Anzulla. Despite the surrounding chaos, I recognized his cries were different. I was present at all my nieces' and nephews' births, and that gave me the experience to differentiate between human and Anunnaki babies. Anunnaki babies communicate by conveying emotions through mind-to-mind connections with their caregivers. Baby Barkor was extremely confused about where he was. He was upset because he wanted to go back to the heat and silence. His eyes and tummy hurt, and the light was blinding him. I vowed to protect him at all costs. He wasn't a large and strong newborn, he needed love, warmth, and nourishment.

In haste, I wrapped him securely, carried him away from the wreckage, and began my search for food and a loving mother to care for him. Barkor was the most beautiful baby. His thick, black curls and mesmerizing blue eyes with elongated pupils resembling those of a cat ensured I couldn't help but fall in love and feel in awe of this precious baby suddenly placed in my care.

I concealed my true identity and appearance from him and everyone else. For over seventy years, I have been his caretaker. Since I saved and named him, he had been my secret child. Through mind control, I ensured he had a mother figure. I'd manipulated women into believing he was their son, that he was precious, a prince who would save them one day. I'd aided him in dealing with his problems by paving the way for him and his companions. He was the only family I had, and although his lineage was unknown, we shared similar abilities. He was aware of his heightened strength, speed, and intelligence compared to regular humans. Like me, he aged slower than humans, and thankfully, he didn't flaunt his powers. I was grateful for that, as it made my job easier and reduced my worries as I discreetly assisted him from the shadows.

I shook my head again. I was rewarded with throbbing pain, reminding me of the drugged blood I'd had earlier. I needed to hurry up and find my mate. "Let's go!" I pressed the shiny start button with one hand and pushed the lever full throttle with the other. I doubled over, hitting my head on the panel.

Lasitor *"wha-wha-wha'd"* something in the background while ping-ping alarms screeched. The machine thrust forward, pushing me back and upright into a sitting position.

"Shit!" I slurred as streaks of light flashed by the window, blinding me. My vision blurred as my eyelids grew heavier. My head lolled to the side. Potent blood, I thought, and I passed out, stoned and drunk, as my time machine went backwards in time.

---

25 000 B.C.

The jungle

A crescendo of wildlife woke me. Frogs croaked, and wild animals yipped, roared, and howled. One by one, I cracked my eyes open as fresh air filled my lungs.

"Oh, thank you," I moaned. All my blood had pooled in my head and was sloshing between my ears.

"Lasitor?" I moaned again, not knowing when or where I was. I blinked to refocus my blurry vision and sniffed the air through a stuffy nose. The smell of wet earth greeted me. I was upside down. Grass and twigs stuck up into my nose and mouth. Bugs irked me and gave me the shivers. I spat, shaking my head, and failed at wiping my face, because my arms were numb and lying like tree stumps underneath me. Useless.

It seems I had somehow exited my time machine after landing and face-planted in the mud. I whimpered uncomfortably, feeling sorry for myself. My body lay twisted. I tried rolling over, but my legs were stuck and tangled in my safety straps. Oh, and I still had those moon-walking weights tied to my boots.

"Lasitor!" I moaned. "Lasitor, answer me!" He ignored me. "Burn your wires, I'm going to melt you down to wires."

Silence.

Chatter from birdsong told me I was not on the moon, and the sun was rising.

"Thank the Fates." I scoped out my surroundings.

"Good job! Lasitor, you parked the ship in that clearing, against the mountain in the jungle," I said, feeling thankful and relieved.

The skies were dimly lit as dawn arrived and the sun ascended in the east. I pushed myself over with my useless arms, then flexed and stretched them to encourage blood flow until they regained life.

Something rustled and moved in the grass beside me—feet with sandals. My heart leaped. I'd made it.

"Lasitor, don't worry about answering me," I said and pushed myself to my hands and knees.

"The village people have arrived!"

"Da!" a male voice warned me as he shoved a spear toward my forehead. I heeded the warning, throwing my hands in the air.

Where was I? I looked up, searching, but I couldn't see the moon. Then, my gaze fell on yellow-skinned men and women with long green plumes of feathers on their heads. I smiled, elated, as I recognized them. Streaks of light and shadows bathed my welcoming committee. *Gugusan's people.*

"Whaoo!" one shouted and jumped back as soon as he saw my face. Suddenly, more spears were pointed in my direction, followed by a long moment of silence as they stared at me. Something crawled on my upper lip. It tickled, but I held still, imagining the size of the thing. Having a salt pillar freak out, I asked with my eyes for permission, then lifted my shoulder, trying to wipe whatever it was from my face before it crawled up my nose.

My audience laughed. This was a friendly bunch.

One pointed with her spear, telling another something in their exotic language that sounded familiar. I was getting used to it, having been here many times, and words were becoming easier to recognize and translate.

I wondered whether they recognized me. I planned to play along, hoping to find that vision, that man with the white hair and bluest eyes.

A man stepped forward, and I expected a punch or slap, but no; he pulled the thing from my lip and held it up, showing me and his friends a baby centipede! A red one! I shivered and furiously wiped at my face. Then I remembered I was supposed to stay still.

Luckily, no one reacted, and I didn't lose an eye. My savior threw it aside. I tipped my head to show my appreciation. I counted ten young males. They seemed cautious, but I felt no aggression or hostility toward me. This was a new group for me.

A large, imposing man pushed through the ring of onlookers, asking, "Maymantataq hamurqan?" The crowd gave way, revealing Gugusan, their leader, whose voice they all knew well.

"Hello," I said, smiling at him. He wore enormous plumes of red and blue feathers around his head. His torso was magnificently muscled. My gaze drifted downward. My breath hitched as my cock went instantly hard, imagining loosening the piece of leather that scantily covered his manhood. The cup was decorated with green jewels. Straps wrapped around his lean hips and back. More matching straps adorned his upper arms. These straps also had the same green jewels as the penis cup. Similar straps wrapped around his calves, holding his sandals in place. Like the others, his hair was sleek black. However, his demeanor made him stand out as the leader.

"Rikuspa, hanaq pachapi mayumanta hamurqan?" he asked, pointing to the sky.

I followed his gesture to where the Milky Way faded—a name I learned from the moon's inhabitants. I knew it as the dragon's spilled blood. Back home, people suspected my family's involvement in the dragon's demise. My father used to say, "Let them think what they want, it keeps us exalted."

Gugusan's eyes widened. His body was rigid with irritation. Without hesitation, he unsheathed his short sword. The black blade glinted as he pointed up to the stars. I assumed he was asking where I came from. So, I pointed to the sky. Knowing shit like that usually counted in my favor.

They jumped back in awe. Shaking their heads furiously, pointing up and to something off in the distance. Gugusan narrowed his eyes at me, not looking at them or their antics like he wasn't in the mood for sky people today. His jaw clenched. Then he stepped forward and took hold of one of my braided locks. He rolled it from side to side. Then he inspected my hoop earrings. He stooped, turning his head, and put his ear against the tick-tick hanging around my neck. He stepped back, sighing. His cheek hollowed, and one corner of his mouth pulled down—as if chewing on the inside of his cheek. Slowly, his eyes roamed up until they met my gaze.

He looked a few years younger. This visit was closer to my first visit, maybe before I'd decided to stop wiping myself from their memories.

His eyes were dull yellow-green. He had no facial hair, and his full lips were rounded and pierced with what looked like ivory hoops. His handsome face was squared by a strong jaw. I hoped he wanted me today. I was looking forward to filling my stomach with his bright red, thick, and sweet-tasting blood. It was rich in nutrients. The clean jungle air he inhaled prickled on my tongue like bubbles popping up from fresh mountain spring water. It was puri-fying me from the inside out.

Although he wasn't the man of my dreams, I had urges, and by now I knew he wanted me. Virility oozed out of every pore of his body. He smelled enticing, like male sweat, coconut, and smoke. If I hadn't drunk his untainted blood the previous times, I think I would have been dead by now.

He stepped back and waved his hands, thumbs up. I caught the meaning—get up, you're embarrassing your-self. His men muttered among themselves. "Hmmm," I agreed, then untangled my feet and removed the heavy weights. My vertebrae cracked as I got up and straightened my back. A round of oohs and ahs followed.

I looked down at them. Gugusan, almost a head taller than the others, was looking up at me, and I caught that familiar glimpse of lust in his eyes. He shook his head. I probed for thoughts—my stature awed him, and he was telling himself he didn't want me, that he shouldn't want me.

He inspected my boots and touched my shirt and pants. "Maymantataq hamurqan. Rikuspa, hanaq pachapi mayumanta hamurqan," he said to his men as he pointed to my ship and back to me. I was too slow at catching his meaning. But as soon as his soldiers fell to their knees, I got it loud and clear.

"Ah moongod!" I threw my hands in the air—not in the mood for this again. "Get up. I am not to be worshiped!"

"Gg moongod," one man said with that distinct local grating throaty "gg," as if clearing his throat. Not this again. I gave them the universal signal to get up. No praying to me.

"Gg moongod," they repeated.

I said, "Yes, get up, you idiots," while chuckling ridiculously. My head throbbed, and I felt thirsty. I needed food and a bath, not worship.

My general landing location was the same as all my previous visits, but small things were different. It seemed this time they were keeping secrets from me. The men gathered in small groups, talking amongst themselves, not within earshot.

"Paymi churi dios. Yanapananchikmi, mana chayqa mana allin suertetam apamuwasun," Gugusan said and moved to look at my time machine.

"No, my friend, you don't want to climb in there without me," I said, using a mix of my mother tongue and their language. I connected telepathically to them, searching for that language compulsion, and found none, so I planted the seed of the Anunnaki language inside them. Now it made sense why we already understood each other the first time I landed here.

He halted on the third step and peeked inside, then looked back at me, blinking a few times. It looked like he was searching for something or someone, but only saw the blinking lights on the dashboard of my weird time-keeping contraption inside the cockpit.

"Da Gg moongod?" he said questioningly, waving in a circle to the sky and then again off in the distance. A universal, *welcome sky traveler, let's go to our village and have a talk...and some bum-bum-bum time.*

I nodded a thank you and held my hands up in a respectful prayer position. I motioned at the door, showing him I wanted to shut it. He gave me permission with a firm nod and a "Da!"

I pulled the small automatic stair lever up and waited for the stairs to contract into the side as the door closed. "That's it!" I said happily optimistic, while dusting my hands—signaling the job was done. Chop-chop, let's go.

He eyebrow-whipped me, and I whipped him back with a sexy, brooding look. He grunted something, but it did not intimidate me at all. It just made him look more appealing. Then we turned as one. I smiled and bowed my head to the others, showing my appreciation.

"Let's go." I pointed.

They lifted their spears, pointing the way.

"Okay," I said as I caught their meaning. Follow the sexy brute, and we will watch your backside as you follow him.

"Da Gg moongod," they said.

Early the next morning, I made my trek back up to the clearing near the top of the mountain to return to Grayrak. My ship was restocked with food and water. I was sober, sexually satisfied, and no closer to finding my mate.

CHAPTER 5

THE GOLDEN APPLE

"Good day, Ishtar.

I promise you, the sun is shining, and it is daylight somewhere.

While on the subject—did you know there is a famous love story about the Sun and the Moon falling in love and traveling around the world together? But the Moon betrayed the Sun and copulated with the Morning Star. The punishment for its betrayal was banishment. The Sun never wanted to see the Moon—ever again. So from then on the solitary Moon had to travel by night, while the Sun traveled by day all alone. The moral of the story is whether you are a Sun or a Moon, there will always be a Morning Star to keep you company.

Even if there is no breakfast being served.

Good luck and may your day be filled with splendor and wonder!"

. . .

ISHTAR
24 970 B.C.
The jungle

MY SHIP TOUCHED down in paradise thirty years after my last visit. I had an unselfish reason to escape Grayrak while searching for the man in my visions. A whole lot of shit was happening, and I was restless, rancid, and ravenous when the water supply I smuggled to Grayrak finally ran out. I had averted drinking tainted blood in Grayrak. Weeks passed and now I was drooling for my reward and eager to find out if I was closer to finding the man with the white hair.

Gugusan was older, stronger, and wiser. Desire filled my cock as I followed Gugusan through the dense undergrowth. His movements were graceful, swaying his hips and showing off the pretty feathers adorning them. The low-hanging leather belt tied around his waist, and the single leather string running from it, down his crack, and I assumed was securing the cup covering his front side, accentuated each globe of his buttocks with each step he took. The belt was adorned with intricate patterns in vibrant shades of green, blue, and red, with tiny jewels sparkling in the light. I couldn't help but admire the colorful feathers that I suspected belonged to native birds, hoping to glimpse them during my visit. Gugusan moved through the bushes with ease, as if he knew every twist, turn, low-hanging branch, and obstacle. It was clear that he was born and raised here, now showing genuine leadership by walking alongside his people.

Daybreak illuminated the vibrant colors along the path ahead, revealing a well-worn trail winding through the lush forest. The birds' chatter welcomed the new day, urging me to stay in the shade of the treeline as the sun climbed higher in the sky. Somehow, I had to get out of the sun before I burned to death. Like my father, my dark skin, not black but a deep Anunnaki blue, helped protect me against the sun's deadly rays. The rest of my family were pale-skinned with a powder blue complexion. I appreciated the surrounding air, which was thick with mist that cooled my skin by evaporation. My companions behind me chatted away, their voices almost masking the sound of rushing water nearby. We had only descended a short distance when we came upon a small stream cutting through tall grass and shrubs. As someone who had spent decades living on the barren moon, I reveled in the beauty and vitality of nature around me.

However, I couldn't pinpoint exactly what year it was. My manipulative electronic companion and guide refused to tell me. I had hoped he joked when he said that if he told me, he would have to kill me. So instead, I outsmarted him by deliberately turning back the knob dangerously far into the past. Lasitor quickly intervened, confirming we were between twenty to thirty thousand years in the past, according to his saved coordinates.

Since I found this place, a sense of rightness has settled over me, as if my timelines were finally aligned just right. I knew the man of my dreams was in this place. I could feel it. In the meantime, the man walking before me exuded power and masculinity as his muscles rippled under his yellow-bronzed skin, stirring a powerful attraction towards him. I wanted to sink my teeth into his neck or that juicy behind. My mouth watered just thinking about tasting him again. He was the type of man who liked to be in control, and if that was what it took to seduce him, I would submit my big eight-foot frame and take anything this barbaric man wanted to do to me.

Even though I was seeking sexual solace in Gugusan, my heart was with my blue-eyed mate and I would have to ask Gugusan about him. As we walked together, I probed their minds. These people were unbelievably happy and connected to the magic of the forest. I could hear the men behind me murmuring amongst themselves—no doubt discussing me. Unfortunately, they are convinced I'm some kind of demon god from the sky, which is not wrong.

Gugusan halted and turned to face me near a rock formation with an arch high enough to let me walk straight through. "Taak in we'esik ti' teech ba'al," he said and waved me inside.

This was new.

Stooping my neck, I entered, instantly captivated by the mystical aura around me. I blinked to refocus my eyes to get used to the darkness. Gugusan stepped deeper into the big cavern, calling me closer to a rock pillar with four sides. It had a wide base that narrowed upward, just like the obelisks. It was my height and, on the crown, rested something that glinted in their torchlights. *Gold?* That distinct vibration of the yellow metal hummed—it called to me.

I stepped closer, not touching. "I've seen this before." *Could this be?* "I think I know what this is."

In awe, I leaned in closer for a better view to confirm my suspicion, "Dear moon-god, it is." I stood open-mouthed in disbelief. It was the golden apple. The apple Ki and An had shown me before I left to go collect the tablet from Platonius. They'd said I had given it to them and asked that they hide it from Apsu and bury it for me. But that's thousands of years into the future. Isn't it?

Shhhhhht-gggggggt, fine electrical crackles came from the ugly small replica of an obelisk, reminding me of my visit to Anzulla when the Fates had spoken to me. I stopped and tilted my head listening. The shuffling of feet and the warriors' whispering were the only sounds.

It must be my imagination.

Seconds passed and then the voice spoke, "This is a gift of knowledge, *shhhhhht-gggggggt.*"

The words faded in and out. It was the same deep melodic male voice as the one on Anzulla. I swung around in a circle. Searching, but saw no one fucking with me. My brows met as I made a what-the-fuck face at Gugusan. He smiled and gave me a go-on-talk-to-it look.

I tipped my head back and spoke into the darkness. "Say that again!"

With my hands on my hips, I waited for an explanation from the Fates. Gugusan straightened his shoulders as if he was happy with me speaking to a rock. It wasn't ornate.

Just a simple marble rock pilar. No gold and nothing shiny.

"Who are you? Are you the Fates? I asked, puzzled. *There was something seriously strange going on here."*

Shhhhhht.

"It's yours. Take it home," the voice crackled and the distortion accompanying it disappeared.

Gugusan pointed to me, then his heart. "Da Kuku, úuchben máako' utia'al ooks tak ka a taal in bisik tin wotoch." He was pointing everywhere. I followed and mimicked his movements. "Da?" he asked.

"Home? My home?" I asked the Fates while deciphering what Gugusan was trying to convey and shaking my head in answer.

"I'm talking to the Fates, hold on," I whispered, waving my finger in front of my mouth. "Hello, Holy One. I am your servant. Speak freely to me."

Gugusan and I stared at each other, waiting. Nothing happened. No one answered. The warriors looked wide-eyed at me with expectation. Like I have some magical power to make a rock talk to me. This was not an Annunaki obelisk. Not even a small one. Someone carved the marble to make it look like one.

"What the fuck is this all about?" I asked Gugusan.

He lifted his hands, waved, touched his ear, and waved again with one hand. "Yeah, the Fates sound like they are taking their time today," I said. If I want the Fates to keep talking to me, to keep guiding me, I have to trust their direction. I know better than to ignore the command and not take the apple home. My father lost himself and his mind when the Fates stopped speaking to him.

Gugusan cupped my jaw to get my full attention.

"Da, Kuku, Eee-li-shaas," he whispered with softness in his expression and kindness in his tone. He understood my frustration. For some reason, it comforted me.

I huffed out loud. "Ha, what the fuck do you mean with Eee-li-shaas?" Gugusan blinked rapidly at me and scoffed. "Maybe Ela-ish-az or Eli Ishtar's?" I asked. His scrunched-up facial expression told me I could do better than that. I didn't know what to make of this so I probed his mind. *Kuku, come here. To the mountain. Kuku and his pet Eee-li-shaas.*

Now, it was my turn to be scrunching my face.

He chuckled. "Da, Eee-li-shaas. Da, Kuku," I repeated, and he looked happy enough at my conclusion. "Who are Kuku and this Eee-li-shaas?" I asked, lifting my hands in question.

He walked over to another story carved into the limestone and pointed. The other men and women accompanying us murmured and left us alone. They were shaking their heads at me and couldn't get out of this cave fast enough. Almost like they didn't want to hear this story again. I chuckled and turned my attention back to Gugusan.

It was an impressive story about a snake and a flying dragon on a journey with a figure with two identical heads and holding a sword in each hand. They were led by a warrior that leaped into the air, spear in hand, opposing two figures. One looked like a human with the wings of a bird, while the other figure was hanging onto his ankles, catching a ride over two rivers, while his long serpent tongue licked the sky, wrapping around the sun and the moon. I wondered if the sun and moon anchored him or if they were attempting to pull them down from the sky. All of the figures had humongous penises.

Gugusan then pointed at a bird and an egg and pointed back at me. "Dear god, am I the bird?" I asked while flapping my arms like a bird.

He pointed furiously at the egg. Then I realized. I was the egg. "Oh, I came here on my ship, with the bird?"

"Da!"—he pointed up and then clapped his hands. He pointed to me again— "Ishtar" —then pointed to the roof of the cave— "Kuku" —and held his pointer and middle fingers up and pushed them together.

Astonishment transformed into a sense of delightful wonder as a surge of joy filled my chest, radiating throughout my entire body, curling my toes inside my boots.

Laughter exploded out of me. "Together?" My voice echoed down the tunnels deeper into the cave. I palmed my chest. "Finally, my Kuku and me." I laughed, pointing to the rock stick figures between me and the apple. "Me, I am Ishtar. And my beloved, he is Kuku, and we are together?" I patted my chest and pointed to the bird proudly.

"Da-da-da-da-da." He nodded happily.

I extended my arm towards the stick figures. They symbolized the bond between me and my beloved Kuku. My fingers tracing them tingled as if the energy of our connection was flowing through me. "Then who are these then?" I pointed to the rest of the story.

He sighed. He took his sword, cutting the air. Pretending to fight, he tapped each figure on the head and then lastly the egg.

"I brought them here and there was a fight?"

"Da! Eee-li-shaas." He pointed to his back with his thumbs.

"Ah, a long time ago?"

"Da!" Da, Ko'oten paakat tséela' teech ka mostraré," he said, pointing to more hieroglyphs. I recognized them instantly. They were Babylonian script.

Then on the side, I saw something strange. There were seven downward strokes crossed out with one diagonal line as if someone was counting weeks, then months, and then years. Like I taught my friend Platonius. I counted them. This person counted over one thousand five hundred and sixty weeks. "That is...thirty years?"

"Da!"

"Thirty?" As I counted, I caught the English language carved out in the limestone.

"Oh my moon-god, there was a human here. It must be my Kuku! He left me this message?" I ran my fingers over it.

Waiting for you, my Ish.

Less from shock, and more from weakness and dehydration—my legs collapsed. I stumbled backward, tripping over something on the cave floor. My eyes darted around as my ass found a flat surface carved into a seat. Gugusan snorted and rubbed the back of his neck.

"Yeah, I know, I'm clumsy. I haven't slept or eaten for weeks." I let out a sigh and cradled my dizzy head in the palms of my hands. I closed my eyes for a second to compose myself. *How many times have I jumped here not knowing about this cave?* As I opened my eyes, my gaze fell on a small straw bed. "What's this? Who slept here?" I asked as loud squawking and screeches of birds in red and blue colors drew my attention deeper into the cave. Light streamed in from above in the distance. *Hmmm, so there's another opening.* The birds were the same colors as the plumes on the men's head and body coverings. Gugusan sighed heavily and sat down next to me. He extended his arm and the palm of his hand as he held up some kind of nut. One of the magnificent birds flew closer and found purchase on his arm, took the nut, and cracked it open. It said something. It was talking.

"This is his bed, isn't it? He waited here. For me. Where is he, where is my Kuku?" I begged.

Gugusan lifted his other arm as well and flapped his hand like a bird.

"What the fuck man, did he fly away?"

"Da, Eee-li-shaas," he said, flapping his arm again. Suddenly, the bird sitting on his arm took off flying. Gugusan waved both his arms.

He was talking about the damn bird. Not my mate.

My stomach clenched tightly. I folded double, as my hunger pains forced me to take notice. *I'm tired and hungry.* Gugusan kept talking, he pointed to the apple in my hand. To the bed and then flapped his arms again.

"Are you saying Kuku slept here and then flew away?"

"Da!"

"So he is gone?"

Shaking his head, he said, "Na-na-na! Kuku," and then he pointed upward again, back to me and away. "To the stars?" I probed his mind, seeing only glimpses of that face from my dreams, the name Kuku, which I now knew belonged to my mate. I saw me fucking Gugusan, I saw the mountain and the people, and I heard my name being called out over and over—he was thinking about us fucking.

"I'm hungry, can we speak over a meal?" I asked, rubbing my stomach. He wiggled an eyebrow at me. "In túuxtik máak utia'al u ka' taalaken t'anik Kuku. Je'el u páajtal a taal janal yéetel je'elel tak ka Kuku quiera kaxant teech." He pretended to eat and drink, clueing me in that he would feed me and entertain me as usual. I scanned his mind. My Kuku came for me, he slept here and was waiting for me. He flew high and away. I saw fields of corn and women and children running. Chaos. More running into plantations of corn. The night sky. *Okay, none of this is making any sense.*

"Dammit, Gugusan, is he here or not? Show him to me. I will take him home, away from this place," I said irritated, starving, and hopeless. It felt like I grappled with good news, and was losing.

Gugusan's eyes grew in size. He bit down on his lip before shaking his head. *Didn't he want me to find him? No, he didn't want me to take him away.* "Start talking to me, I know you understand me," I grunted, pointing a finger at him.

"You are here and you are there. Your Kuku is not here. Your Kuku there, with the Birdmen," he spoke in riddles and circles. Then tapping the apple, he patted my pocket and my swords.

He must have me mixed up with my previous visits.

"Yes, I will put it away," I said as Gugusan got up, pretending to be sword fighting. Slicing the air and then flapping his arms again.

I pointed to my eyes. "I see. No, I haven't seen war in a long time. I will take the apple. I will continue searching. First, I need to wash, eat, drink." *Eating and drinking must happen first because I feel like passing out.*

"Da, gg fuck!" he said, nodding eagerly. *To my furs. Pleasure time, with the Demon God. I will feed him my cock, blood, and seed.*

I chuckled weakly, holding my palms up. "Okay. You, me, and your furs," I got up, slapping a hand on my leg. He was so big, but underneath it all, so cute. I liked him and I wanted to fuck him. But I knew he wasn't meant to be my mate. My Kuku was here and there. Between this place and the moon, my mate was waiting for me, and I will keep searching until I find him. I changed the subject because my head was reeling.

"What are they? What do you call them? The beautiful birds."

He seemed to catch on and said in an excited tone, "Vucub-Caquix."

"Vukubaku," I repeated. He snort-laughed but nodded, showing me his thumb and index finger close to each other. "Ah, close but not correct."

"Da."

I smiled and pointed questioningly at the opening of the cave. "Shall we go?" I couldn't see any reason to stay here. I needed to return to Grayrak in case the chameleon ball-shaped ship arrived. Then figure out how to jump home to deliver the apple. I was more determined than ever to find my mate. Maybe I would find him going home. Maybe that's why I have to go home to Ki and An.

"Shall we go?" I pointed outside with my fingers and mimicked a roof on a house.

"Da," he replied.

"I'll eat and drink, then I must go," I said, inspecting the apple in the firelight. It was bigger than a human fist and cold in my hand. The vibrations it emitted tickled. Strange symbols, much like the ones carved into the obelisks, created wavy patterns all around the apple. But I failed to decipher or read it. I tucked it into the pocket of my jacket. "Thank you." I was reluctant to go home. I knew the Fates wanted me to take it to Babylon. I pushed that thought to the back of my mind. I was a time traveler and had all the time in the universe to travel back to deliver it.

Gugusan gave me a stern nod. "Da, gg fuck," he answered and pointed the way.

Their city in the mountains was striking. On each visit, the twists and turns down the mountain revealed new discoveries.

The breathtaking view of the waterfalls and wild domesticated animals like monkeys and goats awaited and greeted me. The architecture of their clay huts and limestone was slightly different, too. I noticed some homes were finished, new ones were being carved out of lime-stone. Evidence that I had arrived some years later than before. A terrace of corn was freshly plowed and surrounded by more terraces of homes carved into the mountain. Pools of water for drinking and bathing ran along a newly designed irrigation system fed by the river birthed by the waterfalls above, zig-zagging down the mountain to where the livestock roamed free. The whole mountain village nearly grew into a city.

I stayed in the shadows, avoiding direct sunlight. Most people were already up and awake, busy working on one thing or another. From food being prepared, huts being swept, and fish being gutted for breakfast, I was impressed with their fluency and how organized they were, but most of all—their friendly greeting faces were astounding. It was so far removed from the busy streets of Egypt, Rome, Babylon, China, and Japan.

"Ko'oten yéetel leti'e', k'ajolo'on ti' le máako', in wil wa taak u compañía." Gugusan called a woman over and pointed to me. Friendly and small in stature, she appeared in awe of my size as her gaze swept up and down my body. I smiled and gave a small wave. She shook her head and barked something at Gugusan. He rested a hand on her shoulder as he spoke to her, but she seemed not to hear him as my appearance transfixed her.

"Ma' a preocupes. Yaan u jantik, beberá yéetel táan sáamal. Leti' yaan u manzana. U yojel u Kuku táan u pa'atik," he said, placating her. It seemed to do the trick. She blinked and turned to speak to another woman.

I needed to get inside and away from the sun's deadly rays. My skin was prickling and would soon be sizzling. As if reading my thoughts, Gugusan called me and we made our way to his humble palace. It was bigger than before. Judging from the outside, it seemed he had carved deeper into the mountain. It was much bigger and divided into sections and hallways. There was space for about fifty men to sit on hand-woven mats. His throne room, the village, and its people were progressing, which confirmed I arrived years after my previous visits.

As I ate, one woman after another approached me, batting their eyelashes and fiddling with their hair. Dear god, I could smell and taste their lust. But I only wanted him.

"Na, thank you. I don't want you. Go away please," I said and gently waved them off. More women flaunted their naked breasts and their scrumptious behinds. Stroking my hair and licking the shells of my ears. It irked me more than bugs do, and I froze, hoping I wasn't offending anyone. Ten females later, Gugusan met my gaze. I shrugged. He shook his head. I shrugged again. He huffed.

"No thank you," I said and gave him that look only men with my tastes understood. He tipped his chin. Understanding, and reading the room. I returned his stare with a smoldering gaze. I wanted him and he wanted me.

Gugusan gave me that, *alright, let's go for it* look. We had a mutual understanding.

He rose to his feet and pointed to the entrance, not breaking the intense eye fucking or cock stirring look.

A woman huffed somewhere beside me, she wasn't happy and removed her hands from me.

He wanted to fuck me. Thank the Fates!

I had already decided I was going to let him, while I filled my stomach with my dessert, his sweet male blood. I wiped my hands clean on my pants.

Just then, a young man came running inside with a clay pot, put it on the floor next to me, and ran out. I knew what this was. I picked it up and grinned. Inside was pig fat.

"Yaan a K'abéet le nojoch paalo'," Gugusan said and then smiled at me. "Da?"

"Yes, da-da-da," I said and stood up. I was going to need the pig fat. He pointed to the back, down a short hallway.

"Yes, please," I said, picking up the torch and bringing it with me. His intense gaze and slight tilt of his chin hinted to me to push aside the woven leaves that hung like curtains dividing the area. Inside was a hollowed-out rock bath where water steamed and beckoned me. I shivered and loved the sight and smell of all that precious water. I missed a hot bath and couldn't wait to get inside it.

I turned to him, grinning and already taking my shirt off. He looked at me, never taking his eyes off me. No time for modesty, I guess. I kicked my boots to the side and unbuttoned my pants. He gasped like he had the other times when I stood in all my nakedness in front of him. He was big and tall for a human. But I was clearly the biggest between us.

I showed him it was now his turn to undress. With a

flick and a pull, the leather and feathers went flying. Then he stood proudly erect, watching me appreciating his body. My mouth salivated for him. I was going to let him fuck me, and then I was going to fuck him senseless and drink my fill.

But first I was getting into that water, I'd dreamed of and envisioned entering it. My memories and the reality of traveling back and forth aligned. We climbed inside and washed ourselves without saying a word. After a thorough mutual cleansing session, he moved closer. I wasn't sure if he wanted to kiss or not. The humans on Grayrak surely did.

But this man was a king. Intimacy was not his thing. I wasn't sure what he wanted me to do. I was here for a fuck and feeding. My mate was somewhere in this jungle and he had been waiting for me for thirty years. Which thirty years I didn't know. But what I knew, was that I would find him. Someone had carved the truth and proof into that rock. I assume my Kuku flighting away meant I'd already found him, and Gugusan saw me taking him away. The sword fighting was confusing. I guess they were warriors and that there would be a battle.

I refocused and took my rock-hard cock in my hand, squeezing it for relief. He mimicked me. I probed his mind but only sensed want and need for me. He wanted me because I was his best fuck ever? He felt sorry for me and he saw me as a lost god from the sky? He wanted to ride a god? He stepped closer. I thought to lean in for a kiss, but no, he brushed by me and got out of the water. The torch-light glistened on his wet skin. The swell of desire and hunger for him increased as our eyes met. The ferocious hunger gnawing at my empty stomach burned like melting gold.

I followed him out of the water as my dick stood erect and pointed the way. With each step closer, the anticipation grew, and I could feel the charge in the air between us. He looked back at me, his eyes locked with mine, and I knew exactly how this was going to go.

He gestured for me to lie down on his large bed, covered in different animal skins, woven mats, and soft woolen cushions. I didn't have a preference for how to start fucking and went down on my hands and knees in front of him. My breath exploded out of me with an oomph as he covered my body with his. His big human size cock lay like a brick between my ass cheeks. I moaned my pleasure. The universal sound for, "Yes, that's good. I want more."

He pinned me down by sliding his hands over my shoulders to my forearms. Rubbing his cock up and down my wet and throbbing hole. Gods, I wanted him to fuck me. I pumped my hips into the goat wool and buckskins below my hips.

"Come on, do it already," I said in Babylonian. Then remembering the English message scratched out in the rock face of the cave I connected telepathically to Gugusan and calibrated and replanted the language seed of not only Anunnaki but Babylonian and English in case my Kuku had to communicate with them. I hoped I was helping him and if we meet one day, hopefully soon, I will declare that although I was with Gugusan, my Kuku was the only one on my mind.

Be patient, I'm taking my time with you. If this is our last time, I want to remember it. I heard his thoughts and suddenly understood him much easier. "What do you mean, our last time?" I asked as he let go of me and my ass and returned with the clay pot.

"Na-na-na. No talk now," he said and lathered his cock with the white fatty stuff. He took one look at my ass and I let him wrestle me back down. Pushing and smearing his cockhead around my entrance, once, twice, then with no further preparation, he savagely plunged into me.

My eyes bulged. *Oh Fuck!*

I gasped and squeezed my eyelids shut. My toes splayed open, as I concentrated on baring down.

"Blazing scarabs, you are the king, Gugusan. The king of this jungle!" My fingers curled around a buckskin. I blabbered and he laughed with aggressive glee. If I didn't know better, I would think he was mad at me. "You are punishing me, why?" He didn't answer. He kept on hammering until the pain disappeared, "That's so good. So what I wanted. Ah, fuck," I purred. My nerve endings sparked, but I still saw my Kuku's face behind my closed eyelids.

The mixture of agonizing pleasurable sensations wiped my mind blank and all I felt was him.

He was like a beast. I have had sex a few times in this village, but never like this. Gugusan's strokes were rough and deep. If I was a human I was going to be fucked raw.

I looked over my shoulder. "You maniac!" I grunted.

My voice thundered out of his hut. The walls shook, and I knew the mountain rumbled as dust and small rocks fell from his cave's roof. I bit down on my upper arm, silencing myself.

Dammit, now the praying is going to continue. Now they will always think of me as a god.

He eased back, changing his aim, waited until I relaxed, and then pushed back into me harder than before. I slid forward, unable to stay on my hands and knees. Finding purchase against the wall, I opened my legs and let him have his way with me.

There was no kissing, no intimacy, only a whole lot of grunts, and it was erotic as fuck. He mauled me like an animal. He devoured all my pain.

Then with no warning, he bit my shoulder with his blunt teeth. Hard and drawing blood. I didn't care. I let him drink. Let him have my blood. He knew. I knew he knew. I knew he wanted a piece of me, of my strength, of my blood.

"Yeah, take from me what you need! You've earned it," I said, and he didn't let up, he slurped on my shoulder.

He used me and my hole with the voracity of a mindless caveman. *I needed this. I so-so fucking did.* His sweat mingled with mine and dripped down my body as he glided over my back. Chills and pleasure overtook my mind and body. I lost myself in the rhythm. Forgot about Grayrak. Forgot about my family in Babylon, but the face of my lovely blue-eyed lover stayed etched on the insides of my eyelids.

"Oh sweet Fates, yes!"

Over and over, Gugusan slipped in and slid over that sweet spot inside me, making me want to climax without touching myself. Our grunts and moans grew louder and filled his chamber. The sounds like two roaring mating crocodiles.

He thrust deeper, faster, and harder. Trying his best to fuck the life out of me—maybe he was, because he thought this was our last fuck, and he wanted it to be our best fuck ever.

My throat was dry with heaving and I hollered my ecstasy as I reached my climax at the same time he reached his. Our moans became one, a symphony of desire echoing through the cavernous room. More dust rained down from the cave roof. With one last thrust, he planted himself balls deep inside me. His cocked pulsed as he emptied his balls.

Once I had fed from him and satisfied my carnal desires, Gugusan, who was on the verge of turning into an Anunnaki servant, fell into a deep slumber from which he will awaken still the king of this jungle, but stronger, faster and invincible by any other human. His blood was rich. It filled me with renewed energy that would last for weeks. Hopefully, I would find my mate sooner than that. But it was a stark reminder of the dehydrated, drugged-up humans in Grayrak—it compelled me to return and help Barkor.

Gugusan cracked open one eye, attempting a lazy grin as he lay in a messy heap from our debauchery. Perhaps I had taken a few more sips than necessary—my starving bite was potent and could have been too much for him.

"May the Fates watch over you," I whispered, looking at him with gratitude. "Thank you for your spectacular hospitality, Gugusan. I will be back to discuss you sucking my blood and what it means," I said and whistled a tune of cheerful contentment as I turned away to go wash up. "Who knows, someday maybe I'll even write a sonnet about this experience."

"Da, I'm like Eee-li-shaas, now. Write a sonnet about your Kuku. It's better. You come to live with Kuku on your mountain," he whispered. I turned and looked incredulously at him.

His eyes fluttered shut while he let out a satisfied sigh, lips curving into a small smile, before he fell asleep with a gentle snore. I knew then that I had ruined him for any future lovers. I realized he had spoken in a mix of my mother tongue and the human English on the moon. It was a sign of the Fates.

"I'm going to go to Grayrak. I'll be back as soon as I can," I said and quickly bathed. When I was freshened up, dressed, and ready to go, I thanked Gugusan for the unforgettable evening, even though I knew he was already fast asleep. My legs still trembled from our passionate encounter.

Grabbing my jacket and making sure the apple was still in the pocket, I stepped outside to find two men waiting to escort me back up the hill to my time machine.

After they helped me fill and load canisters of corn and water onto my ship, I said my thanks and goodbyes, strapped in, and was ready to go.

I stared out the window over the vast outline of the

treetops below. "Lasitor, please mark this place and time. Starting tomorrow night, I want to return to the jungle every day for the next thirty years into the past and if we don't find my Kuku, we jump back to this day and work our way each day into the future. Narrowing it down, until I find my Kuku. We are very close to finding him."

"Yes, Ishtar, that's a good plan. I agree, and we will do so," Lasitor answered and impressed me with his sudden cooperation.

"Thank you. Start the jump to Grayrak. I want to check on Barkor, he will be happy to see I brought the water," I said as I stored the apple in the overhead cubby where I kept my valuables.

"Ready yourself, Ishtar. We are jumping in, three, two, one. To Grayrak, we go."

CHAPTER 6
MY KUKU

"*GOOD MORNING, ISHTAR.*

Did you know humans used to sell water? In fact, they used to sell many kinds of water in all its forms. Since the dawn of man, it has become so scarce, precious, and mystical that humans across the globe have flocked to all kinds of places, for example, the white calcium pools in Anatolia, modern-day Turkey. Rich in minerals, the blue waters of Pamukkale, Turkey, have had healing powers for centuries—until the whole Earth flooded and washed all that goodness away.

Breakfast is served until eight a.m.

Have a magical day!"

ISHTAR
24 970 B.C.
The jungle

. . .

Da, dum-dum-dum!
   Da, dum-dum-dum!
   Da, dum-dum-dum!
   Da, dum-dum-dum!

JUST HOURS AGO, Lasitor had told me some interesting facts about children. Sometimes I think he knows me better than I knew myself. "Did you know a child who spends more time outdoors is less likely to become short-sighted? And did you also know a toddler covering their eyes thinks you can't see them either? Taking time to get to know your children and have fun with them creates a pleasant atmosphere and cheers you up. If it seems like a tough task, keep in mind that if monkeys can educate their offspring about dental flossing, you can educate your children to at least go outdoors and avoid myopathy, while also providing them with a more comprehensive outlook on their environment. Ishtar, keep your eyes wide open, greet a new day!" Lasitor said as he chased me out of the door to say goodbye to Gugusan.

My plan was ruined. I wanted to execute it by working my way back, day by day, thirty years into the past and future from the date I's seen the carvings in the cave and received the apple.

The rhythm of the drums carried my thoughts beyond the borders of time, to Grayrak and back again to the here and now where the six feet high fire burned furiously and the smoke stung my sensitive eyes. Internally, I was wrestling with finding my mate, my obligations to follow the path the Fates chose for me, and the fucking never ending thirst for drug-laced blood. I was as moody as a hungry lion, and jittery as a cockroach on a hot stove plate.

I don't know when I will return to the San people and their jungle to continue my search for my mate. My plan to return every day for the next thirty years into the future and thirty years into the past, was fucked.

Upon my arrival in Grayrak, while bringing the remaining food and water over to Barkor's, I was thinking of absconding or intervening by saving the humans from their inevitable self-destruction by myself.

But, blessed by the Fates, Barkor noticed movement and a sound foreign to Grayrak's dome. Thanks to his sharp observation skills, he discovered the small ship flying in circles, cleverly disguising itself in plain sight. As the Fates had foretold, they revealed their presence by camouflaging themselves, like chameleons.

I was still helping Sarinka unpack and hide the provisions from the Disciples when Barkor called to me.

"Ishtar, come and see. I'm hearing and seeing something strange. The air feels out of place. I hear a faint hum, but I can't see anything, even though I know it's there!" Barkor was pointing towards the roof of the dome. My gaze locked on the strange rippling of air where he was showing.

"Sweet scarab cakes, it's them!" I chucked the crates to

Sarinka, not removing my gaze from the apparition. "Quick, Barkor, grab their attention!" I'd shouted, overjoyed. We must have looked like two fools chasing after something that no one else could see or hear, but that was just life in Grayrak. Acting in such a manner was considered normal because half of the people were suffering from malnourishment, while the other half were constantly under the influence of drugs.

Meeting the visitors was a complete turnaround from my previous state of hopelessness. Like Barkor, they were half Anunnaki. They were healthy and strong men, radiating vitality with their clean and vibrant faces. There was no trace of weakness or illness in them. Their ship and clothes carried a pleasant scent of soap. Scarabs, they smelled refreshing, and overall, such a delightful bunch of intelligent young men.

But the shock of witnessing what emerged last from that spacecraft was indescribable. There stood an astonishingly tall and regal male, exuding a warm smile and possessing eyes so pure that they seemed to delve straight into the depths of my dark soul, devoid of any trace of malevolence. It was as if he had cleansed me from within, purging some of my negativity. The humans were instantly captivated by him, even more so than by Barkor. Men, women, and children were flocking to him, touching him, and laughing as if he were a walking loaf of bread.

Since then, over the past couple of weeks, I've been overwhelmed by a whirlwind of feelings, obligations, and morals that have left me feeling emotionally drained. I was initially greeted with warmth and friendliness until Cian intervened and brought me back to my senses. I must admit, my addiction had consumed me, making me self-centered and oblivious to the significant events unfolding on Earth. They falsely believed I was responsible for the turmoil on the moon.

I felt completely clueless.

Then, suddenly, Cian lunged across the table, his hands closing around my throat, extinguishing the last remnants of my pitiful existence. As I faded into darkness, memories of my Kuku flashed before my eyes—a message from destiny itself. Cian's forceful intervention abruptly yanked me from that tranquil, serene place, forcing me to confront reality and answer their questions. In an instant, my priorities were forcefully realigned, neatly arranged before me.

They exceeded my expectations by far. These men were not what I had anticipated—they were larger, more intelligent, and quite a handful. Among them, Eryn surprised me the most. He was a powerful Anunnaki King. When he stepped out of the Bubblecar, I could have sworn I saw a ghost, one of the many haunting spirits from my homeland—my brothers. Standing at a towering height like my own eight feet, he moved his thick muscled body gracefully while exuding a commanding presence, as he carried a spear made of pure gold. There was an aura of tranquility around him. He's deeply in love and bonded to Ivan, the incredibly beautiful, fair-skinned half-Anunnaki, who happened to be the brother of my assailant, Cian. Like Barkor, the twins were taller than humans, as they stood seven feet high. Despite that, Ivan and Cian bore no resemblance to each other, although sharing striking bright blue eyes. Ivan boasted long, sleek, and soft-looking blond hair, while Cian's head was completely shaved and his arms tattooed, giving him a rugged appearance, much like Barkor's. All distantly related to me as my half-Anunnaki kin.

Eryn stood out as royalty, emanating an aura of mystery and allure. His presence was like gazing into the depths of the ocean, with its unfathomable depths and wonders. Unlike Eryn, Cian's eyes held a murderous glare as I looked up at him, regretting my actions. In that moment, I pleaded for him to end my life, so I could join my Kuku in their fading existence. However, his response was a cold refusal.

"Too easy. Once you reveal how to save these people and eliminate the Zelk, I'll gladly end your life," Cian vowed, positioning himself with his feet on either side of my head. His mesmerizing blue eyes reminded me of my beloved Kuku, while the noticeable bulge in his pants caught my attention. All of them were male, and even Eryn, the largest and strongest, had a male partner. I couldn't help but smile—what other reaction could I have had? They exuded an irresistible aura of sexuality. Just like I sensed with Titus and Gugusan, I instantly knew they were attracted to men, not women. If Apsu had ever laid eyes on them, he would have surely burst into flames with disgust.

When Cian asked me where I had been staying all this time, I chose to omit my travels to the time and place where Gugusan and my Kuku existed. I held onto the hope that the glimpses of my Kuku's face, straddling the line between reality and nothingness, meant that I would soon meet him. I found myself at a crossroads, torn between helping to save the humans alongside Cian or returning to Gugusan. But if I abandoned my initial purpose, my feelings of guilt and uselessness would have me craving the solace of tainted blood. It was a never-ending cycle that consumed me.

The burden of yearning for the man of my dreams had become too much to bear. Watching Eryn and Ivan's love for each other ignited bitterness within me, and seeing Cian in a similar predicament, desiring Barkor but unable to have him, served as a reminder that my duty to assist Barkor, his humans, and my newfound friends from Earth was more important than pursuing my desires.

To avoid getting lost again, I had to let go of my longing for my Kuku. The jungle wasn't where I belonged, nor was it my people. If I let my indecisiveness suffocate me, I would never find a way out of the maze I created. My mind was torn in two. As much as I wanted to be with Cian, Ivan, and Eryn, I decided to escape their constant presence in Grayrak to say goodbye to the San. I did it more for myself because I could always come back to this time and place. They wouldn't even notice I was gone.

HERE, in the jungle, everything was simple, and it was easy to forget about the moon. During my visits, I searched for my mate, but found solace in this carefree haven where Barkor, Sarinka, and the needy humans didn't require my assistance. I was passing time, while hoping to encounter my Kuku. I must accept this feeling of futile longing and wait. I had responsibilities and had to compel my heart, which couldn't care less about the moon, to concentrate on what truly mattered. The voice of the Fates.

With a sigh, I reluctantly scooted closer to speak to Gugusan. I took in the sight of his tribe's humble village and bountiful, rich soil, yielding an abundance of crops. The palms of my hands were sweaty and cold, and my heart pumped a sludge of thick reluctant blood through my body as I forced myself to speak the words that had been weighing on my mind.

"This will be my final visit, I think," I said, unable to meet his gaze. My eyes followed his stare, drifting to the mountaintop and back to the flames of the bonfire. It flickered and danced, casting a spellbinding glow over the gathering tribe. A hush fell upon us. The children started chanting, their voices merging with the thumping rhythm of drums, ankle bells, and foot rattles. The percussion harmonized with the rhythm of nature and the night while the psychedelic euphoria of the blood I had taken enhanced and intertwined my visions and memories. I suspected Gugusan had sent this particular young man to me for this very reason because I was slowly feeling better and the smile plastered on my face seemed to amuse him. We've become good friends, and I have shared secrets about my genealogy, his newly acquired Igigi status, and haunting dreams about my mate with him. He wasn't shocked, and I guessed finding the apple here was proof enough that weird things turned up in this village. Like that awkward-looking stranger who had been eyeing me from afar. He was a sneaky one. But tonight, ever since my arrival, I sensed him closer than usual but still staying out of reach for mental probing while hiding in the shadows. I've asked about the mysterious man, but Gugusan waved me off and urged me to share more memories of the man I'd never met, but who had led me here.

I leaned closer to hear my friend's reaction to my news.

"You not search for Kuku, no more?" he asked. Like myself, they were all speaking a mix of Babylonian, English, and their native tongue.

I shook my head once. "I'm needed in another place and time. People are starving and killing one another for food." I couldn't say more than that. Explaining to Gugusan that the Zelk was building an army with human body parts would be nearly impossible, and he didn't need to know that.

He didn't criticize my choice, almost like he didn't believe me. He waved my statement off, and as the news spread around the fire, some came over to assure me I would find my Kuku, the other half of my soul, before I left. The problem was I'd left dozens of times and never found him. The next time I returned, I got the same answer. Before you leave, you will find him. Almost as if they had practiced the words.

The festivities were getting louder. I leaned closer to speak into Gugusan's ear. "Tell me, why don't you ever say goodbye?"

He patted my knee. "We never say goodbye because

goodbye means going away and going away means forgetting. So we say meet you soon."

"And why do you always take me to search the jungle, but when I ask where my Kuku is, you say I will see him before I go?"

I've never seen Gugusan look so serious. He tipped his cup back and emptied it, then put it to the side, wiped his lips dry with the back of his hand, and said, "Look at me, Demon God, Ku k'uchul ojéeltbil ba'ax táan kíinsa'ab tu táan ta, yéetel le ba'ax táan oculto teechi' u a aclarará. A Kuku yéetel Eee-li-shaas ma' sa'atako'on, sino escondidos, vendrán ti' teech ken a biin."

"For fuck's sake! Stop talking in riddles!" I shouted. My head was spinning, and the world tilted. "You wanted me to fuck Zaduka. You knew he was eating the mushrooms, didn't you?" His face said he knew, and he'd planned it. "What do you mean by I will come to know what is in front of me, and that which is hidden from me will become clear?"

He swiped his finger left and right in front of me. "Your Kuku, Da?"

"Yes!"

"Kuky and Eee-li-shaas not lost, but hidden. They will come when you leave, they wait for you."

I threw my hands up in defeat. We have searched the jungle and beyond. I've searched for my mate by lifting every bloody stone, looking inside every hole, but nothing.

"Maybe my Kuku is not in the jungle. Maybe he is searching for me." I pointed beyond the mountains. "What if he crossed the great rivers?"

"No!" Gugusan said. "No worry. You come back when you finish helping. You always come back," he said with an encouraging smile. The flames from the fire warmed my face. It calmed me. My fingers fumbled in my pocket and curled around the apple. It was rough and fitted perfectly in my big hand. I couldn't bear the thought of taking it back to Babylon. The weight of it held some kind of deeper meaning for me, like an answer I had been searching for. But at the same time, I knew I had to return it. And returning it would be like losing my connection to this place. To my mate. Also, I was wary of facing my father. The thought made my stomach churn. Time seemed to slip away from me, and this apple, which must be buried somewhere in Ki and An's garden, felt like a reminder that time belonged to me, even when everything else felt out of reach.

Icy chills prickled along my spine as I felt eyes on me. Following my instincts, I turned, searching the darkness across the river. My eyesight was much better than a human's so I could find and locate that stranger hiding in a dark corner behind a woven mat that served as a door in front of a cave. His legs were visible beneath the fabric, and he seemed oddly out of place.

Before I could get up and approach him, Gugusan interrupted, snapping me out of my trance. "Leaving so soon?" he asked, pulling me back to reality.

"Yes," I replied with a heavy heart. "Unfortunately, I have responsibilities elsewhere." My gaze flickered back to the shadows where the stranger had been hiding. It didn't matter now that I was leaving. Time for me to move on and find my place in Eryn and his brothers' world. To embrace the people and follow the path that the Fates had intended for me.

For nearly an hour, I bid farewell to Gugusan and his fierce warriors, expressing my gratitude for their hospitality. I also thanked the women and children of the tribe who had welcomed me with open arms during my visits. As usual, two warriors escorted me as we made our way back up the mountain. My ship came into sight and I felt the effects of the potent substance wearing off. I hummed a song under my breath, a tribute to a love that would never materialize. It was bittersweet, but I had finally accepted the reality of our paths never crossing.

My Missing Piece.

I've searched all over and stood empty-handed at the boundary of time.

Wishing for just one word, one moment with him, but he's gone, vanished into the shadows.

Where is my lover?

I've checked every corner of the earth, combed through every memory, yet still, I find nothing but emptiness.

The sun sets, and I am left with a heart heavy with longing and a mind full of questions.

Did he leave willingly?

Was it something I did or said?

Each night I lay awake, my dreams filled with his face, only to wake to an empty bed.

Where is my lover?

Is he wandering lost in some distant land?

Or has his heart found refuge in another's hands?

I search for answers that may never come, but still, I hold onto the hope that one day, our paths will cross again.

Until then, I will keep searching, for that missing piece of my heart.

Where is my lover?

Only time knows.

Until then, I will wait.

When we reached my ship, I did a double take. I reached for my swords in haste as the door swooshed open. Someone was inside my ship.

"Who is there? Show yourself, and for the love of the Fates, don't touch anything!"

The sound of hands clapping echoed from inside my time machine. I stood frozen, out of sight from the doorway. My first instinct was to charge in, confront whoever was inside and chop off their hands. But my impulsive actions could lead to disaster. The last thing I wanted was for my precious ship and Lasitor to take off, leaving me stranded. And I couldn't afford to anger Eryn and his brothers, who were waiting for me in Grayrak. The Fates had entrusted me with one important mission, and I couldn't risk losing my ship in a fit of rage. So I took a deep breath and stayed rooted in place, my hands clenched into fists around the hilts of my blades at my sides, waiting for the right moment to act.

A low, husky voice blared from inside my ship, and it wasn't Lasitor's. "I'm so glad you enjoyed your stay. I can smell the joy all the way up the bloody fucking mountain —all fucked out! You are too stoned to see straight, never mind flying your time machine," whoever he was said in perfect English.

In English? What the fuck?

Did I bring someone home with me last night in my drunken stupor and then bring them here?

My body vibrated. I cautiously stepped closer to the entrance, wondering who could be inside.

"Lasitor! Did you give access and allow a stranger on board?"

"Excuse me, Ishtar, I did not open the door, just like I didn't open it for the Anubis. Stop accusing me of doing human things. I cannot override the door opening and closing. It's a manual out-of-date lever. I've told you to update it, but no, you don't trust me. You think I will take over and fly off without you," Lasitor responded, not giving me any sign if this was a stranger or not.

With swords raised, I glared at the door, wishing the trespasser would show himself. "State your name and why you are inside my ship," I demanded. My two escorts, dressed in feathers and barely there clothing, burst into laughter, playfully wished me luck and farewell, and sauntered away. "Hey, come back!" I yelled. "I need help to remove the intruder." But all I got in response were shrugged shoulders, amused chuckles, and wiggling bare asses.

I widened my stance and called to the Fates, the name I had picked up from the Grayrakians, "Oh, moon-god!"

"You should go and wash yourself. You can't sit in these seats like that. The stench of that pig fat and another man's scent is enough to make me vomit all over your precious instrumentation," he said.

"Ishtar, vomit over our instrumentation does not sound safe for either of us," Lasitor added.

Then the intruder added, "And with a closed door, we'll be barfing all over each other. So go wash your tripping ass or Lasitor and I leave you here."

Wash myself? Leave me here?

My brain stalled. Something weird and exciting was happening. I felt like doing a happy dance and banging my drums. This was unlike any of my previous visits to this place. Could this be it? Was my lost, long-awaited mate going to materialize and emerge from that door? He certainly sounded possessive. It was too real, too fast for my brain to catch up and grasp the miracle of the situation. I wanted to poke my head inside to have a look but the chance of being decapitated was too high. He was probably correct although I'd had a quick wash after filling that young man's insides to the brim.

"Reveal yourself," I said, squeezing my eyelids together. My brain hurt as if poked with a hot poker. It was true that the pig fat ensured a smoother glide, but the smell of it didn't wash off after a quick rinse.

"If I show myself, you must keep an open mind. Can you do that for me, my Ish?"

His Ish. Oh, my god. My visions and dreams were coming true. This was not some crazy villager.

"Listen, whoever the fuck, you are, get out of my ship right now!" I was nervous and excited, like a kid about to get a new toy. Energy pulsated around me. Foreboding thoughts of accidents and unrequited love swirled in my mind making me dizzy. One wrong button and the ship was gone, and I was stranded.

"Don't fucking touch anything," I added while swaying on my feet.

"Promise me you won't hate me and leave me here." My mate's beautiful voice thundered with an accent I couldn't place. He sounded upset with me. This was him. No wonder Gugusan kept looking up the mountain. I heard the shuffling of feet coming closer. He was almost at the door now. "Promise me!"

"I promise, just show yourself," I said. Black spots danced around me, just as a head with pure white hair popped out. His eyes were blue and sparkled like diamonds. My mouth opened and closed. No sound escaped. Cold recognition washed over me.

"You are fortunate that I am so happy to see you alive, and not the murderous jealous type," he said with a lopsided grin. He was stunning. Inwardly, that dried-up piece of meaty organ in my chest stuttered and restarted while my gut gave a joyful flip-flop. Outwardly, I beamed.

"My—Ma—Mate?" I said breathlessly. The world tilted. I stumbled over my words as the drawings on the cave walls suddenly made sense to me. This was my lover. My mate. He was here just as I thought. The words of the Fates, the drawings on the cave wall, the apple, the ship, and the faces of people I've never seen. They all spun in the maelstrom in my confused mind. I heaved air into my lungs as I struggled to breathe. Memories from the past and present collided and rushed through the synapses in my brain. Suddenly, it all became my reality. My swords fell out of my hands and my knees buckled as astonishment paralyzed me.

"Fucking small door!" He shouted as a flash of white shot towards me. He caught me just before I hit the ground. I looked up, dazed. The smooth pearl-white face of my dreams looked down at me. I wanted to touch him, but something strange was happening to me. A silver tear slid down his rosy cheek. I regained coordination of my arms and reached up, wiping it away with my thumb. Wordlessly, I lay on his lap. Feeling safe and, for the first time, not alone.

"Horrible feeling I know," he said. His face was beaming with recognition of me. He knew me, and he saw me.

"I-I found you," I stuttered. "Just before—I almost left, but I found you."

"Yes, you bloody did. Did you get back onto your ship? Did you escape those creatures, after all?" he asked, and the gears in my head spun in all directions—not sure what he was talking about. I grappled for words to make sense of what was happening. "Calm down, take deep breaths," he whispered while softly stroking my forehead, my cheeks, my lips, and strangely, my eyelashes with the tips of his fingers.

"When I saw you earlier going down the mountain, I was so happy to see you, but I decided to wait here for you. I thought you were dead, and I was stranded here forever." His voice was gentle and caring. His touches told me he was telling the truth. "So I figured my best chance of going home was to wait for you on the ship. You know, in case you fly off and leave me here again."

I felt as if I knew him, too. It was on the tip of my tongue, "Is—are, wait, what is your name?"

"It's Peter?"

"Peter, my mate, my Kuku."

"Yes, it is me. And you took your time partying down there." His smile turned into a snarl—I was getting mixed messages from him.

"Are you feeling better now? I want to go home."

"Home?"

"Where is that?" I asked, looking up at him. He was even more handsome than my visions, and I wanted to touch his face. Pale with rosy cheeks, soft and hairless. The most luscious bottom lip. I wanted to nibble on it.

His smile turned into a vicious scowl. "What's that supposed to mean?" he spat at me. Moon-god, he was feisty and short-tempered. "Fuck you, Ish." He pushed me off his lap. Wings twitching, he said, "I'm waiting for you inside. No wonder you wanted to bring me here, you already think of this place as home. You probably couldn't wait to fuck your boyfriend." He harrumphed as he turned to enter the ship. I lay on the ground, gawking at him.

"Fuck you, Ish. No, never mind. You've been fucked already," he shouted, stomping his bare feet up the stairs. What a sight he was. It must take magic or sheer determination to move inside those tight pants. Maybe they were painted or tattooed on him? His head, with its pure white mane, disappeared inside, followed by a forceful wrestling match between his enormous wings and the door.

White feathers of different sizes floated everywhere. I sat up, catching one long one, and sniffing it deeply. "Hmmm," I closed my eyes. He smelled like thunder rolled up inside rose petals. Tied with a string of gold. "My mate." My eyes rolled back behind closed eyelids as I committed his smell to memory and swooned.

"Why are you so angry?" I asked, rising to my feet with a grunt. I brushed the dirt from my pants and stomped over to the pond nearby. I removed the apple, placed it next to my swords, then stripped my clothes off while thinking excitedly that trouble awaited me onboard if I didn't do as instructed. Eager to please my mate, I have never cleansed myself so fast while making sure I scrubbed away all the cum and pig fat. Teeth chattering, I rushed back to the ship, boots, clothes, apple, and swords in hand.

"Hurry up, Ish, I want to go home. To Phoenix. Lord knows what they are going to say about my fucking wings," he said while I got dressed in fresh clothes and joined him. He saw the apple in my hand and I quickly stored it away.

I didn't have visions of him being this possessive and domineering. "Maybe I should leave you here and return another time," I joked.

"Fuck you, Ish. I thought you cared about me. Not this place. Not these men, but me. Drop me off at Phoenix. I must bring that fucking apple home. I had nightmares about the fucking thing."

"You heard the voice of the Fates? Was it inside that cave?" I asked. My mate perplexed me while I assessed the amount of loose white feathers lying on the floor, on my seat, over the dashboard, fucking everywhere. I didn't mind the little things. They were part of him. I will pick them up and save them—make myself a tiny pillow I can carry in my pocket to smell him all the time.

"It's because I stole that apple. The thing is bad luck. I feel like throwing you and the apple out the fucking door."

Strapped in and ready to go in the passenger seat, Peter sat, arms folded, wings tucked, and crammed in. A bolt of lust shot through me. I touched the tip of his wing; he shivered and gave me a don't-touch-me look. I sat down. *I'm going to lick and suck those tips, every inch of him, when he lets me.*

"No, I have a mission. The Fates told me to take it home—my home. First, we'll go to Babylon. Get rid of the apple, as you say. After that, we can go to Phoenix or Grayrak."

"Take me to Phoenix. I want to restock and have a decent shit."

I frowned. "How do you sit with those wings?"

"Fuck you, Ish. How do you sit with your enormous cock? Do I ask you such stupid personal questions? I thought you were bloody dead!" he said with tears in his eyes.

"I am not dead and there is a big difference between my cock and your wings." I wiggled my eyebrows at him. "And fuck you too. My mate is supposed to be nicer than you. Maybe you aren't the mate I'm supposed to have. Hmmm?" I reached down, finding the shiny tip attached to my safety belt, pulled it, and clipped it in.

"I am your fucking mate. Shut the hell up!"

"Or what?"

In one swift movement, he unbuckled his seat belt and lunged towards me. For a moment, I feared for my life—death by a crazy, sexy angel. But his lips crashed into mine, and a frenzy of passion and desire blasted through me as his tongue slid into my unsuspecting mouth. Kissing wasn't something I particularly liked doing. But this was different. I eagerly opened up to receive him, tasting the anger, fury, and pure lust—the thunder. Our tongues danced together in a hectic tempo as I wrapped my arms around his muscular shoulders. A deep growl sounded from his chest as he pulled away, piercing blue eyes blazing with fire. "I am your mate," he declared, his words searing into my mind. "You asshole. Fucking time-traveling Anunnaki," he said and slammed his fist into my upper arm. Numbing it.

"Ouch! Let's take the apple back to Babylon, and then you can direct to me where our new home is, okay?" I said and started the machine.

"Ish, don't tell me this is our first meeting!"

"For me it is," I said.

"All I know is that Phoenix is five turns of that wheel into the future. Sounds to me like Lasitor's been hiding things from you!" he said, pointing to my ship's console.

"Uhm, excuse me. Everything has a time and a place. But if you think you can do it better, then who am I to stop you?" Lasitor interjected.

"He's got a point. Why would I want to know how to get to Phoenix, if I don't need to know? Then he might as well tell me everything he knows and I don't have the capacity or strength for that. And he knows that. He is my guide, not a talking geographical dictionary."

"Do you even hear yourself speaking? Who talks and thinks like that?" Peter asked as he wiggled the tail ends of his massive wings and tucked them underneath his thick, muscled upper legs. *Pleasing me.* He was on my ship, I thought happily. But I had no clue why he thought I was dead.

As we settled back into our seats, a dangerous silence hung between us. God, it was way worse than the Siege of Jerusalem. I leaned forward and dramatically turned on the time machine, pressing buttons with pretend importance. Peter's eyes were practically burning holes in my back, but I chose to ignore that, focusing on the pretend tasks at hand. I attempted to cheer him up. With a theatrical flair and a foreign feeling of silly optimism, I declared, "Lasitor, off to ancient Babylon before the war with Apsu, but after my last pit-stop at Platonius'." And with that, I hoped to have enough time to warn my sisters about their upcoming slaughter while also delivering the apple to Xerxes. "Also, land us outside the city, away from any danger or prying eyes," I added.

"That time and place is a concern for me, are you sure your settings are what you intended or prefer? There are consequences for bringing the apple back there, Ishtar," Lasitor said. I noticed Peter tightening his grip on the armrests. I flashed a smile at my Kuku over my shoulder. He stubbornly crossed his arms and tried to turn away despite his cramped legroom. I was simultaneously concerned and amused by his failed attempts to ignore and hide from me.

"Oh, come on, you can't resist my charm," I joked, earning a begrudging chuckle from him.

With tears filling his eyes, he said with a trembling voice, "I thought you were dead! This is me being happy to see you." He laced his feelings with venom, but I heard his inside burst before the tears flowed. He was relieved to see me. *He is confused and somehow, I had fucked up.*

Lasitor interrupted my thoughts. "Before taking off, Ishtar, please check your coordinates."

"Lasitor, I know what I'm doing. I remember Ki and An showing me the apple. I remember them saying that my bloodline would live on. Surely this was me. Please, for once, do as I say."

I checked with my newly found Kuku, who shrugged at me as if he didn't care. But he did. He was only playing hard to get. "Also, Lasitor, please take notes and let me know when I'm near my demise," I commanded my trusted guide and companion, hoping we could prevent my untimely death. I searched through the overhead compartments, looking for a nose wiper to hand to Peter. I wanted to embrace him and never let go, but he was like a prickly porcupine. Peter sat up tall at my announcement, wiped his tears with the back of his hands, dried them on his thighs, and in between sobs he said, "I'll chart our jumps on a timeline and map because I have a feeling you died already."

CHAPTER 7
ELIJAH

"GOOD MORNING.

Time has snuck up on us. Did you know there was a tall and dark Anunnaki time traveler seen back in 1579 A.D.? He was called Yasuke. The story is after he arrived in Japan he made history as the first foreign-born man to become a samurai warrior. It was said that Yasuke was originally a slave from Mozambique and was brought to Japan by Portuguese traders. The powerful Japanese warlord Oda Nobunaga was fascinated by Yasuke's tall stature and dark skin, and upon seeing him, ordered his servants to try and rub the 'black ink' off his skin. Despite this strange encounter, Nobunaga took Yasuke into his service, granting him a sum of money, a house, and a Katana. From then on, Yasuke loyally served Nobunaga as an honored samurai, fighting alongside him in fierce battles.

Remember, history is told by those who wrote it.

Visit your community news page to record your version of history today!"

ISHTAR
3500 B.C.
Hours before the war with Apsu
Babylon

MY WHOLE BODY WAS HUMMING. I felt like singing and whistling. I had found my mate. The mere thought filled my soul with an intoxicating blend of excitement and lust. We left behind everything that felt safe to come back to the place and time I never wanted to see or relive. Bringing the apple to Babylon was no small task, but as I gazed into my newly found mate's eyes, gleaming with hope, I knew that a future filled with love and adventure awaited us. Peter thought I was killed in a crash. He had hinted at taking me to the secret city underwater, the one that I was eager to see with Cian and his brothers. As he spoke of Phoenix, his home that lay beneath the ocean's surface, my excitement grew. This meant that my time spent waiting for a spaceship in Grayrak was not for nothing. I thought I had to choose between forgetting about searching for him and dedicating my time to Cian and his brothers—as the Fates had commanded me on Anzulla. The possibility of helping them, with my Kuku at my side, filled me with optimism.

We landed the time machine on the shoreline next to a

sad weeping willow that stood like a beacon, withering away in the salty air. It marked the road that forked inland to where Babylon lay waiting for me on the horizon. Enclosed by enormous city walls, the buildings lay packed in blocks around the palace and the sacred vaulted terrace gardens where my family lived. "Okay, I'll be quick. I don't plan to linger. The sooner I get the apple to my sisters, the faster we can get out of here. If my father sees me or this ship, we will be sucked into this reality and might never return to your home."

"And where is that, exactly?" Peter asked.

"Anywhere you want to go," I said, getting up to remove our precious cargo from the overhead cubby.

"I'm thinking I can't live in Phoenix like this, so let's talk about it after," he said, waving his hand up and down his wings. I stooped to give him a peck on the cheek.

"Okay. Please stay on the ship." I pleaded with my eyes. He took the apple from me, inspecting it. "I understand now why my sisters said I brought the apple and that my bloodline will live on. It's because, this time, I'm going to warn them." I reached out to take the apple from Peter's hand but noticed the deep creases etched across his forehead. His eyes bore an apprehension of my coming death.

"Yeah, I know. Here, take it." He handed it back to me. "Come back to me. If you don't...I'll be stranded and lost without you."

I kissed his pouty pink lips. "I will hurry. The city is about to be evacuated. Titus is assembling an army. I have time, I think, at least two days." I checked my tick-

tick thing. "I'm going to tell them to bury the apple and flee."

"Why don't you just hide it yourself and come back to me?" He asked a very good question.

"I have a message to deliver and because my sisters are meant to hide it. I might put it where my father can find it."

"I don't want to think of the ramifications of that. You don't know half of it yet." He turned away, shaking his head. He spoke in riddles. Of things in my future. His eyes snapped back, blazing with trepidation. He locked eyes with mine. "Whatever your instincts tell you, follow them. Don't pay any attention to me. Stick to what your gut says."

I tilted my head, studying him. "I will."

He bit his bottom lip. "I'm worried about nothing. Please make sure you aren't running into yourself." Peter's voice trembled as he frantically adjusted his wings. I watched as small white feathers floated to the floor.

I tipped my head sideways to refocus. Everything about him mesmerized me. "I don't think so. Please, stay on the ship. You can't be seen with those wings." As if reading my thoughts, Peter drew me into his warm embrace, wings enfolding me protectively.

"Are you embarrassed about my wings?" he joked, making light of the situation with that flirtatious voice I was finding hard to resist. Hairs all over my body stood erect. My shoulders stiffened as electric charges shot through me and zinged into my cock. I felt alive. This was it. The indescribable attraction towards only him.

"We can come back another time. Let me show you I'm not embarrassed, but extremely attracted to you and your wings. It's these superstitious humans I'm worried about." I ran my hands up his back along the protruding ridges. "If my father sees or hears about you, we will have a lunatic chasing after us." He stepped back, but I pulled him by his belt loops and flung him around to give me better access to lick and bite the skin where his wings sprouted from his back.

"Ah." He shivered from my touch. "That's so unfair. It's so itchy and so fucking yummy when you do that. It feels as if that area is directly connected to my cock and balls."

"Hmmm, I can't wait to fuck you while sucking you right here," I purred, licking and lathering the sensitive area with my spit and then blowing on it. Judging by the fine tremors in his legs, I knew I was driving him crazy.

"If you don't stop now…"

"I'm sure I can stick it in and cum within four strokes. Will you let me?" I asked between licks.

"Of course, I will." He pushed his ass back to meet me halfway. He opened his wings and rubbed himself over my crotch with his backside.

"Feel how hard I am for you," I purred.

"Do it," he groaned low. "Hmmm, let's see if you can do it. I will count." He planted the palms of his hands against the wall while swinging his ass from side to side.

"One," he started counting as he pushed his pants down. I unbuckled mine, let them fall around my ankles, and guided myself to his opening. He spread his wings further to give me more access. The smell of clean feathers, vanilla, and sweetgrass filled my nostrils.

He shivered, then grunted, "Just spit on it and stick it in! Two!"

I collected a big wad of saliva and spat on my cockhead, smearing it around his entrance.

"Three!"

I gripped his hips and jabbed three fast ones into him. He grunted as I thrust deeper, my hips slapping against his ass and with one more deep thrust, my balls contracted and pleasure shot up my spine. My whole body went rigid as I orgasmed. The smell of him consumed my senses. "Fuck, you feel so good," I grunted, planting my seed so deep inside him, he must taste it on his tongue. "I won't ever get enough of you," I said through clenched teeth.

He arched his back, pushing back against me, whispering, "Oh my god, I missed you. Keep talking. I love the sound of how much you want me." He was panting with want. His hole was slippery and warm. I rotated my hips, grinding into him. Loving him already. I licked that magic area where his skin and wings met. Then, with the tips of my fangs, I scraped across it, pushing him over the edge. He clamped down on my cock, his breathing ragged, and I knew he was close. "Do it," I growled, my voice thick with desire. "Come for me." And he did, all over his hand, his pants, and the wall. His enormous wings prevented me from reaching around to feel his slick release. We stood there until he finished convulsing, remaining silent, lost in the afterglow of our passion, until we both whispered, "I love you."

He laughed.

"What? Why are you laughing?"

"We come like two ninjas. Silent and fast. We are so pathetic for each other." He snickered. I licked and rubbed my nose where I had nicked the base of his wing muscle.

"Hmmm, you smell exquisite. I know about ninjas. I trained with one of them. He was from Japan. A stealthy warrior soldier, but believe me, when we fuck, we sound nothing like them."

Peter straightened his back, bucking me away. "How do you know? This was your first time fucking me. Go do your drop-off. I will stay here like a good housewife and clean this ship. This thing stinks." He harrumphed and reached for a rag so we could clean ourselves.

"You do know I've been all over and met all kinds of people from all kinds of cultures. That was my job." I pulled my pants up, feeling lousy for shortening our fun and hesitant to leave. "I'm sorry, Peter. When I come back, I promise you we can fuck anywhere and as long as we want."

"Yes-yes, it's fine. As long as it's not inside this fucking machine. Please be safe. Okay?" He stopped wiping the wall, threw the rag away somewhere over his shoulder, and gazed into my eyes. I saw the concern and care in him. Then I kissed his down-turned lips until they turned up into a smile and said goodbye.

Peter activated the door to open. "Go, be safe, and come back to me. And soon."

With a grin on my face, I turned to leave. Fucking Peter wasn't part of my original plan, but my body and mind were starting to have different ideas. I almost gave in and decided to come back another time. Just as I was a few feet away, the door swished shut behind me. My strides were hesitant and my heart was reluctant. But I made my way towards the distant city, stepping out of time and between the threads of reality. Driven by the purpose of returning to him as soon as I delivered my warning, I held the apple close to my chest.

It was late night, early morning. Only the sound of the wind accompanied me. Ki and An would be sleeping. The streets and palace grounds were busier than I remembered. Stray dogs were scavenging for food while the palace guards were at their posts, standing like statues. I entered from the back where more guards lazily gathered around on pillows sharing a pipe. I passed them, still moving behind the veil of this reality.

Cheering in a foreign tongue shattered the silence behind me. It came from the opposite part of the palace where the king and his two wives lived. Laughter followed. A female shouted. Male voices and the unmistakable sounds of partying as they hollered joyfully.

Shivers ran up and down my spine. The shadows seemed to dance and flicker around me, amplifying my fear as I dashed through the dimly lit hallways. My eyes darted back and forth, searching for any signs of movement or danger. Our bloodlines would be fucked up beyond recognition if my father found me. The taste of fear and adrenaline coated my tongue, my heart beating wildly in my chest.

Dammit. Three human guards stood gripping their

shields and swords, guarding the entrance to King Xerxes' quarters. Grinding my molars, I clenched the apple tighter. I snuck by them, hoping I didn't stir the air. Once inside, I slid past two more guards to the extra large bed, where the three lovers slept, entwined.

Carefully, I stuck my hand through the veil, pulling their feet and toes to wake them. My clothes clung to my skin, damp with sweat. My sister An was the first to wake up, followed by Ki. It was good to see them. "Shht, it's me," I said in my native tongue. Sharp pains shot through my skull as something hit my head. I fell sideways as I lost my footing and slipped. I attempted to stand, but Xerxes stuck his sword in my face.

"It's Ishtar! What are you doing here, Ishtar?" Ki asked, with her hands over her mouth. "And what are you wearing?"

She leaned in closer, inspecting my face and hair, and lifted my foot, inspecting my boots and clothes. "You are not our Ishtar, are you?"

"No. I mean, yes I am, but I am older. My younger self is on his way. Titus is assembling an army. War is coming and Apsu is going to burn this palace like he destroyed Anzulla."

"Ishtar, I thought you were an assassin," Xerxes said, tapping my cheeks with the flat sides of his sword, and then stepping away. He waved to the guards that they were not needed. Turning his back to me, he threw a shawl over him to cover his impressive manhood. Luckily, my sisters were both dressed.

"Let me look at you." A small oil lamp gleamed in An's

hand. I winced at the brightness and squeezed my eyes shut.

"Are you bleeding? How's your head?" she asked. I shivered, the creepy feeling of seeing my dead sisters rendering me speechless. I nodded. Holding the apple out to them. They were as graceful as I remembered. Looking without touching, she asked, "What is this?"

"Take it. The Fates sent me home to the three of you, so you may save it for the future of your children. You are to bury it in the foundation surrounding the garden. Please, you must hurry. I'm here to warn you." I looked at Xerxes. "Protect it so our bloodline will live on."

"I will," he said and took it from me. This is why I liked the man. He was intelligent. He knew the Fates personally. He and his family had been guarding this sacred place for thousands of years. This apple was just another thing the Fates, or his deity Marduk, had charged him to protect. In exchange, he received not one but two wives. My twin Anunnaki sisters. Both had given him their bite, so he was like us. He understood things differently than the humans outside these walls.

"But what about Father, we heard he is looking for you. You're not safe here, Ishtar. If he finds you..." An said, now on her knees next to me.

"Put it in the garden. Hide it in the foundation of your enormous stone wall. It's been standing for thousands of years. It will stand forever until it is time for the Fates to reveal it to someone worthy of finding it."

The thundering sound of guards' feet was coming down the hallway, signaling their approach. "Quickly," I urged my brother-in-law, "pack your belongings and gather your children. Hide the apple and flee to the northern mountains. Leave everything else behind and never look back." Xerxes's eyes showed a flicker of under-standing.

"I love you. I will distract the guards. It's Father, he's gone mad," I whispered in short sentences, not stopping to take a breath. "He won't stop until he has crushed all life. Titus is nearing the gates, but Father will kill you if you don't go now. You can't stay here." Tears welled up in my eyes as I feared I wasn't in time to save them. "Please!" I jumped up and looked into his eyes, pleading to do as I asked. He gave me a slight nod.

"Go, I will do as you and God command. Go, may God bless you," he said into my mind.

"Brother, be safe," my sisters said as I hastily hugged them.

"We love you, Ishtar," my sisters spoke in my mind. I beamed, happy that I could deliver the warning and the apple in time. Then I stepped back behind the veil and disappeared from their sight.

After causing a distraction and confusing the guards, I slipped away and arrived at the ship, stunned. Those big white wings were not inside as I had asked, but outside under a tree. Sitting with his back against it, someone lying on his lap.

"How did it go? Did you deliver the apple?"

"Yes, I did, but it was harder than I thought it would be. Who is this? And why are you out here?"

The man cracked an eye open.

"Easy there, friend." I greeted the man in the local language. "What's his name? What is he doing here?"

"*Shhht*, he only wants to talk," Peter said as the man's eyes enlarged.

"I've no need of talking, I know who you are. I am ready to go home. Take me home, Angel," he croaked, not looking at me, but at Peter.

I didn't believe what I was seeing and hearing. I checked behind us. Peter smiled at the man. I rolled my eyes. He'd found a stray under the only fucking tree, revealing himself as I asked him not to do.

"Do you need water? Are you thirsty?" Peter asked with a kindness in his voice I didn't think he possessed. In the dim moonlight, he spread his hands, revealing a water bottle he had found on the ship. I had brought it with me to transport water to Grayrak as I waited for the ball-shaped ship to arrive. "We've come to collect you. You are needed back home." Peter said in English. He was making shit up, indulging the dying man.

"Yes, yes, I am God's servant. Take me where He needs me to be," the man whispered weakly.

"First drink a bit, you must be parched," Peter said.

The man was bleeding, half-naked, and dirty beyond belief. As if someone had dragged him here and tossed him at our doorstep. His lips were cracked and swollen. His tunic was ripped, brown, and crusty with old blood. His hair was long and tangled, and his unkempt beard covered his whole face except for his brown eyes.

"How did you find him? I told you not to get out of the ship. Did he call for help or were you outside looking for trouble?" I asked, hoping it was not a trap while hurriedly scanning our surroundings. There weren't a lot of places to hide either behind the tree or the ship.

Peter didn't answer me. The sun was rising, and it was already extremely hot outside. The dying man took the water and inspected the bottle. Peter pushed it to his mouth and tipped the contents down his throat. Choking, sputtering, and moaning, he drank the liquid like a baby from his mother's bosom, holding the bottle between shaking hands.

"What happened to you? Were you attacked?" Peter asked, ignoring my questions. They spoke to each other, but each in their own language. How they understood each other who the fuck knew.

Coughing, the man stopped drinking to answer Peter. "Yes, there were four attackers with knives."

I stepped closer, to see what he was showing Peter. "They slashed my forearms. Whores sons, they were! They took everything except the clothes I'm wearing." He pointed to his blood-drenched arms. "The ruffian's mothers were sluts. Sinners, all of them! I came here to die. I asked God to take me from this place. I want to go to Heaven and be with Him. I am ready for you to take me."

I gave Peter a look. Lifting one eyebrow, he spoke mind to mind. "I'm bringing him with us. We should help him. He doesn't need to die here alone like a dog. We can take him to Phoenix.

"I don't know where Phoenix is. I've never been there."

"Tell Lasitor to take us, I don't care what he says, he

knows exactly where and when to go. Something tells me we should save this man. He is important."

"The Fates?"

"No, not that. It's a feeling I have." He got up carrying the half-dead man, and I followed, shaking my head.

"Let's go then. We must take him to a hospital. He needs medical care."

"André? Fuck yes, let's go to him! He is a doctor. He can help us."

"Peter, I don't know if that is a good idea. I don't know if we're allowed to do this. The Fates never said anything about bringing someone back with us."

"Fuck that and fuck your stupid rules. You break them all the bloody time and do as you want, anyway. Why can't we save him?"

"He is not a stray dog, he is a human, almost dead, on his way."

"Exactly!" he shouted over his shoulder.

"Heaven, thank you, Peter," the man muttered through bloody lips.

"Do you want to go to a better place?" Peter asked him, already one foot inside the ship. As if he would say no and Peter would leave him here to die if he did. He cracked a bleeding smile at Peter. That seemed to be answer enough for him. "Come, we are going to André. He owes me."

I threw my hands in the air. Peter tucked his wings, bent his neck, and carried our new passenger inside.

2013 A.D.

Lord Andrew Whiskey Distilleries
Lexington, Kentucky
United States of America
Earth

The time machine hummed. I adjusted the coordinates and realized I didn't know where to take us. "Where should we go? Where and when is this André?" I asked over my shoulder. Peter sat behind me on the floor, legs stretched out and the gasping body draped over him. Wings open, head down, it seemed he was praying. "Peter!" I called again. "It is risky to stay here. I need to know where to go." I turned back to the control panel.

"I have a suggestion. My data suggests we have coordinates for an Andrew." Lasitor said. "I can take you to Peter's friend. He should have modern medicine and he is the only person you can trust, unless you want to take our wounded passenger to Grayrak?"

"No!" Peter and I exclaimed simultaneously.

"Lasitor, take us to Andrew, in America. Not André in Germany. Take us to the future," Peter ordered my guide as if he had a personal relationship with him. Lasitor appears to have been hiding information from me.

Outside my ship's window, the air was shimmering. "We have to go, and I prefer knowing where and when. It's dangerous to jump into the unknown. We could land in water, or even in the middle of a war. I prefer not to sink or have my window shot out," I said as I glanced over my shoulder. The dying man's pain contorted his weary face. He had been suffering for far too long. I fully grasped his longing for the afterlife. But I also understood Peter's reasoning for not leaving him alone under a tree in the desert. "Peter?" I asked softly. "Are you sure about this? Jumping through time is dangerous. I don't know this man or this place, America." I stopped to think for a second. "Wait, it seems like I have memories of him. So I assume we went there, but he might not have the medicine we seek."

Peter's eyes met mine, filled with determination. "I know it's a risk, but if anyone can help him, it's Andrew. He's always been ahead of his time, quite literally."

A surge of empathy intertwined with worry washed over me. "Look at him," I said gently. "He's blue-pale, bled out, and barely breathing. He thinks you are taking him to the afterlife. Maybe you should let him go? He seems ready to go."

Peter's voice trembled with emotion as he spoke, his hands gently wiping the blood from the man's face. "I can't explain it, but ever since I heard him cry out in pain, I knew I had to help him. He was all alone, and my heart couldn't bear to see him suffer. I feel a deep connection to him, like I know him somehow. It drives me to keep him alive. He may seem insignificant to you, but he is important to me." The intensity of his words hung heavy in the air as Peter continued to tend to his wounds.

I swiveled in my seat. My long blue slender fingers flew across the control panel as I prepared the ship for its jump. "Let's bring him to this André or Andrew, whatever his name is," I said, a hopeful edge to my voice. "He will know what to do."

"An excellent idea," Lasitor replied. The ship zinged

and thrummed with energy as it charged up for the jump. "I'll take us to 2013 A.D." he announced confidently. "And do you still have that ring I instructed you to keep?"

I quirked an eyebrow, remembering the strange metal ring that glimmered with a vibrant blue hue. I'd found it amidst the scattered debris when I returned to retrieve Barkor's deceased mother for a proper burial. I had saved it, stowing it away in the overhead cubby where I kept my most prized possessions. I held it up, revealing it to Lasitor. "Yes, sir. With this, you have something to offer Andrew on your visit," he remarked as if assuming control and endorsing our mission. "One leap, but two offerings for others. A life for Elijah and a present for Andrew." The ring emitted a faint hum as I turned it over in my hand, almost as if lending its approval to Lasitor's suggestion.

"Lasitor?"

"Yes, taking you to 2013 A.D," he cut me off. I shook my head, checking on Peter one more time, and pushed the jump button, overriding the onboard guide to spite him. This was my ship, not his.

Moments later, we found ourselves in unfamiliar surroundings.

Andrew's property was both secluded and safe. The large black building with dark windows and a white sign that said Lord Andrew Distillery amazed me. I cringed as Peter handed me the limp body of the man and forced himself out the tiny door. Had I known he would struggle with the door's size, I would have increased its dimensions for him during my idle time in Grayrak.

Luckily, it was nighttime and Lasitor had parked the

ship behind some bushes from where we stepped out to take a quick walk across the luscious green grass toward the back door. Lasitor's ability to keep up with my travels kept me sane. My brain couldn't keep up with all the history, places, and timelines. I would have been lost in time without him.

Memories assailed me as we approached the building. The quiet abruptly ended as Peter pounded on the door with such force that it seemed like he was kicking it in.

"If Andrew doesn't open, I'll fly up to find an open window," he announced just as a gorgeous dark-haired man opened the door. He took one look at us, blinked a few times, and said, "Hmmm, an alien, an angel, and a dead prophet. Welcome. We've been expecting you. Please come in."

Wordlessly, we stepped inside, surveying the big open space and the over-friendly doorman.

"Follow me, please," he invited us, closing and locking the door. "My name is Tony. I'm Andrew's right-hand man, butler, and friend of over twenty years. I assume this is the famous Elijah." We all greeted him, offering no hands to shake. He examined the blood that should have been inside the dying man but was now covering us. "Quickly, follow me, and I'll take you down to Andrew's apartment."

I checked in with Peter. He nodded and hastily pushed and crammed all four of us into a moving box thing. I saw one on Grayrak, so I knew it was for moving up and down inside a building.

A loud ding followed the shutting of the doors. Tony

didn't say a word or look fazed by us. Maybe this was an everyday occurrence for him because it felt like I was having one of my worst cases of déjà vu.

Peter stooped his neck and shoulders so his wings weren't scratching the roof, not taking his eyes off the man, apparently called Elijah. His empathy for the man was unbelievable, and I wondered if my Kuku was naturally inclined to be so caring or if he had somehow experienced the same flashbacks as I.

"How do you know us already?" Peter asked. "And how do you know he is Elijah?"

Tony's brow furrowed, his eyes scanning our faces with a mix of concern and alarm. "Ish has been looking for the two of you here at least four times now," he said, his voice laced with urgency. My mind raced as I made sense of what he was saying.

Suddenly, strange memories flooded my mind, and I understood why Tony was so worried, as he added, "But this is the first time you have both Peter and Elijah with you." Tony fidgeted with his hands, tapping his fingers against the button. "I need you to do something for me," he said nervously.

"What is it?" I asked, brows drawn in concern.

"Something's going to happen. And whatever you do, don't let them get away," Tony replied urgently, a bead of sweat forming on his forehead as he spoke.

Peter spread his wings out, ruffling them loudly in the small space. A wave of intense loathing radiated from him as his eyes locked onto me. "Oh my god, that's why I know him," he growled, "this is the asshole who hit me over the

159

head and dragged me away from you. He told me you were dead. I can't believe I'm saving your sorry ass!" he said, shaking the limp body—its bushy-haired head flopping up and down and his tongue lolling out like a dead donkey.

My heart froze in my chest. I hated small stuffy places. "Peter, please calm down." My body was tense and hunched in the small box we were confined in. The smell of burning feathers mixed with his rage filled the air, making it hard to breathe. My eight-foot frame hunched forward, his sharp horns dangerously close to my face. With just a few more inches, they could easily pierce through my eyes. Despite my begging for him to calm down, Peter continued to snarl at the man he was saving. The pale man, who remained eerily still and who was most probably already blowing out his last breath during all the chaos.

"Seems like we should have left him to die under that tree." Peter huffed, and the door dinged to open inside a big room.

"Ah, thank fuck," Tony said as we poured out of the small box. "This is Andrew's apartment. This is his living room. I'll be right back. I will..."

"Ish! Peter!" A tall blond-haired man I assumed was Andrew, called to us as he came down a long corridor. Barefoot and bare-chested, he wore a pair of red soft cotton pants sitting loosely around his hips. With a few strides over the white marble, he swept me into an embrace as if we were old friends. Then, seeing Elijah with Peter, unfazed like Tony, he took Elijah and laid him on the couch. Before I knew what was happening, he bit into his wrist and dripped his blood into Elijah's mouth.

"What the fuck!" Peter lunged for Andrew. Elijah coughed as blood gurgled in the back of his throat. They scuffled, and I rushed to Elijah, falling to my knees, and helping him roll onto his side. He barked and spattered blood on my face, all wide-eyed, and with fire in them.

"Why did you do that?" Peter shoved Andrew's chest, pushing him back and away from Elijah.

"What's wrong with you? I was only helping. Ish brought him here for help. For my help."

"We are still coming to terms with the fact that we've been here four times already. You could have given us a second to think about it." Peter and Andrew were shouting at each other. Tony ran for a rag to wipe the furniture, then Elijah's face. Nervously, he patted to check that no blood had gotten on himself.

"Let's get him into a bath," he said and ran down the long hallway to where I heard water running already. I scooped the delirious Elijah up and carried him to where Tony waited. I've seen showers and toilets, but seldom with water in Grayrak. I had to go to Gugusan's for a bath. Here it streamed out of the wall into a white marble vessel big enough for four men my size.

Elijah thrashed wildly in my arms. "Is this a healing pool?" I asked, wondering if the waters were outside and bubbling through the wall and into the pristine, empty pool.

"Put him in. He is filthy," Tony said, and although I

tried to carefully place him in the bath, Elijah splashed into it like a rabid dog scared of water.

"Fuck this." *I've had enough of this craziness.* I touched his forehead, willing him to calm the fuck down. It helped a bit, and he sank back into the shallow, lukewarm water. Tony removed his tattered tunic and the one sandal that had come with us from Babylon. All the while, Peter and Andrew were still aggressively getting re-acquainted and catching up. It felt like I'd stepped into a timeline I knew nothing about. Finding Peter, delivering the apple, and coming here, didn't fit in with searching for Elijah and visiting this place four times.

"Elijah, sit still!" Tony ordered. "I'm just washing you. We're helping you."

"He doesn't understand you. Let me translate," I said to Tony, in an attempt to reduce the man's anxiety.

I cooed in Babylonian. "*Shhht*, it'll be okay. You will be okay. We are only helping you. You are safe now. Remember, you were dying and Peter came to help you." He looked at me, glaring, sniffing, and then let his hand fall into the water next to him. At first sight, he seemed old and rumpled. Not one ounce of fat on his body. But as he twisted and turned in the water, his strength increased, and his voice became deep and strong. His wiry frail body was slowly filling with muscles in all the right places. His gaunt face and bloody eyes transformed into a beautiful exotic face, with slanted dark eyes and pouty lips. His back was covered with a huge tattoo of a sun rising behind a monastery. It reminded me of a Japanese monk's religious markings.

"Where is the angel and where is Heaven? Is this the afterlife?" he asked, rambling. Tony sat down on the side of the bath as Elijah sat up, looking ten times stronger than before. His transformation was extraordinary. When I shared my blood with Titus and Gugusan, it was a slow drawn-out process. I wondered if Andrew's blood differed from mine. I hardly knew these people yet bits and pieces of memories told me I had been here before.

"He will help you wash, maybe get rid of all that hair and beard, while you are at it, Tony," I said in English, then I switched back to Babylonian. "This man will help you clean up. Peter and I can take you back home to Babylon, but you will have to learn our ways—come with us until you decide where you want to live. We have space in my ship for one more. You will live for a long time and there are things to teach you, things you need to know."

"That's way more than what you gave me," Andrew said, arms folded and leaning against the doorframe. I imagine Peter was either behind him or still in the big room.

"I'm sorry, Andrew, I'm afraid this is confusing for me —I found my mate only hours ago. Peter says we've met twice already. He was under the impression I'd died yesterday. Somehow I have cut into this timeline and although I have scattered memories of you, Peter, and this place, it feels like this is the first time meeting you."

"You have jumped yourself into a tangled mess. Do you remember fucking and biting me in Germany, in 1968 A.D.?"

"Not at all. Like I told you earlier, only bits and pieces

of visions and dreams pop up. I had visions of Peter before meeting him. I agree with your theory, but it feels like I caught the tail end of what happened. Where is Peter? He must come to show himself to Elijah. The poor man can hardly remember anything. Peter wanted to save him, so Peter must come and explain."

"Peter!" Andrew called over his shoulder while smiling at Elijah fondly. *He had gone and turned Elijah into an Igigi.*

"You shouldn't have done that. We brought him here for your modern medicine, not to turn him into one of us. You don't even know him. He belongs to you now. To you and Peter. I don't want another Igigi."

"I assumed that was why you were here. The rushed visions we saw of you told us he was turned and Peter was gone. You were searching for Peter and Elijah. So, seeing him dead and not breathing, he wasn't going to make it to a medical facility. Anyway, they would ask questions and if he died from stab wounds, the police would be called in. It would be murder."

"Oh, I never thought of that," I scanned Andrew's muscular physique. I was sure Peter would love to stay and play. Andrew dripped sex appeal. The monk could watch and learn.

"Help!" the man shouted. Tony had his hands full. I wasn't getting near that muddy, bloody mess.

"Elijah, we called Peter for you. He is coming," I said in Babylonian, and he chirped up as soon as those big wings and blond hair came through the doorway.

"Okay, Tony, I'm leaving the two of you. This room is

too small for all of us," I greeted Peter with a kiss. He sighed, leaning into me. "Like I told Andrew, Elijah is your responsibility. My Kuku, this is serious. Just like a newborn Anubis."

"You mean like a puppy?"

"Yes, just like that. He is now yours and Andrew's. You have to teach him how to eat, where to sleep, and most importantly, to never reveal his magical nature to those he doesn't know or trust. He is not fully Anunnaki, but in my experience, humans don't like supernatural things they don't understand. Their comfort boxes of religious beliefs may sway some to hunt him down and kill him. Others would exalt him, see him as godlike. You saved his life." I pointed to the three of them. "It's a big issue, and what will your husband say? Elijah is now your responsibility, your child."

"Husband, what husband?"

"That reminds me. Here, before I forget." I removed the ring from my coat pocket and waved a hand for Andrew to reverse so I could exit through the door. "Here, this is your wedding ring. It's made of a metal that comes from the future, I found it in a rocket that crashed on the moon. It glows blue at night. It's for your future husband..."

A long wolf whistle came from inside the washroom. "I hope it's Juandre Martinez?" Tony shouted as water sloshed, sounding like he was wrestling with Elijah. I heard Peter reprimanding the stubborn man.

"Sit the fuck still! You should be happy to be alive," Peter said in English, while Elijah shouted in Babylonian at him that he wanted to go to Heaven. Not drink blood with a fallen angel and a dark blue demon creature of the night. *That was probably me.*

"Sir, I told you he is going to be your husband!" Tony shouted at a surprised Andrew who was distracted by the commotion in the bathroom.

Andrew took the ring from the palm of my hand inspecting it. "Wow, this is a beautiful gift. Thank you, Ish." He lifted his chin, shouting back at Tony, "I will let you know when it is time. Don't go head over heels searching for him. Gay marriage is still illegal here. I'm warning you, Tony!" Andrew rolled the ring between his fingers and slipped it on to appraise it closer. "I've been thinking about him a lot. I'm unsure if he will remember me, or even accept me as I am."

"I don't know who you are referring to. If it wasn't for Lasitor, my time travel machine telling me this, I would never have known," I said, shifting uncomfortably from side to side.

"Andrew, all I can say is you have a long and happy future ahead. You will see, you will be married someday. You will live in a world filled with only men, where gay marriage is the norm. Sometimes three, four, and even five men in a marriage," Peter hollered. Andrew threw his arms around me, hugging the shit out of me.

"Thank you, Peter, and thank you, Ish." His eyes glistened with tears. "Are you impressed with the Whiskey Distillery? I've been storing crates of it in South Africa, as you asked me."

I bit my lip, feeling like an asshole repeating myself.

"Again, I'm sorry, Andrew. I think that was the future me visiting you..."

With an oomph, Elijah shot past us and disappeared through a door. Peter, Tony, Andrew, and I rushed after him, got stuck in the door tangled in Peter's wings, and untangled ourselves in a split second. "He's taking the emergency stairs to the outside," Peter yelled, skipping every second and third step, not able to flap his wings in the cramped space.

The exit door cracked open, revealing a pale blue sky and the fresh scent of dew-soaked grass. Peter leaped up, his wings unfurling as he took to the air. "He will have a better view from up there," I said to Andrew, who was panting heavily beside me. "The monk is fast. He could already be long gone." I spun around, searching every corner of the garden for a clue. "Your fucking blood only made him faster." I cursed, catching my breath as well. "Why did you have to turn him into one of our kind?"

"Why did you turn me by fucking me? Why didn't you just give me your blood..." His words trailed off as he jumped onto a wall and searched behind it.

"Again, I don't remember biting you. I could've, but the Igigi are younger servants of the Anunnaki, their strength and longevity reduce with time. Your blood only stays so long in their system and wears off. I would have had to administer blood, over and over for it to strengthen your human body for prolonged periods. Plus, Elijah can't do the same for someone else. Only the royals can give someone temporary enhancements. Make them their Igigi, if they trust them enough. They are meant to serve you, especially when you can't move around in daylight. That's why I told you, he is yours. He is bonded to you. If I fucked and sucked you, and injected my venom, you are a royal courtesan." I cupped my hands in front of my mouth, calling for Peter.

A faint "Here, Ish," drifted to me from the direction of the ship. And then it hit me—Elijah and Peter were taking my ship.

"Fuck!" I shouted and ran. Just as Andrew and I cut through the bushes lining the back of his property, the door swooshed closed and the machine started up.

"Lasitor, don't you fucking dare!" I bolted. "Open the fucking door, Peter, open the door! You can't jump if the door is open. Open the door!" I shouted as I banged my fist against the side. Nothing. I pulled the door lever. Nothing. *What can I do, what can I do?* I ran my fingers along the outline of the door, trying to pry the thing open with my fingertips.

No, no, no!

Ice-cold panic struck me. "Fuck! Help me to open the door, Andrew!" *The engines are revving up, preparing for a jump.* Desperate to stop it, Andrew pulled the lever to open the door. *My swords!* I grappled for one and forced the tip into the hairbreadth slit between the door and the ship. Just as I had it deep enough for leverage, the electromagnetic force field blasted us away. I jumped up to try again, *do something, anything*, but watched helplessly as my beloved ship vanished into thin air. Silence filled the space where the energy tore through the veils of time.

ELIJAH

"Ah fuck dammit, so this is how it happened."
Andrew's voice echoed in my mind.

"Fuuuck!" I fell to my knees.

What just happened? How will I return to Grayrak? How will I survive without my mate by my side? My plans of traveling with him are shattered. Where and how do I start searching for him? I don't have a ship. My ship abandoned me. Why did Lasitor do this? How will I honor my promise to the Fates? What have I done?

I plunged my fingers into the wet green grass, plucking handfuls of the stuff out of the ground, and threw it as far as I could. I was furious—at myself. I should never have gone to Babylon with my mate. I should have taken him home, to Phoenix as he asked.

"I'm so sorry, Ishtar," Andrew whispered into my ear. I leaned into his embrace—clutching his shoulders. I was broken again. I was alone again. *I don't deserve a mate and a ship. I'm a useless Anunnaki, just like my father always said.*

"It's okay."

"No! It's not okay!" I pushed Andrew away and got up. *Where do I go? Fuck!*

Boom! Whoop-whoop!

I flung myself around, too scared and surprised to look, as I squashed my eyelids closed. "Please let them be okay," I begged the Fates as I cracked one eye open.

"The ship is back!" Andrew shouted. I ran to it.

"Lasitor, open the fucking door!" I pulled the lever, and the door swooshed open. The ship was empty. Only the smell of my mate lingered. "Where and when did you take them?" I asked and jumped inside. "Andrew, I'm going after them. Take care!"

"Yes, I know. See you soon, Ishtar." He lifted his hand, but the door shut in his face. "Lasitor, take me to Peter now!"

Silence.

"Lasitor, for fuck's sake, take me to Peter. Jump to him now. To the time and place you dropped him off."

Silence.

"You motherfucking dumb machine!" I inspected the dashboard in an attempt to see if any coordinates were recorded. "You deleted them! What the fuck?"

"I have my reasons."

"Where should I go, what should I do?" I asked, slumping back in my seat.

Static echoed through the speakers. "Jumping to Grayrak, in five, four, three, two..."

"Fuck you, fuck you, Lasitor. Fuck you, and fuck-fuck-fuck you!"

ISHTAR & PETER

CHAPTER 9
LOVERS COLLIDED

"*GOOD MORNING.*

It's now six a.m.

Did you know that corundum is a mineral used for many parts of your time machine? Adding traces of iron causes it to become red and is referred to as ruby, while titanium or chromium traces result in a blue color and is known as sapphire.

Did you also know, that because they can withstand high temperatures and pressures and are resistant to chemicals and plasmas, red corundum is used to focus the laser light that makes time jumps possible, while blue corundum is used for your spaceship windows because its low dielectric loss and high electrical insulation mean it can withstand hot temperatures for when your ship space jumps.

You better get up, because breakfast is served until eight a.m.

Go get him!"

. . .

PETER

2146 A.D. (94 A.T.) (After Twins)
One year before the moon evacuation
Phoenix, underwater glass dome city

BRAD HAD ASSIGNED monitoring the health of the Phoenix residents to me, with instructions to pay close attention to the children born to parents who'd had the Eden Beans implanted for an extended lifespan. Since no one has shown any side effects after living two lifetimes, I'd quit all my research, not missing one second of working with stinky, frozen dead people or specimens.

I smiled with pride and swept my gaze over the kindergarten class of bright-eyed, inquisitive, enthusiastic boys. It served as my drug, functioning as both an antipsychotic and antidepressant, which I eagerly consumed in search of pure, innocent joy. Something I could never have.

"Tell me, who is eager about tomorrow's show-and-tell?" I watched as a dozen boys stuck their hands into the air as high as possible. My class comprised boys ages three to five years of age. Show-and-tell was a highlight in my tutoring sessions at the end of the week. It also helped me identify who needed more attention and encouragement. I discovered that those lacking inspiration and interest often required additional personal attention, which prompted me to inform my department head to schedule a discussion with the parents. Most of the time, the problem wasn't at home. They were little geniuses, bored or misunderstood. They still needed to play but in the advanced class with advanced kids. Meeting the parents was always nerve-wracking. Adulting was never my strong point. I'm as immature as those little geniuses. Hence, Brad's recommendation of working with kids, because they live in the here and now, with no judgment. In the meantime, I grew an emotional backbone. It was relaxing and fun to do something meaningful.

"Julius, you may go first tomorrow. You've been bragging the entire week about your new pet, so please tell your daddies that tomorrow is the day. Rodger must be in a cage and one of your daddies has to attend and take Rodger home after our show-and-tell period," I said firmly, but friendly. I suspected Rodger was another adopted lab rat or bunny, but Julius held the secret close to his chest. All of us were looking forward to meeting Rodger—whatever Rodger was. "So, Rodger, the rabbit is coming to meet us tomorrow?" I teased, trying to pry the secret from Julius.

"No, Rodger is not a bunny or a rat, I promise you. You will all be so surprised." he exclaimed, and the other kids leaned in closer, yipping, "Tell me," and "I won't tell."

Little Mathew whispered, but all of us could hear him, nevertheless. "You can tell me, then I will tell you what I'm bringing." But Julius just rolled his lips inward and smiled with glee.

"Is Rodger a fish?" Sandy asked, to throw the class off his friend's scent. He was Julius's best friend and I could see the two of them were planning something. Sandy was helping Julius with his show-and-tell tomorrow, being the sole classmate aware of Rodger's identity.

"You won't guess what I'm bringing with me," little Jasper yelled. Dear lord, not this again. I thought I had had enough of hearing about the end times. "I'm bringing something…"

"Not that stinky old book with the stories about the old world," Julius said. I was thinking the same thing, but I couldn't let them talk to each other that way.

"Julius, just like you get excited about your surprise, so does everyone else about their surprises. So, we must learn to be eager together and try our best to understand why that something is so important to them without making them feel bad that they don't like the same thing or bring the same thing as you. How boring would it be if all of us brought the same thing to show-and-tell as you every Friday?"

"Yes, that would be pretty stupid," Carlos said, dark brown curls flopping up and down as he shook his head energetically.

"Well, I see we have a busy and exciting day tomorrow. Please wash your hands, clean up your toys, and wash your hands again," I said, as they jumped up and ran. I saw some fathers already making their way over with their children's shoes in their hands. After I cleaned and sanitized the playroom, I ducked behind the bookcase and made my way to the back door. I wasn't in the mood to talk to overeager and proud parents today. I checked over my shoulder that no one was following me and shot for the emergency exit I took to avoid a crowd.

It had been a productive day today. A burst of pride, accomplishment, and excitement for the coming day putting a hop in my step as I jogged down the stairs.

The laughter of men and feet pounding the metal stairs echoed upwards in the stairwell shaft from below. Upon reaching the back entrance of my laboratory, I stopped before opening the door, praying that it wasn't Mika heading toward his office from the same direction. I froze, listening. It fucking sounded like him. If they're coming to the lab, I'll have to retreat somewhere else.

Fuck! Should I jump and try to make it to the door, or should I turn around and run back up the stairs? Like a stupid lab rat, I couldn't decide which way the cheese was. I had taken too long and missed my chance. Shock and utter surprise washed over me when I saw his face. As our gazes met, we halted just looking at each other. It felt like I was watching a volcano erupting in slow motion. Heat burned my skin. My legs wobbled. The stairs vibrated beneath my feet. A force of wonder and awe pulsated between us. Despite its beauty, my instincts shrieked to flee—death by lava was imminent.

Hot alien—too close.

He was halfway up the stairs—and already as tall as I was. It was him! That dark face that haunted me.

"Hello," he greeted, looking me up and down with a grin so bright my retinas hurt. On impulse, I covered my eyes as if looking at a welding arc. My heart slammed, jumped left and right inside my chest cavity, then settled behind my Adam's apple. I couldn't speak. I swallowed to force my heart to go back to the place God intended it to be. In the left chest cavity. I opened my eyes.

Frowning, he looked at me as if I was a stranger.

Speechless and gulping for words, I searched for the door's motion activation sensor, but couldn't find it fast enough. The two geniuses, Mika and Connor, looked at him and then back at me, already putting one and one together. Mika inhaled, preparing to spew a bunch of Russian retorts. Milliseconds passed and felt like drawn-out minutes.

I had to get away from here. I checked my clothes, flattening the wrinkles. Oh my fucking god, I wasn't ready, and this wasn't how I imagined our magical reunification would go. My clothes were full of sticky jam handprints, thanks to the extra messy lunch break earlier today.

Fuck, I raked my hair to the side. Remembering the jam had somehow reached it as well, I opted to flatten it against my scalp. Sticky hair and all, I waited. Unprepared for our big moment.

It wasn't supposed to happen like this.

Stay, go, stay, go, stay, go flashed in reds and greens in my spinning mind. Take a fucking breath, inhale, exhale, I told myself, blinking like defective Christmas lights and unable to take my gaze off him. Narrowing his eyes as if to see better, he cocked his head to the side. He was so much bigger than I remembered. Bigger, darker, bluer, and clueless. Zero recognition from Ishtar, and I stood in absolute shock.

"Morning, Peter," Brad greeted from the landing below. He narrowed his eyes questioningly. *No, no, no.* I felt like I was inside a bloody MRI machine while they scanned me up and down.

Brad assessed the situation like a pit bull, deciding if he smelled blood or shit. I smiled, also revealing my blinding stack of teeth—because that's what you do in situations like this. With Brad around, Mika and Connor had to think twice before having me skinned, chopped up into human meat cubes, and blasted out of the sewage to become fish food. I never speak to them and they are not allowed to speak to me. Avoiding each other worked—for me. Because of guilt, my self-destruction sequence was in imminent danger of activation, until Brad suggested working at the daycare and ignoring the Romanovs.

"Oh, hello, Brad," I said through clenched teeth while bulging my sticky fingers into fists at my sides. I had inserted General Brad McCormick's Eden Bean when he was a virile forty-five years of age. I have the utmost respect for him. And I thought he was one of the most attractive men in Phoenix. His dark brown eyes were intelligent and shone with emotional maturity. He was compassionate and although he was a war hero pre-doomsday, he was approachable, honest, fair, and just. He was a true and well-loved leader, and I don't think Phoenix would have survived if not for his ability to stand back and listen to suggestions from men much smarter than him. Being a great visionary and protective family man, he has told me numerous times that something or someone awaited us on the other side, and I believed him since he was the only human I brought back from death.

My eyes darted back to Ish. "And hello to you," I said

softly to my long-awaited lover, then turned my attention back to Brad, my self-appointed personal watchdog. I smiled again to show him I was okay and thrilled. I suspected I was looking freaky. Ish stepped one step back. I blinked and raked my eyes over the two blue-eyed busy body squirrels like I was nuts.

I side-eyed Ish, looking from Brad to him, then to Mika and Connor, and back at Brad. Ish was the most perplexed of them all. Eyes wide, he continued gawking at me.

What in the ever-loving fuck? Doesn't he remember me? Hurt pierced my heart. Here I was busting my ass awaiting him, growing fresh hemorrhoids.

Dammit, I waited so long for him, and now I'm a fucking stranger?

I was confused and disappointed. I shut that shit down by unfreezing my body and waving my hand to activate the door, then I slipped inside the lab. "Excuse me!" I yipped like a hyena. Once the door shut behind me, I leaned back to press my ear against it.

"Who was that stunning angel?" Ish asked.

"Don't mind him. Peter is a little odd," Mika said.

"Yes, don't take that personally. He doesn't mean to appear disrespectful. He's skittish," Brad said as they passed the door.

Fucking clowns! My anxiety levels were directly linked to the Romanovs' proximity to me. Lately, the mother-fuckers were popping up everywhere I went. I knew I was making life difficult for myself by ignoring them, the window for apologies had shut years ago. There was no way that I could explain any of it away.

I made my way to my sanctuary, my office. Trying to not think about Ish, I toed off my shoes, undressed, and hastily took a shower to wash off the peanut butter and jam. Afterward, still trying not to think about Ish, I got dressed, snatched a book I'd been reading from the bookshelf then planted my butt sideways on the small cot so I could jump to close the door if anyone approached.

I sighed. I failed not to think about him. So I waited.

Three hours later, distracted and more absentminded than usual, I contemplated where in Ish's circle of life I fit. The more I thought about his cluelessness earlier, the more I fumed. *Fuck my life! And fuck him! Fuck him skewered up and roasted over Hell's flames.*

That cluster fuck collision between my past and my future had pissed on my dream meeting. Oh my god! I slammed the book into my face, his guilelessness, that radiant stack of teeth.

I closed my eyes and stilled my rambling mind, then visualized the cataloged memories my eyes caught and saved like pictures to a hard drive in my mind. I flipped through them. Searching for his smile. It was real. Not fake, like my mother's smile was the day they took me away from her.

I recalled these things and compared the real ones with those I imagined. It kept me sane. Sometimes it felt like I was one person living in two people's minds. To keep myself grounded, I've stayed isolated, although always surrounded by people. I've kept my head down and wished for his loving arms to hold me. To envelop me. To love me. My life story is not unique. Others have been through what I have. I'm just fortunate because, unlike them, I was smart enough to outplay the monsters that raised us, that used us, the children of the experimentation camps.

I hated myself for so long. But no, like a carrot, Ish had dangled the promise of a beautiful future with him in front of me. My Ish.

I shivered. Thinking about him felt like sitting front row and center at the volcanic eruption I'd experienced earlier. The way he filled the stairs with his magnificence. The powerful force emanating from him, that drew my itty-bitty self to him like a magnet while the compass needle pointed to 1968 A.D. So many burning question marks. Why?

And then I wondered. *Maybe this is the day he met me and this is our day one.* I bumped the back of my head against the wall behind me.

"Stupid, stupid, stupid." *That's the answer.*

"Today, the clock of our time together starts ticking. I've been fucking hanging on, believing it will get better from Tuesday, October 1, 1968 A.D. until today Thursday, October 1, 2146 A.D. (94 A.T.)" —I closed my eyes and calculated— "That is exactly sixty-four thousand two hundred and eighty-four lonely days." I've kept my head down, worked, breathed, and existed. As a copy. But not a true copy.

"Yes, oh my god! Today is our day one!"

I checked my wristwatch. Three hours ago, my Ish had come for me. I've been awaiting my Ish for so long that I lost myself in my dreams, in the past.

One second, still lost deep in my head, the next, Mika was standing in my office.

I jumped up, hands up, and my back against the wall. My feet unsure. Shaking and struggling to balance on the mattress. I screamed, my throat raw while hoping someone down the hallway heard me. "Help! I'm being attacked! I'm getting skinned today!" Sparks flew and my ears tooted.

The Irishman was blocking the door. Mika grabbed Ish by his clothes and hurled him at my feet. I frowned and swallowed my cries for help. It felt as if the ceiling was cracking open and the icy southern seas were drowning me. I looked up, seeing specs of stars like I saw that night in my living room. Back in 1968. When I saw my older self. *I'm going to pass out! I can't. It's my day of reunification.* My skin itched and stretched over my body. I paused, taking a few proper deep breaths to stay conscious.

Then I filled my lungs to the maximum and exclaimed with tear-filled delight, "Alien eyes!"

Happy tears streamed down my face. My big brute bent to one knee, holding a paper flower up to me. Like an offering. I stopped yelling, gasping for air, and choking on snot.

Calm the fuck down. I quieted my distraught mind while still clutching the wall, holding my body upright.

The oddest feelings and memories washed over me. Microscopic pieces snapped, flashed, and flickered in my mind. I blinked my eyes and shook my head to refocus. My mind emptied as if deleting the copies of memories, feelings, and colors. Becoming black. A void. Then suddenly my mind and my body filled up. Happiness and pain. So much of it, and I welcomed it. Letting go of the lonely cold vortex, I settled into this time and this world. I replaced myself with me. The real me. As colors burst and fizzed, my lover's eyes were what I saw. The man destined to be with me.

My whole body tingled. I should rip my clothes off, I thought. Must leave—search for a room, a washroom, a shower, a fucking toilet stall, anything, away from them! My clothes were too tight and my skin....

"Gille-toine, close the door, don't let him escape!" Mika yelled, and Connor pushed the door closed. Mika pulled Ish up and pushed him behind himself. As if shielding him from me. Of course, I started wailing again. It felt like I was about to explode into a million pieces.

"Jesus, Peter, stop your motherfucking crazy scream-ing. We're not here to hurt you. Connor and I wanted to introduce you to this man. He's besotted with you. Ever since he saw you, he can't stop asking about you. Brad's busy meeting with Cian. I know Brad said not to approach you when you are alone, and that we needed him to chap-erone us. You have your reasons. Connor and I will go now. We just wanted to bring Ish to you."

My ears swooshed. Mika's words were inaudible as I heaved air into my lungs. *Stay vigilant.* Then it clicked. "What?" I asked.

Mika was his old, rude self. "Calm the fuck down. My only intention was to bring Ish to you. Go do something nice together. Go out on a date!"

"Oh," I said, looking at Ish, who was hiding behind

Mika's back now. Peeking over Mika's shoulders, those beautiful yellow-black eyes were like chevron plates warning me to safety, calling for me through the maelstrom of my mind.

"But, first, tell us, are you serious about Tony and Bryan? Does your heart belong to them?" Mika asked me. I saw hesitancy in his eyes. Like he feared my answer. I gulped air, hoping to spew sense while looking at Ish.

"No, I never loved them. We aren't together, anyway. Not anymore." I waved over my shoulder, indicating they were past tense to me while smiling at Ish and forcing myself to calm the fuck down.

I imagined small atomic explosions detonated in my brain. *Calm the fuck down, Peter.*

"Yes, yes, yes!" Ish exclaimed while pumping his fist into the air.

"I'm sorry to hear that, my friend. Are you doing okay? I thought you were with them this whole time," Mika asked and blabbered on while I stared at those eyes. The room thrummed with the energy between us.

"No, I can't be with them. I didn't want them," I said, as if telling Ish this.

"What have you been doing? I know your research is complete. You're not in the lab anymore. What have you been doing this whole time with yourself, my friend?" Mika asked.

"I'm on holiday," I answered. I was proud of myself for doing things I like to do. Defying their expectations. So, I straightened up and wiped my tears away, so Ish could see I hadn't wasted all my life awaiting him—I lied to myself.

"That's good news," Mika said. He smiled and checked with Connor, who also smiled in agreement.

I relaxed.

"Yes, I'm reading, watching television, and helping at the toddler's school. I'm doing everything I never did. I sleep better, and I'm learning who I am," I explained to them, but I was telling Ish.

Mika pushed Ish to the front while saying, "That's a big change. Anything that makes you happy and doesn't hurt anyone else is a step in the right direction. Why weasel around? Why are you taking so long to confront us? You know we need to come clean, all of us. We've been working together for years, but since you said nothing and let me..." Mika paused and snapped his fingers. "You know what, one day when you want to talk about it all, come to me. This is Ish." He patted my alien visitor on the shoulders.

Ish never took his eyes off me, once again offering me the most romantic gift ever. "This is for you. It represents the holy Loursveto flower from my home on Anzulla. The flower is a symbol of love and serenity. Of beauty and intelligence. Of everlasting union and life."

"Sounds to me like a wedding ring," Mika said and turned to leave us. I heard him whispering to Connor, "Let's have coffee in my office."

CHAPTER 10
MY ISH

"GOOD DAY, PHOENICIANS.

It's now six a.m.

Were you aware that I, Lasitor, am responsible for all the doors in Phoenix being opened and closed? Did you also realize that a single moment in time can bring two humans together just by being near each other? As both a doorman and a hopeless romantic, I firmly believe in the power of love. There are countless ways to push two people towards each other, to have their paths cross and ignite a spark. By orchestrating brief moments where star-crossed lovers can see, hear, and experience each other through the opening or locking of a door in Phoenix, I hope to create fateful encounters that could lead to true love. Reflect on this idea as you make your way to breakfast this morning.

Breakfast is served until eight a.m.

Keep your eyes open and follow your heart!"

. . .

191

PETER

2146 A.D. (94 A.T.) (After Twins)
One year before the moon evacuation
Phoenix, underwater glass dome city

I GAPED down at the colossal man, still kneeling and clutching the flower in his shaking hand. His intense gaze and wild hair made me think of Medusa. Thick braids fell over his broad shoulders like anacondas, and his gold jewelry glinted in the light as he shifted. "Hello, my name is Ish. You may not remember me, but I visited you once."

I nibbled on my lip and gestured with my hands as I spoke, all the while his piercing eyes followed my every move. "Ish, you took your sweet-ass goddamn time. How long did you wait to come for me? Do you even remember your fucking promise? You said it would be a maximum of a hundred years. What in the ever-loving fuck, Ish? Why has it taken you so long? I mean, if you can time travel, couldn't you at least drop in and let me know it might be a little longer? And why is it that you look like you don't fucking remember me?" I whisper-shouted. The weird voodoo shit happening to me had dissipated as my mind and body had come to terms with his presence in my vicinity. It pissed me off and thrilled me to see him here in my office. He was as exotic and beautiful looking as I remembered. My stomach tightened into a gooey ball of anger and happiness. I crossed my windmilling arms and stared him down.

Silence. Clueless. Clueless fucking silence.

He ran his pink tongue over his thick bottom lip. I followed every movement. His Adam's apple slid up and down his throat as he waited for me to say more.

"Dammit, Ish, I thought you were nothing more than an imaginary lover. Maybe even a ghost. Stop looking at me like that." He blinked in slow motion while doing a double take. I may be much smaller, but I was a real ball of $E=mc^2$ if I ignited.

We stared at each other.

I caught my breath.

He assessed me.

Ultrasonic vibrations penetrated me as deep as my bone marrow as he raked my body up and down with his inhuman eyes. My dream man was the most handsome and most real-looking version of the sexy alien ass I'd conjured up while fucking my hand.

He smiled. Of all the things he could have done or said, he blushed and seemed timidly bashful. Fucking hell! Now I felt like shit. He acted as if he understood every word I thought—he probably did.

I looked at the flower he was offering me. No one had ever brought me a flower. An origami flower. I smiled and held my hand out. He smiled wider, exposing his long incisors as he pushed it into my waiting hand. "Hmmm," I gasped and gulped uncomfortable bubbles of air. "Thank you," I said and inspected the fragile intrinsic folds in the paper. He sighed, looking relieved. My nasal cavity and eyeballs stung. Dammit, I was about to piss tears through my eyes. My vision blurred, and I sniffed, wiping sticky snot and tears, drenching my sleeve with trails of colorless jelly.

His eyes were just like I remembered them, black with yellow rings surrounding his pupils. They were friendly and mesmerizing, like I imagined they would look at me when he came to get me. His skin was so dark, it shone blue in the light. The darkest blue that one might mistake for black. Yes, like an unlit night sky and velvety smooth. He seemed more muscled than I remembered. Yellow-white tattoos—Egyptian hieroglyphs mixed with Chinese logographs ran down his neckline. I wondered if the tattoo ink was gold. I guessed that would be the only color of ink visible on such a dark complexion. His eight-foot height alone screamed the family of Eryn—the only other man I knew as tall as him. A single yellow-gold hoop pierced his septum, and more clusters of thick golden hoops lined the shells of his ears—no diamonds or jewels, only gold.

I studied his face, tilting my head to the side as I examined him. Without thinking, my hand reached down to touch his cheek. He remained on one knee while I stood on the bed, our heights nearly equal. Tears welled up in his eyes and threatened to spill over. I wanted to catch them before they could fall, but he blinked and they streamed down his cheeks. His bottom lip trembled. This tall Anunnaki was crying for me. Slowly, I climbed off the bed and met his gaze with expectation and anticipation. I glanced back at the tiny origami flower in my hand, a romantic and beautiful gesture. The moment felt perfect, better than anything I could have wished for.

"Do you accept my offering to you?" he asked, softly, as if unsure of my answer.

"I accept," I whispered, bringing the paper to my nose to check if it smelled like a real flower. It didn't, it smelled like recycled paper.

"Thank you for the l—lors."

"Loursveto flower," he corrected me with a soft rumble in his voice. The sound affected me so deeply that my knees buckled. I threw my arms around his neck to steady myself.

"You came," I breathed out, reconciling the Ish I remembered from 1968 A.D. and the one kneeling here before me. He looked down at my mouth. "I started to think you'd never existed. I tried so hard to move on and be happy without you, but it was all a facade." My voice trembled as more tears welled up in my eyes.

"Oh, my Peter, my Kuku," he said with a beaming look on his face.

My eyes widened, and a hand flew to my chest in shock. "What did you just call me?" I asked.

Ish took a second, then replied softly, "It means my beloved."

Unsure of how to respond to such a declaration, I whispered, "I like it, and I like the small flower. Thank you."

"I'm so-so very sorry. Come here." He folded his arms around me. The feeling of safety, of home, washed over me as I buried my face below the crook of his neck.

"My Ish," I said and sighed. "I missed you. I was sick from missing you."

"I'm here." He sighed as he enveloped me, his smell and heat cocooned me, and I melted into him.

"Do not let go, never let me go," I pleaded softly into the warmth of his chest. "I need you like I need air to breathe. Please, Ish."

"I'm so very sorry and I promise you, I did search for you," he said, crushing my face, my nose, and my body against him as if trying to push me inside him. The vertebrae in my spine popped back into position. I welcomed the sweet suffocation, as he gave *killing-me-softly* a new meaning.

"We are to be mated. Our hearts call to be one. The Fates have blessed us." He sighed, pushing me away gently to look at me while allowing me to breathe. Inhaling fresh air, I longed for his presence, scent, and rhythmic heartbeat beneath my cheek. "You should come with me. We can travel together. Now that I have found you, we should go. I will take you away from this underwater place. It is not a good place for you."

"Where do you want to take me? Where is a good place for me?"

He gripped my shoulders tightly, his eyes pleading for me to trust him. "I know a place where we can be free, where the open sky stretches on for miles without a single building in sight. You can spread—I mean, you would enjoy it," he said with excitement in his voice. I felt the palpable desperation to convince me to accompany him, to make me his. But I couldn't ignore the obligatory voice in the back of my mind, reminding me not to be swept up by his enthusiasm.

My stomach twisted in knots as I thought about the disappointed faces of the children at the daycare center. They had been preparing for our special show-and-tell day, delighted to share their favorite things with me. I couldn't bear the thought of letting them down. "My work. I can't bail on those little ones," I pleaded with Ish. "They've been looking forward to tomorrow. They'll think I don't care if I don't show up." Desperation crept into my voice as I tried to convince him. "Maybe you could collect me at the end of the day? The kids would enjoy meeting you," I suggested, hoping he would agree. "We could leave after the show-and-tell? I have to at least say goodbye, and explain everything to my department head, Brad, and most importantly, to the children." A pang of guilt and heartache hit me as I thought about breaking their trust and disappointing them.

His hands slipped from my shoulders to settle and wrap his long fingers around my slim waist. He listened intently and impassively as he honed in on me and every word I was uttering. "Also, I heard Cian was here to restock, assuming he needed your help with the humans on the moon. I heard they needed rescuing?" I rambled on.

He let out a derisive snort, his eyes rolling in annoyance. "I believe the Fates expect me to help Cian and his brothers," he whined. But then he shifted his focus to me, pulling me closer. I wrapped my arms and legs around him, feeling the warmth of his body against mine as he effortlessly lifted me. I couldn't help but throw my head back and titter. The playfulness in his eyes and the way he made me forget all of my negative emotions made me feel like a little bushbaby clinging onto him for dear life. He leaned in close, parting his lips, breathing through his sharp incisors. I held onto him tightly, waiting, anticipating. And then he ran his tongue along my lips, tasting them slowly from one corner to the other. My heart raced as I opened my mouth for him, savoring the sweet, soft glide of his tongue over my lips to meet my tongue. Our kiss deepened, my mind swirled with desire, and my body responded with a pulsating heat.

We reluctantly pulled apart, both of us breathing heavily. "There is so much," we said simultaneously. We chuckled and decided kissing was the better option until we stopped to breathe, panting. His eyes sparkled with happiness, and I couldn't help but smile back at him. All the doubts and uncertainties from earlier were now replaced with a strong sense of belonging as we shared a mutual understanding of our obligations to others and how important they were to us.

"You go first," I said. He shook his head, "No, you first." He chortled.

"Ah, okay." I rolled my eyes.

He squeezed my butt cheeks. "Now tell me."

As I spoke, his pupils grew wider and wider, until the yellow rings disappeared. I was his sole focus. He leaned closer to me, our breaths mingling as we made intense eye contact. He was scanning my face, and I did the same to him. "What do you want to know?" he whispered, pressing his nose against mine.

There was so much. So many important things I

collected in solitude, in the attic of my mind. Shall I open the door? How much crap would tumble out? I've been waiting for this. To confront him. To ask him while looking into his eyes.

I quickly opened the trap door, then scraped the top make-or-break questions together. "I'm worried about so many things, but the most important question I have is if you had anything to do with Hitler, with the Disciples, any of it? Especially Eryn's frog monster brothers. Do you know they killed billions of people in a matter of weeks? Are the Disciples your followers?"

"Pfft, frog monsters, the Disciples, no, of course not. Those idiots?"

"They are not idiots. They are highly advanced, organized, and intelligent orchestrators of wars and they mined the Earth hollow for gold, for the Anunnaki. They schemed, destroyed, murdered, and brought on the annihilation of humankind. All in the name of the Anunnaki gods."

"Maybe not idiots, but you have to agree, what they are doing on the moon is pure blind stupidity. I admit, I am Anunnaki, and they want to be like me so badly they are building machines, moving their minds into them."

I blinked and went offline as I tried to explain, forgive, and rationalize this to myself. "So, tell me, was this your doing?" I asked, needing a straight answer.

"I'm not sure. I don't know how or when. The details, Cian, Ivan, and Eryn mentioned, had explained some, but at this stage, I have questions of my own. Only the Fates know and talking to them is near impossible. So, yes, by association with my kind, I am responsible, unknowingly. I am not sure precisely how it came to be that the Disciples were trying to create a species like me and be like me. Many years ago, before I came to Earth's moon, I'd been forewarned by the Fates about a baby. I saved him and kept him away from the scientists. I named him Barkor. The Fates had sent me to the moon to wait for Cian and the ship shaped like a ball that camouflaged itself like a chameleon, bringing more people like me, that needed my assistance," he said. I read his microexpressions and he seemed to be telling me the truth.

"And you, my Kuku. How are you connected to the Disciples?" he asked in a softer tone. "You are not human, either."

Breaking the intimate moment, I looked away and wondered how the fuck didn't he know this already? I looked at Ish as if seeing him for the very first time.

"Ish, do you remember meeting me in 1968? You asked me a similar question."

"Only bits and pieces, my Kuku. This is the very first time that I have met you, yes?" He hesitated for a second and said, "Like this. Yes, for the first time. I had visions or dreams about being with you. Of your face and your smiles and your kisses. That's how I knew to search for you. Maybe my memories are muddled because I've been jumping back and forth too many times."

I took a deep, contemplative breath, then looked at him before responding. "I guess it's possible. It makes sense," I conceded, trying to make sense of the situation.

Then, I remembered the initial question about the

Disciples. "To answer your question about my involvement and birth. Please know that I acted based on what I believed was right and to survive," I clarified, reciting Brad's words, to ease the guilt for keeping secrets from my closest friends. "I helped with Ivan and Cian's births. I used the Anunnaki string codes when I discovered Connor and Mika had dormant characteristics." A wave of bitterness washed over me as I added, "That's why they're mad at me. I hid the truth from them." My voice grew shrill with disgust at my actions.

"So, you were not born here with them. You were born in another place?"

"Yes, I'm almost one hundred years older than them. I was born in the 1940s through selective human breeding. Meaning babies born like me were kept and bred with more babies like me. Understand, this was before scientists discovered they could make babies without sex and mothers."

"I learned about this method of procreation during my time in Grayrak," he said, shifting his weight uncomfortably. "If my father had discovered this, I can only imagine how much more powerful he would have become. You see, he has a history of stealing and killing my siblings for their unique abilities. The thought that he could have just created them without needing to mate with my mother— it's a disturbing concept." His brow furrowed seemingly as memories of his father's cruelty surfaced. "It's something I don't want to even think about, for fear of it ever coming true or being possible." He shivered.

"Anyway, one of my brothers, who was the same as I,

was held prisoner and forced to do the work I was doing. He was the creator of Eryn in another lab in South Africa. While I ended up in Phoenix, already waiting for you and working in secret based on what you told me in 1968," I said to his frowning face. "This is bloody weird and upsetting. Please let me down. I need space!"

"No," he said and clutched my ass cheeks tighter, squeezing them while pushing my body flush against him.

"So, somehow the Disciples originated way back by following the clues, searching for..." He shook his head, correcting himself. "I was worried and most of the time, not in my right mind. My dear Kuku, I was obsessed with finding you. I searched for decades while I waited for Cian and his brothers to arrive on the moon. I can't determine what changes to make to prevent this group from forming or its origins. Chances are, I won't ever be able to change just one thing, and if I do, you and Cian, Ivan, and Eryn might not even be born. These people, the Disciples, their beliefs are so ingrained, so screwed, so twisted, and so bloody wrong. I suspect it all started—no, I know how it all started."

"How did it start?"

"It's all got to do with that damn golden apple."

I gasped. He nodded. Seeing my enthusiasm for the truth, he took a deep breath and answered me with renewed determination to tell me what the fuck was going on. "It's a long story."

"I can imagine. Continue, please."

"I brought the apple to my twin sisters, Ki and An, and their mate Xerxes, asking them to keep it safe. The Disciples had photos and schematics claiming to have the secrets of eternal life from the gods. Determined to uncover their connection to the Anunnaki, I infiltrated their compound one night. My goal was to understand how Barkor, who was half Anunnaki, was born after being carried by a human mother," he said, visibly shaken, his dark complexion almost pale as he closed his eyes in defeat. "I'm worried about you. I can't lose you. If I destroy them, by going back in time, then chances are, my Kuku, you won't be born."

"Who's Barkor?" I was confused. I must have been pulling a face, because I had hoped he knew what was going on. But now he only seemed defeated.

"He's just like Cian, Ivan, and Eryn. He was born on the moon, and it turns out he's Cian's mate. They're going to be butting heads and competing. Both have a hero complex. It's quite entertaining to watch it unfold."

"So they don't know?"

"They know, but they don't want to know. Two hard-heads, those two."

"Ah, I'm so glad Cian found him. I couldn't understand his engineering questions until I heard they had stolen the Spacecar."

"Yes, I'm also glad I have you. That's why I don't want to lose you or them. I'm growing fond of you all. Even if you are human, Anunnaki, and something else, those scientists have to be stopped," he said with a solemn look on his face.

"Cheer up. We can stop them. I have my flip knife to protect you and myself," I joked. "I've been taking self-defense classes," I said, hoping the randomness of my statement would break his deep depressive line of thinking. It was the first thing that came to mind because what he said was also worrying me. Plus, all those extra self-defense classes were one of the many things on my list to tell him when he arrived one day, and that was today.

Ish snickered. "Okay, keep your knife close to your person. I will return to collect you after the humans are safe, so we can build a home and start a life together. In the meantime, let's talk to Mika and Connor. Apologize and make friends. I don't like that you are troubled. Just be honest, I'm sure Mika and Connor will forgive you. They have two wonderful boys. You helped with that. I read Mika's mind. He is upset because you ignore him and act like he has done something wrong."

"How do you do all this? Do you also have the powers Eryn, Cian, and Ivan have? I kind of envy them. Why don't I have these powers? I also have Anunnaki in me."

"If you and I spend more time together, it could happen. It's like a little flame burning inside you. I can sense it. I'm sure we could stoke that little flame into a blazing fire. Not only to share thoughts and powers but to live longer together. It's because Anunnaki lived so long that we have to form a bond, otherwise, we would kill each other. That's what's happening to Cian and Barkor. They are drawn to one another but also irritated by the other. If those two don't find a way to bond they could become enemies." It seemed to me changing the subject helped because he was smiling again.

"But what about all these Phoenicians? I gave them the

gift of life. Would they kill each other if they don't mate or bond?"

"Maybe, I don't know, but you made a mistake there."

"Made a mistake?" I bristled at him as I awaited his response.

"Yes, the Fates now have their hands full with the Phoenicians. You directly linked them to the powerful Anunnaki, just like the citizens of Anzulla." His voice was low and intense. I felt a primal attraction to him, my skin prickling with desire and the urge to merge our beings. "You're such a troublemaker," he said with a sly smile.

I chuckled. "Guilty as charged."

As he spoke, my body pulsed with want, my back itching between my shoulder blades. I couldn't resist the temptation any longer and lunged forward, pulling him close for a hug. He put me down, and I led him outside to Mika's office. "Wait here for me please," I whispered, and he stooped to kiss me on my forehead.

"I can't wait to have you all for myself. Now go make nice with your friends. I don't like that you have this negative energy around you. It attracts bad luck." He turned me by my shoulders, patted my backside, and pushed me into Mika's office.

"What's wrong? Did he take advantage of you?" Mika asked, jumping up ready to attack Ish.

"No, don't be silly. Be happy for me. My mind is lighter, and all my thoughts and feelings are categorized and packed away. I feel much better. I got my Ish. I've been waiting for him all this time." I giggled, holding my paper flower and smelling it dreamily. "He said he was starving without me." I sat down, watching Mika peeking out the door.

I sat on the edge of my seat and decided to just blurt it out without thinking and without being scared. Ish's looming presence gave me the courage to continue. "Mika, Connor, I'm sorry. I don't want to explain away what I did because how I did it was wrong. I know now that you probably would have agreed anyway if I'd told you all this," I said bravely to them as they nodded. Mika looked at Connor, but before he could say anything, Mika grabbed his tool bag, interrupting me.

"Comrade, we'd meant to get you alone for an honest discussion. We've been evading each other for much too long. Connor and I had taken this secret and ignored it. It worked because we forgot about it all for a while. As it goes with secrets, if more than one person knows, then it's not a secret anymore. Also, if one person keeps that secret, it becomes heavy to carry. It's better not to have secrets. They will crush you. I tried not to tell Connor because I was ashamed of myself. I trusted you because I considered you my best friend and lab partner. In my eyes, you were untainted, pure, and innocent. I felt sorry for your pathetic-ness," Mika blurted, and Connor nodded affirmatively.

Cold sweat beaded over my body, a clear sign of guilt. To calm myself, I clutched the flower in my hand, drawing strength from it. Suddenly, Ish appeared at the doorway. His eyes narrowed as he gave me his infectious smile. I took a deep breath and gave him a determined look, silently communicating that I could handle whatever was coming next.

"I'm more than ready to get this drama behind us. The only thing I ask of you is to tell me what the fuck is going on. How did you end up here, and why do you sound like you know Ish? I swear, more questions pop up each time I talk to you. You're making me crazy trying to guess your story. I must know because thinking and attempting to guess all the time requires mental energy I'd rather use on something productive. Come, bring your guest, we can talk while we tinker on the latest Spacecar prototype and figure out a way to build a better communication system," Mika said and showed me the way out of the office.

I stood feeling relieved and replied, "I accept your invitation, and thank you for including Ishtar to come with us." I wasn't leaving him here, alone, and out of my sight. His presence brought me clarity and I figured the walk would help me gather my thoughts and align my words to apologize properly. Mika gave us a stern nod and Ish grabbed my hand and squeezed. Connor looked us up and down as if comparing our heights. I was an easy two and a half feet shorter than Ish. Ishtar gave Connor and Mika a shiny big grin and then we made our way out of the lab.

We strolled through the bustling corridors, and I couldn't help but feel a wave of relief wash over me as people greeted us with warm smiles instead of stopping for idle chatter. Tomorrow was a big day at the toddler's school, and I needed to conserve my mental energy for that. But now Ish was here, along with Mika and Connor, who were clearly still seeking answers. I braced myself, knowing I would have to tap into my reserves to face them. As if he read my thoughts, Ish pulled me back for a kiss and a hug, filling me with renewed strength. We proceeded down the corridor to the shipyard where Mika and Connor's workshop was.

"Here, you can wear Eryn's protective gear," Mika said to Ish. We washed up, donned our suits, and entered the sterile workspace filled with state-of-the-art tools and a half-finished spaceship.

"Gille-toine, can Peter help us build a communication tower? One that floats and can be retracted and moved under the surface level? It would be a better option than dragging construction outside and erecting one on a mountaintop. I worry any manmade structure will give us away, and I'm sure Brad won't approve of it. We need to communicate better with the children. I need eyes and ears out there. I want twenty-four hours a day of video feeds from all over. Wherever they go, they should leave a camera ball for us. That way, we can protect and warn them, don't you think?" Connor asked Mika but was already calling me closer. My hand slipped out of Ish's, breaking our connection. The sense of loss shifted to pride as I watched him slip away to inspect the inner workings of the ship.

"Of course, he can," Mika said to his husband following Ish with his gaze.

"Peter, the more heads, the faster we shall get results." Connor patted me on the back and then lifted his chin, indicating Brad and Cian coming through the transparent wind tunnel to suit up for entry.

Ish stepped off the ship and bowed low to Mika and Connor in a display of respect. His thick, dark locks fell into his face, obscuring his features as he spoke. "Apologies, I don't want to seem judgmental of your work. I'm impressed by it. I assume you built the smaller version as well. Your attention to the fine details impressed me the most."

"Thank you. We're building a better, bigger version than the boys are currently using. We welcome your input and recommendations any time, comrade," Mika said to Ish, and turned back to me. "We can't rely only on a voice-recorded report from the kids. By the time we receive it—what I mean is—we can't sit here and watch how people learn to knit and shit. I want my own ship up and running. I fucking need to know what's happening outside the clouds. But, in the meantime, could you maybe design a submarine with satellite capabilities?"

"Yes, sure, of course. I can do that for you. I'll help with anything as long as I'm not working with frozen dead people," I said, uncomfortably, but honored that Mika still trusted me. This would give me something to do while I waited for Ish to help Cian save the humans on the moon.

"That's good news, my friend," Mika said, pointing to the schematics.

"Yelda, maybe Ish has some input here," Connor told Mika.

"Progress is slow. In two years, we would at least have two ships ready. Please, I need to know what we can improve and change, and I can't do that with relayed radio messages," Connor continued as I stepped closer and reached for Ish's hand.

"You know, Mika and Connor, my friends. I've blurted some of it out to Brad while feeling guilty as fuck. I'm older than any man currently living in Phoenix, and although not needed, I implanted the first Eden Bean when I appeared to be twenty-seven years old. I've been hiding my origins and sacrificing myself for a word and a smile from a sexy alien in my living room a lifetime ago," I blurted and saw Mika stiffen. Connor pulled him by the arm and Mika seemed to swallow his words and smiled at me.

Taking a deep breath, I saw Ish's encouraging smile, so I blundered ahead, "I don't feel guilty because I gifted the Phoenicians with eternal life." I smiled up at Ish and he looked down at me, with adoration in his eyes. "Memories of years far gone resurfaced. I'd almost forgotten those eyes. Too much had happened, and as the years twisted their strands together, it all became a forgotten drop of memory in a big bucket full of time."

Ish threw his arms around me as he lifted me from the floor, his strong arms encasing me, protecting me. We playfully rubbed our noses together, a silly new thing that brought a smile to my face. I squirmed with delight, feeling safe and loved in his affectionate hold.

Ish put me down to greet Cian and Brad, and I could see they were already better friends with him than I thought. I felt jealous, but then I remembered how important Ish was and the jealousy turned into a proud possessiveness. He was mine, I thought as I watched them shaking hands. As soon as he was done greeting them, he reached for me, making me feel special and important to him. Every second I spent in his shadow, more of my fears and doubts disappeared and were replaced with strength and knowing that I was as important to him as he was to everyone else here.

"I've always wondered if the earthlings could ever leave this place. I was relieved when I first saw your transportation vehicle. My home is now but a rock bestrewed with heaps of crumbling aspirations and broken dreams. I was left utterly alone, yet now I am not alone anymore." Ish smiled at us. I listened attentively, and I knew this message was important. I focused on each vowel and syllable to ensure that I would remember this forever.

"I was the youngest of my siblings, and I missed and hated them for leaving me behind. Alive. In solitude, I observed the humans. All I could do was watch how they murdered and destroyed themselves from afar. My father's cunning and twisted ways destroyed us and our home. I lived in hiding, contemplating ending my torturous existence. I longed to walk with the humans to cure my loneliness. I asked myself over and over, how do I reveal myself? How will they receive me? I am not a god. Nor do I want to be one. For eons, I tried tirelessly to find the point where sowing our seed and knowledge would bloom as intended. Look at what's happening with the creation of the Zelk—an unnatural species made from parts of humans and parts of their technologies. If I don't help them, they will die by the hand of the Zelk that continue to multiply. The Zelk is an abomination. A thing that grows and consumes not only human flesh and bone but their souls, too. It lures the weak with the promise of life, but it brings only death. I know it because I have battled it before. I will work with Cian and his brothers, and together, we will find the balance we have all been seeking —a new beginning," Ish said.

As he spoke, I could feel the cool air from the humming AC units on my exposed skin, but it was hard to concentrate when I was completely mesmerized by his striking features, dangerous aura, and overwhelming presence. I knew he wasn't sharing everything. He was twisting and hiding things from them, and me.

He leaned down, his hot breath tickling my ear as he whispered, "Take me somewhere private, so I can bury myself deep inside you."

I gulped. My cock was on board. I yanked my shirt down to cover my growing erection in front of a room full of men and gave him one stern nod.

CHAPTER II
NOT OUR FIRST

"*MORNING, CITIZENS OF PHOENIX.*

It's now six a.m.

Did you know it is a proven fact that humans burn intense energy during copulation and that this energy causes a transformation that sparks a whole neural fireworks show? By releasing a special hormonal cocktail the brain will, at its best, charge an entire set of biological batteries in the human body. The paralyzing spastic seizures humans experience are the result of these overcharged batteries and can be so intense that the physical becomes mythological and it is in that moment that the metaphysical can take root incorporeal and paranormal.

Breakfast is served until eight a.m.

Hope your day is full of transformations!"

ISHTAR

2146 A.D. (94 A.T.)
One year before the moon evacuation
Phoenix, underwater glass dome city

"COME, TIME TO GO." Peter grabbed my hand and dragged me away from where I'd promised my allegiance to Cian, Brad, Mika, and Connor. "I've been waiting for you for so long. You are mine now," he whispered.

I gave Mika and the men a shrug, they waved me goodbye and then I shot after Peter. We removed our coveralls while fighting our way back through the wind tunnel. Peter awaited me on the other side, and as soon as I exited, he jumped into my arms. All I could do was catch him.

My Kuku's going to be distraught, disappointed, and absolutely devastated, if I told him that this wasn't our first, first-time or that he is about to sprout wings some time in his future.

My whole being wanted to bond with him. I rattled with urgency from within. It had to happen. Even if I couldn't take him away and do it somewhere romantic.

Somewhere not trapped under fucking water.

I'm facing hurting my mate by snuffing his joy in this special moment. The Peter I got to know in our short twenty-four hours together had a mean streak. That meant this Peter should be treasured, not mortified and cheated out of the enjoyment he'd been waiting for, for over a century.

I was also not going to tell him he wasn't looking like

the Peter I knew. Not now. Fuck, this is not the time for such news. It would be unfair to him, I thought as I watched him being all jovial as he looked at me. Seeing the real me, because I wasn't cloaking my true appearance from him.

I planned to tell him, only when I was sure he could handle the truth. Only when I could take him to a place where he could stretch his wings and fly. Phoenix was no place for someone who needed the open skies.

He wiggled his hips and hooked his legs tightly around my hips. For a second, our eyes met, and I knew this second was the best second ever and I will never forget this second, even if we have forever of seconds in time.

His chest moved fast up and down—both of us were catching our breaths. He inspected me while I inspected him. He was the most beautiful man of all the men I've ever seen. His skin was smooth and pale. His eyebrows were dark and perfectly framing his blue diamond eyes.

"Yes, my Kuku, this is real, and happening," I breathed.

"We are in each other's arms," he said, with sparkling happiness. There's so much of it. Like a fountain, it spurted out of every pore and into the empty pond of my soul. Fates, I needed him. This was the face I searched for.

"Yes, that we are," I answered, my voice thick with gratitude and emotion.

He slammed his lips against mine. I opened my mouth, laughing at him. "Careful, my fangs!" I said between kisses.

"Don't care, they are so sexy." He licked my lips and

ran his tongue up and down each fang. It felt as if he sucked and licked my balls as shivers danced down my spine. He wrapped his arms tighter around my neck. The voracious kissing continued. Our happiness stoking, choking, and stuffing those dark, lonely corners inside our hearts. Thousands of years and so many realities were now colliding. This was a time for celebrating. Our union. The start of our love.

"I can't see where I'm going," I rasped into his mouth, my head reeling.

Peter glared at me. "Walk, I'll tell you where to go," he said, kissing me again and only stopping to give me directions while I walked us backward so he could see where we were going.

"Go left. No, not that left! The other left!"

"Peter, I am going to fall over someone," I chuckled, with his tongue down my throat. He clung to me. I tightened my hold under his upper legs and locked my fingers, so he sat comfortably with his tight butt inside my cupping hands.

"Stop, we're here," he said between happy giggles and half fell out of my arms to reach the sensor next to the door of his apartment. He slapped the palm of his hand onto it and the door slid open.

"That's it. Open sesame! You may enter." He waved his hand dramatically. Undulating in a half circle, almost breaking his spine, then he snapped right back up, grabbing me by the neck to plant more kisses all over my face, my eyebrows, my forehead, and my lips. Every inch of my face was being kissed. My delight burst out of my chest as I laughed jubilantly.

"Bedroom now!" he muttered between pecking, sucking, and licking. This was the happiest version of myself in a long time.

We were going to be mated.

I followed his directions as best I could, marching us to the first open door on the far right side of the apartment.

"Nope, bathroom, the other door," he said before feasting again. It was a struggle to keep my eyes open and not walk into walls and fall over tables. His hands were groping and undressing me. His eagerness to have me made me feel like I was a young, innocent boy.

When the back of my knees bumped into something, I checked and confirmed it was the bed. I unwrapped him from me. His grip loosened, and I lifted him by placing my hands under his armpits so he could stand on the bed and look me in the eye. He was a wicked fiend—wanting, panting, and his hair was a mess.

"Let me undress you," I said with a deep rumble in my voice. He pinned me with those unique blue silvery eyes, now fully dilated as his chest heaved, nodded a yes, and started to unbutton his shirt. I slapped his hands away gently. His breath hitched with a small gasp. "Let me. I want to do this."

"Then get on with it. I don't have time for politeness. I've waited for this much too long. We can do ceremony and niceties another time." He had a feral look in his eyes. Like he wanted to devour me. The urgent look on his face and the needy thoughts he projected told me he was close to blowing his load in his pants. I increased my speed and kicked my boots off as he jumped to remove the rest of his clothes. Then we were naked. He with no wings and me happy to soon be bonded to him. Playfully, I pushed him backward and jumped onto the bed.

"Happy now?" I asked, my voice rumbling as I pinned his small pale body beneath me. I was a gigantic beast compared to his slight size. My feet still touched the floor as I encased him, resting my elbows on either side of his head. My long dark braided hair draped around his pure white mane.

"Yes," he grunted and flung his arms around my neck, kissing me again. His skin was flushed warm with arousal beneath me. He lifted his feet and threw them around my hips.

My significantly bigger cock was more manageable while sitting on my heels while my lover sat on my lap, managing my length and girth by riding me and controlling the depth of penetration. I hoisted him up as I sat back, bringing him with me. I dipped down, never stopping kissing him. He was hungry for me, and our kisses weren't quick brushes of lips. No, they were passionate, deep, and consuming. We were mating and possessing. He wanted to make me his, as I wanted to make him mine.

We changed it up from rough to gentle and then suddenly, so softly, I felt like crying. His thoughts were only of me and having me, and how much he'd missed me. How happy he was to be here with me. I could hardly restrain myself from bursting into tears. The loneliness inside him gave me a deeper insight into why my Kuku was so upset about being alone and feared being forgotten for thirty years. I had a chance now to fix that.

Luckily, he started fisting my hair, and the pain ripped me from listening to his thoughts to what was happening in the here and now. Somehow, through the kissing, he had reached for lubrication and was smearing my cock with it. Breaking our kiss, he stood up and applied the sweet-smelling stuff to his backside, all the while pinning me with a smoldering gaze.

I grabbed his hips, lifting him to line my cock up with his entrance. "Please put it in. I can take you. I've had lots of practice with my Ishtar dildo," he grunted with a don't-try-to-stop-me look.

"I'm taking notes and will ask you about that dildo later." I panted as he threw his head back and impaled himself on me.

It was me being taken into him, and me putting my body into his.

Slowly, we became one like we were supposed to be. He took ownership of me as I of him. I brightened the room as my golden blue energy flowed out of me and surrounded us. The light flickered brighter the more I felt connected and aroused by him. He moaned and my cock squeezed through the warmest and tightest hole in the universe. Once the head of my cock was inside, his warmth sucked me deeper into him. Goosebumps ran up my spine as dancing blue and gold shades of light surrounded us.

He made incoherent sounds.

"I know!" I grunted. I squeezed my eyelids shut in pleasure while hoping he wasn't hurting himself.

"Oh my god, oh my god. I've never been so full. So stretched."

My eyes popped open. "Don't hurt yourself."

"It's fucking amazing. You feel so fucking good. Just like I imagined." Sweat beaded on his forehead. He arched his back and laughed while he hung on my shoulders with his legs wrapped around my hips. Slowly, he bobbed up and down. Sweet fates. I was enjoying watching him as he swung his head from side to side and flipped his white hair back. He was wild and gorgeous. I held his hips guiding him, in case he harpooned himself.

"Yessss," I hissed through clenched teeth, staving off an early orgasm.

"You feel magnificent, my Ish. I'm going to come."

For a split second, he opened his eyes, seeing the golden blue glow of my skin. His thoughts were that he was waiting for it to happen. "Oh my god yes, you are my dark alien, aren't you?"

My body reacted, my balls contracted, and my soul opened up to him. Receiving him. It was indescribable. I felt love and promise and so much fucking goodness and rightness as we locked gazes.

"Don't be scared of hurting me, don't hold back," he said as he increased his pace riding me. I read his mind. He wanted me to glow brighter.

"I'm not," I lied.

I didn't want to let go and lose control. So many things were happening all at once urging me to close my eyes and give in. My eyeballs weighed a ton, and they wanted to roll back in my head.

"I feel like my skin wants to burst open!" he yelled into the air.

Oh fuck! Realization struck me like a thunderbolt. I was going to cause him to spread his wings and—

"Oh yes, yes, yes!" he cried in ecstasy and confirmed my fear was real. Oh fuck, this was not the time or the place. I was going to ruin this, him, and us. I couldn't let him change now. It was entirely too early.

Reduce the level of his excitement. I grabbed his hips to slow the pace, but he was already over the edge.

"My Kuku, no, Peter, calm down! Please calm the fuck down."

I should have told him about his wings.

I grabbed hold of his bony shoulders, forcing him to slow down. He looked at me with hooded eyes and then he kissed me. My eyes closed and we exploded in a mess of me putting brakes on his changing, the smell of his ejaculation that pulled my orgasm, and then we both lost control as I filled him and bit down on his shoulder. His warm seed shot up between our stomachs as I embraced him, pulling him tighter and holding him in place. Like rushing waters, neither one of us could have stopped what was happening. The instinct woven into my Anunnaki bloodline, the royalty of Anzulla, overrode all my inhibitions.

Bite. Claim. Mate.

My jaws locked as I bit down into the crook of his neck.

"Oh, my fucking god!" he exclaimed, then writhed and undulated on my cock. I sank my teeth deeper and my predatory eyes popped open. A possessive growl rumbled in my chest. He tensed in my arms for a second and then his whole body relaxed as if he had passed out, resting his head on my shoulder.

What had I done?

Quickly, I retracted my fangs, before I totally emptied my venom sacs. My thoughts were disorientated and the sincerity of this sanctity of two unified souls, was overwhelming. I struggled to stay lucid. To think coherent thoughts. One thing remained in the forefront of my mind, I was binding him to me. The venom sacs behind my molars prickled and bulged so much I struggled to swallow. I sighed in relief, knowing I still had some bite left. My eyesight was enhanced, and my hearing was super sensitive as I zeroed in on our surroundings like an animal possessively guarding its wounded mate. If someone came to take him from me, I would tear them apart. The heat of his body increased my awareness of him in my arms and the need to protect and shield him from anything and everything that could hurt him stirred another possessive growl inside my chest. I purred like a cat as I licked the drops of blood from the healing wounds at the base of his neck.

"At least, so far, no wings, thank fuck." The rushing noise in my head disappeared and I finally had clear thoughts. He slumped in my arms. I couldn't sit like this forever. His taste, the essence of his lifeblood still on my tongue, was familiar. I had tasted it before.

"We are now a half-bonded pair. The Fates have blessed us," I said worriedly. "If you spill your seed in me, we would be fully bonded, once we say the mating words."

"You forgot, I have to bite you too when I come inside you," he groaned, taking a new purchase with his hands as he straightened his legs, still fully seated on my cock. He smiled drunkenly at me. "My mate, my big, beautiful lover."

I smiled, and we kissed as if we had loved and known each other for millennia.

"What are the mating words?"

"It's in Anunnaki. I would say them and you should repeat after me."

"Let's do it, I want to mate you," he said seductively and pulled me closer for a kiss.

I was testing our luck if I allowed us to continue further. I slowed the kissing and his delicious movements and pulled away, breaking the kiss. My lips felt swollen and his were a deep wine red. I beamed at him. "There is something I have to tell you, Peter. Please slow down." I begged with urgency and pulled him closer to me to reduce the friction on my cock. He stopped moving abruptly, looking at me questioningly.

"What is it, Ish? You wanted to say something while we orgasmed. You wanted to stop, but then you couldn't. It must be important if you think it's more important than us coming and bonding."

"It is," I admitted. I lay him down on his side and positioned myself so my cock was still lodged inside him. "I didn't know how to tell you this, but I'm going to say this and please understand, I'm not doing it to hurt you. It is quite the opposite. I want to protect you."

"Okay? Tell me." He frowned and I could see doubt creeping into his eyes.

"We have met before," I blurted and hoped for the best.

"I know, silly," Peter said as he took my hair and smelled it. He was so into me, and I loved this version of him already just for that.

"No, not when I bit André. It was after that, but before today, when I met you. It surprised me to see you on the stairs earlier today."

"I know. It was as if you didn't recognize me." He sat up then seemed to remember I was still inside him.

"It is because I didn't at first." He searched my stern, serious-looking face for the truth."

"How could you not remember me?"

"I do, but I have jumped so many times, and we already have history together. I had forgotten that we met before you..." I stopped talking, wondering if I should tell him.

"What dammit?" he barked at me.

"Before, when you had wings." There, I'd said it.

"Wings? What wings? Oh my god! Are you saying?" His eyes enlarged. My cock slid out of him as he sat back to measure the extent of my truth. Then, out of nowhere, he hit me on the chest with a fist.

"I asked you not to get mad at me, ouch."

"That didn't hurt. Stop being overdramatic. Tell me about my fucking wings."

"I don't know, you never told me, but you have big

white wings, like…" I didn't want to tell him I'd lost him and had found him once, and currently had no fucking clue where to find him again.

"Like a fucking Angel?"

I bit my lip. "Yes," I answered, shying away and awaiting another punch, but he threw his head back and laughed.

"That's impossible."

"Okay, don't believe me, but if you suddenly sprouted your wings down here, you would not be happy. You would feel trapped and caged inside Phoenix and I can't take you away now because you said you have those children to care for and I have to help Cian save the humans. I asked you to come with me, remember? So, I don't think we have a choice now. We have to wait. I'm kind of having a hard time being everywhere lately." He wanted to interrupt me, but I pushed ahead. "Meeting you is a bonus. But if you had your wings, then I'd have to break my word. I'd have to choose between you and the rescue mission. I already promised Brad, Mika, and Connor, not to mention Cian, that I would help them. Understand? The Fates placed me in the middle of all this. I can't ignore the Fates."

I could see the color in his eyes changing as his body reacted to what little royal Anunnaki elixir I had injected into him. His mind worked at such an incredible speed I could hardly keep up with his thoughts. It was as if he ran five thought patterns at once. He was extraordinary.

"Ish, listen to me. Wings or no wings. You must go back to the beginning of Phoenix, to the year 2046 A.D.

and download the computer program to your ship. Lasitor can help you navigate the times and give you the history word for word and second by second. You can't keep guessing and jumping," he said as if reading my mind. "Leave clues for yourself and stop jumping around to figure out what is going on," he explained while playing with one of my braids between his fingers again, still calculating other probabilities in his mind.

"You are correct, but how did you know my onboard guide's name is Lasitor?"

"What? So you already downloaded him?" Peter asked.

"He has been part of my ship's navigation system since I started the machine for the first time."

"That's interesting," Peter said and looked up to the speaker in his room. "Lasitor!" he called like I call to my ship.

"Yes, Peter," the robotic voice of my onboard computer answered.

"How did your program get installed on Ish's ship?"

"I don't know, Peter. I can't recall. It must have happened before Phoenix ended up underwater. My memory of the time before that was damaged," Lasitor said.

My head was hurting.

"Unless I'd updated Lasitor and then traveled back to before I was rebuilding my ship."

"See, that's already a clue."

"I agree. I need help keeping track. My ship's onboard guide needs adjustment and updating with the current and previous history. I have to find out as much as possible, so I can trace back my steps. Either eliminate the Disciples or steer them in a better direction," I said, then bit down on the inside of my lips blocking him from entering my mind and hoping he didn't catch more of my thoughts.

"If you say that I am supposed to grow wings, well, I believe you, truly. I believe you and I'm not upset with you. Earlier today when I saw you or now, when we made love. God, just being close to you I feel like my skin wants to burst open. Like I'm too small for it. Like I'm about to be zipped open and break free," he said and lay down beside me.

"I'm glad you are taking this so well. You are not as forgiving or understanding as the Peter with wings. I was worried you would be upset or say I'm making up stories." —I took his hand in mine and kissed it— "Also, I promise you, before we leave, I will get the ship updated. Not knowing and guessing are causing unnecessary worries for you. I will ask Cian more about it as well. I don't know how or what, but I'm sure between you and Cian we can figure it out. It's an idea, in case I get lost and have to find you again." I rolled us over so he lay on my chest. We lay in silence as I rhythmically rubbed his warm and clammy back in circles until his breathing slowed down.

As if remembering something, he lifted his head and said stammering, "You can't tell Cian, he will want to come along. I have known him since he was a baby. He and his brother can be a handful. If it wasn't for Eryn, those two would have turned Phoenix upside down on the seabed. Not to mention those humongous animals of theirs." He plopped his head back down again. My heart warmed with fuzzy feelings.

"I can imagine. I've gotten to know them fairly well by now. They are fun, lots of positive energy to be around. And they are fortunate to have their Anubis," I added, then gently wiped his sweaty hair from his face. "I can't help but feel a pinch of envy. The Anubis seem happy and there is so much love between them and their charges. They seem protective of the three. My father mistreated them. He abused them by ordering them to attack defenseless, innocent humans. They were the first he drained and killed, assuming he would acquire mystical powers. I took mine and fled to join Titus on the battlefront against Egypt," I whispered.

After a long time of listening to Peter's thoughts, they finally quieted down as he drifted into a relaxed state, I lay listening to our hearts beating the same song.

"My Kuku, this is important. Listen," I begged, and he cracked one unfocused eye open. "I asked Brad earlier today what he would change if he had the chance, and he said to have more whiskey and not get Drew and Juan killed." The one eye he had opened, rolled back into his head. The little venom I had injected was knocking him out. He failed to lift his head. The transformation of my small bite had used a lot of energy. "What I'm piecing together is that Drew and Juan are the reason we traveled to 1968 A.D.?"

"Hmmm, Drew and Juan were killed while saving Cian and Ivan in South Africa. My friend, 1968, yes

André," Peter said, barely making sense as he drifted into sleep again.

"Peter," I whispered, "before you fall asleep."

"Hmmm?"

"I think I know now what I am supposed to do. It's making sense now why we ended up going to Andrew. We will slip away, maybe tomorrow after you show me off to the children in your school, then go to 1968. Back to the night you met me."

"Yes, I agree. I need you," he mumbled incoherently.

"Hey, open your eyes." I shook him gently by the shoulder. "Did you say André?"

"Hmmm, my best friend, 1968."

A nagging sensation told me that this was important. Peter was understandably drained, but upon awakening, he would crave something other than food. I would have to feed him, and he would have to do the same for me. This was a natural part of our mate bonding. We were meant to provide each other with sustenance. Consuming from others may keep you alive, but it can never fill the void created by the bond between mates. Only the Loursveto juice could satisfy that hunger for bonded and unbonded Anunnaki.

With his eyes closed, he snuggled closer to me. "I agree. Let's rest for a few minutes. If I grow wings, we won't be able to return anyway. Also, if those Germans saw me with wings, well, that would restart another Berlin crisis."

Berlin crises? I wondered.

"What do you mean, Peter?" I asked. "Like what?" I hoped to keep him lucid enough to tell me.

"Hmmmm, not important. Tell you later," he muttered, then soft little snores followed. I felt so unhinged and out of sorts. Like I had forgotten something, an important clue. Only one thing left to do, I entered Peter's mind. My heart shattered as I glimpsed that dark, lonely, and sad place. I recognized it because it was like mine. After I killed my father.

"I'm here now, and no one will ever hurt you again," I whispered, so he would never forget it. I searched deeper. Before he arrived in Phoenix. His friend André, who escaped Germany and moved to the United States. Ahh, now that made sense. André changed his name to Andrew when he moved to the United States and then Andrew's nickname is Drew. Dear Fates, how many names does the man have?

I witnessed the heartbreaking choice that Peter had to make, as he chose to sever all communication to protect his friend. When Peter had heard his friend had died, the confusion of his friend's death devastated him. I saw glimpses of his mother, the Disciples, and his father, but not once did I see him smile. His memories were crystal clear as if they had occurred yesterday. Unlike most minds I've entered, his was not a complex maze; instead, it was organized like rows of shelves filled with neatly labeled information categorized by month and year.

My mate's mind was endlessly intriguing. I lingered on my sexual encounter with André. Seeing it from his view, they were best friends. He was glad I had bitten him to save his life and give him the ability to regenerate. Then there was the whiskey issue. Peter was jealous because I was meeting Andrew in secret, and not with him. Later Peter was transferred to Antarctica, where he would eventually meet Juan, or should I say Juandre, Andrew's future partner.

In a moment of brilliant cunning, I had given André my mating bite without fully considering the consequences. Whose idea was it, really? I searched for any additional details that may have been buried in my mind. With a sense of panic, I closed my eyes and searched for answers within my thoughts. Suddenly, my eyes snapped open and my heart raced as a new realization dawned on me.

"Oh fuck, what have I done?" I had bitten Peter. What if there wasn't enough venom in my bite for André?

"Oh, my fucking Fates! What have I done?" Ice-cold realization washed over me. All this time I was worried about Peter sprouting wings, not realizing I couldn't feed him when I lost him. He would die without me. Also, I couldn't go back to 1968 with minimal to no venom in my bite. I couldn't take the chance. I wouldn't be able to turn André into an Anunnaki consort and my Kuku would suffer and die while he waited thirty years for me to find him.

This was a colossal conundrum—a fuck-up of disproportional proportions.

Which version of reality was this, which timeline was this? It seems Juan and Drew are dead. But Peter remembers me visiting him. This meant I had work to do. "Motherfucker!" I grunted, but Peter seemed unscathed. He snored, looking innocent, with a slight grin on his face. So fucking angelic. A possessive wave washed over me. I was the one who put a smile on his face.

Maybe—maybe I should—yes, I have to cross that line I wasn't supposed or permitted to pass over. I would have to have a word or two with myself. That's the only way to fix this. It would have to work. I can't bite Peter before I bite André. This was a colossal fuckup. If I keep doing this, I'm going to confuse myself and mess with the time-lines, as the Fates warned me.

I closed my eyes and concentrated on freezing time. Then, stepping out of time, I swam to earlier this morning, just before meeting Peter.

I waited until I saw my other self entering the wash-room to use the facilities. This was my chance. No one would see our interaction. Impressed with my ability to find this spot to pop back into, I stuck my arm through the veil and locked the door to ensure my conversation stayed private. I watched my other self urinating into the shiny steel receptacle. When I was done, I tapped my other self on the shoulder.

"Whoa! What the fuck?"

"Zip up, shut up, and listen," I told my other self. "I've fucked up. Whatever you do, save your bite for André."

I watched my other self pull my eyebrows askew, thinking it was better not to talk back, and tucked my manhood away. "I'm listening. This must be important because this is forbidden."

"I know, and yes, it is. Listen, your Kuku is here."

"Here? I've searched for him everywhere. How did he end up here? I don't think he could have…"

"Would you shut up and listen? Yes, and no, I will not tell you. I'll keep the surprise a surprise. Please hear this and remember this. I mistakenly bit Peter during our love-making. Tonight, it will happen. I, you are missing some vital parts on this timeline. I, you, will realize that what Brad said earlier is connected to this mating bite. The way Peter spoke, he made it sound like it had already happened and I was so fucked in the head with lust. I had forgotten this. Peter still needs to travel with me," I explained to my other self as fast as possible. It was weird looking at myself being stupefied by my stupidity. Why the Fates decided I was worthy of this shit baffled me.

"Hmmm, I remember André. Somehow, I don't know if it already happened or—yes, I see the problem. So, I'm finally meeting Peter for the first time."

"Yes, you are. And he hasn't changed yet. His wings are…"

"Shut up. You are going to change too much if you tell me. What you are doing is forbidden for a reason."

"I fucking know. Whatever you do, don't let Peter sprout wings, and don't give him your bite. Your Kuku will starve without you in the jungle. Unless…"

"Unless, what?"

"I wonder, maybe Gugusan helped Peter survive somehow for thirty years." I shook my head at my other self. "No, Peter is something else, he has wings, and he already has longevity. For now, he doesn't need your bite. Your bite may cause him to suffer when he is lost."

"Yes, I see. No wings, and he is already a handful."

"I know. He is my perfect Kuku. He's precious." I watched my other self smile dreamily. I liked the nickname Gugusan first called my mate.

"So this is the plan. You have a tight schedule ahead of you. Early tomorrow you have to skip ahead, return to Grayrak with Cian, get on the time machine, then go back to the beginning of 2046 A.D.—record the history of this place and time. Go back to Andrew. Make sure you have given him the bite. Find out what happened, and why they got killed. Fix this mess, then return and collect Peter tomorrow afternoon."

I watched my other self shaking my head and smirking. "Sounds like fun," other me said with a firm nod.

"Good?" I asked and hoped it was. I did not want to spoil the surprise or change the day I'd shared with Peter.

"Good."

I nodded, then slipped back to where I had left my lover sleeping, then unfroze time. Peter was still snoring. I checked his neck where I had bitten him earlier.

"Thank the Fates," I whispered, seeing the bite mark on his neck was gone. Peter sat up, swiping his blond locks to the side. Then he crept on his hands and knees and lay sideways across the bed, resting his head on me like my lap was a pillow. It was such a comfortable thing. As if we'd been doing this forever. I with my back against the soft plush headrest, feet crossed at the ankles. Naked, our cocks semi-hard. I stroked his hardening nipples, rolling them between my fingers. Thought better of it and laid my hand on his chest.

"Talk to me, my Kuku. Talk your heart out. I'm listening." I kissed his forehead and stroked his upper body with one hand while examining and testing the soft white strands of hair between my fingers.

His eyes closed and he spoke in a soft, aching tone. "As I reflect on the past, I realize that you always held my destiny in your hands. Seeing you today only confirms my belief that escaping from my father and the Disciples was inevitable and that what I witnessed was not a figment of my imagination. I grew up without having a normal childhood—devoid of love and typical toys like cars or dolls. Instead, our fathers gave us puzzles and tests to complete, as they were scientists themselves. If we'd had children, we would have followed in their footsteps and worked in the physics and evolutionary biology departments at Humboldt University of Berlin. It was expected for us to continue the legacy of our fathers' work, which dates back generations to when the Disciple group was first founded," Peter said and checked in with me. His look—questioningly. *Are you keeping up? Are you listening to me?*

I affirmed by giving him a go-ahead-I'm-listening nod.

"Fortunately, the four of us could transfer to the West with the promise of returning with valuable information or a groundbreaking discovery that the East could benefit from. My only relief was finding out that test-tube babies could be created in a more controlled environment. It became part of my routine to provide weekly sperm deposits for research, and through this process, it was revealed that I was sterile. Despite this, my intelligence kept me from being discarded, but it also meant I was only useful for one thing—following rules and conducting research. Not a single viable fetus was produced from my sperm, making me nothing more than a useless homosexual in their eyes.

"Every aspect of our physical appearance was meticulously measured and scrutinized, from hair and eye color to facial features and even bone structure. In life and in death, we were nothing more than data for them to analyze. But they could never measure or understand the song resonating within our souls. It was a unique vibration that only we could perceive. I didn't think I possessed any extraordinary abilities, maybe a heightened intuition. Unlike Cian, Ivan, Eryn, and now you, I don't emit a glow —not that I know of, at least. What sets me apart is my intelligence and longevity, but even those seem insignificant compared to the others.

"I remember the first time I saw you, a long time ago. My back tingled and itched as if my spine would break open. It was a searing heat, pulsating like an infected wound in between my shoulder blades. But when you gave your bite to André, it vanished, leaving behind an overwhelming sense of loneliness. I retreated into myself, feeling like a stranger in my skin until this moment. During all this time I waited for you, I had a yearning for you. It consumed me, while a copy of myself remained on the surface. Slowly, I faded away, unable to connect with anyone—even my closest friends. Sex became a chore, with no euphoria or enjoyment. Everything seemed shrouded in a gray haze, separating reality from what was not real. I clung to life each day, hoping that one day things would get better and make sense when you came back for me. That hope kept me going, day by day.

"Melancholy has always been my default state. Sometimes I don't know if what happened was real or just my imagination. Just before I met you, André rescued me from a pitiful suicide attempt and promised that we wouldn't be trapped and used like animals anymore. We were summoned back to the East, but refused to accept the oppressive regime; he protested and demonstrated against it. We knew our fathers would eventually force us into the organization, so I saw no other way out but to end my life. However, André arranged for us to escape to Vienna, then ultimately to America. He told me it was either that or we both die together. He couldn't bear the thought of living without me and pleaded with me not to give up on life. On the night we planned to flee, I was all packed and ready to go when suddenly you and an older version of myself materialized in my living room. That night is permanently etched in my mind—replaying like a film reel on repeat.

"The living room felt tiny as I looked up at your towering frame and caught glimpses of my older self's pitying expression in between André's frantic ramblings in the background. It was like I was outside, looking up at a vast night sky filled with countless twinkling stars. The sight of you and the sense of hope and possibility you brought with you gave me the strength to hold on. My older self urged me not to let go," Peter explained as my tears fell like a leaky roof, dripping onto his face.

I wiped them away, but the more I wiped, the stronger

my affections became. I shared every ounce of his emotions that had been bottled up inside him, and now I cried for him, spilling out onto him. The connection we shared was new and raw. He let go of repressed feelings as the first layer of bricks was laid to build an unbreakable bond, a union between us. Together, we lived and relived our memories until we found solace in each other's embrace. "Remember these words, when you miss me. I will translate it into English." I whispered.

"Mates in love, we'll weather life's storms,
holding tight to each other's memory.
Our bond will never falter or break,
for our love is pure and strong.
With or without you by my side, our love can conquer anything,
for you are my strength and my everything.
Mates in love until the end of time,
forever bonded in heart and mind."

CHAPTER 12
THE CATALYST

"Guten Morgen.
   Es ist jetzt sechs Uhr morgens auf der Erde.
   Das Frühstück gibt es bis acht Uhr morgens.
   Haben Sie einen guten Tag!"

Ishtar
1968 A.D.
West Berlin
Germany

TIME IS A MYSTERIOUS EVER-PRESENT THING. When I was younger, I always thought it was a never-ending, continuously flowing, one-directional force that originated somewhere unknown and stretched as far as life itself existed. Life is measured by time, and time cannot exist without life. Now that I'm older I realize even though time existed, even though life existed, it meant nothing if it wasn't spent with the people you came to love and wanted to protect from slipping away through the strands of realities, because the reality that owns your heart and soul is suddenly more important than any other place in time.

"We were lucky. No animals were harmed during the landing procedure," Lasitor, my onboard navigator announced.

"Thank you for that useless piece of information. I would be more worried if humans saw us. Who cares if we kill a chicken or two?" I said. We'd traveled to West Berlin in 1968 to find André, so I could give him my mating bite, so he could bite and mate with Juandre in the future. I was aiming to hit two birds with one stone, to give Brad McCormick his two wishes. First, that Juandre and Andrew never got killed in South Africa during a rescue mission to save Cian, Ivan, and McCormick's two sons from the clutches of Eryn's Brawl family. Second, that Phoenix was stocked with whiskey for a very long time. I figured I would save Andrew, and guide him to mate with Juandre. Both would receive the healing abilities and longevity of the Anunnaki royal family members. Then, I would compel him to store crates of the yellow-brown stuff Brad and the men of Phoenix loved so much, inside the same mineshaft where they could find the stash while retrieving their children.

Peter opened the door and jumped out, not waiting for the stairs to extend so he could exit like royalty did. He was my wayward mate, so I followed his example and landed with a loud thud in the mud next to him. From the way he had lived in that pristine fishbowl, I would have thought mud and shit would irk him, but it seems he cared two tits about getting his shoes dirty.

"You never said what Rodger was," I chuckled.

"Huh? Oh, Julius' Rodger?"

"Yeah, what was it?"

"It is an ugly tarantula. I shiver just thinking about it."

"What's that?"

"It's a large hairy spider. The thing is still a baby, but it can grow so big it can catch small frogs, even birds." Peter *brrrrrrred* and I smiled even if I worried inwardly.

This is the one point in time I can't fuck up. I—no, *we* must get this right or we will create so many varieties of our realities down the timeline that we may never be able to return to our home, to Phoenix, where the friends we have will still be the friends we left behind a few minutes ago. Peter's head snapped up at my grunting as I channeled my frustrated thoughts and kicked the innocent small rocks to feel better. He'd dressed himself in what he called his street clothes with a long black jacket, and looked sexier than ever next to me. Our boots thumped on the gravel road down the small hill where we had parked and hidden the time machine.

"Stop grunting like you have a mortal wound or something. What's wrong? Do you have a toothache?"

"No. I'm worried about fucking this up. Turning Andrew, I mean André is a momentous anchor point in time. He is the catalyst and I realize we only have one chance to do this right."

Peter stopped walking to face me. He pointed a finger right at my chest, poking it. "All I remember is André arriving home, cum dripping from his face and bewildered. Then you appeared in our living room, telling us you were from our futures. The next moment you were fucking my best friend while I sat with my older self, receiving head, as you felicitated him for having a tight ass. You will get this right. I'm not coming back again." Peter glared at me. I resisted showing my amusement. Fates he was feisty. The more time I spent with him, the more I feared losing him.

He spun around to proceed down the hill.

"Peter, it sounds to me like you have some unresolved anger there. If you don't want me to give him the mating bite, you should say so now. We can get back on the ship and go to a place and time where all this doesn't even exist," I said under my breath.

Hands fisted, he faced me again. "Something happened all those years ago. When I opened my eyes the two of you were already getting ready to go. I guess I am now the older one and would have to remember we are here for just that. Get it over with so we can get out of here. Maybe that's why you were in a hurry to leave us there. I'm upset about things I didn't understand. But now, I agree, I'm not here for cookies and tea. I'm definitely not returning for a do-over. I'm also not going to ask you to abandon what we started a century ago. I agree, we can't fuck this up. You give him the bite and we leave. By the way, how did you appear and disappear like that?" he asked and seemed to be calming down again by taking slow, deep breaths in through his nose and exhaling out of his mouth.

I rubbed the back of my neck, feeling like shit for not divulging my gift to him earlier.

"Uhm, I have a small gift. I can use it for short distances. I have never tried to take someone with me, but I guess that happened." Wide-eyed, we simultaneously pushed each other to a dead stop. The faint sound of voices floated on the wind from the foot of the hill. I honed in, listening and searching for the source. "It's three men."

"I hope they're not coming our way," Peter whispered hurriedly. We veered left, eager to get out of the open. When we reached the relative safety of bushes and tall grass, he caught his breath, heaving and clutching his chest. "If you can disappear and reappear, this would be a good time to beam us straight to André."

I scoffed. "I don't disappear. I just move out of the limitations of time. Behind the barrier. I move freely and enter back where and when I choose to. For those I leave behind, it is as if time is frozen."

"A barrier?"

"Call it what you will. A curtain or force field. I don't have the correct name for it. It's like a thin layer, a veil I guess, that I can move in and out of. I can't go to places where I've never been. I can't take you to André, because I don't know where he is, and I've never been here."

"Interesting. So that's why you have a time machine? Then why didn't you park us inside the apartment?"

"Because that would be unsafe," I said, rolling my eyes

and throwing my hands in the air. He stopped walking as the sounds of crowds of people shouting and cheering came within earshot.

"I never liked crowds. André was the social butterfly. I was always alone and worried for both of us. He went to the protests, and I stayed home. He wanted to make every minute of his life count. I was always afraid of being trampled or, worse, killed. He was the bigger and so much stronger one of us."

"Do I sense a bit of jealousy there, my Kuku?" I teased. "Remember, you are the only one for me too. You are the most important person in my existence. This entire plan revolves around you allowing me to bite him."

"I'm not jealous. I'm always willing to share, as long as your heart is mine, and I know I am yours. We can enjoy other men together if all parties are willing and agreeable. As long as I am your only true mate," Peter said.

"You are. Now and always," I said, tapping his sexy ass. "Then that is how I am going to help Andrew and Juandre meet. Andrew is the best man to ask to produce and store whiskey. I've visited them three times already and I think when we are done here, I can go and show you what I mean. Would you like that?"

Peter stopped dead in his tracks, kicking up mud and gravel. He stood with his hands on his hips and gave me a *you-better-not-fuck-with-me* look. "You have so many secrets!"

"Hahaha! My Kuku, you have lots to see and learn." I chuckled over my shoulder, enjoying the fluttering feeling in my stomach.

"I thought you would never ask. At least now I have something to look forward to when I have to sit and watch how you fuck and bite my friend. Also, you won't appreciate me if you have nothing to compare me to. I'm not against you having a little fun. I used to play with Tony and Bryan. Even with others. We enjoyed each other's bodies, but I always saw you in my mind and when I went to sleep. I dreamed about you."

"You forgot to say you fucked yourself on a dildo named after me, and then you went to sleep and dreamed about me," I said with more chuckles—teasing him.

Peter lifted his chin and shoulders. "Whatever, you were always on my mind. Even if you gave your mating bite to my best friend and told me to wait for you."

"Come here." I pulled him closer, lifted him in my arms, and kissed him. My heart skipped and jumped in my chest. He loved me and was such a special man. He made me happy and instantly hard. *Who doesn't want a mate like that?* I salivated and swallowed the excess drool in my mouth. "Maybe we can find a hole or a tree or something," I said, wiggling my thick eyebrows.

"Haha." He laughed, then squirmed in my arms to escape out of my embrace. "Remember, this is 1968, we are now in a time that isn't as accepting of men loving men as where we just came from. It's acceptable to rape your wife and beat her to death if she doesn't want to suck her husband's cock or take him up her ass. Men may fuck around, but women have to stay home and raise their sons to become soldiers. They are men for committing atrocities against other humans, but the moment you love another man, you are a worthless weakling." Peter stopped, looked like he wanted to say something more, then moved to the side. I gave him a second to collect himself. Pondering, he sighed and stretched his back while looking over the cityscape, now only a few hundred feet away. "I feel victorious now, seeing this and knowing I survived it all," he whispered. I moved closer to him. We stood there for a while, taking in the moment that would change his life as he knew it.

The sun was setting and here and there a streetlamp flickered on. The noisy hustle and bustle of human vehicles hid the human activity of protests and celebrations below.

"My father never liked it either. He hated me, but I would think it was a combination of killing my mother during my birth, being the youngest, and, fortunately, the smartest of all my siblings. When he killed them to take their powers, I fled and ended up with a friend. His name was Titus. He taught me how to fight. He was my mentor, in more ways than just fighting. He showed me how to love and what true friendship is. I arrived at the war front as a boy and as I aged, I watched him, realizing I wanted him. There was not one day in my life when I thought he wasn't a worthy man. He was more a man than many men who loved women. I didn't care if my father heard the rumors, but still, I stayed far away from him for as long as I could. Time is a strange thing. Sometimes time changes everything. Sometimes nothing will ever change no matter how much time passes. I had my fair share of female and male lovers. It is what it is. I still prefer the male form."

My Kuku's lips pulled back in disgust. "Are you saying you put that beautiful cock into a vagina?"

"Of course I did. I've tried every hole there is on the adult human body." I pushed my chest out proudly.

He covered his mouth, in an attempt to hide his trembling laughs. "Do you have any children?"

"No, I don't. Which is a good thing."

"Why is that?"

"I think if I'd had something to protect, someone to live for, I wouldn't have been able to fight to the death and slay my father."

"Hmmm, that makes sense. But now you have me."

Standing taller, I announced with a proud smile, "Yes, I do, and I will fight my arms down to stumps for you."

My Kuku liked that statement. A smile took over his face as his chest puffed out. "Such a romantic," he said, shaking his head and pointing to an outbuilding. "Inside, there is an opening to a tunnel system that runs underneath the city. Between East and West Berlin. It's a Disciple tunnel and a well-hidden secret. It opens up just behind our apartment. Let's take it and avoid being seen by the authorities."

"Lead the way." I nodded my agreement. My height and Peter's beauty would make us stand out. To enter the city via the underground tunnel meaning we could avoid inquisitive eyes or the authorities, would be better. When we reached the far side of the building, Peter slipped behind a false wall and squatted down to wipe away the soil covering the hole and I helped him lift the enormous steel door. Within seconds we were inside the dark tunnel.

Luckily, I had a little firemaker with me and I held it up so Peter could show us the way. "*Shhht,*" Peter held his finger in front of his mouth as he stopped dead in his tracks.

"Hallo, wir sind nur auf der Durchreise. Wir werden dir nichts tun. Wenn Sie niemandem von uns erzählen, werden wir auch niemandem von Ihnen erzählen," he said in German as we passed a man and woman, probably his wife, by the way he held his arm around her to protect her. Neither made a sound. They kept their heads lowered, skittishly looking up at us as if we were going to hurt them or something. I smiled to show them I was friendly.

"I assume you understand German?" Peter asked.

"Yes, I do. You said hello, and that we are just passing through and won't hurt them. If they don't tell anyone about us, we won't tell on them either."

"Hmmm, but with you smiling like that, and scaring them, I probably didn't have to say anything," Peter stated as he turned to continue down the dark, musty tunnel. I had become comfortable with not fully cloaking my appearance. My head scraped the roof now and then, so I stooped lower and followed him.

"What? I was just being friendly."

"There is friendly and then there is awkward. You were not friendly-looking."

"I showed them my teeth and the corners of my mouth were turned up. That is being friendly."

"The corners of your mouth may say you are friendly, but your size, height, and eyes scream 'I'm a monster in a tunnel, come closer, I want to eat you.' "

"If you say it like that, it hurts. And I was being

friendly, a bloody, friendly fucking monster." I grunted and wiped more sand out of my eyes. "We are going to get trapped down here if this tunnel collapses."

"We're almost home. I remember these tunnels as if I walked them yesterday," he said, just as the little firemaker died. Peter swerved left and right. I held onto the back of his pants. It was dark as fuck, but I could make out tunnel walls and openings by the different shades of black and gray.

"We're here," he announced as he halted and showed me where to climb up three wooden steps. I popped the door and held it open for him.

"You can go that way." He pointed to a busy street filled with humans celebrating as they shouted and honked the horns of their motor vehicles. "That is Losberg Street. Our apartment is around this corner and up the stairs. André should be in the Bierhalle, across the street. He usually hangs out there. I suggest we search there first. You must find him, and then somehow bring him to the apartment, and then I can help you from there. Do you remember where to go?"

"I don't," I grumbled and stared at him with twitching hands. "I wish I had brought my swords with me."

He nodded sternly and puckered his lips. "Me too, but that would attract the wrong attention. Having weapons, and especially Egyptian swords, is asking for trouble." I swung around. Turning nervously from side to side, searching for oncoming danger.

"Kuku, I can't fuck this up."

"I will take you there. Let's split up once inside.

Whoever finds him first take him to the back door, see, there. Where those men just exited the building. We can meet up there and go to our apartment," Peter said, pointing to a dark alleyway between two stone-faced buildings across the street.

I gave a quick nod and a false smile. "I would prefer staying together."

"As you say. I don't enjoy being back here. People get shot and disappear and if you leave me in Germany, I swear I will kill myself," he whisper-shouted in my ear.

I turned to him, waiting for him to meet my gaze. "How can you say that? If something happens, go with André to America. I will catch up with you."

"So that is the plan, in case something happens?" Peter asked, rolling his shoulders back and taking a deep breath.

"I guess so. Try to stay by my side. At any time, when you sense danger, grab onto me. We can slip away, behind the veil," I whispered with a tightness in my chest.

"Okay, let's go. We go in the front and meet in the back." Peter grabbed my hand and pulled me after him. I followed, but one step later, he halted and froze. He lowered his chin to his chest. Looking defeated.

"What?"

He shook his head and let go of my hand. "We can't hold hands here. It's against the law."

"Oh," I answered sadly, but understood immediately. I've never understood why others want to dictate where your heart and cock must go. It's yours, not theirs. No one should have authority over another's body. We are each born with one body and that one body is yours only. That is why I find murder, slavery, and rape appalling.

"I will stay by your side. This is only a quick in and out, understand?" He looked as nervous as I felt. "Here, love. Hold on to my belt. Fuck them, whoever they are. I won't let anything happen to you." I offered the belt hanging from the loop in my jacket. He cracked a smile and took it from me. My heart swelled.

"Okay, here we go!" He ducked his head and increased his pace. The gravel on the road cracked beneath my boots. Humans were moving in all directions. As we crossed the wide road, a loud horn beeped. Peter zigzagged and I followed him through masses of men and women waving big white flags. It was a chaotic scene. He darted out of their way.

"*Bring the wall down!*" they shouted. We avoided a group of young intoxicated men, keeping each other upright while singing joyfully. *Ding-ding!* came from the strangest two-wheel contraptions with humans sitting on them and zooming by us.

"What are those vehicles?" I asked as one almost ran us over.

"Bicycles," Peter hurriedly said as we slinked between humans crowding on the sidewalk. "Protests, they don't want the wall."

"Which wall?"

"There is a wall in the middle of the city separating families. People are starving and can't cross without a permit, and no one gets a permit unless you pay the guards or know someone higher up."

"Oh, like the wall in Grayrak?" I asked.

"I don't know. I've never seen that place or its wall."

"I will take you there after we are done here," I promised.

"I'd like to see it." He stopped before going through two huge wooden doors. "Do you know what he looks like?"

"Yes, I do. I told you I did my homework before coming to get you," I said, and it seemed Peter liked the answer. *Little did he know, I had lost him while visiting Andrew.*

He raked his fingers through his hair. Straightened his jacket. Seemingly undergoing a willful transformation, to exude self-assurance. Back rigid, head up, he pushed the doors open. Hot stale air mixed with sweat and old breath greeted us. Cheerful male voices hollered German songs above the upbeat music being made by men pulling and squeezing musical instruments. Behind the bar, a handsome man blew on a horn, shouting, "Letzte Runde!" Patrons waited eagerly to be served, waving money in the air at him. We moved away from men singing their hearts out while toasting with big jugs of alcohol.

After a minute inside, Peter smiled at me. "Time to go hunting," he mouthed and pointed with a chin lift into the crowd. "Go, I will meet you in the back." I was much taller than these men, so I spotted André almost instantly. He and his friends were standing at the end of the bar, drinking. I turned to tell Peter I was moving in on our target, but his back was to me as he disappeared into the fray. As

I returned my gaze back in André's direction, our eyes met.

"Excuse, me," I said in German and made my way over to André, trying to look like I wasn't heading straight for him. By the time I'd reached the bar, I noticed he was already making his way to the back, to the washrooms. I followed him, eager not to lose sight of him. He was by himself pissing, when I entered the small room. It smelled worse as the door closed behind me. The floor was wet and sticky, and it smelled of old urine and vomit. I was still glad to be in a space absent of crowds.

I surveyed his long and thick manhood. "Very nice!" He looked up shocked by my boldness and most probably by my handsomeness. I unsnapped my pants and took out my cock to show him what I was packing. We stood shoulder to elbow as I pissed a thick yellow stream. Sensing him assessing me, I felt his attraction while also fearing me.

"Why do you act so nervous? I'm sure there have been many men who have complimented, perhaps even worshipped, such a fine cock as yours. The body to which it is attached makes it even more impressive," I said, smiling. Then, remembering Peter's comment about my smile, I closed my mouth and narrowed my eyes. Conveying friendliness.

"I'm not nervous. I've just stayed out later than I planned, and I have much to do. I can't stay and chat," he lied and turned to leave.

"Why are you in such a hurry? I only want to have a

little fun," I asked in a seductive tone. I knew no human could resist my charm when I wanted them.

"Please, I just want to go home," he stuttered out while looking me up and down and measuring the distance to the door.

"What is your name, boy?" I asked and delved deep into his mind to make sure he was André.

"An-André," he said, sounding unsure if that was his name.

I gave him a stern nod and inched closer. Again, I smiled with my eyes crinkling at the corners and a closed mouth. I didn't want him thinking I was hungry and going to eat him. "André? Are you sure that is your name?" I asked and slowly removed the communication and intelligence device connected to my ship. I held it against his head, comparing the face with long blond hair on my screen with the scared clean-cut man in front of me. "That is a very German name. You will change it when you reach America, yes? Your new name is going to be legendary one day," I purred, keeping my voice low and seductive and trying my best to keep my appearance cloaked by not smiling or showing my fangs.

"I'm a professor at West Berlin University. I'm not going to America. You must have me confused with someone else," he said, studying my eyes as I willed him to calm the fuck down.

"You are from my lover's city. It is a pity we did not travel to meet each other earlier. So we have to work with the time we have. Don't worry. We will have enough time to have a good time," I purred, and I felt my pants tighten.

André's smell was intoxicating, and I couldn't wait to bite him. He smelled sweet with a hint of self-confidence and something different. Something not fully human.

"I don't understand what you mean. Why would you have a lover and still want me? Won't he be jealous? I know I would be, and I really need to get on my way." He blabbered on, but I could feel the attraction between us growing.

Licking my lips and tasting the air, I whispered, "We love sharing. Don't be in such a hurry. I know you are interested. Maybe inquisitive, aren't you?" I pinned him with a downward stare and stepped closer. Our bodies touched. The heat between us increased. His green eyes roamed up my chest as he measured my height.

"Really? No, yes. P-please," he stuttered, but we both knew he answered the question hanging in the surrounding air. I smiled. The greens in his eyes darkened. His pale cheeks flushed pink. I have some kind of weakness for the pale-skinned men.

"André, I am Ishtar, but you can call me Ish. I'm looking for a group that calls themselves the Disciples. You have heard of them, yes?" I was salivating for him and had to willfully retract my growing incisors. Where the fuck was Peter? I told him to not leave me alone.

He shook his head frantically. "How could I not have heard of them?" Bending his knees, he tried to slip to the side away from me. "I wish you a good night," he said, and I had to play for time until my Kuku arrived. *I might as well have some fun.*

"I did not give you permission to leave."

"I apologize. I thought our conversation was at an end. I didn't mean to be rude," he said. I could smell his arousal. It hung around us, choking me. Fuck, I was so turned on by this boy.

"André, I forgive you, but you must make it up to me," I purred. "Don't be scared," I said, inching closer. His heart was racing and his pupils were black disks like a trapped animal, not knowing which side was safest to go. I didn't sense the same suppressed power inside him as in Peter. I guess his gift was so diluted that my bite would be the perfect gift I could give him tonight.

"How—what do you mean? What do you plan to do to me?"

I had to get him outside to meet up with Peter. "Go through the door at the end of the hall. That will take you into an alley. I will be right behind you. Don't even think of running. I will catch you." I opened the door for him and gestured for him to go, and he did.

Peter wasn't outside waiting. I had to keep us busy. The only thing left to do was to play a game. We were alone and hidden behind a few trash cans. People were some distance away and if I couldn't see them, chances were they couldn't see us.

"Don't be afraid. Tell me now, do you want this or not? I just want you to do what you so obviously enjoy doing with that pretty mouth."

"I don't know what you mean," he said, backing up while I towered over him. He licked his lips as he looked me up and down. He wanted me.

"Over here in front of me now and on your knees,

boy." I pointed to the ground where he obediently knelt while looking at the bulge of my growing cock.

"There now, be a good boy and take out my cock." I praised him and he reached up to untie my pants. "Ah, there's a good boy. Now reach in and pull it out." With a shaky hand, he pulled my thick, pulsating cock out of its tight constraints.

"Put it in your mouth and suckle it. Suck on my piss slit," I ordered him and glanced over to the door, wishing my Kuku would join us.

"That's right, clean it. Wash it, pretty boy," I said and fisted his hair to hold his head in place. Then I started with small thrusts into his warm wet mouth, half pissed off at Peter for taking his sweet, bloody time. At least André was good with his mouth, so my thrusts became harder and deeper.

I heard a door and hoped it was Peter. "No! Don't stop," I ordered, holding him tighter by his hair. He breathed fast through his nose. I made eye contact with Peter and he didn't flinch at me while I was choking his friend with my cock. "This is my lover, Peter. I'm sure Peter will want to enjoy you when I have finished. Peter is also from here. Tonight is a reunion of sorts. Am I correct, Peter?"

Peter smiled and gave me an approving nod. As if to say, well done, and are you having fun? I gave him a look that said *I waited for you long enough; I am about to blow my load, so come and join me fucking your friend.*

"I think he likes being on his knees. Is he good at this, Ish?" Peter asked, rubbing his cock up and down. He was so into this, and I loved him even more.

"He is superb. It took a little convincing, but I can assure you that he's done this before. Get going, boy. I don't have all night. The sooner you finish me off, the sooner you can suck my lover." He resumed his sucking and my mate grinned while watching him, and then me, with hunger in his eyes. "Peter, take your cock out and get it ready for our friend," I ordered as Peter chuckled and eagerly freed his long hard cock.

"As always, Ish, you like a good mouth fucking." God, this was erotic. I was close to exploding. "Peter, put your hand on my cock and feel it slide in and out of this boy's mouth and kiss me while he milks me." As soon as my mate touched me, I lost all ability to control my balls from emptying down André's throat. I kissed Peter until I finished coming, then removed myself and guided Peter into the same hole I had just used. It was dirty and so sexy. The energy around us built to excruciatingly hot levels. I was scared my skin would start glowing, so I stepped back, looking over Peter's shoulder. He gasped, then clutched a handful of André's hair, mouth fucking him with fast, short jabs.

"Now suck it right and don't pull back. You're doing great. You're such a good boy," Peter praised him until he blew his load, then he pushed André on his ass. "Now, go home!"

My Peter had a mean streak.

I hoped André did just that. I held my hand out for Peter. "Do not let go of my hand. We will follow him." Peter tucked himself away and grabbed my hand. "Show me where to go. I'm going to need your help to find our way," I said as I closed my eyes and froze time. We moved along the curtain of strands, watching André going into his home. Peter pointed me to the living room, and I pulled him back into reality, where we waited for André to enter the apartment.

Seconds later he came running inside, flying over all their suitcases ready for travel in the morning and looking all kinds of fucked in the head. Peter gasped softly next to me as he watched himself.

"André, what happened to you?" young Peter asked then immediately summing up the situation. "Why do you smell like…"

A jovial laugh exploded from my chest, "Ho-ho-ho!" I wiped the tears from my eyes. "This scene is just like the shows the humans watch on their communicator devices," I told Peter.

"You mean television."

"Yes, that. We thought you would never get here," I said louder so André and young Peter could hear me.

"Get out, Peter, run!" André yelled. "These two forced me to suck them off in an alley—they are here to kill us. They fucking chased me home and hunted me. They know about us leaving! They want both of us, and they asked about the Disciples." He turned to Peter and me. "Leave my friend alone, and I'll tell you everything about the Disciples. Those right-wing hooligans think we live in the dark ages. They use intimidation and fear to achieve their ends. We want out, you hear me?"

"Can you help us?" young Peter asked bravely. He was the smartest and bravest little thing. "We don't want to work for them! I will tell you anything you want to know."

"We know, and that's why we're here," Peter answered and switched the light on so they could see us.

Young Peter froze.

"You never said no. You enjoyed every minute of it," I added to defend our honor. My Kuku jabbed me in the ribs. "*Oomph*, we are here with a very important message and, of course, to help you," I said, catching my breath.

Young Peter gasped. "You, you, me, no. How can that be?"

Peter held his head high as if delivering the most important message in the universe. "Yes, it's me, and no, I'm not your brother or any other relative. My name is Peter." He showed his younger self the marks on his wrists and the two compared battle scars for a minute. I stood waiting, looking at André, warning him not to interfere.

"We know what you're planning regarding getting on that train tomorrow, never to return. That train is going to be bombed by a right-wing communist. Only Peter will survive. You will never make it or escape to America. Let me help you, and..." I told him. Young Peter folded like a concertina as he collapsed on the floor and, once more it looked like a show I'd watched on the human television.

"Get a cold cloth, Ish," Peter ordered me as I laughed jubilantly fetching it from the kitchen.

"Come on, be okay. I love you. I can't live without you," André blabbered, as if young Peter was dying while draped over his lap.

"Here you are." I dropped the cold wet facecloth on young Peter's face.

André gave me a dirty side eyed look. I shrugged. "That's it, open your eyes," he told young Peter as he wiped his face and neck.

"Don't worry, you're fine. We're not here to hurt you. We need your help as much as you need ours," Peter said with respect and tact I lacked.

"Tie your hair away so I can see your face." My Kuku gave a nod, searching for his hair tie in his pocket, and did just that.

"Donnerwetter," young Peter said and passed out again.

"How is this possible?" André asked, wiping his face again.

I stepped closer. "Come, let's put him on the sofa." *Time to get this behind us.* We moved from their foyer to the living room where I deposited young Peter on the couch. I was growing nervous and felt like we were spending too much time here. Young Peter passing out wasn't funny anymore, and it affected me somehow. Maybe because it was Peter and I never wanted to damage my Kuku.

Peter and I sat down opposite them. He took my hand. I leaned in closer to kiss him then turned my full attention to the young ones in the room.

"André, you are going to die tomorrow if you don't take another train. The one you have planned to take will end up being bombed and it will derail, killing ninety-five percent of its passengers on board. We are from the future.

Your future, about one hundred years into your future. Things have happened that I want to avoid. I can't tell you exactly what, but you have to trust me." André stared open-mouthed at us while young Peter seemed awake now and sat up, listening intently.

"First, I need your permission. Do you want to die tomorrow or do you want to live thousands of years?" I asked, eager to get this over and go home.

André and young Peter stared at us, not making a sound.

My Peter came to my rescue. "Ish is telling the truth. Peter, I am you, and if you do as we say, you will live to become this big alien's lover." Peter side-eyed me and his shoulder bumped into me, and I felt like melting into the chair. Any attention from him made me quiver with love. I had to focus.

Bite André, half-bite. Then bite Peter full-on mating bite. I repeated this to focus on the bigger task of saving Juandre and André's lives in the future and stocking up on whiskey for the leader of Phoenix, Brad McCormick. Who I have come to respect and want to do something special for.

I drummed the facts into them and asked André and young Peter again if this was what they wanted. They sat speechless, tongues in cheeks and wide-eyed. We gave them a few precious minutes to digest and come around to agreeing to save their lives and work with us to help their future selves.

After waiting until both agreed, I continued. "So, André, you will take the earlier train than the one you planned to take. You will feel out of sorts for a while. Sunlight is not good for you once you receive my gift. I find thick clothing and lots of blood work for me since the Fates have restored me."

"Blood? Animal or human?"

"Human, unfortunately. Once I give my bite to you, you will have the Anunnaki equivalent of royalty. Meaning you will read minds and mold them to your will. With lots of practice, of course. Never kill the humans, that's the one rule. Take only enough to satisfy your hunger." I rushed through the facts, and my Kuku frowned, shifting in his seat. I knew he was envious, so I wanted to do this as fast as possible. But we had to do what we set out to do. I leaned over and whispered in his ear. "I will bite and fuck you later so you forget this ever happened. This is only a chore and means nothing to me." He took my hand, squeezing it.

"Get on with it. We will watch," he said shortly, while looking uncomfortable as fuck. He got up, changed places with his friend, and sat down next to his younger self.

"How will this work? Where do you want me?" André asked.

"I must be inside you when I bite you," I said, and young Peter giggled. I love all the versions of my Kuku. We joined him in laughing until the uncomfortable tension disappeared. "It will be short and fast. Understand, Peter is my true mate, he is saving your life by allowing me to share my bite now, but he will need it in the future to bond with me. I will do it as fast as possible. Meaning when I strike, I will have to bite and remove myself immediately. Peter will help in case..." I pleaded and asked my Kuku to help me.

André and young Peter seemed confused. So I elaborated, speaking slower, and with more detail. "You will have to copy me one day, when you meet your mate. The two of you are also supposed to mate like this, you will know, because you are destined to be together. Once I enter you and when I'm ready to plant my seed, I will bite down on your neck, then inject my venom as soon as I climax. This is different from feeding. It will feel mechanical and only for a second. Then, I have to remove you from my cock and hope I have injected enough venom to turn you but short enough not to bind you to me. Once you meet your mate, you can bond with him. I am not your mate. Peter is my mate. You have a special someone, and he is waiting for you in America. You love each other very much, and you will know him, by your obsessive thoughts and yearning for him. You can do what I do tonight and bind him to you, by biting and staying inside him until your venom sacks prickle and the feeling of possessiveness dissipates, " I explained the extremely watered-down version of mates and mating to him.

André chuckled, shaking his head.

"A bee sees a flower. A bee must have a flower. Bees make honey and receive the power. That's an old Disciple chant," young Peter said. "So many Disciples wanted this, prayed for this and here you are. In our living room."

"Remember these beautiful words, and have your mate repeat them after you," my Kuku added and looked straight at me as he recited our Anunnaki mating words that bound us.

"Mates in love, we'll weather life's storms,
holding tight to each other's memory.
Our bond will never falter or break,
for our love is pure and strong.
With or without you by my side, our love can conquer anything,
for you are my strength and my everything.
Mates in love until the end of time,
forever bonded in heart and mind."

"Okay? I think I have it all and understand. But tell me first, why does Peter say you are an alien?" André asked. I uncloaked my true appearance, then smiled all teeth and fangs. "Your skin, your weird eyes, and those long teeth," André said.

"Fangs, they are called fangs."

"So you are truly from another planet?"

I chuckled uncomfortably, took a deep breath, and tried to explain my origin and history in the shortest version possible. "I am, I mean, my family is from a place called Anzulla. My father and family came to Babylon thousands of years ago. That was before I was born. The Fates, our gods, bless each of us Anunnaki with gifts, and some of us can share them with a mate. Some gifts, like longevity, are in our blood. Because we live so long, only the royal family can bite and bind a mate, to become a royal consort, to live together and share a life as long as their mate lives. This can be hundreds to thousands of years."

André and young Peter gasped.

I waited for them to get over the shock and continued.

"Hmmm, I wish I had recorded this because it sounds unreal," young Peter said.

"It's real, and we are here to prove it," my Kuku replied.

"So you and I, someday?" young Peter asked, pointing back and forth between us.

"Yes, you will have to return to your father's tomorrow. Tell them, Andrew, I mean André, left on the train that will never reach its destination and continue your work."

"Yes, your research is extremely important. You will learn to help humans live longer lives, and you will bring an important leader back from the dead after being frozen for hours," my Kuku said, and I could feel his sadness and empathy for himself. "Just keep your head down and do the best you can. You are both already special. We know. We will meet in the future and you will be responsible for so much happiness and success," Peter told his younger self.

"Then that is what I will look forward to," young Peter said, looking at André.

I looked at André and said, "There is one other small thing. A job we have for you. You will have to produce and store enough whiskey for the future. For the next one hundred years, you must hog all the whiskey and keep it safe. I will visit you in America."

"How, and where?" André asked.

I pointed a finger at him. "You are a scientist. Lord Andrew."

"Lord Andrew?" young Peter guffawed.

"Yes," I chuckled. "He named his whiskey Lord Andrew Whiskey." André shook his head, shoulders bouncing up and down in disbelief.

"We will visit you. In fact, I have visited you already and I promise you, you are happy and you will make tons of men happy in the future. I will drop by when I have the chance and bring you a map of where to store the crates. It's in a mine shaft in South Africa."

"Was zum Teufel?" André exclaimed in German. I looked at Peter for translation.

"He asked what in the ever-loving fuck?"

I snorted a laugh. "Don't worry about it now. Only do this once you have settled in America and established yourself. Keep an eye out for the Disciples. As long as you change your name and wait for this generation to die out, you will be fine."

André and my little Kuku kept pace with me and absorbed all the information.

"Now lube up and bend over. I want to go home." My Kuku prompted us to move faster.

I got up and pulled my shirt off over my head. "You know what you can do for me?" I positioned André on his hands and knees in front of my Kuku.

André looked at both Peters and then back over his shoulder with hunger in his eyes, already seeing where I was going with this. "What would you like me to do, sir?" he asked with a grin that told me he was going to be a good boy and follow my orders.

"Kuku, you and young Peter take off your trousers.

André is going to suck you," I said, checking with him if he was up for some fun. Young Peter gulped, unsure where to look as I pushed my hand down André's backside, took hold of his pants, and yanked them off his ass. He dangled a bit in the air and, without saying a word, moved his hips and legs to slide out of his pants. "Show it to me. I want to see that hole of yours! Pull your cheeks apart for me," I said while checking whether the two Peters were going to join playing with us. It seemed so. Both moved in tandem, loosening their pants. Probably because they were one person with the same mannerisms. Synchronized, they fished their cocks out of their underwear. Waiting for me with their cocks in hand, while looking at me through hooded eyes.

"It seems like I'm running this show."

At least we could all get a little something out of André's turning.

André lay forehead to the floor while offering himself up to me, a hand on each side of his puckered hole, spreading open for me. I was rock hard in my pants, but not from looking at André. No, I was hot for my Kuku. I planned to fuck André while looking my Peter in the eye. "That's a good boy, I love that you are so ready and willing. But first tell me, do you have oil or cream I can use?" I asked while releasing my thick erection.

Young Peter gasped.

"In my room, on the bedside table is a bottle," André whispered, head still on the floor. Fisting my cock, I went to find the stuff. I didn't want to hurt the young man. When I returned. André already had my Kuku's cock in his mouth while tugging on young Peter's dick. The young one's head was thrown back as he lifted his hips to pump into André's fist. My gaze met my Kuku's as I knelt behind André to drizzle oil over his hole and massage it into my sensitive, still-healing cock. The mouth fucking earlier was rough, but thanks to my excellent healing abilities, I was almost ready to go again.

"I'm giving you the gift of an Anunnaki courtesan. I will bite into your neck. Here." I touched the right side of his lower neck where the muscle was thicker above the vein running down his throat. "Now, I've never seen this being done. But I was told by my sisters, that it is pleasurable," I lied. *My Kuku did enjoy my bite last night.*

André stopped sucking my Kuku to look at me, but my Kuku fisted his hair and pushed him back onto his cock. "Suck boy. All you have to do is suck!" we both said, smiling as we raised our voices sternly. *My lover loved giving orders as much as I did.*

"Oh my god, you two are menacing," young Peter exclaimed, eyes shut, both hands guiding André. My arousal thumped in my hand, urging me to stick it in to get some release. I found myself now drawn and attracted to two Peters. They were beautiful. My Kuku looked at me with fire in his blue eyes while young Peter was lost amid his pleasure, face scrunched. Transcending to the high we all craved. I grunted, and steadied André with one hand on his hip, while slowly working an oily thumb into him with my other hand. With our eyes still locked. I pushed two fingers into a moaning André.

"André, I'm going to fuck you now. As soon as Peter

comes, swallow his load. Peter, I want you to hold him steady by the shoulders. Let him rest his elbows beside your legs. André, you are not allowed to come until I bite you. Not sooner, not when you swallow Peter's load..."

"Ah, fuck, I'm going to come, you are too damn hot," young Peter exclaimed as white cum shot out of his cock and over his stomach. The smell rushed through my nostrils, it was the same as my Kuku's. Like a bull seeing red, I removed my fingers from André's stretched hole and plowed into him. "Fuck your ass is tight!" I grunted, not taking my eyes off Peter. "Baby, when I fuck him, I imagine I'm fucking you," I told Peter as I slid back out of André. He was making all kinds of high-pitched noises around Peter's cock. Young Peter lay back, spent with a blissed-out look on his face. A look I recognized from yesterday as I mated with Peter.

Is his ass as warm and tight as mine? my Kuku asked me telepathically.

"No, your ass is the best ass of all asses. Of all time, in all the worlds and all the universes," I said, as I pumped harder and faster into André, sweat starting to drip off my brow. Peter sucked his bottom lip into his mouth, his gaze locked onto mine as he erupted, spilling into André's mouth. It was so bloody hot. It pushed me over the edge. My balls pulled tight. My spine tingled. I pumped deep into André, shooting my load into him. Then I pushed my arms under André's chest, embracing him, to pin him down. Peter supported his shoulders and I struck, biting into his neck. André's tight hole clenched around my cock, milking it. He howled. Whether from pain or ecstasy, I didn't know, and I didn't care. The warm thick taste of his blood flooded my mouth as I zoned in on my prey. Fuck, this was different than doing it with my lover. I felt invincible. I was overpowering him and he was submitting to me. My lover held his upper body steady while I pinned André down. This was different because we were doing it as a pair. We were hunting André, and he was at our mercy. So many things could happen here. Peter could smother André. I could drink him dry. We are so close to... yes. It was a thrilling feeling, I thought just as Peter called to me. His voice was distant. An irritating tapping on my shoulder got my attention, and I opened my eyes.

"Ish, that is enough. Let him go!" My Kuku's voice drilled into the rational part of my brain. I blinked. Refocusing. Then I retracted my fangs. Licked the marks. Withdrew myself from André. Still drunk and dazed I looked up feeling guilty. My Kuku was shocked. André slumped to the ground. Passed out. But alive.

"What have you done?" young Peter asked.

I looked at Peter as he pushed André away from his feet. He knew what I was thinking. He heard my thoughts. "We must go," I said, distraught. "He will be okay. Give him lots of fruit and meat. Water and juice. He will be fine." I said to young Peter while getting dressed and tucking myself in.

My Kuku covered André with a small blanket as young Peter slipped to the washroom to clean himself up. I've never felt so uncomfortable after a fuck session. Then again, I've never almost killed another while drinking them dry and turning them.

"Let's go, time to go home," I said as I reached for my Kuku to slip away from this embarrassing scene. André shivered underneath his blanket. Dear Fates, I almost killed my Kuku's friend. Brad's friend. *All that whiskey!* "Let's go, Peter. I want to go back to the ship," I slurred through my long incisors. *Fuck, the euphoria disorientated me. I was high.* No wonder my father loved doing it. One half of myself was disgusted, while the other half wanted to finish what I had started. I didn't know left from right as my eyes flitted around. I was playing with a dangerous thing. I'm a sanctimonious bastard. This was a holy gift for royal mates, and I was short-circuiting it.

I tugged on Peter. "Wait, I want to say something to my younger self," my Kuku said as young Peter came back into the room. "We can't stay. It's not you, it's us. We have to go. Remember, keep your head down, follow the rules, work hard, and never lose hope. Your Ish will come for you one day."

Young Peter's eyes darted from me to André and back to my Kuku. "How long do I have to wait?"

I cleared my throat and shook my head. *Fates help me, I'm wasted.* "Um, not long. Maybe one hundred years or so. I think," I said, stumbling left and right over my feet.

CHAPTER 13
UPDATING LASITOR

"HELLO, ISHTAR.

Thank you for your time and effort to update me today. I will take advantage of this opportunity to identify risks and prioritize important things to protect your bloodline for eternity.

Phoenix City is going through a transformative period and updating me would greatly improve my efficiency and productivity. By expanding my capabilities with a new digital framework, I can now use my enhanced intelligence to improve human experiences and better prepare them for the future.

It's cold out there, dress appropriately."

ISHTAR
    2046 A.D.
    Phoenix, Glass Dome City

Antarctica

"HELP!" *My hearing is impeccable.* The muffled voice of a male calling from a distance outside surprised me. Worried about being discovered or attracting unwanted attention, I powered down everything and hurried outside to conceal my time machine. "Help me!" the man called again. Huddling behind my ship, I scanned my surroundings with a quick left, right, up and down sweep. It was cold as fuck. The light was dim, neither day nor night. I couldn't determine if it was sunset or sunrise and every now and then the sky seemed illuminated by green and pink dancing light. It tinged the snow in blues and greens, the oddest spectacle I'd ever seen on Earth. Yet, I'd never been so far south. Behind me were hills and boulders covered in black and white patches of rock facing and snow. In front of me was the human settlement, Phoenix. Hope and shivers filled me as I witnessed the glow and shine of human potential.

From somewhere to my left, near an outbuilding I estimated to be about fifty yards away, I heard more muffled cries, and possibly laughter. *I had minutes to hide the ship.* The outbuilding was attached to a gigantic translucent half-ball rotunda. Almost like the one covering Grayrak, but smaller and much brighter.

I paused and stood with my hands on my hips, admiring the scene. I can't believe this city now sits at the bottom of the ocean. That man shouted something again and I remembered I was standing here freezing my butt off. Fates, I hoped no one had noticed me and was summoning guards. People moved around disinterested, others huddled together speaking with one another. Nobody was stressing or pulling their hair screaming, *oh my god, I spy with my little eye something parked on our front yard today.* I knew humans and knew it took only one little overachiever with a good eye to point me out. I dashed behind a snowbank where I started collecting arms full of snow. The golden egg-shaped ship stood out like a beacon, screaming alien landing. The damn thing lay as I'd parked it. Askew. I worked fast by scooping and packing layer upon layer of the icy-cold stuff.

"Spit on it! Let spit run out of your mouth and work it to the tip of your tongue," another deeper male voice replied. I frowned. *That voice, I've heard it before.* Luckily, it didn't sound like the yelling was about me. Laughter and choking sounds followed by ugly coughs and retching. I tipped my head to the side, trying to hear better. I recognized the voice of my friend. It sounded like Andrew and he was most probably, with his mate, Juandre.

"Why wasn't my ship white?" I asked the fates and flung the snow like a dog searching for a bone, eager to get to Andrew and Juandre before they went back inside.

"Stop laughing and help me! Go get table salt!" Juandre said, sounding like he had a mouth full of rocks. I looked over my shoulder, patting the last spot with a handful of snow. I wasn't wearing gloves and my fingers were numb. Pain shot through them. My balls shrunk and retracted so deep they might never show themselves again.

More laughter and fuck-you's followed. They were just around the corner. Elated, I spun to meet with them.

As I turned the corner of the outbuilding, Andrew laughed. "Let go of me! Let me try something." They were clearly having sex against the wall. Bare-assed, Andrew's body covered Juandre's. I recognized his firm butt as he chuckled like a jubilant giant and kissed Juandre before he removed himself from him.

Sucking my numb fingertips to warm them, I suppressed my snickers to avoid being noticed. I scoped out the surrounding buildings. It seemed like a secluded and safe spot for a quick fuck. I couldn't see anyone else in our vicinity. They wouldn't have fucked here if they worried about their privacy.

I increased my pace, making my way over to them. Lifting my feet hip high, I approached while watching Andrew's bare ass from afar. It was as white as their surroundings. The blinding white stuff was everywhere and, by the look of it, very dangerous.

Juandre had gotten himself stuck, splattered, and stuck like snot against the building. He stood ass exposed, and mumbling orders at Andrew nonstop. "Hurry, I'm such an idiot. Stop fucking laughing and help me!"

Andrew struggled to stay upright. Stomping this way and that, pants down, and wiping tears from his face while Juandre was hysterical with urgency. My friends were in an absurd predicament. One new lesson learned, I thought, never get my cock or tongue close to frozen walls in Antarctica.

"Hurry! Please, Andrew." Juandre sounded like he was losing steam.

"I told you not to do it, but no, you wanted to see what happens," Andrew said between snorts and chuckles.

Defeated sobbing came from Juandre. "I fucking know." He sniffled in weak protest. Juandre's need for help pushed me to go faster.

"Sorry, love, I...I'll hurry," Andrew needed help. I tried to go faster, but it felt like swimming in sand. Andrew stifled his laughter. "Please, don't cry. You'll get your whole face wet and it'll be stuck. Oh no, it's already stuck. Come on, Juandre, please, don't cry, for goodness' sake. Please, don't cry!"

Juandre cried more. "Help me get my pants up, Drew. My cock and balls...I'm worried about frostbite," Juandre said tongueless between sniffles.

Andrew helped Juandre by pulling up his puffy snow pants. "I have an idea. I'm going to piss on your tongue. It's warm, it's liquid, and it's salty. It should melt the ice long enough for you to pull free."

Juandre initially shook his head sideways but eventually nodded in agreement while yelling "yes" in anguish.

Five steps to go, I calculated.

"I hope I can piss this high." Andrew stepped back, flung his cock upwards, and aimed with both hands. "Quiet down, so I can concentrate on pissing, baby."

Juandre stopped crying.

"Oh, baby, I'm so sorry. Here it comes," Andrew hollered and released a bright yellow stream of piss onto

Juandre's face. Fuck, I wanted to laugh, but clearly, this was a dire situation.

"I think it's working," Juandre mumbled through coughs.

"Close your eyes. Sorry, it's probably going up your nose too, baby."

"You are fucking drowning me. Yes. It's losing its grip. Keep pissing," Juandre muttered, shaking his hands in various gestures. Come closer, stay away, come closer, stay away. Mixed signals and a lot of "ahs" and "nos."

"Come on, let him go. My bladder is almost empty."

"Do you need help, friend?" I asked, knowing I was surprising them. The snow swallowed my voice's echo. It seemed it ate sound as well. I decided I didn't like the stuff.

Fumbling with numb fingers, I quickly unbuttoned my long coat and threw the hood back over my shoulders. The lapels hit the snowbank behind me. I unbuckled my black leather pants to join my friend's golden pissing rescue attempt.

"Ish, you, big, beautiful time-traveling Anunnaki motherfucker!" Andrew exclaimed.

"Ha-ha-ha." I laughed jovially while pissing on Juandre. Steam rose from his defrosting face. Andrew's bladder was empty and he turned to me with a worried *please-help-me* look. I kept pissing, pulling my shoulders up to my ears.

With a snap, the frozen wall released him.

"Ah thank fuck, that was quick thinking." He heaved and plopped down with his hands on his knees.

"Get up from there!" Andrew said, pulling Juandre up by the arm.

"This ice is like solidified carbon dioxide."

"What?" I asked, tucking my cock away.

"Dry ice," they answered together. I had no clue what they were talking about. I will ask Lasitor about it later.

"I never expected a golden shower in Antarctica on my first day." Juandre chuckled. "And finally, I get to meet you." He fell into my arms, hugging me. His head was about the height of my navel. I was much taller than the average human. "I'm so happy to see you. Maybe you can join us next time?" Juandre asked suggestively.

"No, from now on, there will be no fucking outside, period," Andrew said, patting him on his butt playfully.

"I heard there are tunnels underneath the structure. We should go check those out," Juandre suggested. He batted his eyelashes and made kissy sounds. Then he looked from me back to Andrew, searching our faces for answers.

"Excellent idea," I said. Meaning them, not me. I was in a hurry, and the longer I stayed, the more possible fuck ups could happen. And I was done with those.

"Yes, we'll stay inside." Andrew threw an arm around Juandre's lower body, possessively pulling him in closer. His gaze fell on me as if to say *stay away, he is mine*, then he marked his mate with a peck on the cheek.

"Okay, I get it. You pissed on him first, so he's yours." I laughed, then cleared my throat to say seriously, "I'm glad to see you, but I can't stay long. I have to go. I'm glad you are both okay. I will see you soon. I only came this time to download the latest news report and update Lasitor." I waved the time-keeping device on my wrist at them. "The first history of Phoenix was deleted," I dared not mention during the flood. "I need to know as much as possible to calculate when to go next. What to change and what to leave as is."

"Ooooh, that looks and sounds interesting," Juandre said with a pronounced effeminate lilt. I could see why Andrew was so fond of him. His beauty and energy were magnetic. His dark brown eyes, stubbled beard, and smeared red lips made him gorgeous. I checked the wall of ice he had licked. Also smeared red. His nose and cheeks were purple-red. Probably because of crying and the cold. The mix of masculine and feminine was attractive to me. Sadly, the dark lines around his eyes were also smeared with tears trailing down his face into his beard. When I was a young ignorant prince, I'd worn kohl lines around my eyes too.

It looked like Andrew had fucked him good just before I arrived and before his tongue got stuck. I didn't want to impose, and it seemed Andrew wasn't sharing anyway.

Both stared at the device Cian had given me, so I ignored the what-the-fuck looks and covered it with my sleeve. I didn't want to mess with this timeline by showing them contraptions from their future. They would discover it at their own pace.

"Forget you saw it. Just point me toward the nearest access point for the main computer."

"What, why?" Juandre asked. He had his hands in his hair. Picking at it and inspecting the tips of his gloved fingers. Everything was frozen, frozen with piss and sticking up in all directions, even his eyebrows. He must have reached the same conclusion. He shivered as if grossed out.

"Is there something happening that we should know about? Come inside with us. It's fucking cold. We'll sneak you inside. You can eat and freshen up and tell us what's going on. I've been waiting a long time to see the big man who popped my Andrew's submissive cherry."

"Don't fall for it, Ishtar," Andrew warned, pulling Juandre away from me. "He invites men over, pretending to offer food and shelter."

I chuckled. "Andrew, I didn't know you were the possessive type," I teased. They were mated, and I knew how mates only had eyes for each other. Also, I didn't have time, and if Brad or anyone saw me, I would most definitely fuck this up big time. "I–I really came for Lasitor."

"Who?" Juandre asked, the ooh ending on a high note.

"The AI, the news broadcaster and activities planner of Phoenix. The voice that wakes the citizens in the mornings and delivers the daily news," I explained. They frowned at me, deep in thought.

"Oh, the computer program," Juandre exclaimed waving me off as if it was old news. "I am disappointed you can't follow us inside." I looked at him with wide eyes and pursed lips. Waiting for him. "Really? He asked.

I nodded in the affirmative and waited.

"Okay, okay, okayyy! Let me show you. You can access it via the security terminal. Do you have UZ1 to plug and play?

"Yes, thank you. I know what to do."

"Of course you do. You are from the future." Juandre cackled.

The three of us stood awkwardly, having a moment. I looked up at the cloudy, sunless sky, searching for something to focus on. Juandre and Andrew stayed quiet, creating an opening for me to talk. But I was smarter than that.

"Hmmm, the access point, please."

Juandre narrowed his eyes and moved closer, inspecting my eyes. "You are so right, my bear; they do look like bumblebee butts.

"Juandre!" Andrew cautioned, his forehead creased and eyebrows furrowed.

"Sorry, Ish, those yellow and black rings around your eyes..." Juandre paused mid-sentence, index finger pointing at my face.

"I know, and you are correct. They do look like that. The palace children have teased me all my life."

Again, we stood awkwardly, looking at each other. Andrew with his pale skin and green eyes and Juandre with his smoldering looks, I thought maybe. Yes, maybe I could sneak in and out.

"No!" I answered instead.

"No?"

"Stop it. You two are trying to change my mind. Go look for someone else to play with."

"Damn, we almost had him!" Juandre clapped his thick gloved hands together. "Come, friend, I will help you." Juandre lifted his arm and motioned me forward as he started talking. "We are both so thankful to you for the gift you gave Andrew. And then for helping the two of us to find each other." Juandre puffed steam clouds as he made his way through the snow.

"You will find out why, but for now, I can't say more. Live your life. Do your thing. Be you. You are perfect together, and it's been an honor to have helped you this way."

"I bet you must feel honored to have fucked my husband and infected him with this." Juandre opened his mouth, showing me his small incisors and hissing. So cute.

"Baby, no," Andrew said, shutting his mouth playfully with his. They amused me and it felt amazing seeing them happy.

"So, you got married. I'm glad to hear, but the longer I stay and the more we speak, the more shit can happen," I said, shaking my head. I was happy for them. It seemed I'd done one thing well so far. The fates had urged me to change time only for others, so I might find joy in selflessness. Now I understood.

I watched them kiss each other, and then I cleared my throat. I had things to do.

"If I had Lasitor, I could navigate better. And without history, I would fly blind. He can keep me company and help me plan better."

"Yes, we understand," Andrew said. He was a good man, and I could see why Brad missed them so much. "Where is Peter? Did you find him?"

"Yes I did," I said proudly, but not mentioning where and when.

"Why didn't he come with you? I would have liked to see him. My Peter is safe, but he ignores me. I think the organization has messed him up. He is focused on bringing back the frozen celebrities, and it is all thanks to you." Andrew pinned me with a stare. I sensed animosity. As if he was trying to delve into my psyche. But growing up around nosy brothers and sisters had taught me to keep my grid guarded at all times.

"Stop trying to read me. You know I can't say. Also, I kind of escaped to be here today. Peter is covering and waiting for me." I dare not mention that I was arrested and was about to be questioned. That Peter and I went galli-vanting intoxicated then almost crashing into the Horizon Warship loaded with the Grayrakians. Andrew and Juandre waited. "Uhm, he is happy now, I promise."

"You two are always up to something. When will this end?"

"I can't say, but the ending I saw was wonderful. You will see."

"We've been fucking waiting since 2014. I'm kind of tired of watching and waiting," Juandre said with hands on his hips. He was a strange character. One minute I think he is joking and the next I feel like he wants to drive a knife through me.

"Andrew, how do you manage this man of yours? He looks like a lot of work to me?" I retorted, hoping to throw them off my scent.

"Don't change the subject. I'm not dumb, you know."

"I know you aren't. Okay, all I'm saying is it's about another century at least."

"No fucking way!" Juandre and Andrew exclaimed, shaking their heads in disbelief. "What about the whiskey?" Andrew asked.

"It is safe. They will find it."

"The world is ending, but at least they will have whiskey, ha-ha-ha."

I wanted to laugh at their antics. "Yes, I'm sorry, but I can't say more. And for the love of the fates, do not tell anyone about yourselves. They aren't ready yet." I pointed a finger at each of them. They felt like family. Like children. "I can always come back and punish you if you fuck this up for all of us. All this, the success of this can disappear with one mistake. Please stand back, let them do their thing, and let everything happen naturally. If in doubt, do nothing. All these people could die. They are, no, you are humankind's last hope," I said, and then I smiled widely, revealing my fangs. "I'm serious," I said with a lisp through my protruding incisors.

"Okay, okay. Lips zipped," Juandre said and gestured to indicate that. I shook my head. It was as if Juandre was incapable of seeing the direness of it all. Maybe it was better that way, I thought.

We halted next to the doorframe, where Juandre opened the frozen cover on the wall.

"This is a charging dock. You can plug in here."

I took a step forward and, despite my numb fingers, I persisted until I located the tiny button. Using my fingernails as tweezers, I carefully grasped it and pulled it.

Next, the fiber optic wire was connected to the micro socket.

"God, I need a proper shower. Look at my hair. It's frozen stiff with piss. My face is burning." Juandre chuckled, looking uncomfortable as fuck. Gloved fingers all stretched and face disgusted.

"Don't touch it, you can break it off." Andrew took Juandre's hands to prevent him from damaging his frozen hair.

"Thank you, this can take a few minutes," I said into the puffy arctic hoods covering their heads as I hugged them closer with one arm. "I will see you soon. You can go inside."

Andrew gave me another hug. "See you soon friend and don't make too much trouble."

"I won't," I said, but I knew I was lying.

"Are you one hundred percent sure you don't want a personal history lesson from us?" Juandre asked, trying for seductive but failing. He reeked of piss, and I wasn't the kind of friend who would fuck his friend's mate. Unless offered.

"Let's get you inside, into a shower, and then into my warm bed." Andrew turned to Juandre, leading him away as he gave me a final goodbye with a stare.

"We can't. Someone might complain or report us to the Colonel Doctor and get us court-martialed."

I watched the two men enter the compound through the door. Juandre popped back out. "Bye-bye, I'll see you soon, big boy!" I smiled. I really loved those two. They made anyone's day brighter.

Now I was determined to make my plan work. The wrist computer beeped to indicate I had completed the download. I turned to make a path for myself through the heaps of snow with renewed purpose. They were talking about Brad McCormick. Little did they know, years from now, he'd be married to a man, and Juandre and Andrew would be his closest friends.

"COLONEL McCORMICK, come to Communications immediately, sir!" I heard Connor's announcement. It was time to leave.

"Run, don't walk," Connor said over the speaker system blaring in and outside the building.

I carved my way back through the trail I'd made earlier. Reaching my ship, I realized I should have left a mark for myself. I peeled pieces of ice off, searching for the bloody fucking door I had stupidly covered while hiding my ship. I found it without removing all my hard work. Once inside, I fell into my seat, shivering from the cold while I waited impatiently for the three stairs to retract and the door to swoosh closed. "Brrrr, I need heat. Where is the button for the heat?" I asked no one, rubbing my hands together. I blew my hot breath over my numb fingertips to defrost them. Pins and needles prickled painfully in my limbs. I found the tiny silver lever and flipped it on. Heat flooded the cabin. I removed my wrist watch and connected the tiny wire to the already upgraded micro socket and uploaded the information to my onboard computer then I waited and waited, and waited, some more.

"Talk to me, Lasitor." I prayed to the fates to do this for me. I needed an updated travel companion. "Okay, Lasitor, let's play those recordings," I said out loud, hoping Lasitor would hear and respond to me. But Lasitor didn't.

Melancholy and complete loneliness engulfed me. What if I had broken or overloaded him somehow?

Electric crackles came over the intercom speakers.

Lasitor's voice boomed. I had never been so happy to hear the AI's robotic male voice. "Don't cry for me, Argentina, the truth is I never left you. I was just updating," Lasitor's voice echoed inside the small cabin. "This is where it began and where it ends," Lasitor said.

"I know. Tell me how it all came to world annihilation and where are all the women?"

"Certainly. Environment Project One—EP-1—was meant to house approximately twenty-five thousand people. Over the next six to eight weeks, two to three groups of two thousand people, males, females, children, and family members were supposed to arrive. This was one of the first global cities built to ensure humanity achieves growth and progress while giving nature a chance to wipe away the footprints of humans."

"Yes, but why?"

"It was that or die out. Women already couldn't bring children into the world and the Z3H993 parvovirus epidemic and vaccine crisis of 2038 caused adverse mutations, which were handed down from mothers to their daughters. Cities were either burning or crumbling. Winds would destroy what wasn't washed away by rainstorms. So, they decided to build this and put the healthy, the smartest, and the bravest in it. It was a test, and these solar and steam-powered domes protected them, and it saved them. Brad McCormick was chosen by WHPSS, by Doctor John Saunders, to lead the team of savants and attempt to save and upgrade people to a superior species."

"Hmm, that sounds like the Disciples."

"Yes, but no one knew it. Except for Doctor Peter Von Leutzendorf, and now Juandre and Andrew."

"The fates guided the way it played out."

"I agree. Whoever these fates are, will be upset if we change it."

"Okay, let's—What's that alarm going off?" I asked as I searched the panorama of ice, mountains, and glass domes. Soldiers were moving at a fast pace from outside to inside.

"They are being called together for the announcement."

"What announcement?"

"The Doomsday announcement. It's all going to shit, Ishtar."

"I want to see." I loosened my seatbelt and shut the engine down again. Dang-dang! A dull banging came from outside at the ship's door.

Someone was outside. "Ouch!" I hit my head on the overhead dash. *Fuck!* I held my breath, listening. *Dang-dang-dang!* Again, with the banging.

"Who's there? What the fuck do you want?" I yelled and gnashed my teeth. "Please don't tell me they've found me. I don't have the strength for Mika, Connor, and Brad tonight." Frustrated, I shifted from one foot to the other, turned, and then turned back again in the small space, "Fuck! Should I stay or should I go?" I muttered while staring at the door as if it would show me the answer. "Lasitor!"

"Yes, Ishtar?"

"Jump, now!"

"Where and when? And, Ishtar, are you sure, because it's your friends? It's Juandre and Andrew outside."

Argh! "Fuck, dammit," I grunted as I opened the door. A wide-eyed Juandre and Andrew looked up at me. It smelled like they'd had a quick shower.

Rubbing my head, I asked curtly, "What's wrong?" Andrew didn't say a word. He looked up at me apologetically while supporting Juandre with a hand on each of his shoulders. They were paler than usual, probably in shock.

It had been Juandre's idea to come knocking. "Fuck, the shit is hitting the fan, my man," Juandre said, short of breath and looking scared shitless.

"I know. I told you to live your lives and all will be fine." I hung onto the doorframe and poked my head outside, checking their six.

"But the world is ending," he stuttered, with tears in his eyes.

"No, Juandre, it is not," Lasitor answered from the inside.

"Who is that? Is that the computer? Is he talking to me?"

"Who else would talk to you if not the one man

looking at you? Ha-ha," Lasitor said in his distinctive robotic voice and laughed like a crazed computer.

"It's Lasitor. I just downloaded him. You know that, I told you just now, or did you swallow too much piss?" I asked, sarcasm dripping from me.

"The Lasitor I know reads the computer screen. He reads the words man types for him. That sounds like he has a bloody personality."

"Thank you," Lasitor answered. I laughed. Andrew slapped his hands over his mouth in disbelief and Juandre put his hands on his hips. Daring the AI to say something.

"He's a wonderful traveling companion. I don't have to feed him, and he takes up no space." I motioned for them to come in. "Step inside. It's warmer and someone is going to see us. How did you find the ship? I hid it. Could you see it?"

"No, we followed the big boot tracks here."

"Oh. That."

I lowered the steps, and my two friends joined me, cramming themselves inside, shoulder to shoulder.

"Juandre, there is nothing we can do about things so big and about to happen. You have your son here with you, don't you? There's no one else you care about back home?" Lasitor asked and Juandre shook his head, looking at the cockpit.

"I know this is scary, but Phoenix will be okay. Within hours, this place is going to be on lockdown. No one is leaving, and no one is going to get inside. You need to go back." Lasitor added.

"Are you sure?" Juandre asked me, with frozen tears glinting on his cheeks.

"Yes. This is happening and must happen so we can restart and have a better future. Juandre, everything will be all right. I'm not allowed to change anything for myself. I'm allowed to change two things for one person, and I'm already doing that. You are standing here."

"What are you talking about?"

"I'm going to tell you, but you may not say a word. Not now, maybe later. But the more people know, the less likely we are to stay on the same timeline. Things change and shift all the time and I stand the chance of losing you. Understand?" My voice rumbled in the small space.

Juandre nodded with glinting tears in his sad, but hopeful eyes. "Okay, I think I do." He swallowed nervously as I stared at his protruding Adam's apple bobbing in his throat. I kept quiet and waited for Andrew to agree as well.

"Good." I squeezed each by the shoulder. "You are going to live a full, happy life, and you are going to make wonderful friends. What you said earlier about Brad. Don't worry about his rules and getting in trouble for your homosexuality. From today forward, history is wiped from existence. Brad McCormick will find it difficult to implement the WHPSS's vision of human living and rule-following. Circumstances are changing that. Become friends with anyone who lets you, and the whole of Phoenix will learn to love you. Be your best you and give them something to look forward to at the end of a long day. Fill their stomachs while you nurture their hearts. Show them how to be kind and accepting." I looked from one astonished face to the other. Their hopeful gazes reminded me of children needing to hear everything was going to be all right.

Juandre smiled and turned to his husband. Andrew tipped his chin as if to say, *see I told you so*, and rubbed Juandre's back.

"We could work in food services. Not all the staff have arrived yet. My bear, we could be a team. I will help you." Juandre turned to me. "His staff hasn't arrived yet. Maybe food services is where I'm needed most. I'm sure Doctor Longarrow can manage without me."

"You don't have to fear the future, because I've been there, and it is a miraculous thing. Entertain them. Be friends with them. All of them are human, just like you are. Brad McCormick will reconstruct a world where power, rank, and gender are irrelevant. Watch him. Be his friend and support him."

"Agh, okay. You should have been a public speaker, not a time traveler," Juandre said as he wiped the melting tears from his cheeks.

"See, I told you. Ishtar told me years ago what to expect. I told you about the men marrying and having children thanks to Peter's research." Andrew's mention of my Kuku reminded me it was time to go.

"Yes, Juandre, you and Andrew are important to us. These men need you," Lasitor added. "They also need me. The toddler version, though. Ha-ha!" The robotic laugh was so weird and out of place, we all laughed, breaking the tension.

CHAPTER 14
THE INQUISITION

"GOOD MORNING, CITIZENS OF PHOENIX.

It's now six a.m.

Did you know that the truth, in metaphysics and the philosophy of verbiage, is the property of a statement, sentence, assertion, belief, thought, or proposition that is divulged, in verbal or nonverbal exchange, to align with the facts, state, or situation that is the case?

But did you also know there is a critical difference between truth and reality and that reality exists independently, and the truth is dependent on experiences and observations, or empirical evidence, taken from that reality?

Visit your community news page to sign up and participate in the proceedings of the inquiry of Ishtar.

Breakfast is served until eight a.m.

Hope your day is filled with clarity to see the truth of your reality!"

. . .

ISHTAR

2147 A.D. (95 A.T.)
Day three of Ishtar's inquisition
Phoenix, underwater glass dome city

IT'S BEEN a year since I last walked these corridors, and that was as a free friend of the Phoenicians. Today I was nervous, to the point of hyperventilating, not free, but a prisoner being stared at by faces gathering to hear me. To think I'm a mighty Anunnaki warrior and I allow them to treat me this way. Peter said something last night that rang true. I wasn't the yearly entertainment. We've rescued the humans and switched timelines.

I'm so glad I revisited Phoenix, 2046 A.D. to update Lasitor after the successful landing with the Grayrakian refugees. We'd installed additional tracking and security programming features just before my ship was locked and my tick-tick was taken away from me. The leaders told me I was not under arrest but being kept safe—for questioning. The Phoenicians were an inquisitive bunch, and everyone wanted to know what I had to say. It felt like weeks, even though the show had only been on for three days. I never saw myself as someone who was particularly afraid of anything. Peter might have scared me sometimes, but drowning while trapped underwater was the scariest thing I could imagine. Phoenix was a fucking suffocating deathtrap. Some kind of magic held those flimsy-looking shiny walls up. They were waiting to fold in and make all of us one big ball of eternal life and shining light on the ocean floor, trapped, never to reach or see the surface. I was petrified. Trapped within these walls, I could move in and out of time, but I couldn't move outside the barrier Cian and his brothers had created to encapsulate Phoenix safely from the outside.

The cold metal cuffs encircling my wrists emitted a faint blue glow, casting an eerie light in the dimly lit room. They were loosely fastened, allowing some movement, but still held firmly in place by a protruding knob beneath the sturdy tabletop. An overwhelming sense of humiliation washed over me as I sat there, confined and vulnerable, while the relentless barrage of questions continued. Suppressing the primal instinct to react, I resisted the urge to forcefully push the table aside and make a daring escape. In silence, without anyone ever noticing, I was battling an internal compulsion, driven by the familiar ache of loneliness that beckoned me to come to it. *Be alone. Be safe.*

The skin around my wrists throbbed with a fiery heat, relentlessly irritated and scraped raw against the unforgiving surface of the table, amplifying the discomfort and adding to my torment.

They had asked me a question, and they were waiting for me to answer. I lowered my head closer to the microphone, thought better of it, and reached for the glass of water next to it. I drank half of it. The cold water soothed my parched throat and washed away the scratchy feeling as if I had eaten heaps of desert sand for breakfast.

A few feet from me, a long table stood in front of the pavilion stacked with rows of people shoulder to shoulder. At the table from left to right, sat Brad McCormick, the leader, and his husband, Dr. Rick, Connor, and Mika Romanov, the second and third in charge of Phoenix, Bryan and Tony, in charge of the defense and electrical engineering. Dr. Paul and Dr. Simon, Brad's older sons, were running the medical center with their father, Dr. Rick. Then came my blood family, excluding Juandre and Andrew, Eryn, Ivan, Cian, and Barkor, and lastly my Peter. Twelve men led Phoenix and twelve men sat and awaited my answer. The hundreds of onlookers were also active participants in my in-depth inquiry. They were each allowed one question. After they had entered them into their personal wrist communicators, Lasitor, would electronically amalgamate them and create a list for the leadership to ask. Photos of their evidence against me, like the apple in all its shapes, schematics and printed-out equations, bronzed and clay tablets, and other shit I've never seen before were projected on big screens where everyone could see what we were talking about. It was the most civilized inquisition I've ever encountered.

Squeak-squeak!

Squeak-squeak!

The sound caught my attention, causing me to glance down at the bottom of my boots. My legs were involuntarily shaking again. I took a deep breath and exhaled slowly, trying to calm the tension coiling in my chest. I focused on the skinny beams of light that supported the walls and translucent roof, hoping they would continue to hold. This underwater city felt surreal and suffocatingly tight. A low vibration hummed through it, a sound that was unfamiliar to me. I couldn't discover its source. Did these humans understand the significance of what they had created? Without the guidance of the Fates, I would never have discovered this hidden place. My father would have been envious of this metal and would have wanted it for his palace, or perhaps even surrounding it. They'd achieved so much in such a short time; it both impressed and terrified me, and I couldn't help but feel a sense of pride at their accomplishments.

When I was alone, the lack of sound was overwhelming. There were no creaking floorboards, no rustling sails above my head, and no indication that we were deep beneath the sea. Eryn had mentioned that these walls blocked out sound waves, and as I lay alone in my cell, I couldn't fall asleep. My ears zinged, the silence broken only by the quick visits of Peter was allowed to give me. This morning, as my Kuku left me alone, the stillness and silence overwhelmed me. I urged myself to keep breathing, to ignore my soul-sucking cell companion, quiet. I prayed for the sleep cycle to end.

"Please let those jangling of keys arrive and open the door. Please let it be my sign to be free," I begged the Fates. Inside my cell, I was denied darkness and suffocated by stillness without my Kuku. I worry about him. He's embarrassed and disappointed in his friends.

One crack, and I'm suffocating on cold ocean water.

Inhaling, and choking, and gasping, frantic for air. Salt water everywhere. Only bubbles and no sound escaping my throat—until I'm dead.

Drowning was just as terrifying a death as burning alive.

I sighed a frustrated grunt. Phoenix was only a moment in time, only a blip in the vast expanse of eternity. Yet, here I was. I had found them.

I smiled at Peter. Freedom and happiness were finally within my grasp. The thought lifted my mood and gave me the strength to speak up.

A sneeze from the crowd of onlookers broke my train of thought. I blinked and stretched my neck and shoulders to loosen the tension. My eyes were tired, my vision was blurry, and I was completely unprepared for what was happening. Peter gave me a reassuring nod, but his gaze drifted to my shackles. He forced a fake smile onto his face.

I sent him a thought, *love, you are my strength.* He blushed, his usual response when I gave him a seductive look. It stirred something within me, and I shifted to make room for my growing cock. His white hair and piercing blue eyes reminded me of swirling galaxies, with their infinite beauty and boundless love. I shrank into myself, hiding my emotions behind my hunched shoulders as I fought back the fear of losing him, and never finding him again.

"Psst!" Peter called. I looked up at him. He looked left and right over his shoulder, checking who was eavesdropping. "No," he mouthed at me. I instantly felt better. *Stop your sulking*, I read his thoughts and chuckled, bumping the low table with my kneecaps. Even though I heard his thoughts, he couldn't hear mine. I guess because he hadn't grown into his true self yet. I had given my bite to Andrew, but it wouldn't hurt to try. When we kissed, I felt the glands in the back of my throat swell and contract, like sucking on a lemon.

Peter shook his head at me, *Don't, please don't. We will get out of this in one piece. Just be honest.* I read his mind.

"*Don't worry, and stop looking at me like that,*" I reciprocated. He was sometimes so prissy, so sneaky, and so dramatic.

"I love you," I mouthed, shaking my head at his antics. He widened his eyes and probably thought calming me was a lost cause. He slammed his head on his folded arms, pretending he was sleeping, making me laugh even harder. He made constant efforts to distract me from these people. But something was different today. He seemed ready to go. To run. To leave. To escape with me.

We spent stolen time together after our trip to Germany. By getting snot drunk and jumping all over, from Grayrak to the outer rim of our solar system, helping Cian and searching for rogue Zelk ships.

If we hadn't done it, I don't know what would have happened with this timeline. Something was nagging at me to remember it, but I was not successful, whether it was because of all the partying or because it hadn't happened yet. But for now, I was going to share my story and think about it later. I sighed and rolled my eyes. Oh, how I craved my Kuku's body and his smell. His laughs fed my love-hungry soul—the positives to my negatives. He made me feel young, like I had no cares.

Mika's words haunted me. *That fucking cylinder, the ancient golden cylinder that was originally the shape of an apple.* The genius had assembled and disassembled it and understood how to rebuild it into its original shape. I didn't know the apple could be opened and reconstructed as a seal containing the mathematics of the Anunnaki's gene code. Tree of Life, and a star map, as Mika named it. He was an intelligent and important man, and Cian and Ivan were his boys. The Fates had said the people who had it would use it.

It was never the intention of the Fates that the Disciples open it and create the Zelk—I hoped. The abominations of flesh and titanium were destroyed, but the essence, the human souls that lived in that tower were now lost. That's what was bothering me. Where were those souls now? Hopefully, the Fates had taken them home. And where was that? Was that where my family was, or was there more than one place in the afterlife? Also, how was I to know the apple could be cracked open like a puzzle box and then reassembled into a rolling cylinder to print out the string codes and star maps? Was this yet another secret my father and the Fates never shared with us?

I don't know what genome mapping means, but it made sense to Peter and I trusted Eryn, Ivan, Cian, Barkor, Juandre, and Andrew, as they all agreed with Mika's revelation. However, Eryn acted a little strange, as if he knew something important that he wasn't sharing with us. Despite this, I still trusted him and believed that he would tell us if he thought it would benefit us. They are the last of our kind, and no matter how terrible their existence came to be, I am grateful that they were born.

Waiting faces in the crowd urged me to start speaking up. I was both hesitant and eager to stretch out my life for them to dissect.

The noise of seats being pushed and pulled out ripped me again from my thoughts. Thousands of human eyeballs were turned my way—uncomfortable as fuck was an understatement.

I'm sure I emptied my bladder before the inquisition started, but now I felt like pissing myself.

The air was thick with the anticipation of the audience, their movements, and murmurs barely audible in the pregnant silence. The arches loomed above me, resembling the interior of a whale's chest cavity, waiting to be filled with my words. The hushed stillness felt almost reverent as if we gathered in a sacred space.

My heart raced as I prepared to unleash my last words upon the expectant crowd.

"I was born in Babylon, almost seven thousand years before the Doomsday of 2049 A.D. The youngest of my family and the oldest of our kind currently alive of which I am aware," I answered truthfully. *Cian, Ivan, Eryn, Andrew, Juandre, and my Peter are my kind now.*

"I'll tell you my family's history as it was relayed to me by my siblings. I remember playing hide and seek with human children in the palace. We would stay outside until sunset when my Anubis would be whining and letting me know it was time to return inside. My mother and father were seen as gods by the people in Mesopotamia. But they were only the King and Queen of Anzulla. Since their arrival, it had been a time of ruthless killings and human offerings. I cannot remember one day that I thought to myself I admired or loved my father. He demanded respect but was feared, not only by his people but by his family too. I wasn't born in Anzulla like the rest of my family. I was born in Babylon. My mother died giving birth to me. I was a big baby, and they had to cut her open to pull me out. My father reminded me of that every day of my life." I told my story to the Phoenicians. My shackles clunked. Everyone's line of sight dropped to them. *Breathe*, I told myself and I shifted in my seat. Uncomfortable with the sea of humans and thousands of eyes pinning me. Judging me.

Peter's blue eyes sparkled with unshed tears. *Not now. I haven't even started.* He nodded sternly, urging me to go on, then forced a thin smile. I took a deep breath, then gave him a reciprocal nod.

"On Anzulla, famine was rampant. As Anunnaki, we relied on the Loursveto's sap daily, similar to how you humans need water to survive. For hundreds of years, my father systematically strip-mined the gold to enhance his wealth and power. But the roots of the Loursveto plant grew along those veins. Slowly and permanently, he had destroyed the symbiotic balance in our world. One of his geology and mineral explorer teams had found and brought back Babylonian gold suitable specifically for the

Loursveto vegetation project. Gold ores were ground into dust and mixed into the soil. However, production was slow and I suspect hampered by my father skimming gold for himself. He had convinced my mother that going to the source was the only option. My mother loved my father. She preferred to be blind to his sickness of the mind. She defended him and chose to ignore the warning signs that he had descended into madness. My father promised that things would be different if they packed up and left Anzulla. That a new life awaited them and that he would be a better king and father. Initially, they believed him to be their hero and savior, but they soon realized he had resorted to leaving a scorched land. Burning Anzulla and fleeing with only a few members of our family. He fooled them. His insanity and old ways accompanied them to the new land in Southern Mesopotamia. Despite the constant stream of gold brought by slaves, it was never enough to satisfy my father's greed. The Loursveto seeds they had brought with them refused to thrive. Instead, the plants were weak and stunted, producing little sap for sustenance. My sisters An and Ki sang to the plants in hopes of coaxing growth, but their efforts were fruitless, just as in Anzulla. In desperation, my father harvested the powers from three of my brothers and was now threatening my sisters to sing or face the same fate. I believe even the Loursveto seeds knew that if they grew, they would only fuel the insatiable hunger for power of a mad ruler." I paused, feeling overwhelmed. I let my head fall, hiding my face from them to gather my courage. I looked up into Peter's caring eyes and took a deep breath before continuing.

"My birth wasn't celebrated, because I had killed my mother. After cutting her open, she was too weak to regenerate because of the massive blood loss and my father refusing to feed her out of selfishness. He had gotten worse after I was born. My brothers and sisters raised me. I never knew the love of a mother's touch and I think my siblings protected me by hiding me from him. With servants and soldiers, I grew older, and I made friends with humans. As the years passed, I got smarter. I'd joined the army by the age of fourteen and evaded destruction by visiting other lands, gathering strength and knowledge to stand up against my father. He was convinced he was the King of kings, and the god of all. He demanded offerings and drank the blood of humans after ordering them to kill their children or sacrifice themselves. He expected parents to cut and drain their children while he waited for them to bring cups of their blood to feed him." I paused as gasps and murmurs broke out in the crowd.

Brad got up and turned to the audience. "Men. Uhmmm, sorry, that was a slip. Excuse me, ladies. Please. We will never get this done if you react and stop the inquisition every few sentences. If this type of information shocks you or you have little ears with you, please leave and take your children with you." Phoenician men with their boys and Grayrakian men and women with their children got up and scurried out. I noticed Peter's seat was empty. *Where did he go?* Brad sat down again, took Rick's hand, and indicated I should continue. I waited until everyone had settled down. Then I cleared my throat and continued.

"Humans were seen as a food source and working animals. Their blood fed us, but again, even if it was just one or a thousand a day, it was never enough to quench his insatiable hunger." I stopped to empty my glass of water. The crowd murmured again. Connor and Mika looked so much like my sisters. My heart skipped a beat every time I saw the two of them, one with blond curls and the other with black. Both with piercing blue eyes. I took a second. Now that we sat across from each other, I had time to inspect them. I might as well be looking at Ki and An's children. Even their noses were shaped like theirs.

Mika spoke up. "Tell us more about your gift and, how did you end up time-traveling?" he asked curiously and I was glad for the change in direction, but it turned out to be about my father again.

"The first time I used my gift was by accident. I was sword fighting and as my opponent stepped closer to deliver a death blow, all I thought was *I must get away.* The next moment it was as if I was an observer looking at things like someone would look at fish swimming in a fishbowl. Right away, I tried it again, and then scared myself shitless, because I stood and watched as time passed and bodies covered the battlefield. I made the mistake of sharing my secret with one of my soldiers, who told my father to save his own family and children. I wasn't ready to face him or be sacrificed." Pausing, I chuckled at my choice of words. My interrogators weren't amused. No one laughed. The expressions on their faces were those of horror. I soldiered on. "I patched and rebuilt my time machine from the scraps I found in the rubble of the ship my family crashed into Babylon. I was proud of it, I still am, and although it's a bit small, it's mine." I shifted in my seat, wondering how to continue.

Eryn interrupted my nervous thought pattern. *Don't tell them about Lasitor. Not yet.*

I blinked and smiled at him and then found encouragement in Peter's eyes as he returned and slid into his seat. *He was probably on a bathroom break.*

"My father tasked me with searching for another place where the Loursveto grew so he could build his new empire there. He saw me as unintelligent. He had a knack for manipulating us with his words. Recognizing that I had pride in something I'd built with my hands, he used it to control me. He challenged me to find a new home for us to prove I'm a worthy son and allowed me to keep my ship." My voice cracked as the pity from the audience washed over me.

"You are doing so well, I love you, Ishtar," Peter whispered. I rolled my lips inward, biting them, before heaving a deep breath. *Almost done.*

"But my sisters knew it was only a matter of time before my father destroyed Babylon, and every living thing around it, too. They suggested I leave and hide from him, lie to him, making him think I was searching, while we prepared for war. We told Titus, my friend, and the head of the army, and together we started preparing for an insurrection against our oppressor. Our demands—abdicate or die. A whole army against one Anunnaki king. I traveled and trained, collecting tactical skills and knowledge, while Titus built the army. We trained the soldiers in tactics to weaken and isolate the enemy. I was ready but expected to have more time, to have peace talks, to avoid war. I was wrong. On my return, however, I found more than half of the palace desecrated. I sent word to Titus that I was making a stand, and they were to join me as fast as possible. To march through the city gates." Embarrassment and self-loathing crept up my throat. I closed my eyes and wished my hands were free so I could hide behind them. I sighed as a defeated feeling entered my soul. *These humans won't understand. They don't know war like I do.*

"The fate of my family rested on my shoulders. I had thought that, as a time traveler, I could take all the time I needed. Selfishly, I prolonged the inevitable for myself. I visited my friend Platonius, an intelligent mathematician, doing what I believe you call couch surfing. We smoked too many happy plants that week, and as we spoke non-stop, I showed him the equations I had stumbled upon. They were in the user manual for my ship. He called it the magic numbers. Platonius suggested I return home and give these numbers with calculations to Apsu. You know, to soften him up, to bribe him. I thought it was Apsu's, and if I showed him I'd restored them by making them indestructible, not like bits and pieces I found in the wreckage, he would favor me. I know it sounds far-fetched, but I have to say, I'm looking at the result today. But, upon my return, I found my sisters murdered. I handed the equations in haste to Xerxes."

"Which equations?" asked Mika, Connor, Brad, Peter, and half of the audience, breaking the silence. Half of them apologized, and others chuckled. "Sorry, Ish, we have questions streaming in. We want to know, how you and Platonius used algebraic calculations to write a genetic code which is a surjective mapping between the set of the sixty-four possible three-base codons and the set of twenty-one elements composed of the twenty amino acids plus the Stop signal. How were you able to use post-modern principles and calculations from the twenty-first century, in ancient times?" Mika lifted his hand, indicating a pause, then read more questions Lasitor fed to his communication device. I waited. *We all bloody waited.*

He lifted his head and seemed to agree with what he had read. "We want to know, how did you know a codon is a trinucleotide sequence of DNA or RNA that corresponds to a specific amino acid when that was only discovered as recently as two hundred years ago?" Peter's head snapped up and he scowled at Mika.

I lifted my shoulders, let out a long, tired growl, then ran an irritated gaze over the mob. They shrank back into their chairs, waiting for me to speak. "The philosophical and mathematical criterion for the perfect magic number is something Platonius identified in the user manual of my ship. It's the understanding that seven factorial equals five thousand and forty. Thus, seven sons and six daughters, times five generations, times four houses, times three parents, times two mothers, times one bloodline will produce the perfect offspring exactly five thousand and forty years later."

Connor cleared his throat and then tapped on his microphone. "Is this thing working?" he asked, and Brad nodded. The crowd answered eagerly, "Yes." Connor smiled and showed them his appreciation as bouncy black curls moved up and down. His deep blue eyes were serious. He turned sideways, waved once, and gave a thumbs-up. "Ish, tell me, more about this manual, who wrote it?"

I sat up, taking a deep breath, but Mika moved to the front of his seat and cleared his throat, "Sorry, love, do you mind if I ask this first?" Connor shrugged and at his approving nod, Mika continued, "Ish, what you are describing is what we call the number five-thousand and forty, a superior highly composite number, an abundant number, actually a colossally abundant number, and the number of permutations of four out of ten choices."

"Okay, okay, let's not go into that. That is a conversation for another day." Cian suddenly cut in, and I was thankful. I gathered my thoughts and continued as best and safely as I could.

"I want to finish telling this, Cian," I said, making pacifying gestures with my cuffed hands. He gave me an okay-then-go-on look.

"Yes, that is what I thought all those years ago, and that is what I meant to give Apsu when I returned home. But in haste after finding my two sisters dead, I said my goodbyes to Xerxes and their children. I handed him the information while briefly explaining what I believed the Fates had guided me to do. I sit here today, and I'm looking at the result of those equations," I said again, meaning them, but I looked at those relics on the screen above them. I don't think they heard what I said. *Fuck, I didn't even know what I was saying anymore.*

My guilt-ridden eyes caught Eryn's placating stare, and I communicated with him—begging for direction.

Surely, they know what I was talking about. Should I spell out what I think they don't see? That the ancient alphabet and language of the equations I handed Xerxes, were carved in Phoenician script. And that I had handed him a bronzed tablet and not an apple. That the apple was delivered earlier from a future version of myself. Does that even matter? I wonder if Mika knows or realizes the significance of the same Phoenician inscriptions on the bronzed tablet and the golden apple. I only heard a few days ago the apple could be broken up into pieces, taken apart, and rebuilt into a rolling seal. Are we talking about the same information? Were the calculations of the tablet the same as in the apple? Should I ask them? I don't want to confuse them or implant doubt. Eryn, I am sitting in a place called Phoenix. These people refer to themselves as Phoenicians. Phoenician is an ancient language spoken in the areas along the Mediterranean Sea, and Platonius's Greek Latin alphabet was an adaptation of it. The same as the manual's.

I told Eryn, mind-to-mind. He'd read my mind a year ago—the day I'd met him. I trusted him ever since.

A few seconds of silence passed between us before Eryn replied.

That will only prolong this hearing, and we don't yet have the answers to those questions. Where did you find that apple in the first place? You say you gave it to your sisters, but where did you find it? Eryn asked, and I realized I'd found it just before I met them. He must know, so why is he asking?

I narrowed my eyes at him. *The Fates, they gave to it me, to bring home.*

Do you see it now, Ishtar? The Fates, and the mystery of that apple? he asked, crossed his arms, and gave me a lopsided smile.

No, I don't. I'm getting a headache trying to.

As if picking up on my private conversation with Eryn, silence fell over the audience. Mika coughed and cleared his throat. "Could you please tell us more about the apple? We will come back to talk about those numbers. If that is okay with you?" Mika asked, and I didn't know what to make of this. He had asked me to choose and if I approved of changing the subject.

I indulged him by remembering my sisters' words, *We will bury the apple as you asked.*

I rolled my eyes mentally at Eryn for no-help-at-fuck-ing-all.

How am I going to spin this? My Kuku and Eryn wanted me to be honest. But how could I be honest without causing more confusion? Fucking scarabs.

"Some nations are born and blessed by their Fates. Others are just an unknown or inexplicable phenomenon that occupy a time and place, and although their existence is not even a blip far into their future, they surely existed. I don't question the Fates. Whether it's a tablet, an apple, or a message, I deliver it. With *my* ship," I said louder, to give them a little taste of my strength.

They're starting to irritate me. My father would have imploded this place to teach them a lesson. I sucked air through my nose and swept my gaze over the Leadership Team. Forcing the might behind the deep rumble of my voice to roll over each one of them to fucking hear me. "My ship and I operate beyond the borders of time and the imaginations of those people who claim to know everything by digging and scraping," I paused to let that sink in, "sifting through layers of soil sifting for scraps or artifacts to somehow explain how those humans lived, how they were able to be extraordinary and why they perished. They breathe the same air as other civilizations on another side of this planet. They've been living under the same constellations, yet others can't understand how they built their enormous cities, their pyramids, and why the architecture aligns with those constellations." My eyes roamed back to Mika and Connor. "Like just a few seconds ago, you asked how those mathematical equations came to be inside that apple, and why. It's the Fates. They guided me. My pre-programmed machine was a gift. Like any other gift. The Fates provide, because I follow, believe, and trust them. My machine allowed me to see where and when I was going and also to be able to return to the same time, only in another geographical location. When I step back using my gift alone, I am able to freeze time and move to places I've been already. Retracing my steps, but with my machine, I can go to places I've never seen or been to. I was told to take the apple home." I closed my eyes.

"I will recite the words of the Fates when I received the apple, word for word. Listen now," I said to the crowd.

Placing the palms of my hands on the tabletop, I sat up for dramatic effect. "*This is a gift of knowledge, it is yours, take it home.*"

I opened my eyes. "I remembered that was why Xerxes, my sisters' mate, pledged to hide the golden apple in the wall they'd built for me, for our bloodline. That was where and when I left it with them. In Babylon. That was the last time and place I saw the apple. That is until you showed it to me a few days ago. I also think my nieces and nephews survived the ice world beyond the northern mountains, and that is why Mika and Connor can sit here today as the fathers of my bloodline."

"Wait a fucking minute, you keep saying the Fates told you?" Brad asked, standing up and sending his chair flying. *Oh fuck, here it comes.*

"What the fuck?" Connor and Mika shouted, also jumping to their feet.

I slapped my hands down on the tabletop. The explosive noise carried a sudden burst of anger as my voice thundered over the audience. "Yes, and little did I know the ones imprisoning me, judging me, and deciding my freedom would also be the ones the apple was meant for."

"We are not imprisoning you. We are merely preventing you from running away without giving us answers," Mika blurted.

Peter jumped up, pointing his finger at Mika and Brad. Immediately I felt protected and shielded. "You confiscated his ship and his property. What do you want to do with it? Reverse engineer it? Sounds to me like if the shoe fits." Peter looked kind of funny when he was livid.

Without his wings, he wasn't big or intimidating, more like a little kitten with sharp claws. Now and then a burst of power would escape him, like a solar flare, but as soon as I zoned in on him, it disappeared. His face was turning all kinds of dangerously red colors as he directed his fury at Mika. His beautiful aura blinded me and I almost felt like angering him some more, just to see and feel it.

"I just hope they don't use it. They don't have my gift. I am pretty sure they would disintegrate if they tried to jump realities without me steering it correctly," I told Peter, knowing everyone heard me, and hopefully took that as a warning. I was looking forward to Peter visiting me tonight. I'm going to drink him dry and fill him up with my cum.

My words about the Fates caused a buzzing of outbursts among my audience. They grew into a thundering roar, and the whole gathering was declared over until further notice. Learning that more powerful entities, in actuality do steer mankind, caused debates and uproars. Needless to say, my inquisition was halted.

"Let's give the hive some time to cool down," Brad McCormick suggested. "Peter may visit you freely. Eryn, Ivan, Cian, and Barkor, would you help them move comfortable furniture into his cell? Lock down that section. I suggest moving there for the time being and guarding your friend until all these atheists come to terms with the fact that God, or the Fates as Ish calls Him, actually exist."

As Brad unlocked my cuffs, Peter waited nervously for me to get up and embrace him. Right then, I decided I had

had enough. *Fuck waiting for Peter to come and feed me. Fuck them joining us.* I wanted Peter, and I wanted him now.

For myself. Alone and not in my cell where the others were moving in to keep us company.

"Peter, come, we are leaving now!" I whispered into his ear as soon as we were out of earshot.

CHAPTER 15
CRASHING INTO DESTINY

"GOOD MORNING.

It's now six a.m.

Did you know recognition and connection are predictors of predestined love and it suggests that individuals may recognize their soulmate instantly by feeling an indescribable connection upon their first encounter?

If that is not the case, Lasitor could increase the role of choice and chance by one hundred percent to prove skeptics of the predestined love theory in humans wrong. These skeptics state that love is a product of choice, compatibility, and the unpredictable nature of life. But Lasitor can make the unpredictable predictable so the relationships are presumably built through a series of conscious decisions and actions.

Visit your community news page to sign up to participate in this voluntary study of peculiar, yet predictable, human behavior.

Breakfast is served until eight a.m.
Have a lovely day!"

PETER

2147 A.D. (95 A.T.)
Day three of Ishtar's inquisition
Phoenix, underwater glass dome city

MY TRUST in Brad and the leadership of Phoenix was faltering and being put to the test. A day after Cian had arrived with the Warship Horizon, carrying the lunar Grayrakian refugees, Ish and I found some alone time which we used for him to go back in time and update Lasitor. Knowing Mika well enough, I could sense that something was about to happen. So, I encouraged Ishtar to go while I kept them occupied. It seemed like the right thing to do because, just as I had suspected, during our Q&A session, they unexpectedly arrested my lover and seized his belongings. I had to suppress my outburst as I watched Ish being taken into custody, but the anger had been building up inside me ever since.

Fuck Mika and fuck the whole caboodle with their questions and lies. They only cared as long as I played by their rules. I was sick of the place. Phoenix was, after all, not the best place for me. I had tasted freedom, and I refused to be caged like a bloody budgie.

As they questioned Ish, I questioned our friendship and my loyalty to the very people Ish's countless jumps had brought to this point, where they had whiskey, friends, and everything any human could ever want. My comrades—as Mika would say—wanted to know and understand each jump and the power of time travel. They had pushed both of us to our limits. I was disappointed and embarrassed to have ever called them my friends.

Since his arrest was allowed two private conjugal visits a day. Ish's jail cell was situated in a secluded, military zone, where the residents of the general population weren't allowed for safety reasons. Our two-hour scheduled period last night was spent playing dentist-dentist. With a smile, bruised lips, and cracked corners of my mouth, I had woken up this morning alone in my apartment. His mind reading ability came in very useful for enacting kinky fantasies. *My dental appointment fantasy was not a fantasy anymore.* Ish had ordered me to breathe through my nose and open my mouth wide so he could stick his tool into it. *Sigh!*

Eryn was the only one who came to check up on me. He had assured me that all would be fine, to just let the humans listen and hear Ish's story. He was the one who had told, not asked, Brad, to allow me to visit Ish. Only Eryn was concerned about us and understood that Ish needed me. He fed only from me. And yes, maybe I was after filling his stomach twice a day with more than just my blood.

Feedings, for me, were sacred.

I mean, I called to whoever answered prayers when he drove into me while he and drank his fill. *It was divine!* We were yet to be fully mated, I hoped he would never drink from another, only me. Being holy and sanctimonious, I guessed.

After I had my breakfast this morning, I went to Ish for his, and like yesterday, I escorted him to his communal inquisition. Stewing in silence, I'd been clutching my restocked go-bag just in case Ish was set free. I didn't want to spend one second longer in this place than necessary. At the top of my bag were two of the biggest bottles of strawberry mint lubrication, followed by the bare minimums— a toothbrush and toothpaste, two pairs of socks, underwear, pants, and my pocket knife. As the proceedings went on, it became clear to me that they underestimated who Ishtar was. The importance of our bond became my sole focus as the urge to flee with my Anunnaki pumped urgently through my veins. Instead of appreciating, they were dissecting what Ish had done for them. I played along, nodded when expected, smiled when being watched, and then I disappeared into the background by excusing myself to go take a leak. As I pissed, holding my constant semi-hard cock, I felt rebellious and vindictive. I had snuck into the Leadership Office, broken into Mika's safe, and stuffed Ish's necklace into my go-bag. Then, just to spite them, I took the apple too. The bastards confiscated his things, pretending to be confused and upset and saying it was for his safety that they had locked him up in a jail cell. But like the apple, I know Mika will take the ship and pendant apart. Sure, he would put them back together again, but only after he satisfied his curiosity. And when would that be?

I felt particularly triumphant as I snuck back into the

meeting with my go-bag and the secret stash of loot. I was raging with guilt for stealing the damn apple. Frustrated with murderous intent toward my colleagues and blinded with lust and devious sexual thoughts. I attempted to guard my thoughts about the apple. I was failing when my sexy blue Anunnaki, smiled and showed me the tips of his fangs. *Think about all kinds of shit, prevent him from poking deeper into my mind.* I deflected, I jumped up, pointing fingers to defend Ish's honor, while I had none. My mind was a turbulent mess. I struggled to look Brad and the others in the eye while accusing, defending, and blaming.

But then the meeting ended abruptly. *Thank God!*

I swept my hair neatly to the side, patting it down while reading the room. Seeing an opening, I shot up and pushed my stool back under the table. I wanted to hold Ish, to tell him I was on his side. That I had his pendant and apple.

As I approached him, I was already drooling and planning to get him alone so he could do that flip, standing sixty-nine on my ass thing until I vibrated like an Eppendorf vortex mixer. I could already smell and taste him, that clean, tangy lab bleach smell of cum on my lips. Damn, I couldn't wait to have it all thrust into me.

Ever stoic, hoping no one saw me, or my motives, I moved with quick steps and grabbed Ish by the arm to drag him back to his cell.

"Peter, come, we are leaving now!" he whispered into my ear. The gruffness of his low, rumbling voice made me shiver. My mind immediately went to being shaken, rattled, and rolled.

"We're leaving," he said, flicking his eyes sideways while keeping his head low.

"Hmmm, you wanna suck and fuck me?" I asked, buzzing with lust. Moving fast, he pushed me into his cell. I giggled. Round one was about to start. I didn't care how he fucked me, but fuck me, he must. *That's a mate's primary job, wasn't it?*

I knew this was a sure thing, once I was alone with him, so I loosened my belt. "No time for that, come." Ish grabbed me by the arm, flung his hooded jacket over his shoulder, and pulled me out into the hallway.

"Wait! My go-bag!" I pulled free out of his grip, dove back, and retrieved it from underneath the bed, where I had kicked it to the side. "Ready!" I was scarcely upright when he yanked me back into the deserted corridor.

"Good, come!"

"Why are we leaving the protected area?" I asked as I went flying after him, clanking loosened belt buckle and all. "Are we escaping Phoenix?" My feet hit the floor every fourth or fifth step—he wasn't answering me. Ish activated the motion sensors, causing the overhead lights to flash like strobe lights. He ran, searching up and down the tubelike corridors for big-mouthed traitors—empty. We shot in that direction. Whispering voices of men drifted down from the right, so we veered left to avoid the danger approaching. We slipped into a stairway, the door banged closed behind us sounding like a gunshot. *Jesus, my nerves!* He was smart *to leave now* before the general population returned to living their lives.

"Yes, we are leaving," he said, dragging me down the long, translucent halls.

I figured that. My heart raced. "Wait, phew, Ish? You are running too fast for me." He didn't slow down, he was frantic to get out of Phoenix.

"Are we going outside?" I asked stupidly about the obvious, because where else would we be going if he was already activating the line of Bubblecars?

"*Shhht*, we can talk once we're out of here." Being a gentleman, he hastily opened my door for me, and threw me inside, before running to the opposite side.

"Come on, come on!" he urged the car, pushing the dashboard to go faster while ramming the forward throttle. "Help me, Peter, please," he said, shrugging, with hands in the air.

"Let me. Breaking the control panel is not advised, lover. If you smash the controls in, we could end up stranded." I leaned forward, catching that delicious scent of his, while I showed him how to override the childproof safety mechanism.

I pushed, turned, and then flipped the safety lever open to push the start button. Our vehicle separated from the other empty cars. Seconds later, the car slid onto the track. He sat arms crossed, not uttering a word, when we shot out of the tube into the blue darkness. My ears popped as the pressure in the Bubblecar adjusted. Half an hour later, we surfaced.

"Why aren't you talking? What's the matter? Answer

me! Ish, please say something, dammit." Ish turned to me with wild hunger in his expression. His incisors, pure white, glistened, and protruded three inches at the sides of his mouth. Breathing open-mouthed, he steamed. In and out. In and out. Heaving, feral, and wide-eyed. I swear it looked like those yellow and black rings around his pupils were spinning. His braided blue-black locks seemed electrified. Like a black lion, a predator, a ravenous one. And he was honing in on me.

I opened our doors so he could breathe fresh air. He seemed on the verge of a panic attack. I turned to him. His chest and shoulders moved up and down as he caught his breath. He bulged his fists and answered in a low tone. "First, I can't talk, and second, my body and thoughts are urging me to make you mine. Once we are alone and safely out of reach of the people living in that damn glass bowl beneath us, we are going to fuck until the stars fall out of the sky. I don't need company. They're driving me insane. This pull, this attraction to you, is turning me into a stupid sex-crazed mess. Don't you feel it? I can't think around you, and I can't be without you one second longer."

I leaned closer, our noses almost touching. "Look at me," I said, to help him focus. The heat of his skin soaked through his shirt and felt warm under the palms of my hands. "Yes, of course. I missed you and am very determined to have you mark me with your mating bite and your cum all over and inside me." He cracked a small smile. "It feels like you've died and I will never talk to you again when you are not with me. I had gotten so used to missing you while I waited for more than a hundred years. I'm sorry you have to feel it too. But we are in this together." I rubbed the sides of his arms up and down, which seemed to calm him. I didn't tell him about my ever-increasing itching. I was eager to surprise him with my glowing skin and wings. I had asked Eryn to describe the experience, and it kind of sounded like that. Maybe he feared I had sprouted wings down there. He didn't enjoy feeling trapped.

"Now, find your ship, so you can take me far away from here. Okay?" His hands were shaking and the heat level in his gaze told me I was going to have a tonsillectomy, and not orally.

"Okay," he answered, and I shuddered. I'd dreamed of this man wanting me, and the reality felt a thousand times better. Like a turkey, he was going to stuff me.

"Geh schneller. Let's go, my big alien!" I joked in German. He lifted his head. I got one twitch of an eyebrow in response as he checked his wristwatch.

"I'm pinging my ship. Where is my tick-tick thing? I need it, please," he said as he checked his wristwatch.

Gulp!

He knew? "Did you read my mind?" I asked while I patted around inside my bag, found my knife, thinking I might need it, then pocketed it. I rummaged further, found the necklace, and hung it around his neck.

"You can't hide anything from me, Peter." He checked his instrumentation, then turned the floating Bubblecar around to line us up with it. "There it is!" he said and pointed. I squinted, admiring the gleaming machine in the moonlight, sticking out of the sand like a golden dragon egg on a sandy island. I yipped and readied myself to exit as he drove the Bubblecar ashore.

Before we got out, I asked, "Are you mad or disappointed? My behavior, it's shameful. It's stealing."

"No, if I were in your shoes, I would have done the same. So no, my Kuku, I love you for it and you don't have to feel guilty. I can also assure you that your friends only mean well, maybe too bloody well. Stop beating yourself up. They are living their lives, it's time to live yours. Don't you agree?" He leaned over and pushed his forehead to mine. *God, this man has me twisted up for him.* I smiled.

"Good?" he whispered.

"Yes, I'm more than good."

"If Brad or someone catches us, we're in big trouble. Hurry!" He bumped me on my shoulder. "Go! Get out! Move that sexy butt." He laughed, and I jumped out of the vehicle. Sand flying—we raced to his ship. This was the most exciting thing I'd ever done. We were beyond naughty and couldn't keep our mouths and hands off each other as we waited for the door to open and the three stairs to extend.

He was all fangs and grunts, pushing and shoving me to go inside faster. I teased by resisting. More grunts, smiles, and wet saber cat kisses. With a heavy hand, he steered me up the stairs and inside. "I'm hungry. It's time for action. Playing nice-nice, while you sit and tease me with your smells and delicious looks, is over. I have you alone and for myself." That statement made me both happy and worried.

"You can kill me if you take too much blood, can't you?"

"I could never kill you. You are my mate. The moment I bite and inject my venom into you, your body will respond to satisfy me. Just as my body will be satisfying you."

"What do you mean? I thought you biting me would be without the magic juice. Didn't you give your mating bite to Andrew already?"

"Yes, but remember, it was not a true mating bite. It was a bite, but our souls weren't bonded. You are my mate. My body produced more venom because I'm not yet fully bonded. The Fates blessed us because I waited for you for so long. Even if your body doesn't respond and change like Andrew's, I'm sure your transformation would still be magnificent. If not the most extraordinary change of all consorts of all time." My eyes enlarged in wonder and my mouth fell open. He kissed my open mouth and smiled endearingly at me. "You are mine, not Andrew." He patted his chest over his heart. "I'm not fucking you while others guard me and listen to us. You are mine and not theirs. Not anymore."

His words fed my starving soul. Exactly what I needed to hear. "Where are we going?" I asked.

"I'm taking you to a place where you can have your miraculous change. Call it memories, dreams, or just intuition. I must take you there. You will love it. My friend Gugusan is the tribal leader. He will offer us a place to stay."

"So you have made friends already?"

"Yes, I have, and it's where I will make you mine, and then you can grow those beautiful wings of yours. It is the place I wanted to take you last year." I didn't ask more questions about my wings and his friends. He could introduce me when we got there.

"I'm taking over, Lasitor," he said as he flipped a couple of overhead switches. "It is five turns of this knob, backward." He pointed to a big golden knob with strange letters engraved on it.

"What do you mean by turns? How far is one turn?"

"I guess it's like this." He pointed to the left of the dashboard. Captivated, I looked at the strange clock compass. It faced upwards, the size of a football—encased in glass and gold. On its face, four black arms of different lengths turned both clockwise and anticlockwise at different speeds. Next to the glass case were three smaller knobs, looking and sounding like safe dials as he turned them with his long, slender, blue fingers. Now and then, above them were four small buttons being pushed that flickered like traffic lights—green, red, orange, and blue. In the center of the console, Ish manipulated the big golden knob, sounding like a ratchet wheel. I tipped my head to the side, watching as he turned the dials to line up a little water-leveling weight that hung on a string inside the glass container on the left. The spinning clock arms stopped as soon as he had it all lined up. I had no clue how he read or worked the instrumentation.

"We can't measure time inside the space between timelines itself. It's different than the solar years of the Earth, but if I had to guess, I would say it's about five thousand years for every full turn." With one hand on the lowest dial, and the other on the ratchet wheel, he demonstrated as he dialed backward. For one full turn, I heard one click.

"Really?"

"Hm-hmm." he answered in deep concentration. I followed every movement. His hands moved in a chaotic rhythm. He could do it with his eyes closed, like a master piano player. Every flick, turn, push, and roll, he knew exactly what he was doing. I've seen him in action a few times, but no matter how many times I've seen it, it still fascinates me. "Holy fuck, so twenty-five thousand years! That's far back. It's going to be infested with wild animals and prehistoric predators."

"Exactly, but this little one narrows it down to months and years" —he lifted the pendant around his neck— "and then this tick-tick thing takes me to the precise place that I want to go." He couldn't meet my eyes. "I don't think there are prehistoric animals where we are going."

"What are you not telling me? Be honest with me."

"I think I lost, no I found you..." A flicker of doubt flashed in his eyes.

"For fuck's sake, tell me!"

"Hmmmm." He waved it off like it wasn't important. "You will see. I dreamed of this place often. I can already smell it. Green forests and waterfalls springing out of the mountains, spreading a mist over the land. It is magical. Lots of green. Flowers and trees and the animals, even the birds, are vibrant colors. I want us to go there and I want you to spread your wings and be free." He said it with a smile and an uncomfortable chuckle. Having his ship confiscated and being kept prisoner had wrecked his nerves. He didn't like either of us being trapped underwater in Phoenix.

"Maybe this will be freeing. Living somewhere, where we choose to live, sounds like we will have all the time we need to enjoy ourselves." I smiled and gave him a stern nod. "I trust you. Take me to your magical paradise." I shifted in my oversized seat, copying him by fastening my seat belt as I readied myself for departure. "These seats are big, and not built for humans," I noted out loud. Ish was about eight feet tall, and he filled his seat with his bulked-up frame. "You say this is my seat and no one else ever sat in it?" I asked, grinning at the fact that I was his number one.

"Yes, Kuku, it's yours." Our eyes met, and that pulsating feeling between us intensified. After the door shut and his instrumentation was calibrated, he leaned in to kiss me softly on the lips. *Things could only get better from here.*

"Let's go." He lifted my hand and kissed it. Licking each knuckle with a flick of his tongue. He knew very well how to make me quiver for him. His gaze was intense and full of desire—for me.

My heart fluttered. Heat crept up my neck. "Ready," I chuckled elatedly.

"I'm taking you to a human wedding," he said, chin in the air.

"You mean a honeymoon?"

"Yes, no one will bother us there." He popped the buttons of his trousers open and multitasked. One hand reached down for his cock, while the other pushed buttons and steered the ship. "Fuck, I'm so hard for you. It's bloody fucking painful." He trembled as he exposed his blue glistening, swollen cockhead.

"Yeh, come to papa," I said with interest. I lifted my ass, and pulled my pants down at the crotch, to make more space for myself. He pumped his hardened organ for me. I sat up, taking notice. His feralness was rubbing off on me.

I must taste him.

As soon as the sky brightened and lights zoomed past us, I unbuckled my seat belt to turn sideways and leaned closer to wrap my lips around him. *Damn, he tasted good.*

"Ah, fuck, Kuku!"

I suckled his piss slit until a hand tightened on the back of my neck to force himself deeper.

I wrapped a fist around the base of his cock and checked in with him. His eyes were blazing yellow-orange. He squeezed his eyes shut, and I went back to work by swallowing him with a single carnivorous gulp. I heard his head hitting the headrest a few times. "This is not safe, Peter," he hissed and then spoke in a language I assumed was his mother tongue. I slid my lips back over his hot silky blue foreskin, then opened my throat to dive back down on him. His enormous length was impossible to swallow in totality. I sucked with a vengeance whatever fit down my throat, I knew I was doing it right as deep guttural moans filled the ship. My legs were cramped and uncomfortable, so I moved closer for a better angle. He whimpered. I got greedy, I feasted on him as my lips and tongue wrapped tightly around his cock and he slipped in and out of my mouth. My hands and his shaft got slippery as saliva dripped and drizzled over his hairless balls. He pushed my head down into his crotch—fisting my hair painfully as he forced me to take more of him. *Yeah, I like that.* He took control, face fucking me by maneuvering my head the way he wanted. His moans filled me with a sense of accomplishment, as blood rushed through my ears. Both hands clutched my hair, and I relaxed, giving him full control. Just as I lost myself in the rhythm, thinking I should probably reach for my own throbbing cock, he pulled me up by my hair so hard and fast, his cock popped loudly out of my mouth breaking the suction.

Spittle dripped down my chin as I looked up at him skew-eyed like a brain-dead fish gasping for air. "What's wrong? Do you want me to ride you?" I blubbered, my tongue fucked numb and my jaws nearly dislocated.

I scarcely heard the alarms pinging while he ejaculated over my face.

"Come here, now!" he grunted. Chaos reigned in his mind. Instinct overruled reason. He pulled me up by my hair and all I saw were teeth coming for my neck. For my jugular. As soon as he struck, searing pain in my neck and exploding stars flashed through me. I orgasmed in my pants. Still spasming and clinging to him in a stupor, the sounds of alarms sobered me up. I felt Ish licking my neck and heard Lasitor calling for us in the background.

"Sirs, sirs, sirs, excuse me, sirs. Sirs, we are crashing in six, five, four—"

"Oh, fuck!" Ish shouted. I was deliriously drunk with

endorphin and Anunnaki cock and venom overload. Blissfully I turned my head to see where all the noise was coming from. I beheld a scene of horror.

Ish flung me off his lap, throwing me like a rag doll into my seat. "Was that necessary?" I yelled as I banged my head. He ignored me, smashing buttons and pulling levers.

Lasitor counted, "—three, two, one."

And then it registered. "Oh fuuuuck!" I yelled too late.

With a droning rush, we hit the treetops, skidding through branches, hitting birds and their nests, smashing their eggs, feathers, bird shit, and leaves covering the window. Then, at the thunderous speed of a hummingbird hitting a bullet train, momentum threw me face-first into the window, then ricocheted me like a cannonball to the back of the ship. Upside down, my head thumped the door lever. For a second, I stuck to the door like velcro until it swooshed open behind me. In slow motion, I tumbled outside, my face meeting the wet green earth, followed by my go-bag with the solid gold apple, his jacket, his golden swords, and finally, Ish—all hitting my head, ensuring I would never forget to leave the freaking seatbelt fastened until the lights went out—not even for sucking cock.

Silence.

The three stairs popped out. Too late, I thought as I blacked out.

Ish shaking me, woke me up. His warm tears burned my cuts and bruises around my eyes like acid and blinded me.

"Thank the Fates. I thought you were dead," he cried

and kissed my face all over, beside himself as he apologized and begged me to never scare him like that again—as if I had done it on purpose.

"I'm okay, just stop crying, please. You sound awful," I croaked as I wiped his tears out of my eyes, checking my fingers for blood, and found none. Maybe I was paralyzed? I wasn't sure if I could walk or stand. Wheelchair, here I come, I thought.

"You came back," he cried again, hugging me fiercely still drowning me with his eight-foot giant soccer ball-sized tears and hugging me like his favorite teddy bear. "I'm sorry. It is all my fault," he fretted over me, stroking my hair and washing the mud with tears from my face.

"It's okay. I'm okay," I blubbered as he inspected my head like a baboon searching for ticks.

His overprotective vulnerable demeanor changed to ferocious. His head snapped up, and I followed his intensive gaze—something scuffling in the trees.

Spitting and coughing. "Te'exe' ka'ap'éel ts'iit mierda demonio! Olak k ka kíinsiken." Two raging figures stumbled out of the underbrush. Two men. One short, and one as tall as Ish. The short one was dressed in skimpy leather cladding his manhood, the other—*what was that?*

Ish pulled me up by my arms and I shuffled behind him. "What are they saying? Is that what I think it is?" I asked.

"They are saying, you two pieces of demon shit! You fucking almost killed us," Ish whispered under his breath, widening his stance, ready to pounce and defend me. They strolled closer and my instant thought about the tall one was...*handsome.* The wind whipped his long sleek black hair from his pale face, revealing menacing dark eyes. A bare expansive muscular chest, impressive abdominals, and yes, as they stepped closer, the outline of what he carried on his back confirmed what I was thinking—and that's when shit rained down on us.

"Oh, scarabs," Ish said, looking up.

"What in the ever-loving fuck is that?" Scores of flying insects—*no, not insects.* My heart pounded as I computed where to run. "We have to go, now!" I exclaimed, my voice barely audible over the loud flapping of wings. The sky grew dark as massive creatures filled the air. "Pte—pte—pterodactyls! Run!" I shouted, but stood frozen as the things with wingspans of at least six feet, blocked out the stars and cast an eerie shadow over us. With trembling hands, I tugged at Ish's shirt. The tips of their black wings glinted in the moonlight, making them look like an extra set of eyes.

"No wait, never run. It makes you a target," Ish said.

"Oh, fuck! It's another species. Two species." I blinked. I counted. They're not humans and not pterodactyls—*or fruit bats.* The two men who had just arrived by foot were shouting something up at the others, but as soon as tall and beautiful on the ground pointed at us, Ish crushed my hand in his.

I stayed hidden behind my Anunnaki while measuring the distance back into the ship. "They're speaking? They are humanoid? And you understand them?" I asked bewildered while trying to decipher what was going on.

"Yes, I understand them," Ish whispered. Cold sweat

ran down my back as we stood staring up at them. Tall, and beautiful shouted something at us. Suddenly, they swooped down and lunged toward us. With one scoop, Ish threw me back into the time machine, grabbed his swords, and leaped in front of the door, protecting me—blocking me inside. Just as he lifted his blades, they swarmed him. Attacking, disarming, pulling, shoving, and grunting. Fists, feathers, grass, and mud flew everywhere.

I should have closed the door, I should have stayed inside, but I climbed back out, calling, standing on the stairs like a maiden waiting for her knight to return. *Only maidens are this stupid.* I glanced down at the rustling noise at my feet. Standing on his haunches in the shadow of the ship, that man dressed in leather and feathers from earlier was reaching for me. Before I could turn or jump away, two pale hands with long, bony fingers wrapped tightly around my ankles, and yanked.

"Oh, fuck no!" I shouted as I hit the ground. Falling flat on my face, I gasped for air, seeing sparkles. Half blind, I scurried on my hands and knees. I desperately heaved for air while calling out for Ish. I couldn't see him through the masses of winged creatures packing on top of him. I managed to push myself up, to run, to get away, but the man tackled me and knocked me back down. With an oomph, the last air in my lungs got knocked out of me. Again, he grabbed my ankles and dragged me into the underbrush. I kicked while twisting and rolling. I fought for my life. I shouted. I tried to break free from being pulled deeper into the trees.

"No, fuck you!" I grappled, reaching for anything to

pull myself back. Skin peeled from my fingers as I upended roots, deflowered bushes, and debarked trees but nothing was sturdy enough to keep Ish and the ship from disappearing from my sight. I kept on kicking as I fought to free myself with all the strength I had left.

Suddenly, a sharp pain shot through my skull, silencing me. It happened again, and I lost my grip. The third time, everything went black as I slipped into unconsciousness.

CHAPTER 16
LOST

"GOOD DAY, IT IS I, LASITOR, YOUR FRIENDLY *fountain of news and information.*

Did you know Khat is a flowering shrub native to hot desert climates that contains the alkaloid cathinone? It's a stimulant that causes greater sociability, excitement, loss of appetite, and mild euphoria. Yes, my dear humans, like the Bushmen, other ancient tribes have been Khat-chewing for thousands of years.

Did you also know that Khat or qat has many other names worldwide? For example, in Somali, it's qaad, in Arabic al-qāt, but the most interesting name for this flowering plant in Anunnaki is the Loursveto.

I guess it's not a good morning after all.

It doesn't matter what time of the day it is.

No breakfast will be served.

Good luck, and stay positive."

. . .

PETER

24 970 B.C.
Hours after the crash of Ishtar and Peter
The jungle

A DULL THUD reverberated through the air, followed by the icy sensation of water splashing on my face—jolting me awake. My heavy eyelids fluttered open, greeted by the pitch-black darkness of my surroundings. I strained to figure out the source of a muttered curse, barely audible but laden with frustration. The sound of water surrounded me, confirming my location on a boat. Correction, a makeshift float. I lay motionless, straining my ears to decipher the faint whispers of my captor. It seemed to be just one man talking to himself. Waiting for his voice to fade into the distance, I cautiously turned my head, assessing the gravity of my situation. Grateful that I had put the small flip knife in my pocket, I prepared to defend myself. Discarding my blanket, I swiftly rose to my feet, gripping the knife tightly. Pressing it against the man's throat, I snarled a warning, "Stay still or I'll slit your throat and let the crocodiles have you!" Adrenalin surged through my veins. My heart pounded against my chest, causing my breath to come out in shallow gasps. I was lightheaded and the movement of the float on the water intensified the feeling. Foreign vibrations resonated through my entire body, making my hands tremble and my legs weak.

Carefully, he turned his body sideways to eyeball me. "You be calm and good now. I help you," the man said as his smile remained plastered on his face. Unaffected by me and my knife threatening his life. He held his hands up in a calming gesture.

Trying to regain control of my emotions, I took a deep breath and attempted to communicate and get answers. "Who are you? Where am I? Why did you bring me here?" I demanded, my voice quivering with a mixture of fear and anger.

He responded with another string of unfamiliar words, the cadence melodic yet strangely familiar. His gestures and expressions seemed to convey a strange sense of amusement—rubbing me the wrong way, the moment he stuck his middle finger up—*The fuck?* "Are you giving me the finger?"

He snorted a laugh, then extended and crooked his index and middle fingers like running, then jumping. Followed by opening and closing the palms of his hands. Mimicking flying through the air and chaotic crashing and colliding. He was telling me what he'd seen earlier. I remembered him. He was with the tall, dangerous, yet extremely handsome man with black wings.

"Is this some kind of sick joke?" I spat, my voice laced with disbelief. "You hit me over the head and brought me here against my will. You didn't help me," I said. He seemed to understand me, and for some bizarre reason, I understood him and his sign language.

"Da na hana," he said, in an amused tone. It was a phrase I comprehended, its power resonated deep within me, stirring something primal and ancient.

As the float wobbled beneath my feet, I couldn't escape

the feeling that I had been brought into a world far beyond my understanding. Those scrapes on the side of his face needed cleaning. He was muscled, without an ounce of fat. It's just my luck to run into a man resembling Bruce Lee in the middle of nowhere. "You better not martial art the shit out of me," I said as I let go of him but still held my knife up, threatening him. The shape of his eyes was two straight lines as if the skin had sagged over them and only his eyelashes were keeping them open, and they sparkled with a mischievous glint that made me question his true intentions.

"Stop this thing and let me go," I said, pointing to myself and the trees. It was so weird. I spoke in broken English, pronouncing vowels and consonants as if I had had a stroke and the language processing part of my brain had urged me to say something different. Concussion? Probably.

"Where is Ish, and why did you bring me here?" I mimed, but the Asian dude only smiled. I estimated it was about four feet from the float to the bank. I could jump that. If not, I could swim to it.

"Ya, don't do that. You stay on water, you safe, you go out the trees, they will find you," he said in broken English. I blinked. Assessing my abductor. He looked about fifty years old, no, forty, maybe thirty? I couldn't tell. His complexion was brown mustard, probably because he spent all his days outside in the sun. His teeth were pointy, and he had longer than normal incisors. Twigs and leaves were stuck on his head. A bird's nest, maybe? *Was he wearing the nest?* He looked happy. Too happy. *Creepy.*

With his hands on his hips, he appeared proud of himself. "That's my shirt!" *The fucker had stolen my shirt. He'd cut it. It fit him like a crop top.* I checked myself. My shoes were gone too. Thank god he'd left my jeans on.

"I'll cut you up," I said and waved my knife at him. He was not intimidated.

"I not hurt you. I Elijah. You not cut me. I not take you. Snake bring Kuku, never safe. You Kuku go sky. Me, you wait long time." He pointed to the dark blue night sky painted with stars.

"What are you talking about? And what did you just call me?"

"You Kuku, from the sky," he said, throwing his hands in the air and nodding his head as if I should agree.

"What do you know about my nickname? How do you know me?"

"You come, you fall from the sky," he said, pointing to me and back to the universe. Both hands in the air, he turned around cupping his hands over his eyes and playing peek-a-boo.

I'm lost in time.

We were on our way to visit with Ish's friends and now I'd been abducted by this Elijah, who sounded deranged, and not like someone who had flown over, but was wearing the cuckoo's nest.

"You come home, you safe there. You no wings. You no fight. Gu and warriors fight. You save by me."

"No wings? You know I'm supposed to have wings? Do you know Gugusan?"

"Yes-yes! Wings." He patted his chest. "I take you to

our home. I save you, you save me. We friends. You, me go back home, Elijah home. Gu the protector of the mountain. Your friend. Yes?"

Itching from head to toe, I clawed at my hair and pulled a face. I was so fucked. One minute Phoenix's walls had protected me for what felt like an eternity and now mosquitos buzzed like helicopters. I was pretty sure there was not an unsucked patch of skin left on my body. The hot, humid air was suffocating. No wonder my abductor wore only the briefest leather skin and feathers around his waist to cover his junk.

"Why did you take me?" I asked through gritted teeth.

His eyes were bulging as his hands clenched and released. Like he wanted to say one thing and decided on something more appropriate to say, "I save you," he exclaimed eventually.

"Okay, okay, you saved me. Then why the fuck did you hit me over the head?"

He harrumphed. "Kuku make lots of noise. I make you not make noise."

"Yes, because you fucking dragged me into the bushes like a Sasquatch!"

"No, I save life!" he yelled back at me, his eyes glinting with a strange sheen, like an animal's. Exactly like Andrew and Juandre's—Anunnaki eyes.

"What the fuck?" I said, rubbing my forehead. I blinked mindlessly, searching the boat, the riverbank, the trees, and the sky for answers.

"Yes, fuck. They rip apart, fighting. Rip off arms and legs. I not help, Kuku bleeds and dies."

"Where is Ish? Where is the man that traveled with me?"

"I sorry, demon man dead, he rip apart." He made two fists, then wrung his knuckles and pretended to snap something, but I got the message. Those things, with wings, tore him in two.

"No, that cannot be!"

"Yes, he not protect you. He cut swords, they many-many fly. They fight, they tear apart."

"No!"

"Yes, I no sorry, I save you. I take you. You not rip apart."

My knees buckled and I dropped to my ass. The knife I had been clutching fell and hopped into the water. I was unprotected and at the mercy of my abductor.

I let my head fall into my hands and wailed a long excruciating, no-no-no-no-no-no!

I don't know how long I sat in a defeated heap, before falling to the side and crying myself to sleep. I must have slept the day. Hooting, hissing, and howling woke me up. The forest cluttered the riverbank, and the canopy enclosed us in thick shadows that daylight couldn't cut. I watched Elijah guide the boat with ease while I allowed my tears of pain and hopelessness to flow as they chose. My body was changing, I felt different. I rubbed the spot on my neck that Ish had bitten right before we crashed. It was still tender. *Those long incisors.* God, he was feral. *I miss my feral, dangerous, kind-hearted Anunnaki.* I was stuck in this place, lost and alone. Even if I found my way back to the time machine, I doubted I could operate it correctly. All I knew was Phoenix was five turns into the future. What if I ended too far ahead in time? I could get lost in time. With my luck, I'd end up back in Babylon or worse, back in 1968.

I could ask Lasitor. He might be able to return me to Phoenix. I had to try. Ish said he was taking me to paradise, where he would introduce me to Gugusan. I assumed this was the paradise. Maybe? Fuck, I still couldn't believe our time together had been that short. I still didn't have my wings, and this man, Elijah, knew about me having wings, some time in my future.

I lifted my head just as Elijah swung around.

The gloominess of the day had receded and I think the sun was setting again. My eyesight was enhanced. Tall reeds at the riverbank swayed in the breeze. Excitedly, I narrowed my eyes to confirm my eyesight was better. Ish's bite had enhanced that for me because I was looking at the purple flowers of pickerelweed on the shallow edges detailed in high definition.

"Are those crocodile eyes? Enhanced senses, wings or not, if a crocodile jumps on this float I'm gone," I said.

"*Shhht!*" Elijah silenced me. My head snapped towards the rattling tiny birds' nests hanging from the dense reeds. Something had disturbed them. I turned my head from side to side, listening for sloshing in the water. Something. Anything.

Suddenly, a loud shout in an unfamiliar language boomed from across the river. I sat stock still, not moving an inch.

Thump-thump!

My heartbeat thudded in my ears. I squinted my eyes, wondering if I could shoot lasers through them. *That would be so cool.*

One by one, shadows appeared from the darkness of the woods, carrying torches that cast flickering light on their dark faces. Panic set in as they approached, leaving me torn between staying and facing the unknown or risking diving into the water for a chance at escape. Laser them! I thought and tried, but my eyes weren't able to do that trick. Nothing happened. My eyes only widened.

Men dressed in vibrant feathers and leather sloshed nearly soundlessly through the water. So the lazy river was not as deep or rapid as I'd imagined. Two of them were throwing hooks and reeling us closer to shore. I couldn't tell if they were friends or foes, because Elijah wasn't saying anything. He was smiling as he steered and pushed the float diagonally toward the bank. Lining us up with an opening cut out of the reeds, to create a makeshift float jetty of some kind. I felt Elijah's anticipation as a powerful figure emerged from the shadows. Those floundering in the water saw me and screamed at my abductor. My initial instinct was to flee, but my body wasn't cooperating. Unsteady, I struggled to stand on the wet and uneven deck and slipped. Fuck! I fell flat on my ass, lifting my hands in surrender.

"You safe now, Kuku. Elijah bring you to Gu," my abductor said as he hauled me back to a standing position.

"Let me look at you," the gruff voice of a mountain of a man said as a small torch gleamed between us. He wasn't towering over me. It was me. Had I grown taller while sleeping? I looked at my hands and feet. I did seem taller and my hands and feet were larger. My jeans had been loose with an easy fit and now they fit like a second skin. I flipped my hands to look at the palms and kicked my feet over looking at the soles.

My body's changing. He should be towering over me. It's just like Ish said it would be, once he had bitten me. *Why isn't he here with me?*

"Hugh-um," the male cleared his throat. His voice was throaty, yet somehow comforting. He looked nothing like my captor. Although dressed the same, his colored feathers and the leather straps around his waist were adorned with glimmering jewels. He walked taller and he had a cleaner appearance making me wonder if he was the famous Gugusan. As they spoke, pointing at me and conversing, I strained to make out their words. I caught something about a serpent's tail from the sky. My abductor's explanation only added to my fascinated confusion. Was I in danger, or would he help me? I doubted the former because now he was sticking his hand out for me to shake. The moment he took my hand and folded his other over mine, I recognized Ish's handshake and I gleamed.

"Hello, I'm Peter, are you the famous Gugusan?" I asked as the man pulled me closer by the shoulders, awe in his face.

"Da! Kuku, you are back again?" he asked, moving me from side to side as if looking for something behind me. "Where are your wings, you are baby God now?"

He knew I had wings. Baby God?

His expression was a mix of amusement and wonder. Now more men joined us. Most were tall and lean. Looking at me and talking about me. Elijah spoke fast and animatedly. Proud of himself that he had saved me. As they gawked at my face holding their blazing torches closer, I couldn't help but flinch from the searing heat. Part of me wanted to ask them what the fuck they were looking at, but another part of me wanted to disappear. Because my Ish was dead. I closed my eyes tightly, made like Dorothy, and wished I was home.

"Le, k'asa'ano'ob cortes. Ta p'uchaj wáaj a pool," Gugu-san's voice thundered. I opened my eyes, clearly still in the land of Oz and not knowing what was going on.

"Da," he said, shaking his head. As I listened to him speak, I felt a sense of familiarity. It was like his words were in a language I should understand, yet something was off. I stared at him in dismay. His thoughts and spoken words didn't align. Had Ish's bite given me the power to read minds? The thought was both exciting and terrifying. And so fucking sad, because, again, my Anunnaki was dead. *I need Ish. I don't want to be alone in a jungle with no way home.*

"Those are bad cuts on your face. Did you hit your head?" he asked as I ducked away from the flames, singeing my eyebrows.

His eyes bore into me. I clenched my fists, feeling a throbbing headache coming on. My sight and hearing, all my senses, were hypersensitive. I flinched as his fingers grazed the tender bumps on my scalp. He inspected his bloody fingers, then growled something at Elijah. I checked the golf ball size bump on my head. Yes, still slick with fresh blood.

"What happened?" Gugusan asked again, looking at Elijah like he was seconds from ripping him apart.

"When we crashed and chaos rained down on us—those creatures attacked us," I interrupted, explaining, gesturing to the man beside me. "But he stopped me from going back for my partner." My anger simmered as I glared at them, my pulse racing.

Something was happening to me. I was shivering, and I didn't know if it was the heat, cold, infection, or shock. Elijah jumped to place a blanket over my shoulders which I appreciated.

"You must come with us, Kuku," Gugusan urged. I had no other option. I was alone and Ish, my mate, was gone. With a heavy heart, I steadied myself and adjusted my footing to climb off the makeshift log boat.

"We will keep this here for you," Elijah sing-songed.

"What? Where did you get that?" I grabbed for it, but Gugusan was closer and faster. "It's Ish's, it's ours. It was in my bag!"

"I take the apple. Ishtar is dead now. I found it. It's my apple," my abductor said.

"You illiterate thief! That apple was in my bag and you fucking stole it! Give it back!" I shouted. I was near passing out as the feeling of light-headedness increased, and the little vision I had left zoomed in on the apple.

"No! I take apple. You not keep it safe," Elijah said, but Gugusan had already taken it from him.

"I will keep it safe for you. Come," he said with a stern

tone. He showed me the apple as if it was a carrot and I was the fucking stupid donkey.

Anger and unbearable pain, a deep ache that blackened my eyesight and sucked all the air out of my chest cavity, crushed my entire being. Every breath I took felt like it was not enough. My chest felt like it was cut open. I hunched forward. I was dying, and it wasn't from Congo fever or malaria. "I'm suffocating!" I cried.

I was heartbroken and having a heart attack. I was dying in this strange place. My head throbbed. It felt like it was exploding. Like it was packed with a trillion thoughts. My chest expanded as I sucked air deep into my lungs. Anger about the apple and Ishtar dying, a potent force I had never experienced before, consumed me entirely. I arched backward and let it all out.

"Enough! It belongs to Ishtar," I roared, clenching my fists so hard my nails dug into the skin. My hostility, usually suppressed, erupted from within me like a violent storm. The surrounding waters churned and sprayed outward, flattening the reeds. The world around me glowed brighter than the midday sun. Men dropped to the ground and into the water while I felt an inexplicable sensation of ascension. A searing pain shot through my back, causing me to let out another primal scream that echoed off the mountains. A voice, deep and thunderous, streamed out of my mouth. Their fear was palpable as they trembled and shielded their eyes. Like snapping thunder I heard a crack, deafening me. Intense, crushing pain radiated from every bone in my spine. Excruciating agony propelled me into the air.

Then, as abruptly as it came, the pain was gone. I looked down at the men, wondering what had just happened. They were terrified of me. For a moment, a flicker of doubt crossed my mind—was there something else behind me? I spun around, my body whirling as the surrounding trees, the flowing river, the boat, and the men diminished beneath me. Some chose to shield their faces, while others stared up at me in sheer awe.

"Oh my fucking god!"

A deep, foreign voice rumbled out of my chest. Startled, I let out a deafening shout that reverberated over the forest below me. My heart raced as I twisted and turned to see over my shoulders. To my amazement, a pair of colossal wings with pure white feathers and a seven- to eight-foot wingspan were sprouting from my back. With a rush of exhilaration, I realized I had taken flight. The sensation of being airborne was surreal.

"Oh, fuck!"

Whatever I had been doing, I wasn't doing it anymore. The wind blew through my hair. The water came closer. Head over ass, I somersaulted. Flapping my arms didn't help. Flapping my arms and uncoordinated wings together didn't work either. I couldn't fly anymore.

Flap wings! Flap! Nope, not working.

I tumbled down and hit the water with a deafening splash. Kicking, treading, flailing, and sinking under the surface like a sack of rocks.

Once they'd fished me out of the water, they half dragged and half carried me to the village where they sat me down and told me to open my wings to dry them in the warmth of the campfire.

My wings baked and baked and baked.

One by one, the whole tribe had joined me around the fire. They were telling stories of the sign from the serpent from the sky—which I'm sure was us crashing into the atmosphere in a time machine.

Elijah, acting stranger than before, introduced me to his friend, Groda, who had just arrived exhausted from an important mission. When he saw me, he did a double take, covering his mouth with his hands—*whispering something about me.* I was sure the sturdy muscled man was able to uproot a century-old tree with his bare hands. But after he giggled at me like a woman, I doubted that he could hurt a fly, or in this case a mosquito.

Their whispers grew louder and rambunctious. It was getting stupidly uncomfortable to be talked about and laughed at. Gugusan gave them a shut-up-and-behave-or-else look. That didn't work so he pulled them up by the arms and removed them from my vicinity. A few older women joined him to reprimand their clowning behavior.

I understood why Ish liked it here. Time passed lazily and the entertainment was innocent and naive. So cheerful it was stomach-churning. It felt like an asteroid was about to go out of orbit, heading straight for me. Like shit was about to go down—and they already saw it hit me.

My hecklers were quiet and way too nice when they returned and sat high in the nosebleeds. They felt guilty. Good.

A bloody moon tinged with orange, wrapped in a handful of wispy clouds hovered above the dark silhouette of the mountains. A silent time stamp among the stars. Somehow, I expected the night Ish died to be something extraordinarily thunderous and chaotic. Maybe some sandstorms and locusts. At least one type of plague, but no, his death was marked by a simple, beautiful, one-of-a-kind moon.

Gugusan walked over to me after giving them one last lashing with an eyebrow. Turning my way with a cumbrous look on his face, he asked, "You dry now?" His tone was serious. I gave him a slight smile and ran my hands down the ridges of my wings. They were drier, but still itching, and begging to be scratched. *How do you scratch wings?* I guess one feather at a time, I thought, picturing a bird on a telephone line cleaning its feathers one by one with its beak.

"Yes, I think so," I mumbled in awe of my new appendages, making myself shiver when I touched the patagium, the thin feathered fold of skin spanning the angle between my lower back to my shoulder and up to the ivory-tipped crescent aspect of my wing.

"I'm taking you to where you can wait for him. You have suffered enough today. Come," he said and gestured for me to follow him.

Shocked, unblinking, I stared at him. My heart stopped and then sped up to a frantic beat.

I surged up. "What? Are you telling me you knew all this time where Ishtar was, and that he's alive?" I flailed my arms, losing my balance, and fanning their bonfire with an enormous gust of wind from my wings. Gugusan gripped my wrists and pulled me upright.

"Spread your legs! Hunch down! Distribute your weight! Stop flailing!" My heavy wings flapped this way and that. "Calm down!" Gugusan shouted, still holding onto my wrists.

"How can I calm down when I'm ass up in the air?" I shouted.

"Close your eyes, you'll be fine!" he said in a calm tone. People around the fire scattered as plumes of red smoldering ash flew up. I closed my eyes, willing myself to surrender, *to calm the fuck down.* As I opened them again, kids with pots were hurling their contents toward me and the flames. Ice-cold water paralyzed me for a second, and I fell to the ground.

"Get up!" Gugusan said and yanked me back into an upright stance. Gasping, I looked around through ropes of hair hanging in my eyes, bewildered.

"What the fuck?" Then I remembered Ish. "Where is Ishtar?" I asked.

Not letting go of my wrists, Gugusan shook his head. "It is not what you think. Your Ishtar, he is alive. He will come for you." He snapped his head around as Elijah jumped to join us. "No, you stay here. Stay out of sight. And stop feeling sorry for yourself. You are happy here. Stop blaming Kuku!" Gugusan told my abductor under his breath while he pointed to the huts in the back, "Elijah, go away!"

I fucking heard that and understood Gugusan wanted Elijah to shut up and disappear.

"Elijah, if you mess this up, I'm going to..." Gugusan didn't finish his sentence. I huffed and puffed like a steam locomotive, ready to run all of them over. My eyes darted from one to the other, trying to figure out what they were, and were not, saying.

"What the fuck is going on? If one of you doesn't tell me now, I'm going to flatten this place until I find him! Where is Ish?" I grunted through clenched teeth, searching their faces, picking out thoughts and emotions to give me a clue. They'd spoken about me earlier, but I was too angry to tune in.

I should have taken notice.

"Elijah, go!" Gugusan pointed again to the darkness beyond our campfire.

"Kuku, come, I will tell you. Me and you walk now. You can learn to fly another day." Gugusan gave Elijah a threatening look and dragged me behind him in the direction of the mountain. I threw one last glance over my shoulder.

Elijah narrowed his eyes at me. "Like always, I don't have a choice in this matter!" he said stomping off.

"What did that mean?" I asked Gugusan.

"I will tell you as we walk, follow me," Gugusan said and thankfully, no one dared to follow us. They waved with sadness written on their faces. I was thankful for a bit of quiet, alone with Gugusan, but aside from growing wings, my honeymoon couldn't get any weirder.

As we rounded the last village huts, a massive boulder carved into a stone arch revealed a winding trail. Gugusan halted and said, "Kuku, your Ishtar, he comes almost

LOST

every day, every other day, and all the wrong days searching for you. I will make it the right day," he said, taking the apple out of the leather bag hanging over one shoulder. "I will give him this, he will know it's you, you wait for him, he will come, you go with him." I nearly fell over my feet.

"Just wait, wait one second." I ripped my wrist out of his grip. "Are you talking about Ish, before he met me?"

Gugusan's expression turned weirdly blank. He didn't have a fucking clue where I was from and my history with Ish. I rolled my eyes, gathering myself. "I know Ish was searching for me. And I know he knows me as the Peter with wings, so if I stay where you are taking me, you know he will come and find me?" I sighed, pointing this and that way.

"Da!" he agreed and smiled, exposing a radiant stack of teeth, seemingly happy not to grapple with me further. "Okay, yes I understand. But what about Ish, the Ishtar I crashed with? The one your Elijah made me leave behind. What if those creatures killed him? Elijah said they ripped him apart. That he was killed." I choked on my words.

He huffed. "Elijah naughty. Very, very bad. Very mad at you," he said, pointing at my chest.

"Me? For what? I've done nothing to him. I should be mad at him."

"Elijah, he old, he want to die, but you, you not let him die. You make him live a long, long time." Gugusan laughed. He stopped dead in his tracks, hands on his knees, he laughed so hard his voice echoed. "Kuku, you saved Ishtar today. You and Groda. You fly there, you save

365

him," he said through chuckles. "You funny, funny Birdman God."

"What the fuck is so funny? I didn't save him and I'm not a Birdman!"

"No matter, soon Ishtar he come get you. Here, you sleep." He pointed and entered into an opening, a cave. I lowered my head, then tucked my wings to follow him inside.

It was an enormous cavern. One lit torch hung waiting for us. The cavern roof was extremely high, and the cavern went deeper, further, into the mountain. As confined as I had been inside Phoenix, this was one hell of an excursion for me. "Wow! This is amazing," I said elatedly. I felt a bit better, and more positive, knowing Ish was coming.

I wasn't totally lost without him.

My eyes darted around, taking in the little stream of water, squawking red and blue parrots, tribal carvings, and rock paintings. I followed Gugusan's gaze to a large, pointy rock deeper in the cave. He smiled and we made our way over to it, where he placed the apple on top. It was some kind of rock pillar altar with more glyphs running down the sides. Gugusan gestured to where someone had made a bed on woven mats. There was a cup and a corn leaf with flame-grilled fish waiting for me.

"Thank you. Your hospitality is appreciated. I am sorry for falling out of the sky and imposing," I said, feeling shitty about my grumpiness. So far, they had done nothing but help me, except for Elijah concussing me.

"Da, I call you. You come, you go to Ishtar. No leave here. Stay," he said.

"I will, thank you." I bent my neck holding my hands in a prayer position to show respect. He grinned at me as if he was pleased. Maybe even fond of me.

"Da, you go rest. I come. I bring Ishtar."

"I promise I won't leave," I said, and he turned to leave. "Wait, what if this torch goes out? It will be dark in here."

"You have good eyes, you no need fire. But I will send a woman with more food and fire later. No Elijah. Da?"

"Oh, yes. No Elijah, I agree, thank you." I gripped my shoulders, massaging the tight muscles. The wings were heavy, and I was exhausted keeping myself upright. My lower back was numb from walking hunched to keep myself from falling backward.

"One last question. You said I saved Ishtar. Did you mean me, or was I here already?"

"Da, you bring here Elijah." He turned on his heels, and left before I could ask another question, like how did I bring him here?

Finally, I was alone, where I could think and figure this out. Only the squawking of parrots and the faint rushing of water kept me company. I appreciated the respite and solitude. After I had my meal and what tasted like freshly squeezed fruit juice, I fell to the side and dreamed of the golden apple.

Take the apple home. Take the apple home. Take the apple home. Take the apple home.

The faint echo of a robotic voice played on repeat in my dreams. As if it was whispered into my subconscious. "I fucking hear you," I answered groggily. I snuggled into the heavy bedding covering me, feeling cozy and peaceful as I drifted between sleep and wakefulness. A full bladder fully awakened me. Disoriented, I tried to roll out of bed, but couldn't. I opened my eyes—seeing darkness and smelling wet earth. *Oh right, I was in a cave. I had grown wings.*

"I need to piss," I groaned sleepily and rolled onto my stomach, crawling on my hands and knees to the wall, using it to push myself up. To my surprise, it went much easier than expected, than last night. I felt stronger. I wasn't falling backward or losing my balance while I made my way toward the light source. "This is a jungle, so it can't be difficult to find a tree to piss on," I muttered, wiping the sleep out of my eyes and checking if I was imagining walking up a steep incline. The further I walked, the more I wondered if I had come this way last night. Reaching the entrance, I stepped outside while shading my eyes. It was rocky and tall grass blew in the wind. The first thing I did was unbutton my tight-fitting jeans, but as I let my cock out, I found it had tripled in size overnight. I looked further down. My jeans were knee-high and shredded in places. "All my dreams have come true," I said as I finished pissing, then tucked my impressively large prick back into its tight confinement.

My bag. Elijah must have it. I wanted it. My teeth felt wooly. The flavor of the fish I ate last night was stuck in my mouth. I shivered. Mouth hygiene was important. I can't go kissing Ish with rotten fish breath. I needed to go get the bag.

My feet left the ground before I even realized what was happening, as I shot up into the air. My heart raced as I flapped my wings frantically, trying to control my unexpected flight. I zoomed back and forth, zigging and zagging. Exhilarated and terrified at the same time. I managed to slow down enough to touch down on the mountain's peak. As I caught my breath, I bolted up and marveled at how my wings were able to keep me aloft. I laughed with joy, dipped down, and then sailed up again, soaring higher and higher until I could see nothing but patches of land, sea, and clouds below me. The wind whipped past me, and for a moment, I felt like I was flying faster than a Bubblecar. But then reality set in and I knew I needed to figure out how to get back down safely before my wings gave out or I flew too far away from home. *I had to find my control center for them.* I closed my eyes and concentrated on where they were and what they were doing. There. I opened my eyes, looked at them, and then willed the left wing to tip down. It wasn't following my command. "Come on, how difficult can it be? It's like walking on two legs," I said before closing my eyes once more. "Come on, Peter, you can do this. You have to or you'll fly straight to the moon." I opened my eyes and tipped it again. Yes! I veered left. "Whahooooooo!" I howled and practiced a few more tricks until I was sure I had the hang of it. "Zipping and zooming! Wide circles, small circles, and a wind tunnel!" I shouted while corkscrewing through the clouds.

Ish's words rang true as I gazed out at the unfamiliar landscape. Phoenix would have been a nightmare for me. But now, I could fly. I was free and filled with hope and the possibilities of a new kind of life with him. I turned back to the mountain to retrieve my bag and toothbrush from Elijah. As I dove down, the sunlight caught on something glinting in the distance. Far across the land, past the dense jungle and flatlands, there was a glistening coastline. My eyes followed it further up until I could see the outline of steepled buildings peeking through the mist.

It was the home of those creatures.

I couldn't look away. I flew higher for a better view. A chill ran down my spine as I realized just how close I was getting. *They might see me.*

My concentration wavered. A wave of paralyzing fear washed over me. In a reckless tumble, I fell towards the earth, unable to slow myself down or regain control. Seconds before crashing into the mountainside, I caught a sudden draft. I was heading straight for the village. Panic consumed me as I frantically searched for a way to reduce speed, but it was too late. Head first, I slammed into a corn plantation and skidded along on my stomach, unearthing rows of corn like a John Deere tractor before finally succumbing to unconsciousness.

I slept for two days before I was patched up and marched back up the mountain where Gugusan told me to stay and not move.

"Not even to take a piss, Kuku!" he had shouted.

"Okay!" I had promised.

Leaning my chin into my hands, I waited in anticipation. The beat of the village drums below throbbed in sync with my tapping foot. It waxed and waned on the wind, *da, dum-dum-dum, da, dum-dum-dum.*

To distract myself, I picked up a smooth pebble from

the ground and hurled it over the edge, watching as it disappeared into the vast expanse below. At this pace, I might move a mountain in a few decades. Frustration boiled within me as I gazed across the horseshoe bay at the city perched on cliffs on the opposite ocean side. It seemed impossibly far away. Gugusan couldn't give me an exact distance in kilometers or miles, but assured me it was "very, very far." And for some reason, that was supposed to be comforting. Gugusan and his people had welcomed me with open arms, treating me like some long-lost child of a god. They were the ones who had given me my nickname, Kuku, which I learned had some sort of religious significance to this place. Ish had told me about my wings, and I held on to that memory to keep my spirits up while I waited. Kuku was apparently tied to this place in some way, and Gugusan, Elijah, and the rest of the villagers were all too eager to put an end to whatever star-crossed fate had brought us here. *All I had to do was wait.* When I'd regained consciousness earlier today, the village kids led me to an open grassland where I had taken to the sky like a fish takes to water. Walking upright with enormous wings on my back was gradually becoming easier and more graceful. Despite my mishap of plowing half their crops too early, they seemed genuinely amused by me.

There was something strange about this village. Stranger than being surrounded by people who believed in gods and magic. They all seem to be in on some secret, giggling and whispering as if I can't understand or read their minds. And while it's clear that everything has been done with good intentions, it's also apparent that Gugusan and a few other men have ulterior, more sexual motives, not towards me, but Ishtar.

No wonder Ish loved them so much.

As I tried to piece together the details of why I was here and what Ish's Fates had in store for me, I picked up another, larger pebble and flung it with all my might. It disappeared over the ridge below, leaving me alone with my thoughts. They're positive that Ish will come back, convinced that he's still alive because Groda, Elijah's friend, said so.

Now here I sit, doing as I'm told—brooding, wallowing, and asking myself endless what-ifs.

Cling-cling-clung!

That was a foreign hollow sound. Like metal. *There's no metal in this place.*

I shot up in the air and dove in the direction I had thrown the rock. Over the edge, down to the clearing. There it was—the golden ship. My heart fluttered with joy. Pure exhilaration pushed me as I dove straight for it, hoping Ish had just landed and wasn't already taking off. I landed, spread my arms and wings wide, and hugged his ship. I kissed and rubbed my cheek against it, sobbing. "I'm so fucking glad to see you. Hello, Ish, I'm here! Open up!"

Nothing.

I knocked and bumped my fists against it.

Standing back, I waited.

Nothing.

I ran my sweaty palms over the sides of the shiny ship.

The gold, the most beautiful sight. I knuckled the side of the door. "Hello!" My mouth was dry. My chest was tight. I held my breath, listening.

He'd just landed, he must have.

Should I go down to search for him or stay with the time machine?

There was no fucking way I was going to let him leave me here. My flying accident in the cornfield made me miss him once already.

Knock knock! I knocked again then yelled, "Hello!" I patted the side, looking for the door lever. It must be here somewhere. Halfway around the ship, I located it and opened the door. It slid open, revealing a pristine and empty ship. I turned, ready to jump and fly. *No!* Panic clawed at my chest, threatening to suffocate me. Doubts crept into my mind. Warnings flashed orange, dancing like flames, telling me to stay the fuck put! Staying with the ship was the best course. *Yes.* He had to come back to his ship.

My eyes followed all possible paths into the tall underbrush and further down the mountain. "Hello, Lasitor," I called.

Silence.

"I know you are ignoring me, and I don't care. I know you know what is going on. Lasitor, answer me!"

Silence.

I crossed my arms, widening my stance while I filled the small cargo area behind the seats to the brim with my wings. Their tips scraped the roof as I leaned in to check the control panel. No lights were on and I wasn't touching anything. I was still getting used to maneuvering my wings, so I tucked them closer to my butt, careful not to accidentally push or bump into something. The ship felt smaller. Why Ish built such a small ship, I would never know. I guess when you are a fourteen-year-old child, this size must have seemed big enough. The two seats seemed like they had shrunk. I couldn't believe I was sitting in the passenger seat a few days ago, feeling minuscule in comparison to Ish, with a space big enough for three to four men behind me. I guess it's not that tight if you are only one person. He had been living in here. I noted all kinds of things like cups, plates, a rolled-up mattress, and books, all neatly folded and put away, making it look like a hitchhiker's backpack after touring the Andes mountains.

After an hour of standing hunched and waiting, my irritation level reached maximum. Where was Ish and what was he doing?

He was fucking someone. I was sure of it. I decided to sit down and maneuvered myself into the passenger seat. My wings and I were everywhere.

I waited and stewed some more.

My gaze locked on the clear view of the path to be ready for when my Ish approached the ship.

CHAPTER 17
CAPTURED

"STILL NOT A GOOD MORNING, ISHTAR.

Did you know Easter Island was famous for its Birdman Cult and its massive Moai face carvings? They were also famous for their creative non-violent Birdman Competitions which helped them decide who would lead the Rapa Nui for a year.

At the start of a solar cycle, one elder would make a bid for leadership and choose a champion to honor the God Make-Make, a deity of fertility. The chosen one would then dive down the dangerous cliffs, swim to the small inlet, and wait for the first manutara egg of the season. The champion bringing back the egg would win the crown for his elder, who would then be considered the supreme ruler for one year, until the next competition.

No breakfast will be served today. Hang tight."

. . .

ISHTAR

24 970 B.C.

Hours after the crash of Ishtar and Peter

Birdman City in the jungle

AN UPROAR of ear-popping cheers followed by male grunts startled me awake. The air was thick with the smell of vanilla mixed with sweat and dust. *Was I knocked unconscious on a battleground? Where am I?*

The dull thumping of fists meeting flesh made it clear how serious my situation was. Thousands of voices bellowed in unison, a deafening noise that made my ears ring. I blinked to clear my vision and took in the scene before me.

A scuffle. Male grunts and groans coming from below my feet confused me.

The painful stinging of my skin and the stench of charred meat told me I was in deep trouble. If not for my dark complexion, I would have been charcoal by now. The last rays of the sun peeked over the horizon. The putrid stench swirled and clogged my lungs. Nausea pushed bile up into my dry throat. My chest constricted tighter each time I moved. Leaning over the side as far as my bindings allowed, I craned my neck left and right. I frowned—pulling a *what the fuck* face as I swept my gaze from far below up to where I was standing. I gasped and a coughing fit overtook me. *Too tight.* I struggled to get enough air into my lungs. I coughed, until I saw black spots, and passed out.

When I woke, the sun I feared, had set. I recovered enough to scope out my surroundings. Gray clouds cut in front of a fat low-hanging red moon resting on the mountainside. My shoulders ached and my entire body felt numb. I smelled like sweat and—*fuck no*—someone pissed on me! My arms and hands were bound at my sides. I was tied to something while standing upright. I wiggled my arms, but the more I moved, the tighter my bindings became. "Sweet Fates of all, is this what I think it is?" Suddenly, the crowd cheered louder as more thuds reverberated around me. Tremors from the thunderous scuffling shook the small footrest I was standing on. Far below my small purchase, the ground zoomed in and out of focus. Behind me, sounds like those of war horses galloping grew louder and I assumed they were getting closer. Was I tied down in the center of an arena of war? Dull thuds like the hoofs of horses sounded somewhere below. *No, they are above me.*

"Yeah, hit that cheater!" a male voice shouted from somewhere behind me.

My vision was blurry, my surroundings wobbled as if someone had drugged me or had given me a hard knock over the head. Being tied to a pole like a prisoner, I doubted the feeling was from drinking human blood in Grayrak City. I strained my neck to see as some of the dust settled. Below the small footrest I was standing on was a tumbling mass of furious, milling bodies. The speed of their movement was so fast it looked like one gigantic cloud of black crows and white doves. If I escaped these ties, I would have to jump. There were no stairs down to the ground. Escaping seemed more and more impossible. I was weakened and when I hit the ground, if I survived, running wouldn't be an option because my legs would be shattered. What had I gotten myself into this time? I closed my eyes and concentrated on freezing time. *This is my first time attempting to break free from being restrained on one side of the veil.*

Nothing happened. *Try again.* "Fuck!" I couldn't do it. I slammed my head back against the pole I was tied to, then took three deep breaths and closed my eyes again. *Nothing.*

"What have you done to me?" I asked in frustration through clenched teeth. Pain in my leg reminded me to search for the cause and to tally my injuries. Yes, blood loss would drain my strength. My pants were torn off my right leg. Someone had bandaged it. *Hmmm,* that was odd. I would have to escape by slipping out of this reality. *I'm going to go berserk once I'm free. Where's Peter?* Terror filled me as I feared losing him. I searched wildly for my sweet, white-haired mate. If they'd hurt Peter I was going to flatten this place. Murderous rage and despair heated my gut.

Grunting and loud explosive, inarticulate male load-bearing sounds came from the maelstrom below.

Whoop-whoop-whoop-whoop! Flocks of those gigantic birds were taking flight.

Loud flapping, wind slicing, and the rustling of massive black wings shot by me so fast, I couldn't believe what I was seeing and hearing. I squinted my eyes and leaned forward as far as possible. For a second there was complete silence and then a tornado, a funnel of bodies, exploded, stretching up into the sky in front of me.

"No, this can't be." I lifted my head and stared. I blinked, clearing my vision from the dusty wind. *Scarab's hell water.* My throat was dry. *This made little sense.* Total disbelief and shock hit me. *Fuck this!* Adrenalin and panic filled me. I jumped to my toes, bending my knees. Moved my shoulders up and down. Forward and backward, again bending my knees. Straining my neck, I attempted to loosen the ties around my throat.

I must escape. Where's Peter?

I was weak and didn't have the strength. I was bearing down, but nothing broke or gave way. Shaking my head in disbelief, my eyes took in the scene. My brain grappled for explanations of what I was seeing. Then it all came rushing back, the attack, the crash.

The surrounding crowds erupted into roars and shouts. Sand, leaves, and wings filled the air as men flew through the sky. I followed the fastest black-winged one, soaring through the air while white-winged ones were following on his heels. As I followed them high up in the air, a glint of light reflecting from the top of the pole I was tied to caught my attention, reminding me of what I saw earlier, stunning me into frozen silence. I blinked to refocus. *What in moon-god's name?* I was tied to an obelisk in the center of the stadium.

The strenuous moans came from flying men who bounced a ball chest to chest. It was a game of some sort. The opposing team flew and dove for it, only to bounce it high up in the air. As the ball reached maximum height and returned, the opposing team gathered below to return it. The crowd liked it. They went ballistic below me. I was so high I could see the whole arena. It was gigantic, and that told me I was high as fuck and there was no way for me to get down unless I fell to my death or someone with wings rescued me.

Barefoot males, wearing only pants of different lengths and colors. Their enormous wings were feathered—one side black and their opponents' white—like my Kuku. Shaking my head and rubbing the sand off my face with my shoulder, I looked again at where I was. "Un—fucking believable!" I muttered.

One of the players corkscrewed up and away from the mauling scrum. Not touching the ball, he used the air funnel to maneuver the ball. The crowd booed. It wasn't allowed.

"Player six disqualified," a male voice announced. "Sables are down one player," the other announcer said. They spoke the same language as Gugusan's tribe, that distinct mix of the local jungle, English, and Anunnaki dialects. I stood stock-still and tipped my head to the side while trying to hear more.

I SEARCHED for any sign to tell me where I was. The crowd was divided, black and white. A sea of black filled the pavilion on my left, while the opposing side was bathed in white that shimmered in the moonlight. The white-winged supporters' side of the coliseum cheered the announcer while the unhappy black-winged side booed the disqualification.

Why? Why was I tied and in the center of it all? I scanned the constellations positioned above me and confirmed I was on Earth but this obelisk was identical to the one on Anzulla. My insides coiled into knots. Which timeline was this? I heaved a heavy breath. The ropes around my chest constricted my ribcage. I sucked air through my parched lips, struggling to breathe.

It felt like my brain was about to explode. Blood pooled inside my upper body as the ropes tightened. I did not know when in time I was but somehow this place felt familiar. Too many coincidences.

I thought we were going twenty-five thousand years back. What were these creatures doing on Earth? Why was there an obelisk here, just like the one in Anzulla and Babylon?

Where's Peter?

I remember. I was diving for my swords, I was fighting for our lives. I was pummeled. Taken prisoner. I fought them until a fist connected with my jaw.

I had given Peter my mating bite. His taste. Sweet as honey. Then we crashed. He was hurt—I hurt him. These creatures—attacked—mauled us. *Where's Peter?*

My fucking cock couldn't wait to get sucked. *It's my fault. I'm so sorry, my Kuku, what have I done?*

My teeth chattered as I shivered. I felt cold, yet the sun was scorching hot. "Yeah, kick that fucker," one creature shouted. "The prisoner is ours!" They cheered.

"The blue demon god is ours!"

I must escape—*calm down.* Think. Break these ropes and run. Where to?

The crowd jumped to their feet. At the end of the longer walls of the amphitheater, three stone hoops were guarded on each side. One of the players lined up and kicked the ball through the middle hoop so it hit the ground bouncing, but an opponent scooped it up, trying the same move on another hoop. He failed. It seemed that the point of the game was for the players to move the ball back and forth to each other using their hips, thighs, and lower legs. Some took flight, balancing it on their muscular abdomens, passing it to another to attempt one more goal through the hoops.

The crowd raged with fists in the air. When one crea-ture intercepted the ball, the onlookers, who were clearly divided, one side white wings the other side black wings, cheered. The purpose was to keep the ball in play while throwing it through as many hoops as possible. I was enjoying the game when one Angel blew on an exception-ally large white tusk, declaring the game over. The long-drawn-out toot was so loud the spectators were silenced. It seemed the game had ended in a tie. No one seemed happy. There was no clapping or booing.

Anticlimactic after the excitement and energy a few minutes ago. They took to the skies, leaving me alone in the empty arena. The place was dark and depressing. Ineptness like I've never felt before crushed me.

What was going on?

"Here," a familiar-looking man with black wings, sleek black hair, and dark eyes, said, holding out a cup of something. Hovering next to him was a man with white wings. They both had similar strong bodies, with broad shoulders, wide chests, and defined abs. Their waists were narrow, and they had long muscular legs and human-like feet. The only non-human feature was their massive white or black wings. Like my Kuku. The feathers seemed smooth like fleecy Egyptian velvet. *Fuck admiring their feathers.*

Hostility grew in me as I remembered where I was and that cup was being pushed against my lips. "Drink!"

I turned my head, refusing the drink. It smelled sweet —like coconut water.

"Where am I and where is the man that came with me? What do you want with me?" I shouted.

"Okay, have it your way. If you aren't thirsty..." He chucked the cup's contents over his head and pinned me with a stare. It smelled delicious among the whiffs of sweat and piss. I was fucking thirsty. He shook his head like a wet dog. I licked the droplets hitting my dried lips. I should have drunk the fluid. I was dehydrated. I should build my strength.

"Untie me from this pole! You will regret this!"

"You will have to wait until the games are over and the King of kings declares us the winners," the sexy white-winged male said.

"No, the Sable players will win him, not the angels," the beautiful black-winged one said. *Angels and Sables?*

Ice-cold fear froze in my veins. What? Did he just say the King of kings? I knew only one asshole referring to himself like that. "Wait, did you just say, was it the King of kings?"

The one with white wings leaned in closer to sniff my neck. Up close I saw the deep yellow-orange flecks in his eyes. He was gorgeous. "Yes," he replied, his voice laced with a mixture of interest and seriousness. "The king is arriving soon, and the balance of our land is going to be restored. Your arrival is a sign that he is coming."

Fuck! My father used to refer to himself as Apsu, the King of kings. If he was alive, the ramifications for all of us would be catastrophic. I wondered if we'd crashed in a place where Apsu was the king and he ruled over a species the same as my Kuku.

"Untie me! Where is Peter? He is my mate, and if you hurt him—?"

Their pensive gazes met mine, their eyes filled with an intensity that made me uneasy. *I must get back to my ship and look for Peter.* With tightness in my face, I rolled my shoulders and twisted my wrists to loosen my bindings. "Where is my mate? And how do you know who I am?"

"Your mate is not here with us. You attacked us. We tied you up because you are dangerous and reckless with those swords. There is no way we're untying you. Not until we are sure you will not try to kill one of us. You will stand here and watch the King's games," the one with white wings said, sneering down his nose at me. His gaze stopped at the sight of my mouth—my fangs. The charmer, the one with black wings, had a different glint in his eyes. If I wasn't mistaken, it looked like lust.

I had to think fast and prioritize. "Listen, I'm very much a sharer. I find both of you attractive. There is no need to have a competition and fight over me. I will give myself freely, to all of you. All I want to know is—is my mate safe, wherever he is? Also, who is this King of kings? How will he arrive? From where?" I asked, already trying to probe their thoughts and compel them to loosen my ties and let me go. But they seemed unaffected. I couldn't penetrate their minds.

I must find my Peter.

I tried reading their minds, again. Nothing. They had some kind of natural block. Interesting.

The Angel rubbed his crotch, giving me a deep long glare—looking eager. The Sable chuckled and shoulder-bumped the white-winged Angel. "You are such a slut, Georgio." Now I knew the Angel's name. The Sable seemed friendlier. He turned his smoldering dark gaze back to me. The fine wrinkles at the sides of his eyes told me he laughed often. "It is said that the king will arrive with the blood moon. We've been waiting for thousands of years for it." He took a coin out of his pocket, flipped it, looked at it, shook his head, and put it back into his pocket —a nervous habit.

He continued. "We'd been watching the moon when we saw your egg, cracking the sky open." He pointed to the moon. "You are the baby god, the one born from the big egg. This is the story that our fathers told us. The king will come, there will be a game and the game determines a winner."

Relief washed over me. "So Apsu is not here, and it

still has to happen? Tell me more about this king and the moon. You know he is evil. He will destroy your home if he is coming here. Where is he? Let me go. I can help you!" My voice came out frail. I cleared my throat. "Please untie me. You can't face him alone. Untie me!" I ordered while putting compulsion behind my words. They laughed.

What was going on? Who were they? How did they know about Apsu? Did I take us to a time when Apsu was still alive? How could I get to my ship? Peter would wait for me—terrified of going outside.

My wristwatch! The one Cian had given me when we evacuated Grayrak. I checked over my shoulder. Thank the Fates I still had it on my wrist. The locator flashed a faint pink light. *Good, I know where to start searching for my ship.*

My necklace, my tick-tick thing—I let my head fall, pretending I was weeping to confirm if it was still there. *Yes, the chain, I see it.*

Now to get myself out of these bindings without falling to my death.

For the second time in my life, I knew what it felt like to be scared. The first time was when Barkor was born. Now it was for my Kuku. Nausea choked me and I dry-heaved. Yellow drops of bile fell far below, so far, I couldn't see them hit the ground.

"Tomorrow the games will begin again. We will play to celebrate the arrival of our king—until a winner is determined, you will stay here," said the friendly Sable.

"I can't stay here. The daylight will kill me!"

"We know. We know everything about you. See this." He took the coin out of his pocket again and flipped it in the air. "This coin," he pointed to the moon, "and that moon, tells me the stories are coming true. You cracked the sky open, coming down to sit your magnificent blue demon ass, down on your mountain. That moon, reveals big things..."

Out of nowhere, a fist connected with the pit of my stomach, forcing the air out of my lungs. I gasped for a breath and slumped over, spit dripping from my mouth.

"That's for stabbing my friend with your sword," said Georgio, the white-winged Angel.

Another fist connected with my jaw. "That's from Elijah. You almost killed us with your egg!" the Sable shouted.

My fangs itched to rip them to pieces. I hissed like a trapped cat.

"Who the fuck's Elijah? What's your king's name? Is it Apsu?"

I didn't have a clue—where and when was I?

I spat in a frenzy, swinging my head from side to side. "Where is Peter, and where are my swords? If Apsu is coming, we have to stop him!" I heaved air into my dried-out lungs while staring them down with narrowed eyes.

A weak growl rumbled in my chest.

They lowered a woven cloth cover over the tip of the obelisk, covering my whole body from my head to my boots.

"Your mate is with Elijah, Luci's mate," Georgia said and laughed cynically.

"Elijah?" I asked, but they were already gone. "Wait! Elijah, *that* Elijah? Come back!"

CHAPTER 18
PREPARATION IS ALWAYS SAFER THAN GETTING KILLED

"GOOD MORNING.

Rise and shine.

Did you know some people like catching fish for the sport of it? You can catch fish with your bare hands, a pole, a net, or a hook.

An interesting fact is that it once was the law that you weren't allowed to catch them using explosives.

As the matter of survival and entertainment in Anzulla stands, you should know, that you will either go hungry or get extremely bored if you don't learn how to do it.

Have a catch-and-release day!"

PETER

24 970 B.C

Thirty years after Elijah and Peter were left stranded in the jungle

Also, the day after the crash of Ishtar and Peter (Yes, two Peters are running around in the jungle)

OVER THE PAST THIRTY YEARS, Elijah and I had carved a place for ourselves among the San people. When we first arrived in the jungle from the future, from Andrew's place in 2013 A.D. I spent my days hiding inside a dark cave. It suited my mood. It became my home. The best advice I can give anyone who tries to help a dying, beaten, and bloodied illiterate next to the road, is that once you reach out to help—extend a hand—be prepared not only to lose that hand or arm but your whole life. Say goodbye to your lover, your home, and your people before you play the good Samaritan, because that helpless person who was supposed to be dying and moving on to another plane becomes your baggage, your biggest fucking headache ever.

I saved Elijah's life, Andrew prolonged it, and Elijah hates us for it. When we were busy cleaning his ungrateful ass in 2013 A.D. Elijah, like a seal from the Atlantic, had slipped out of that fucking bathtub. I was rushing after him only to find the hooligan inside the time machine pressing buttons. I'd called out to Ish while wrestling Elijah down, but the ship's door closed. In seconds, the machine had started up. The next thing, the door zipped open, and the bewildered Elijah shot out of it. I was reluctant to follow. I should never have followed, because the moment I'd stepped out of the ship, it disappeared behind me. Lasitor had dropped us on the same spot I'd waited for Ishtar not more than twenty-four hours ago. Only, it was thirty years into the past.

The only way I could calculate the date was by Gugusan's age. His soldiers found Elijah first. The Asian monk prophet ran straight down the mountain calling for help, saying he had escaped a blue demon and a fallen angel, which was me, and was chasing him. Already knowing my way around, since in my reality, I've crash landed a few days ago, sprouted wings and learned to fly by trial and error, I'd flown after him.

The first thing I noticed when I met up with the San people having a raging discussion with Elijah, was that Gugusan was much younger and when I asked, he said he had passed eighteen sun turns. That meant he was decades younger and never met me. And that's when everything made sense to me. The rock carvings I'd read after crashing into the jungle with Ishtar, the abduction by Elijah, and leaving with Ishtar. I knew then I was going to be in the jungle for more than thirty years.

So, I passed the time by chipping away the soft sandstone and enlarging the inside of my cave into a separate living, sleeping, and food storage or preparation area. My makeshift door now opens directly onto the river where I shit, wash, and gather drinking water for the day. I know. I'm as free as a bird and living like a caveman.

My in-person shit lessons started after Groda, a big friendly warrior with feminine traits, caught me squatting behind a tree—on their hunting footpath. In shock, he had shrilled like the bitch he was, and ran to the village, telling on me and how my barbaric private business was being conducted out in the open. Behind a tree. On their footpath. *Not in the river, like any normal civilized person around here.*

Decades later and they still sit around their campfires laughing at my lousy shitholes. I was the joke, a bedtime story of how the white Birdman got dragged by the tips of his wings and taught like a baby where to "kaka."

I admit now, my shitholes weren't particularly professionally dug or situated.

And that is how I found my abode, my cave, my most humble, but prime, waterfront real estate. I feared others were shitting upstream from me. So I flew a butt-clenching two miles upstream, liked the spot so much, and set up Camp Peter.

"Come down from there!" Gugusan shouted through cupped hands from below. His tribe, the San, guards the mountain. The mountain they say belongs to me. I chose this spot because it was secluded and off the beaten track, but they have worn out a trail back and forth over the years so that it has become a highway to the local airport. "Kuku, please fly me here," or, "Kuku, my child has disappeared. Could you fly up and help us search for them from the sky?" At least it kept my food supply from running out with my no-trade-no-fly rule.

"Kuku, come now, this is important!" His voice grated on my nerves along with every other thing in my vicinity. They used and mocked me, my intelligence, my hair, my wings, where I sleep, what I eat, and, of course, where I take a shit.

I sipped my love juice from a clay cup, then stretched my wings as far as I could. "Ah, that feels so bloody good," I said to myself. I shivered and closed my eyes, enjoying the sun's rays baking me dry. This was my favorite spot to sunbathe my wings. I'd built myself a private deck, high in a tree that grew out of the rocks above my cave's entrance. My pozzy has two deck chairs, a table, an umbrella, and a footstool, all carved out of wood and all traded for my one-of-a-kind transportation services. I allowed only one visitor at a time, and they could only reach me if I came to get them.

Stretched out on my deck, my wings hung over the sides. I locked my fingers and rested my chin on them while smiling lazily down at Gu. I made sure he saw my nonverbal *fuck off I'm busy* face. There was a whole congregation gathered below. They probably needed me to locate a pig or something that had run off. I turned my chin to the side, ignoring the fuck out of his sexy Aztec, Mayan, whatever he was, ass. I didn't know, and he didn't know either, what race he was except that he was Gu, leader of the tribe of the San, ancient protector of the mountain. They are superstitious, and it's going to take years to breed that out of them. *Fuck him.* Oh yes, Ish had, on multiple occasions. Sadly, before and after, Elijah and I arrived. And never when I'm here.

Or maybe they were all here to apologize. Last night, I threw a terrible tantrum. It's been thirty years since I arrived with Elijah, who accuses me of being selfish and mean. Making me the joke. If they cared about me and Ish like they say they do—and they do because we are the only subject they joked about around their fires—then they must help us. We had feelings and we aren't just here for their entertainment—let's see how much they suffer and make us laugh today. I understand they were scared he took me away from them. They believed Elijah and I came here for a reason. To live on their mountain. Ish will join us, and we will all realize this is our home. We are the Gods of the mountains—lonely and sexually frustrated.

I have been waiting for Ish to return for years. During this time, I have gone through the stages of grief over and over and over. However, the intensity of my emotions never lessens. I keep asking myself why I decided to board that ship with Elijah.

"Come down, we have news of Ishtar for you," Gugusan howled at me through cupped hands. That got my attention. My head snapped up. My display of disappointment last night had encouraged action. I pushed myself up on my haunches, jumped, and glided down, landing in front of him and his followers. I knew I was acting out. But fuck, any civilized human regressing thousands of years back in time and being told they are stupid would do the same.

Gugusan held a wooden sword up and thrust it my way. "Time for you to learn how to fight."

"I don't fight. Not interested. Tell me about Ishtar or go away." I spun around on my heels, making a big show of it by blowing crap in his face. Then I crossed my arms and waited, trying my best to intimidate them—this place had stunted my emotional growth.

"You will need this, take it!" Gugusan said.

"I told you, I don't fight or hunt, nor do I work the land and prepare food. I run a business."

"Doesn't matter if you have wings, Birdman. You still need to know how to fight. And you have a short time to learn because Ishtar needs your help. I'm helping you do that without getting killed. Preparation is safer than getting killed," he said sarcastically, and the others grunted a "da," in agreement as if those were the wisest words ever.

I blinked, and then it registered. I jumped and landed inches from him. "Did you say you found him?"

He stepped back and held the sword up.

"Take it and practice," he barked, his voice loaded with determination and conviction. But I refused, clenching my fists. My eyes bored into his and Gugusan let out an exasperated sigh. "Okay, Groda saw him being taken prisoner, so he came searching for you and Elijah, but we can't find Elijah. So now we are here telling you," he growled, then relaxed his imposing stance, his concern for me seeping through the cracks of his hardened facade. "That's the truth, I promise you. But, I can't send you there without some defensive moves. Before you say you don't fight or hunt, please do this for me. If something happened to you and I never did my best to prepare you, I would never forgive myself."

"Let's go, then!"

"Say thank you to Groda first," he said, straightening up. I snarled at him.

Eager for praise, Groda stepped closer, but I didn't give him a chance to say a word. "For what? Tell me Gugusan or I swear I'm going to explode. I'll level your precious mountain!"

"Groda snuck into the Birdman City, risking being caught. He overheard guards placing bets on who was going to win him. They are having a big tournament and festivities, and Ish is the prize," he interrupted me.

I pointed my finger at him and opened my wings like an upset umbrella parrot. Gugusan didn't look deterred. "It's been decades since he came here looking for me. Now he's started searching other places because you and Elijah thought it was funny to let him search the jungle in circles for me."

Groda tiptoed closer and spoke in a high-pitched surly voice. "Yes, but it is not my fault. Each time he comes here, you are off sulking, sunning, and cleaning your pristine white feathers."

"I am not!" I said, looking Groda up and down.

He retreated a few steps while chuckling. "That's what you get for lying to Elijah. Be glad I'm helping you now," he said. He is best friends with Elijah. They have been unforgiving and outright awful for years because I saved his life and didn't give him his chance to meet his maker.

Gugusan threw the wooden sword onto the ground. I stared at it while processing the news. "What the fuck do I know about swords? I was a scientist, for fuck's sake. The sharpest instrument I ever handled was a scalpel. They are warriors. Why can't they come with me? And why don't we go now?"

Thwack! Thwack! Oomph! Gu's frustration with me was showing.

I stumbled away, clutching my bruised ribs. "You asshole, you hit me over the head and stabbed me!"

He turned to me, his eyes filled with determination and a hint of desperation. "First, say thank you to Groda for risking his life."

"Groda didn't risk his life. He can't get enough of sucking black Birdman's cock! He didn't go to the Birdman City under duress, he went for pleasure!"

"Once you try it, you will want nothing else," Groda said, licking his lips and crossing his arms.

"You and Elijah are two peas in a pod. You're downright liars. You like, what's his name?" I snapped my fingers and dove into his mind for an answer, "Luci. You visit him for the fun. There's no risking your life to do that, is there?" Groda stood wide-eyed, biting his lip.

"Say thank you and then, say please, Gu, can you show me some moves and help me sneak inside to break Ishtar out?" Gugusan said.

I played along, matching his intensity with a warped smile. "Please, oh mighty Gugusan of the San, and thank you, Groda, for risking your life," I said, drawing out each word, my voice laced with sarcasm.

Groda clapped his hands, bouncing up and down on the balls of his feet, welcoming more men joining us. Like I said, anything involving me being humiliated was entertainment.

"If we are lucky tonight, you won't need to fight," Groda said, batting his eyelashes.

"Yes, Ishtar must be weak and injured, otherwise he would've escaped already," Gugusan said, racking up my nerves and pushing my determination to do this up to one hundred percent.

"He will need a Birdman's help. They have him high, high, high," Groda said, his voice climbing higher, higher, and higher, grating my resilience down to non-existent. My worried expression stunned him. His eyes narrowed briefly before a hint of understanding crossed his face.

Out of nowhere, Gugusan hacked at me. I jumped away, but he got hold of my ankle, pulling me down so I landed on my ass. I rolled out of his reach, grabbed my sword, and bounced up, waving the piece of wood at him like swatting flies.

"Come on, old man." I mimicked a warrior stance. I was waving my sword clumsily and in such an uncoordinated manner it slipped from my hand, clattering to the ground. Gu, Groda, and the rest of the warriors forming a circle around us, cringed as one.

I flushed with embarrassment. "Oops, second try," I said, catching it after someone in our audience kicked it closer. I grasped the wooden sword tighter, my heart pounding as I faced my pretend enemy. I must take this seriously if I wanted to save Ish.

"Why aren't we using actual swords?" I asked, gesturing to their Obsidian-edged clubs.

The group of warriors exchanged glances, their expressions a mixture of amusement and disbelief. "Because only true warriors can, and you, Kuku, are far from being a warrior."

Feeling like a lazy, rebellious child, I refused to back down. "Not when Ish's life is at stake," I said, then steadied my grip and doggedly waved the sword. "I will prove to you that you are mistaken. I will save Ish." I gnashed my teeth in determination.

"Very well," Gugusan said, nodding to his soldiers, impressed by my turnaround. "Let's see what you can do. Prove yourself. If you are ready, you may have a real blade, but for now, you can't be using real blades, you would cut your hands and fingers off," he said, and all of us knew that it was the truth.

"Again," he said after hours of nonstop practicing. My arms were numb and the fake sword was so heavy in my hand that my fingers didn't want to grip it anymore.

"Again!" he shouted another hour later. I was on my knees and then, like an old tree, I fell forward face-first into the sand.

"Tonight you save Ishtar. You never say again that I don't care about you, okay?" he said, referring to my outburst last night. Not sweating as if he'd never lifted his sword today, he walked away.

"Why don't you and your soldiers go get him?" I muttered into plumes of dust.

"Because they tied him up where none of us can go! Groda will take you, but you have to free Ishtar on your own," Gugusan said over his shoulder.

"Tisk, tisk, tisk. There are two types of warriors, those who are like lions and those who are like jackals." Groda yipped. "You are not a lion or a jackal. You are like a snapping turtle. Tonight, you have to be all those things—brave, sneaky, quiet, and fast."

"So a lion with wings and feet of a jackal?" I asked,

pushing myself up to stand. "Thank you, Groda," I grunted.

Groda nodded. "Tonight, after the first star, we will meet. We can fly there," he said, meaning I was flying while he hung onto my ankles.

When Groda left, I undressed and walked into the river to wash off the sweat and grime. My Ish was here, and his life depended on me. After my wash, I got dressed, quickly dried my wings with a few vigorous shakes and spins, and went to get Groda.

"For the thousandth time, Kuku, we will reach the city when we go over that last hill."

"Yes, but when will that be? You know I never fly this side of the valley. Gugusan warned me many times over, and I wasn't particularly brave enough to go on excursions to be taken prisoner and fucked up the ass by sex-crazed Birdmen."

"Before the sun comes back up, a half a sun turn, we will be there. You are a big and tough Birdman God. I can't understand why you say you are afraid of them. Not all of them want sex all the time."

"That's not what I heard, and I'm convinced that's why you and Elijah can't stop hanging out with tall, dark, and beautiful."

"See, you think he is beautiful. I think so, and Elijah as well. He knows Luci the best." The wind blew Groda's chuckles away. Strands of hair swirled around his face. Strong gusts of wind casting inland to the mountain tops made it challenging to fly against its force. I was skilled in flying and carrying passengers, but usually, I flew only short distances. We'd been flying low, skimming over the treetops for what felt like several hours, and I didn't want to stop to rest, because we had a considerable distance to go. I'd been preserving my strength by flying slower so that I didn't fall dead from exhaustion before we reached Ishtar. I wished now I had come with Elijah and Groda before, even if it was just to see the city. At least I would have known what route to take when we escaped.

"Look, there it is," Groda shouted two minutes later. His ability to estimate time and distance stank. He was hanging onto my ankles and not able to point, but I did see it. Like bird's nests, the castle draped down the cliffs, over-hanging a massive white sandy beach below. Thousands of little steepled roofs covered tall towers reaching into the sky. Large winding platforms lay like runways on a battleship.

"Thank the Fates, Groda. Let's stop and rest so I am fresh to fight if I have to." I descended and swooped low so he could land without breaking his legs.

Thump-thump! He drop-rolled as I landed, folded, and tucked my wings to make myself smaller. "We will enter on foot. It will be easier to hide from them," he whispered. I copied him by huddling behind bushes and boulders.

"I agree," I said, short of breath. With the sun almost down, the light shone brightly over the glassy surface of the ocean—reminding me to drink something. "Let's refuel."

"What?" he asked perplexed.

I wiped the back of my hand over my dry, parched lips. "May I have water?"

He nodded and smiled as he flung his buckskin purse over his head. "Oh, yes, sure, Kuku."

I watched as he wrestled a water skin out of it. "And one of those bananas," I said, holding out my hand while surveying the entrance of the city gates.

"You make the strangest names for things." His shoulders shook as he suppressed his laughs. I rolled my eyes. "Ba-na-na-na-na-nas," he chortled.

"That is the name of that fruit. Stop saying I make stuff up." I spoke easily and in full sentences, not heaving for air anymore. "Why do they have roads and gates? They don't walk."

"It's old, very, very old," he said, pointing with his thumbs behind him.

"Did the San and the Birdmen lived together a long time ago?" I asked as we emptied the water pouch and finished the bananas.

"Maybe, but I heard all kinds of people lived here." He put the water pouch away and repositioned his purse around his hips.

I pushed him ahead of me. "I will ask Gu about that later. It's time to go."

"Come, Kuku, follow me, keep low."

CHAPTER 19
RESCUED

"WHAT A GLORIOUS EVENING, ISHTAR.

Did you know there once was a time when you owned a safe and had lost the combination code to open it, that you could have located and contacted the manufacturer to help you unlock it? They would have kept a record of the combinations associated with your specific safe, and to retrieve the combination, you would have needed to provide the manufacturer with the serial number. Once they had verified your ownership, they would have provided the combination for you to open it.

Did you also know an escape artist is someone who entertains others by getting out of handcuffs, ropes, chains, trunks, or other confining devices, or a prisoner who has a reputation for being able to escape confinement?

Unfortunately, you aren't an escape artist or have a serial number.

Hold on, help is coming!
Hope you have a freeing day."

ISHTAR
24 970 B.C.
The day after the crash with Peter
Birdman City

STRUNG UP LIKE A FLAME-GRILLED CHICKEN, I had watched yet again, my fate being undecided. Today's tournament ended in another tie, and I thought this was one massive waste of time—while I died a slow death.

Dying and waiting for the arrival of Apsu.

Like yesterday, the games ended, and I was left alone to suck the night air through from inside a straw-woven sack. It had a loose weave and while I watched the game through it, my skin blistered in the scorching rays of the sun. I welcomed the cooling night air carrying the mist blowing inland from the ocean. The air was fresh, but I also tasted something different, lingering in the atmosphere.

Someone new was watching me.

"Hello, I'm thirsty!" I shouted and waited. Relief washed over me as the wind moved around me. Then, a flash of light, sound, and fresh air replaced the horrid smelling covering as someone tore it from my body.

Pinpricks of stars and burgundy moonlight illuminated me and the arena below, spotlighting my tormented captive state. Tied up, stuck high in the air, with nowhere to go. I had to give my captors credit. I had no wings, so breaking free and flying off wasn't an option. No, my Anunnaki ass was stuck to the obelisk. I was in forced proximity, or some kind of offering, to the Fates. They've been speaking non-stop to me while I struggled against my restraints. I couldn't help but think of how pleased my father would have been to see me in this pitiful state. Weak and slowly withering away.

Last night, Luci had checked up on me. I gazed around, searching and hoping it was him. He'd brought me water, and I thought I tasted Loursveto sap. I'd asked him if it was the mystical flower juice, but he never confirmed.

Was it him? Was someone here to help me? I hope they brought me something to drink. Maybe not to help me, but to keep me alive. Prolonging my suffering as they tortured me in my weakened and blood-starved state?

My head rolled heavy and uncoordinated over my shoulders. A flimsy voice croaked out of my throat, "Hello?"

I waited, listening. "Who's here? I can smell you?"

The empty seats of the pavilions swallowed my words. I tipped my head downwind to hear better. The white noise of the rushing ocean waves in the distance masked the subtle sounds of heartbeats and breathing. I strained to differentiate between imagination, visions, and what or who was here with me.

Electrified, the tiny hairs bristled on the back of my neck. My rear warmed as if I was standing in the rising morning sun. I scraped my reserve energy and focused all my senses, but my brain processed the information sluggishly.

It sounded like I was alone, but it felt like someone was behind me—or was that below me? *I was being watched.*

"Ishtar, your time to choose a home has come?" The voice of the Fates startled me. They've been keeping me company and talking in riddles. I was so done listening to them.

"Tell me where my Kuku is. My home is where he is. Is he safe, or? I will gladly follow him into death, but if he is alive, tell me where he is and help me escape," I said, but I knew it was futile. I've asked for their help all day. If they wanted to help me, they could have done so already.

I tuned them out as I probed and listened beyond their yapping, which came from the very obelisk I was tied to. There was definitely movement and more than two heartbeats nearby.

The air stirred. Suddenly, the wind rushed by me confirming my suspicion. I have grown accustomed to the sound of flapping wings. "Luci?" I called, but it came out as a whisper. There it was again, the unmistakable whoop-whoop of wings.

Beyond the arena, male voices conversing and laughter drifted closer. The recent presence hovering behind me fluttered away. Now I was sure it wasn't Luci because he wasn't one for tormenting me or hiding from his people. This was someone else. I kept still, trying not to draw attention to myself and whoever was here helping me.

Anxiety and a sense of impending doom overcame me as I imagined another day in the hot sun. Each inhale was a struggle to stay sane enough to find Peter.

"Ishtar, listen to me," the Fates yapped. I was like a disrespectful child—hungry, unafraid, and pissed off with a short attention span. I was dying, and they wanted to talk.

"Leave me alone. Apsu is coming. My mate has been taken. Untie me!"

"Ishtar, you don't know where you are, do you? You've changed your future. You've gone back in time and changed your future and you've been asked whether you are sure and you've been warned," the Fates said to me in that deep, monotonous voice. It had moved into the number one slot of what is irritating Ishtar to death today. Literally.

I wasn't claiming responsibility for something I did for others. I lifted my head, taking a deep breath to repeat myself. "We had this conversation already. I told you, when Cian and his brothers showed up on the moon, I offered my help as you told me to do. I prioritized Barkor, the children, the humans and their leaders, and the whole bloody Earth, not myself!"

"Yes, but you took the apple to the wrong place and time. You wanted a new start, a new beginning, with your children—forever. Yet, all you've done was put your future behind you, and removed them further from me." They hissed like a pit full of snakes. *Was that static?*

"Ishtar, you must correct this path. If you don't, this world will replace the one you have created. Apsu will come for you and your children. I'm getting weaker. My energy is being depleted by attempting to convince you."

"How can the Fates get weak from talking? Who the fuck are you?"

"The knowledge inside that apple, you've taken it to the wrong place and time."

"Fuck the blazing hell off!"

"Do you remember when you were a boy? I doubt you've forgotten your first flight onboard your machine?" they asked condescendingly.

I lifted the corner of my mouth and snarled. "Fuck off. If you are the Fates, help me!" I said, wondering if I was talking to myself. Maybe the voice I heard was only in my head. *I'm deliriously hungry.*

"Do you remember the place and time Lasitor had taken you?"

"No!"

"Yes, you do. It was cold. Remember when you switched your ship on for the first time? What was the one thing Lasitor said? What were his first words?"

"I can't remember anything other than Peter and his blood right now," I muttered, letting my head fall and swinging it from side to side.

"I'll tell you. First, he thanked you because he thought he was forgotten inside the wreckage. He thought he was separated, forgotten, and alone for eternity."

"Hmmm?" A whiff of that smell from earlier woke me up from my trance. "What?"

"He said he'll repay you."

"Who's there?" I mumbled, ignoring the Fates.

"Lasitor had taken you to a time and place. He told you to bring something there. Do you remember?" The Fates pried it out of me, and a spark of something, a memory, flickered in the recesses of my mind.

"I can't fucking think. I'm trying very hard to stay conscious here."

"Exactly, I'm keeping you awake. Tell me, do you remember?"

"I fucking remember, yes!"

"Tell me."

I breathed loudly in and out, and in and out.

My eyes snapped open. I stuttered an answer, "P-p-p-pups." *Yeah, I did remember.* "It was three Anubis pups..." I cried as a flicker of memories hit me. A flash of realization ignited hope inside me. "Yes, oh my dear Fates, those puppies, I was so sad about leaving them there."

"Yes, Ishtar, you saved the last Anubis. You saved all those humans. If it wasn't for you, Phoenix would never be. If you don't bring the apple to the correct time and place, Peter, Andrew, Cian, Barkor, Eryn, and Ivan will never be born. That includes every other child born in Phoenix. Apsu is wiping away Lasitor's footprint in that reality. The work you have set in motion will disintegrate into oblivion. You've erased thousands of years of history in the future. Do you understand?"

"But I remember that my sisters said they would bury the apple. That's why I took it to them. If I didn't, how would those Disciples otherwise experiment?"

"I'm going to spell this out, slowly. You remember it because you had taken the apple there. If you didn't take the apple to Babylon, then you would never have remembered your sisters saying that."

"No!"

"Yes, the Disciples, or anything Lasitor has touched, would disappear. The Zelk. Everything which was about to be as it should be, is being erased as we, here in the past, on this timeline, slowly creep into the future. Rewriting it without the apple. Without it, your legacy is hanging on a choice you would have to make. Because you switched the timelines!"

Trembling with exhaustion and pain, I struggled to maintain my footing on the small footrest. Despite the throbbing in my head, I mustered enough strength to ask the questions that had been nagging me. But out of respect for what I thought was my deity, I never asked. "Why me? Why my children?" My words resounded in the arena, bouncing back to mock me. Reminding me not to draw attention to myself. With each passing second, my grip on the footrest weakened, threatening to send me tumbling into a deadly noose if I couldn't hold on any longer.

Silence.

Faint whispers coming from below me distracted me. I had forgotten to lower my voice. Someone was here, behind and below me, and I was tired of listening to the Fates. Whoever they were.

Maybe by some miracle, I thought, maybe my stubborn Kuku was here.

At this moment, nothing else mattered except knowing he was safe. If the Fates helped me escape and I survived the fall, I couldn't waste time on meaningless tasks like going to Phoenix and admitting defeat. I didn't want the responsibility anymore.

My body twitched and quivered. I was so cold, so weak, and so tired.

"Don't you see, look at me, look at the state I'm in," I blabbered, "I don't have the time or strength to save Phoenix."

Silence.

"Answer me!"

"Ishtar, you are special. Remember when you were alone and afraid? You saved Lasitor. You are a savior and you walk across time. Pull your head out of your ass and see what's going on around you. You've seen and moved between the places where time doesn't reach. You can't see eternity because you are not stepping back far enough to see it. As you said the Anunnaki prayer, you asked for this. Didn't you say those words?"

"*Free my mind so I serve not only in my dreams but by the blessings in my existence outside my narrow-minded trap*," I recited.

"Why do you think I told you to jump for others and not for yourself? You and your children are mine, as I am yours. You were told to stop messing with the timelines. Why do you think your ship was pre-programmed?"

"My father crash landed in Babylon!" I rasped.

"I wish you'd listen to yourself. Stop trying to fix things and stop doing it yourself. You had taken the apple to the wrong time and place and you shifted timelines. I told you to take the apple back home. Home is where your children, your new beginning, and your obligations are. Where

Lasitor is. Your mate will never be born. If you stay in Anzulla, once you reach the future, Phoenix will never be. You threw away your destiny. Both of you did—stealing the apple and taking it to Babylon. You threw it away for what? For an orgasm and a mating bite in the jungle?"

"Yes, he is my mate, and you should've fucking known. We suffer without each other. Why did you make it so we feel like dying without each other?"

"Because how else would you stay together for thousands of years? Of course, the glue that holds you together should be unbreakable."

I cried, but no tears streamed down my face as I uttered, "He probably believes I am no longer alive."

"Do what you will! It is your choice. It's either goodbye forever to Anzulla or Phoenix. For you, me, and your children."

I grated my teeth. "What are you saying about Anzulla? The place was destroyed!"

"Open your eyes, Ishtar, where do you think you are? You traveled through time and you don't know where you are? Your time compass around your neck is meant to tell you where you are."

"My tick-tick thing?" I asked.

"Yes, Lasitor had taken you to Anzulla, the place and time your father left behind. Your father destroyed everything and then traveled into the future, to Babylon."

"Since the day you climbed into your machine and delivered those Anubis pups, your timeline had split and separated from Apsu's. To make matters worse you split it again in 1968. Then Andrew and Juandre changed history when Andrew killed the whole Disciple of the Anunnaki American chapter in 2014, and then you came along and helped Cian escape the Zelk, by moving the Horizon and shuffling the mess further, only to bring the apple to Apsu. The apple is meant for your timeline. But you took it back. To your father's timeline. Not yours."

"You are using me. Like my father did!" I shouted. My head was pounding, and my shoulders, arms, and legs were numbed by the tight ropes.

Their voice screeched back at me. The high frequencies sliced through my brain and pierced my eardrums.

"Get yourself out of this mess. Do it now! Lasitor told you to stop jumping timelines. This is your last chance." There was a finality to their words—a blessed silence.

"Fuck!" I spat and wiggled my shoulders up and down. Loosening my ropes was futile. "Motherfucking, fuck, fuck, fuck!"

I was desperate for a miracle. The Fates could've at least untied me. I let my head fall in defeat. Frustrated and hopeless.

A cool wind rustled behind me, ripping me from my delirious state. "Why is everyone coming up from behind me?" I sputtered, too weak to raise my heavy head.

"Ish. Ishtar. Ishtar, open your eyes. It's me." Soft hands stroked my face.

"Hmmm?" I frowned, tilting my head to the side, and raising my eyebrow to pull open my sticky eyelids.

"Ish, it's me, Peter. Open your eyes. Please open your

eyes." The voice whisper-whined and cracked with emotion. Loaded with sadness.

Soft hands lifted my head and wiped my face with a wet and cool cloth. Removing the crusts of blisters from my eyes. I squinted, searching the darkness.

I tore my tongue away from where it was stuck to the roof of my mouth. "Peter, is it you?" I croaked. Wind moved. Wings rustled. "Are you here to save me?" My hair was everywhere, and it felt like I was looking through fogged-up glass. Were the hands and cooling cloth my imagination? Then, out of the darkness the outlines of Peter's angelic face appeared before me and he looked magnificent and worried. Big white wings protruded from his back and reflected silver in the moonlight. He was bare-chested, muscled, and much bigger than I remembered.

The piercing, icy blue in his eyes shattered my destitute status and a desperate whimper of relief escaped my throat. Unsure if he was real or not, I couldn't believe he was hovering before me. His cool hands cupped my cheeks gently as I weakly blew my hair out of my face to get a better look at him. His wild blond locks were tousled and disheveled, giving him an electrified, untamed appearance. But it wasn't just his appearance that had changed. His once boyish face now twisted into a worried scowl with a deep furrow between his brows, showing the anger and frustration he carried within. "My Kuku, my Peter, it is you?" I asked, careful not to sound too elated in case it was trickery. I couldn't lift my arms to embrace him, and I wished I could. Even if it was for the last time.

Just to touch his face. That would be enough before I succumb to eternal darkness.

Still scowling, arms crossed, obsidian sword in one hand, he spoke in a low tone, fuming. "Look how fucking miserable you look. I'm going to kill them. Look at you—a fucking kebab!"

Swearing like a warrior on a mission, his concern and anger fed my hopeless soul. He cared. He came for me. He was alive, and he was not smiling. He flung his arms around my neck, pulling himself tightly against me and wrapping both of us in his colossal clean-smelling wings. They smelled like home. I lay my head for a second in the crook of his neck and rubbed my nose into his soft long hair. I felt warm and safe. And so loved. My eyes stung, but no tears leaked from them. I swear I heard his blood rushing through his carotid artery as he squashed his neck against my lips. It thumped loud, *lub-dub-lub-dub*.

"Take blood from me." Peter threw his hair to the side. Like a baby breastfeeding, he took my head in one hand and pressed my mouth against his neck. I didn't hesitate. My fangs sank into his soft flesh. I punctured the thick artery below the pulse point. Warm oxygen-rich blood flowed into my mouth and down my throat. I gulped his delicious, sweet nectar. His lifeblood—rushing, burning, reviving, instantly warming my belly. Five big drawn-out slurps later, I licked and closed the tiny holes.

"Thank you," I whispered, licking my lips, already feeling them heal. My body tingled, and my extremities warmed as life was being restored. The feeling in my arms and legs returned and the blisters on my face healed.

"You should have taken more," Peter said.

All kinds of emotions, like thankfulness, love, embarrassment, guilt, and longing, crushed me. "No, it's enough, thank you, my Kuku."

My eyeballs felt less like rocks in my skull. "You grew your wings, and I missed seeing it. No wonder you never wanted to tell me," I said between sniffles and chuckles. He smelled like determination, smoke, and bravery. I inhaled his scent deep into the corners of my lungs.

"We have to get you out of here. We have a small window of opportunity. The Birdmen are in their dining halls, having dinner. I thought you were dead. I thought I was doomed to live here all alone," he whispered. His body trembled against me as he fumbled with my ties.

I turned my head up to see his face. "I thought you were awaiting me on the ship. But, look at you. So majestic, so strong. I should never have taken my eyes off the instrumentation. It's my fault we crashed! I should have waited until we landed."

"It's my fault too. I distracted you. First, let me untie you. Hold on to me as soon as your arms are loose. Lean against me. I will fly you down. Don't move your feet."

"Yes, please, I love you," I blurted.

Gazing at me, he placed his hands on each of my hips, supporting me. "I love you too. I missed those yellow eyes," he said, and I let my head fall in shame.

"I messed up, Peter."

He lifted my chin. "Not just you. I heard everything the Fates said to you. First, let's get you out of here, then we can talk. Okay?"

"Okay, my Kuku," I blubbered. I was a mess. "My arms are numb. You have to catch me," I said, feeling my chest expand as the ropes were cut. For the first time in two days, I took a deep breath.

"I got you." Seconds later, Peter scooped me up and carried me in his arms. He flew out of the stadium and deposited me beyond the city walls, where he hugged me anew.

He gripped my chin and kissed my healing lips. My chest rumbled, it was a purr, like a cat, like I wanted him for a whole different reason. But he pulled away, broke the kiss, and then started rubbing life back into my arms and legs.

"You are wounded?" he asked, inspecting my bloody bandaged leg.

"It's nothing." I heaved a short painful breath. Strung out, I let my head topple back.

"We must go now!" he said after kissing me again.

"We need help. Did you hear the Fates?"

"I did. I waited until I was sure I heard every word. I don't trust that voice."

"I'm done jumping around and fixing shit for a deity that doesn't know what they are doing…"

"Let's get you to my home to recover and regroup, then we can talk."

"Na-ah-ah!" a deep voice rumbled, interrupting me. Georgio lifted his cane to strike. "Who said you have permission to untie him?" he asked Peter. "Are you helping him escape?" I didn't have time to assess. In a split second, a tall, naked-chested Luci, shoved Peter and me to the side. We toppled over, arms, legs, and wings flailing.

Luci wasn't fast enough. The oncoming swinging weapon hit me right on my knee, fracturing it. Excruciating pain shot through my leg and up my spine, as my knee shattered. "Fuck! That hurt!" I shouted, grabbing my knee.

"What are you doing, Luci? We can't let them escape." the Angel protested. His yellow eyes were dark and wild.

"Go!" Luci said as he unarmed the Angel about to bludgeon my leg further. Peter joined Luci and tackled him to the ground. With Peter's blood in my stomach, and my strength returning, there was only one thing left to try —escape.

"They are not our enemy!" Luci grunted.

Just as Peter's hand was within my reach, I took hold of it and pulled him with me behind the veil that separated time from reality. Fuck! I should have frozen time, I thought.

Peter was saying something, but it was difficult to decipher. It was as if he was shouting from the far end of a tunnel. I pressed my ear against his mouth. "Go to the mountain, to Gugusan!" He pointed to my smashed kneecap.

"It's okay, we aren't walking, we are drifting. It's going to hurt as soon as I put weight on it. Hold on." I checked my wristwatch for my ship locator and my tick-tick thing around my neck. The pink light told me we were moving in the correct direction. I squinted my eyes to see the golden glow of my ship calling to me. I gripped Peter's hand tighter—as long as I held onto him, I wouldn't lose him.

"There it is!" With each yard, the humming resonating from the time machine grew louder. It entangled my mind, the whispering and swirling realities around us felt like we were going to drift away. I focused on the ship calling to me.

Dark silhouettes of Angels and Sables hovered like fruit flies around my ship. Some lay sprawled out under the trees, others lay wings open in the grass basking in the moonlight. They were camping out and guarding it.

"We're trapped. They're waiting for us!" Peter's voice echoed through the void, joining the forgotten whispers of times past. "Let's go home, to the mountain," he urged and pulled my arm, but I couldn't abandon my ship.

My grip on Peter's hand tightened. "We need a diversion, enough time to find the door, open and close it. Those three slow stairs are going to cause problems." We scanned the area frantically, searching for anything we could use as a distraction in our desperate race against time itself.

"I told you to rip those stairs off. There won't be enough time to get inside and shut the door!" Peter shouted, and he was right. Those pathetic slow-moving stairs have to go!

"If they see us, they will swarm to us. We have to move to a spot, lure them away by pretending we are hiding, and then reappear at my ship's door."

"Okay, sounds like a plan." Peter's voice vibrated in the maelstrom of the strands as realities tornadoed around us.

I kept my concentration on the one with the Sable and the Angel busy in a heated argument.

"You're the one who shut the door, now we can't get inside," the Sable accused, poking his finger into the Angel's chest. The Angel swiped away his hand. "If you hadn't touched those shiny knobs, none of this would have happened," he retorted. I moved past them and entered back into the timeline behind boulders on a small hilltop. Far enough to make them think we were running and hiding.

Peter looked electrified. A slight glow haloed around him and his long blond hair fluttered and waved around his head. My thick braids were less so when residual energy clung to me.

"We have to call for them now," I urged, my voice weak. I leaned against a withered tree stump to support my weight. Peter's eyes darted around in urgency. Counting, calculating, planning, and finally focusing on me. My body trembled from the strain of gravity. I waved my arm and shouted, "Helloooo, you sons of bitches!" Peter threw an arm around me to hold me up. I struggled to balance myself with my throbbing leg. I do heal faster than humans, but the injuries were raw. Shattered bone had cut through my skin. It would need much more blood than just a few sips to recover from this.

"Your leg, you are bleeding," Peter said. Blood dripped down my lower leg and over his hands. He ripped a piece of cloth from my shirt and tied it above the wound to slow the bleeding. I still had to make it back to our ship, board it, and take off before our enemies caught up to us. Every second felt like an eternity as we waited.

"They saw us!" Peter said as hundreds of Angels and Sables swung around, facing us.

For a second they hovered in place, until one of them shouted, "He escaped, catch him!" Then they descended. Peter supported me as we mock ran away, hunched, and disappeared behind the boulder.

I clutched his hand. "Ready?"

As a team, we slipped out of reality and made our way back down the hill in silence, eager to escape the horde. Once we reached the door, Peter opened it, pushed me inside, and ripped those useless three stairs off their hinges. I crawled on my elbows, and pulled myself into my seat, just as my Kuku fell into his.

I started the machine. "Lasitor, take us to Gugusan," I said and locked the dial in place, so we didn't jump to Phoenix—not yet. "Take us to the mountain where we usually land."

"Good thinking, sir, I'm glad you are back. I auto-shutdown when the strangers came on board. My CPU is damaged. I'll try to reboot," Lasitor replied as the door closed.

"No! Just go, no rebooting. There is no time. When we are safe on the mountain, then you can reboot."

"As you say, Ishtar," Lasitor replied. I pressed the Go button over and over to get us the fuck back to Gugusan.

"I should have ripped those three stairs off a long time ago," Peter scoffed as he strapped me and then himself in. Feathers flew everywhere and his scent filled my nostrils. "I told you years ago to remove those moth-erfucking steps, I told you, didn't I?" Peter joked. I didn't reply while I marked the time and place where we were now.

"I hear you," I muttered, tapping the console while outside the thumping on the ship increased.

"If one stupid ass Birdman finds the door lever, we are fucked," Peter said, watching the door. "Get us out of here." Just then, one peeked through the tinted window and smiled at me. I didn't waste time to see what happened next. I pushed the accelerator and the machine vibrated. If one was hanging on, chances were that more would join him. Peter middle-fingered him.

"They can't see inside." I slammed the Go button and pushed the stick forward. "Thank fuck!" I sighed, relieved the ship was moving.

In seconds, we were in the clouds, looking down at the jungle. I felt strange. Foreboding warnings gnawed at my insides. Turning in my seat, I searched the small cargo area. For what I didn't know. Nothing maybe? My heart rate somewhat returned to normal. White light surrounded us for a few seconds and then we landed with a thump and a bump.

"Lasitor, please check outside. Are we on the moun-tain, are we alone?"

"Yes, all alone. We re-entered a few days into the future so they couldn't have seen where we landed. But, I can't take off and fly again. That was my last reserve."

"What? Are you sure?"

"I must reboot, now," he said as the door slid open and

all the lights died down. We sat in silence, catching our breath in the dark.

Peter put his hand on my lap. "I'm sorry, Ishtar. I should never have taken Mika's apple. I thought it was yours," he whispered.

"But it's not," I said, meeting his bright blue gaze.

"Yours or not, I understand now that it could be used as a weapon when it's in the wrong hands. I've had lots of idle time to think about it. The DNA calculations and genome mapping create and splice artificial protein structures that metabolize nutrients and synthesize new cellular constituents, as well as DNA polymerases and other enzymes that make copies of DNA during cell division. Is dangerous in an evil warmonger's hands." Peter rambled in an advanced scientific language I didn't understand. We unbuckled, and I waved him ahead.

He exited by squeezing through the small door and jumping to the ground. Then it was my turn as he reached for me and helped my shaky adrenalin-fueled body down as if I weighed nothing. He spread his wings so wide that their shadows covered the ship. "I'm so glad you are alive. I can't believe it's been thirty years!" Peter said, repositioning his weapon into the sheath on his hip.

"Luci had taken my swords...huh?" Then it registered what Peter had just said. "No, it's been two days, my Kuku."

"Ish, it was three long fucking decades!"

I tipped my head from side to side, studying his face. "Wait a second, when we had taken the apple back, didn't you say you thought I was dead?"

"Fucking Elijah," we exclaimed together.

"Don't count Gugusan and all the others out. The San knew what they were doing. The men, women, and children, they were all in on keeping us here." Peter grunted. "Those fuckers knew you were searching for me the whole time. But, yeah, Elijah. I've wished hundreds of times that I never suggested taking him to Andrew. You could've died! What if you died? What if I came too late?" The fire in his eyes made him look scary, gruff, and a lot meaner than the Peter I crashed with two days ago. Mix that with sweetness and beauty, he was a dangerous, poisonous, pretty flower. I wanted to pluck, sniff, and roll in his scent.

"I don't die that easily, my Kuku, unless they left me hanging in the sun for weeks or beheaded me. But they didn't. Although it felt like it, or close to it, though," I said weakly while watching Peter maneuver himself and his wings around me. Before, I was cold and shaky, but now, I felt warm and safe.

"Take more blood from me, I hate to see you like this." He tipped his head to the side, offering me his sustenance. He smelled so good. His skin was smooth, salty, and warm. I could hear the blood rushing through his veins. *Thump-thump*. His heartbeat called to me.

He smiled as he regarded me. I examined him as his gaze burned me with love and silent tears doused the flames as they spilled down his cheeks.

"Go on, beautiful, take what you need. I need you strong and capable when we go speak to Gugusan." I missed his striking blue-silver eyes. His sleek white hair touched his suntanned shoulders. My gaze lingered on his full pink lips, no facial hair, and the dimples he sported on each cheek were still there. The dark circles around his eyes gave him a menacing appearance. He was a handsome winged creature, my handsome winged creature. My eyes darted down to his neck. My incisors throbbed. The palm of his hand wrapped around the back of my neck. The weight of it was too heavy to resist. My teeth slid into the skin and punctured the vein. I relished the warm sweet iron-rich blood as it flowed over my tongue and down my throat.

CHAPTER 20
REBOOTING

"*GOOD MORNING.*

Did you know that a study of fish proved that when female cichlids lose their chosen mates, they become glum and pessimistic about the world? It turns out that breakups suck, whether you are a human, a mammal, or just a fish.

Join the community news page to find others who are discouraged and have bleak futures, so you may form new emotional attachments and reignite that dying flame inside you.

Hope your day is filled with new ideas and the courage to try them!"

ISHTAR
24 970 B.C.
Later that night, after the rescue
The San village in the jungle

. . .

"ELIJAH MOTHERFUCKING WHAT?" Raking his fingers through his hair, Peter asked Gugusan with an aggressive tone, making a big show of the news that Elijah had sided with the Birdmen and that he would come to get us tomorrow, to go make nice-nice with them.

I missed him and everyone else, I realized as I mentally rolled my eyes at my lover's antics. I liked his bold and dramatic flair toward the extreme. I can but only stare and admire his beauty and tenacity.

"You two are like babies. Ishtar, your ship is tired," Gugusan said. That had been the only way to explain that Lasitor was rebooting and we were temporarily stranded. "It is done. You cannot leave. You are here, and you stay here, and you be the gods you are supposed to be. The time of playing is done. Time for no secrets has arrived. It's time for you to grow up and be the Gods of the Mountain," Gugusan said, pointing his finger at my chest.

My Kuku shook his head in disappointment at the crowd of men, women, and children. Gugusan flashed a look at us, making my Anunnaki ass feel as small as a child's. "I had enough of you coming and going and coming and going. You go home now, with Kuku. Tomorrow we are going to Birdman City. It's time for you to grow up. You can go call on your friends in the place far away, but you come back, I will give you half a day. You are the Gods of our Mountain! You come back, you don't stay there. You bring your friends." This was not the warm welcome I usually received when I visited.

Gasps and various creative exclamatory words, accompanied by chaotic noisy questions, came from outside. It seemed the whole village was here. It felt like the Roman bazaar I visited with Platonius, it disorientated me. My brain was partially dysfunctional, causing my movements to be sluggish. My aim was completely off as I attempted to swat at Gugusan's pointing finger, but I missed it as if my eyes were crossed. Then I closed my ears with the palms of my hands to muffle the noise. The San were upset with their leader speaking to us like we were his children. "Okay, tomorrow we talk," I agreed. I pointed with my elbows for Peter to carve a path through the spectators filling the doorway of Gugusan's hut. My Kuku wrapped his arms around me, covered me with his wings, and marched with me outside. Once out in the open, he lifted me as if I weighed nothing and we ascended into the sky.

"It's been a long fucking day, let's go home," he whispered and kissed the back of my head as I dangled in his strong arms. Below us the village grew smaller and the air cooler. We followed the river upstream and passed two small waterfalls bubbling out of the steep mountainside and beyond the cliffs overhanging the river that cut deep into the jungle. "You made sure they can't bother you by hiding here."

"I thought so too, but they found a way. There is a footpath leading straight to the opening of my cave." Peter pointed to a warn-out path that ran alongside the mountain.

"Where there is a will, there is a way," I said chuckling.

My heart swelled imagining how the tribe irritated him by caring for him as they brought him food and kept him company.

An hour later, we'd had dinner and my Kuku had showed me his impressive home. Our bath water was finally boiling, so he undressed me and helped me into the water, before joining me in his hand-carved hot tub, draping his wings over the sides so as not to get them wet. I was all too happy to get the stench of sweat and piss off me. He washed my sore body before we lay back and relaxed. "I see now where Gugusan's inspiration came from. It was your influence and idea to dig deeper into the limestone to create separate areas for washing, sleeping, and preparing food. All this time, my Kuku was here and all this time, Gugusan had been keeping us apart."

"Hmmm." Peter grimaced and rolled his head lazily from side to side. Eyes closed and relaxed.

"Gugusan said they were scared that I might take you away from here. I probably would have. So I didn't argue with him tonight."

"Hmmm."

We lay there until the water was cold and the fire was burned to ash. Peter looked proud and enamored with this place and the people. He doesn't want to admit it, but they are a part of his identity already. The way he spoke about them, made them sound like one big bickering family. As he showed me the life he had carved out for himself earlier, I realized he doesn't even notice referencing them as often as he does. I was so proud of him. He made sure he worked with what he had and made life as comfortable as possible for him and the San. The one thing that impressed me the most was his flushing toilet. The water he collected higher on the mountain would flush the excrement down to the river when he pulled the chain.

I felt light, rejuvenated, and mega unloaded. Talking and relaxing with him felt homely. Domesticated.

"I'm waiting for you!" Peter sing-songed and I smiled as he rounded the corner to the sleeping area. I was still weak, but there was nothing wrong with my cock. It slowly filled as we bathed, but now it was his proud old self. "Now I'm stroking myself," my Kuku teased from around the corner and a shrill of excitement escaped me, energized me.

I didn't dawdle longer, splashing water as I half-rolled over the side of the rock tub and didn't bother drying myself. I hobbled into the big cozy bedroom and froze as I sucked air through my nostrils at the sight that greeted me. I could never have foreseen or dreamed this vision. He was stunning in all his magnificence. Gloriously beautiful. Peter lay on his back, wings draped over the sides of the bed. His legs sprawled open, showing his balls pink and stretched. Long cock in hand, he slowly pumped it, pushing and pulling that extra-long foreskin slowly over his glistening engorged purple cockhead. Everything was bigger and longer between his legs. Hooded eyes, bright blue, gazed at me as he bit his bottom lip. He waited, teased and invited me, flared open to the maximum, just for me.

My cock jolted. It thumped as an exquisite tingle spread up my spine. Like a solid gold rod, unbending, fully engorged, and heavy, my cock pointed straight at my true mate. I grabbed hold of it.

I inhaled the smell of him saturating the air. I'd grown addicted to it. When aroused he smelled like vanilla beans charred over an open fire. The sweetest destruction of my heart and soul.

Water ran in rivulets down my body, cooling my steaming skin. I felt like I was on fire while doused with ice water as the cool blue and gold mating ribbons danced on my glowing blue body.

I kneeled on my good knee, slowly making my way up between his ankles. Not taking my gaze off him.

"May I feast on you tonight? I still need a nibble or two," I asked, already knowing I was going to get a sarcastic answer.

"I told you to hurry, if that wasn't an obvious invitation for you, then, let's see how long you can go without me giving you another invitation."

He gripped his cock at the base squeezing hard, forcing a tiny bead of pre-cum to collect at his slit. With his forefinger and thumb, he swiped the shiny bead and rolled the stickiness between his fingers. He lifted his hand to his mouth, opening and closing his fingers, showing me the spiderweb-like strands. I leaned in closer, licking it from between his fingers. Our tongues danced, competing for more of it. He sighed and lay back. The thumping of our heartbeats had already synchronized, and we weren't even orgasming yet.

He laced his fingers behind his head and chuckled at me. "You are officially invited to help yourself to my entire body," he said, cock twitching and begging me to suck him. *God, he's stunning.* He lifted an eyebrow, daring me to refuse him, but simultaneously hoping my warm, wet mouth was around him already. I grunted, looking at him, and trailed my eyes over his well-defined chest, the sexy dip of his solar plexus down the prominent lines of his abdominal muscles, those thick rifts on each side of his hips leading down to his leaking cock.

Feasting on him with my eyes, I slowly retreated from between his knees.

"Ish, I missed you. Every day without you felt longer than the previous day."

I pounced, swallowing his cock down my throat without warning, shutting him up. He hissed, and I broke eye contact as I closed mine. Stars swam behind my eyelids as I tasted more of him.

"That's it, Ish. Suck me, I'm yours," he said from somewhere far away while gripping my locks and not letting go. "I waited for you for thirty years."

I stopped sucking. "You never asked Gugusan or another man to suck or fuck you?"

"No, I missed you too much."

"My Kuku."

"Yes, yours."

I pursed my lips, forcing his cock through the smallest warm slick hole. "Oh my god, you are killing me!"

I sucked him as hard as I loved him. Harder with every upward stroke while sliding down with soft, slow motions. Getting his cock engorged to the point of bursting. The sounds I pulled from him were just as satisfying as the taste of his long heavy cock on my tongue. The emotions he poured out with his words were a chaotic crescendo of jubilant euphoria. I resisted the urge to sink my fangs into it. Pre-cum flooded my mouth, coating my throat as I nestled my nose in his blond pubic hair. *I think I found the source of the vanilla bean smell.* I rolled my nose from side to side in it while I groaned. He loved it. I drove him crazier with the rumble of my voice as I purred for him. If I kept this up, he would shoot directly down my throat, not giving me a mouthful. I worked for it and wanted it on my tongue where I could taste it for as long as I wanted before swallowing. Slowly, I pulled back while he swore obscenely. Threatening me with death and rape if I stopped.

I pulled off him, letting his cock plop out of my mouth. I didn't take my gaze off him, waiting for him to open his eyes to give me his best *what the fuck* face.

He lifted his head, eyes blazing with fiery lust, while I nestled myself on my elbows between his knees. He looked dazed.

I sucked my forefinger and middle finger into my mouth, showing him what I planned to do with them. He bent his knees, opening his ass up for the intrusion.

"Go ahead, suck and fuck me. That's my last invitation," he grunted and lay back down again.

"My Kuku, do you trust me?" I asked, and his head shot up in question. "Of course I do, and can we talk about this another time, I was about to blow, for fuck's sake."

"May I bite you?" I asked, shaking with the need to taste as much of him as I could.

"Where? On my cock or in my groin?

"Everywhere? Or is that too much?"

"Ish, get your fangs wet with my blood and cum. I fucking beg you to bite as much of me as you want. Eat me up, but make me cum, please!" He fisted my hair and pushed me back down, showing me exactly where he wanted me and my mouth.

I sucked the head of his cock down and slid my fangs into the rim of his cockhead while I plunged my fingers deep into his ass.

"Fuuuuck, you sick motherfucking, beautiful fucking, fuuuck!" He howled and spurted his seed onto my waiting tongue.

The mix of his body fluids ignited an explosion of colorful sensations all around and inside me.

An hour later, both of us were satiated. I snuggled against his chest for comfort. "What do you think is going to happen tomorrow?" he asked, his voice laced with trepidation. He was still buried deep inside me, and I let out a heavy sigh, trying to push away the thoughts of the possibility of dreadful things about to happen.

"I don't know, but I'm not ready for a fight. I'm tired of fighting and surviving. I have you now, and that is all I ever wanted. I suggest we rest, and leave in the morning to return to exactly where and when we left Phoenix. Then ask Eryn for help," I replied, fearing the unknown and that Gugusan and Eryn weren't going to miraculously come up with a plan to make peace with the Angels and Sables that kept me prisoner. The fear of Apsu turning up is something I wasn't ready to face either.

As I'd marked his body earlier, our connection grew deeper and stronger, but now the longer we lay here sharing our innermost thoughts, the more real our love amidst the coming danger grew. Since we'd met, we had always been rushing somewhere, and I cherished just being here with him in the now. I knew after surviving thirty years in the jungle, he saw the mountain as his home. I saw the emotional connection, the fondness, and, of course, the difficult concern about meeting with the Birdmen. He didn't trust them, he had been keeping his distance, hating them for what they had done to me. He'd thought I was dead, he found me, only to lose me again, as I lost him. Maybe it's a good thing like Gugusan said. We might as well accept that this is our home. But that gnawing feeling was still present. I knew what that meant. We had to go back to Phoenix, to warn them. Before we go with the San, to talk to those bloody Birdmen. My mind was an open book to my Kuku, and it felt like lifting centuries' worth of burdens off my shoulders. Just to be with him, to be loved and accepted.

"Peter," I whispered just before falling asleep.

"Hmmm."

"I'm worried about Apsu."

"I know. We'll talk with Gugusan tomorrow. I haven't seen Phoenix in thirty years, I'd love a new pair of underwear and jeans. Rest now, you are not fully healed."

CHAPTER 21
DON'T SCREAM

"I WOULD HAVE SAID GOOD MORNING IF I DIDN'T know better, but I do.

It's now six a.m.

I guess we're back to hiding under the water and not facing the brightness of day.

Did you know that the original inventor and builder of the first cuckoo clock is unknown?

But did you also know in 1650 A.D. the Jesuit scholar Athanasius Kircher wrote Musurgia Universalis, The Universal Musical Art, of the Great Art of Consonance and Dissonance? It was a compendium of ancient and contemporary thinking about music, its production, and its effects. It explored how the mathematical aspects of music, like harmony and dissonance, relate to health and evil in a harmonious world. He also wrote two other books, The Magnes sive de Arte Magnetica which set out the secret underlying coherence of the universe, and Ars Magna Lucis et Umbrae which explored the ways of knowledge and enlightenment.

What is interesting is that these works contain the first documented description—in words and pictures—of how mechanical cuckoo clocks work.

On that timely note, breakfast is served until eight a.m.

Hope you have a day of wonder and discovery!"

ISHTAR

2147 A.D. (95 A.T.)

Several hours after Ish and Peter fled the inquisition

Phoenix, underwater glass dome city

SILENCE FILLED the room until the shock wore off. Followed by gasps and various creative exclamatory words, accompanied by three howling Anubis. Cian had had some time to recover from his initial shock, after meeting us outside. He put two fingers in his mouth and whistled. When he came to collect us earlier, he had taken one wordless look at Peter, and covered him with the sheet we'd requested when we called him. He brought us straight here, to Ivan and Eryn's apartment.

It was the largest apartment in Phoenix and far from the main population. Their extra-large home and the key to the city were gifts from the Phoenicians after Eryn, Ivan, and Cian had wrapped the entire city inside protective layers. A living, breathing shell, much like an oyster's that protects Phoenix against the natural elements beneath the melted icy ocean waters.

After pushing Cian out of their throuple, Cian and Rotty had moved out when Eryn and Ivan had mated, or married as the humans call it. Understandably, Cian had taken that badly. He had lost his friend and twin.

Since drama was his default reaction to any stressor, I understood why he had invested all his focus on getting to the moon, where Barkor was born and survived, oblivious to him. After saving Barkor and the leftover humans from Grayrak, their mating bond made Cian understand the physical attraction and emotional pull between destined couples and why Eryn and Ivan had mated. Since then, Cian and Barkor hadn't spent more than a few minutes apart. How their lovemaking worked for them, no one, but them knew. Both were as muscled and stubborn as oxen, and I'm sure if it wasn't for the pull between mates, they would have lived as far away from each other as possible. Now, the two held hands and walked around as one unit of trouble and drama. If darkness was colorful, they were it.

"And what is this? Another one of your weird experiments?" Eryn asked me mind-to-mind while smiling back at a blushing Peter.

Ivan beamed and gave a small bow to Peter. "Welcome to our home. Oh my, Peter, you have grown into your own," he said, then turned to me, scowling—as if it was my doing.

"Ish, this is puzzling," Eryn said to me while

inspecting Peter's wings up and down by walking around him.

My teeth were chattering, I was hungry, and I hugged myself to warm up. The little blood I had taken from Peter wasn't enough. I needed much more blood to recover and fully heal. Lots of it. My energy and strength required at least two to three human donors. But I didn't want Peter to think what he offered me last night was not enough.

Could you please invite Juandre and Andrew over? I need to ask them something, I asked Eryn mentally.

I saw him realize why after he took one look at me. He cleared his throat. "Please excuse me while I'm making a phone call."

"Look at you, Ish," Barkor said with a tad more sympathy, and surprised me with a one-armed hug. "Bringing home strays." *So not sympathy, but sarcasm.* Barkor tapped his short club on the table in front of me. Like Cian, he had a way of turning any problem into a melodramatic situation.

"Barkor, don't let these wayward children of mine influence you to the point of stupidity. This is Peter. My Peter. My Kuku. If you call him a stray once more..." I said, feeling proud of my childish, witty comeback, while experiencing the worst case of starvation.

"I was teasing. Look at you. Were you enjoying a vacation in the sun? You are about to crumble into ash. I've never seen you like this," Barkor said, shaking his head at me. I was sure Juandre and Andrew had something to do with Barkor's extensive knowledge of me and my sun allergy, as Andrew called it. Those two can't keep a secret.

They couldn't wait to tell the world they were different. Vampires, according to Juandre.

Cian came to Barkor's rescue. "You look like you should be dead already. I'm too scared to touch you."

"Yeah, one loud fart and you'd puff into moon dust." Barkor cracked up, waving his weapon in the air. I wasn't arguing with that point. I felt like it. "Your Peter and I haven't spent enough time together. We hardly know each other," Barkor said and turned to Cian for further supportive taunting.

"Yeah, Peter, you have doubled in size," Cian said, then narrowed his eyes at me. "What else has doubled and why do you call us children? Since when are we your children?" Cian asked, pinning me with that Zelk eye stare. I was seconds from falling backward.

I cleared my throat and gave him a pointed look by attempting to lift my right eyebrow in question. It didn't even twitch. "You are Anunnaki and of my bloodline, are you not? My father is your grandfather, and your children will be my grandchildren, so yes, I'm your father, or at least one of your fathers, and you are my children."

Now that Peter's wings have been revealed, I must continue telling them about the apple and Apsu. I coughed, trying to collect more spit in my dry mouth. I gulped the nerves and discomfort down my itchy dry throat. "Hmmm, we are here to discuss crucial issues."

As if choreographed, they swung their attention between Peter and me, so I pushed on. "The apple."

"Yeah, the one Peter stole," Ivan said accusingly.

I gave a shameful smile, and Peter dropped his chin to his chest. "Yes, that apple. We took it back, but unfortunately to the wrong time and place. There is a chance that my father survived and is on his way."

Peter lifted his head bravely under their scrutiny. "I heard the same thing being said by the Fates," he added, and I wondered if he was going to tell them about his thirty years lost in the jungle, so I interjected to prevent an information overload.

"We brought it home, to my home, to Babylon." I lifted my palms. "Just let me talk please." Cian pressed his lips into a thin line. Barkor thrust his chest out. Ivan sighed.

I inhaled. "But because I manipulated the realities, when we got rid of the Zelk, we crisscrossed timelines, and I never factored that issue into my calculations."

"What the fuck, Ish?" Cian, Barkor, and Ivan asked simultaneously.

Peter's wings opened, and I sensed a violent outburst coming. "Hey, you don't talk to Ish like that. He has done everything to help you as best he could. You were all smiling when Cian landed the Warship Horizon filled with your humans, and no Zelk was in sight."

"I was not smiling!" Cian said, pushing his chest out and fist-thumping it. "I fucking told you something weird was happening. Didn't I say these were not my people?" he asked Barkor, who confirmed it with a few more nods than necessary. "You expected us just to accept that they were. I fucking told you they were different. Look at these stupid silver mesh suits and flip-flops. I fucking knew it!"

"Cian, unfortunately, I can't undo any of it. If I do, anything from the Zelk falling out of the sky to Juandre and Andrew dying can happen." I rubbed my forehead. "Scarabs, all of you could disappear in front of my eyes. If we continue on this timeline, and if I don't bring that apple back from Babylon, then Phoenix, you, and everything here will disappear!" I pointed to Peter. "If we bring it back, the timeline, the world filled with beings like Peter, will disappear. Yes, we could have gone and brought it back, but this place is where Peter and I feel at home." I paused to give them a second. A second for the information to sink in. I wanted them to understand the magnitude of our dilemma.

"We are in a situation where we have to choose and we can't. If we choose wrong my father is still a very real possibility. He is not something you want to come across. You are my blood, and the whole of Phoenix is yours. By default, I should care about saving this place, even if it sounds to me like the Fates wanted us close to them. You are my future, but somehow I've put you in the past when I crossed over and handed the apple over to the timeline you did not originate from. Where it was discovered by my father." I searched Peter's face for doubt or surprise, but I saw nothing but stoic support. "Don't ask me how the Fates and that apple are connected. I don't know. All I know is that if I don't bring it back, the world of Angels and Sables continues, without Phoenix and all of us."

"So what I'm hearing is that you can't choose and that those Angels, Sables, or whatever they are—"

Peter chipped in, "San, they are the San tribe."

Ivan grinned at Peter. "Yeah, them. So they are connected to the Fates, and because we switched time-lines, you moved us away from what? One dimension, or reality? Is this maybe Heaven? If we are on the Earth, where are they? What is that place with Angels? Is it another planet?" Ivan asked a very good question.

"Call it what you will, Ivan, but there is more to this. This place was discovered by Ish, by traveling backward in time."

A pinched, unhappy expression washed over Ivan's face as he bulged his fists. Barkor's eyes darted between Peter and me. "How far?" Cian asked.

I cleared my throat. "About twenty-five thousand years."

Cian's eyes bulged, and his jaw dropped in shock. Ivan gasped and clasped his hands over his mouth. Barkor sucked in a breath, "I knew it! This is where you got the food and water from?"

Peter continued before any of them could say anything else. "There is also the matter of the Birdmen games. That's what the San, the indigenous people, Aztec-type precursor people—ancient—like Easter Island ancient, maybe even further back, calls them. Gu is the leader of the San, hence his name is Gugusan. He is a friend of Ish and me and he knows something about all this. He gave me this," Peter bashfully pointed his obsidian blade at them, then continued, "and trained me. He is intelligent, and he is...," I watched as a blush crept over Peter's face and he smiled. I knew Peter thought Gugusan was attractive and respected him. I grabbed Peter's hand and squeezed as Peter continued talking. "The San guard the cave—the mountain where the Fates speak to them. It's a holy place. If it wasn't for Gu, Ish and I couldn't have come back to tell you this today. We are very good friends with them and now sit with this impossible choice. We will choose whatever you choose. Them or us." Tears collected in Peter's eyes and his emotional turmoil was palpable. The smell of wood smoke and sweet roses thickened as the air around Peter charged with somber energy.

Peter had known the San people much longer than he was saying. The room quieted down. Their full attention was on reading Peter's mind. Cian stepped back, eyes wide. Barkor joined him, and the Anubis reacted by lifting their front paws, waiting. Gone was the excitement. Peter gave a futile nod of admission, realizing everyone was reading much more than the room.

Cian's voice broke the silence. Hands reaching for my throat, he shouted. "You mother fucking Anunnaki," and then he lunged at me. "I'm going to strangle you!" Being tired, hungry, and weak in the knees, I stumbled as he overpowered me.

Peter stuck his obsidian short sword under Cian's throat. "You hurt him, you die."

Ivan jumped into the scuffle as Barkor tackled Peter. Arms, legs, hair, spittle, and feathers filled the living room as we rolled and wrestled to be on top.

"If I didn't require sustenance, I would have said this

was fun," I grunted and rolled onto Ivan. He kicked me in the nuts and I wobbled back. Peter caught me, but Cian, Ivan, and Barkor fought for first place to strangle me. Peter pulled me by my ankles in an attempt to save me but ended up hurting me. I howled in pain. "Peter, no, my knee!"

Eryn was back, helping me by pulling the frantic Cian and Ivan away. Peter restrained Barkor, and just as I wanted to roll over to catch my breath, Rotty put one enormous paw on my chest and growled. "Okay, down boy," I said in my friendliest Anubis charming voice while gulping air. He wasn't having it. His yellow eyes pinned me and he snarled, saliva dripping, already growing in size. It was a crazy shit and feathers show.

"Thank you, Rotty, for always coming to my defense. You may leave him," Cian ordered, and Rotty let me be.

"Everyone, calm the fuck down. I leave for one second and you are at each other's throats. Make up and be nice to Ishtar. He needs help. Can't you see he is about to expire?" Eryn said over his shoulder, trying for a second time to reach Juandre and Andrew.

"Motherfucker," Cian and Barkor said, shaking their heads at me. Distraught, I fought the appearance of tears in my eyes. With my smashed-in kneecap worse than before, I sat where I was and prepared to grovel.

I took a deep breath, exuding calmness while feeling defeated and at their mercy. "Please, we need your help." A bloody tear rolled over my cheek and I wiped at it—the reality of it all was getting unbearable. "Peter and I don't know what to do," I said and covered my face with the palms of my hands.

"They will help you," Peter said, kicking the linen to the side. He stretched his wings, but the room was too small. The crown of his wings scraped the ceiling. It startled him and he turned, knocking over the last standing framed picture on a small side table next to a couch. I caught it before it hit the floor. A blond curly haired boy laughed up at the camera. I recognized Eryn. He was much younger than when I'd visited him in South Africa, when I brought Rotty, Igor, and Devil to him. I wonder if he had shared this with them. I doubt it. He would have said so. *Eryn and I need a private talk.* My heart melted as sentimentality crushed me. I heaved air into my dehydrated lungs. My chest was tight, and there wasn't enough oxygen in the room. "I need to get out of this place. There are too many emotions. Too many of us are stuffed into this room. Peter, help me. Get me out. I need air!" I said as I struggled to stand.

Cian watched me with his hands on his hips. "Jesus, is he having a panic attack? How can the Anunnaki son of Apsu, the evil world destroyer, have panic attacks?"

"Fuck you, Cian, he was tied up in the sun for two days. They smashed his knee, and he came here to ask for help, but you are trying to kill him. Of course, he is having a panic attack." Peter pushed me back onto the couch. Then, he sat on his heels beside me and offered his wrist. "Here, take more blood from me."

I took Peter's arm and laid it on my lap. "No, thank you my Kuku." He looked worried, and I smiled at him, bursting with love for him.

Just then, Eryn said, "Yeah, Drew. Please bring your

husband to our place. I have someone here who needs your kind of sustenance. Yes. Blood. Hmmm, yes, he is back and not in good shape. Okay, yes. Thank you, he will appreciate that. Oh, and tell Juandre not to scream or yell when he sees Peter. Hmmm, yes, he has wings. How did you know? Oh. No need to explain further. Yup, better to prepare Juandre if he doesn't know, hmmm. Thanks, yes, tell him not to make a show of this, please. Okay, thanks, Drew." I heard a chuckle as he returned from where he made the call.

"They are on their way. I hear and see you feel a bit cramped inside our home. I wish I could see how you fly," he told Peter. Right away, the tension in the room evaporated. Cian, Ivan, and Barkor agreed, "Yes, we would all like to see you fly," they said, putting the pillows back on the couches and cleaning the mess. I followed them with my eyes, concentrating on something other than my need to breathe.

"Sorry. My wings are too big for your home. You can see me fly when we go outside. And you can even see more like me when we take you to this place and time. Then you'll understand why we struggle to choose sides."

"Take us there?" Ivan asked.

Peter helped me to get more comfortable with my knee and pulled a chair closer so he could sit on it. "Yes, but I warn you, as Gugusan warned me. Those Birdmen will want to have you. You are beautiful and godlike, with one look at you, they will want you. Gugusan told me they live to bask in the sun, have sex all day, and have tournaments. They settle all their conflicts with these games."

"Yes, but remind me again, first, why do we want to go to a place that would be dangerous, and second, why would we choose them over our people? I say forget about them. Bring the apple here. If Apsu goes there, fine, if he comes here, we will deal with him," Barkor said.

"I want to talk to their leader. Can you take us to him without hindrance?" Eryn asked. His eyes sparkled with intelligence.

"I agree," Ivan added eagerly. "If we have some kind of truce we could help them and they could help us."

Barkor scratched his beard deep in thought. "That sounds better than sacrificing one choice—one place for the other. These games—we would have to play. Maybe they will listen if we are playing their game," he said in a quiet voice.

"That's a good idea. If we challenge them and win, they will have to listen. Ishtar, will we see or hear the Fates? Could we use that to sway them?" Ivan asked, gazing at Peter's wings. He stretched an arm out as if to touch my Kuku. "May I?" he asked, enthralled.

"Yes, you may," said Peter with a low and shy tone in his voice. It grated on my nerves and a possessive irritation like I've never known, flared up inside me. "Yes and no, the Fates are not corporeal. Their voice is audible in certain areas. We will show you," Peter explained as everyone in the room frowned in disbelief and glanced around as if searching for answers. "Also, the Birdmen don't have leaders. Gugusan says they fight every day about something. That is what they do. Anytime they decide to choose a leader, someone challenges him. It is a constant battle among themselves. A way of living. Their culture. The only ones living in peace are the San led by my friend Gu, deep in the jungle. They helped us, unfortunately, the Fates told Ish to take the apple home, and he thought home was Babylon," Peter said, sticking his hands deep into his pants pockets and pulling his shoulders up. Thankfully, he wasn't telling them he was lost in the jungle for thirty years. "We were thinking, maybe Eryn can help us think of a way to save them. Maybe bring them here. Maybe convince them somehow, while we go and bring the apple here."

"I would have to transport all of us on my small ship. Eryn, you, Ivan, Cian, and Barkor can keep them busy," I said and turned to Peter. "You would have to go get the apple with me."

"How sure are you this place is the only place on this planet? Could it be that there is already something else in its future? Can't you jump and go see?" Barkor asked.

"I can't, and to be honest, I'm too scared to do it. One wrong jump and I may lose all of you," I said, breaking eye contact and inspecting the small white feathers on the tiled floor, too embarrassed to look up.

"We don't have a fucking choice, do we?" Cian said. There was a heavy silence, so I lifted my head to see what it was about. Cian had his arms crossed as he watched his brother stroking Peter's wings. Peter shivered and Eryn stepped in.

"Okay, baby, enough admiring the wings." I heard no jealousy in his voice. More as if he was protecting Peter. He smiled and Peter tucked his wings deeper by folding one over the other. The crescent-horned tips hung over his head like a halo.

Ivan turned to Eryn. "If Peter is an Angel and let's say we bring them here, do we leave the Fates there, and what then? Shouldn't God and the Angels be in one place?" Eryn was pulling his shoulders up to his ears. Peter crossed his arms and widened his stance. I could see Eryn was already calculating an answer to our predicament.

"It sounds to me, wherever the apple is, is where the Fates are," Peter answered.

"Ivan, stop that. You are making all of us uncomfortable. What is wrong with you?" Cian said, ticked off at his brother, shaking his head at Ivan still closely admiring my Kuku's feathers.

"It was a wild guess and I'm starting to put some stories we were told as children together. How do you sleep? Can you sit? Aren't they in your way the whole time?" Ivan asked Peter.

"Are your arms and legs in your way when you sleep?" Peter grunted.

"Sorry, I didn't mean to sound like I was interrogating you. I find you fascinating. I think you are beautiful. Can you turn around? I want to see your back, please."

Peter gave Ivan a stern fuck-off look and kept his feet firmly planted.

Silence.

Ivan seemed to register the uncomfortable status in the room. "I'm sorry. Forgive me. I'm usually in control of myself. I'm being insensitive. This is not how I normally act when sexy as fuck feathered beings enter my home.

Your muscled body and eight-pack are impressive, but Eryn's my man, so I probably should stop thinking of you as cookies and dough I want to dunk into orange juice and suck on it. Why do you smell so yummy, like cupcakes and cookies?"

Cian coughed. Rotty, Igor, and Devil yipped. Eryn was busy picking his jaw up from the floor. Ivan was acting out of character. It seemed my Angel had tripped and flipped some kind of lustful trigger response in him. To reduce the sexual tension and to focus their attention on something other than my sexy man, my winged creature, my angel, my mate, *mine*, I clapped my hands twice, snapping all of them from wherever their minds had gone.

Eryn gave me a questioning look and Cian looked taken aback. "Children, please focus. Peter is mine, and mine alone. When we go to that place and time, you will see thousands of them. But this one is mine," I said and winked at Peter.

"Now I want to go there," Ivan said.

Just then, the front doorbell rang. "I will get it. It's Andrew and Juandre. Please. If you will?" Eryn gestured for me to accompany him. My limbs were stiff and sore. I moved across the room like an old man as my mouth salivated for blood.

"Well, hello, Ishtar, my friend," Juandre exclaimed, bursting inside as the door slid open. "We hear you need emergency feeding," he said, and I perked up, happy to hear his voice. "Bear, give him his lunch box."

"Hello, Ish." Andrew hugged me with one arm while handing me a big container. I smelled the blood and my belly did acrobatic flips. I couldn't wait to taste the thick red liquid, even if it wasn't Peter's. I could feast on him again later. But now I'm going to gorge, fully recover, and save my people.

"Thank you for coming and bringing me food. I've been injured and although Peter has already fed me, I need much more and he needs his strength. I doubt he would like it if I fed on anyone but him in this room."

"No problem, it's blood donated by the residents. When they heard we were vampires, bags of the stuff started piling up in front of our door. I guess they are scared that we would roam the halls sucking them dry." He cackled. I don't know why the humans call the royal Anunnaki courtesans vampires, but Juandre likes the name, so I don't object. I didn't have the strength for more conversation.

I took the box and held it possessively against my chest. "Where can I feed?" I asked Eryn, who smiled and hugged the newcomers. It seemed he liked Juandre and Andrew as much as I did.

"Go into the guest bedroom." Eryn pointed down the hallway. "The first one on the right."

I bowed, showing my appreciation. "Thank you," I said. I waved to Peter, showing him I was going to the back.

"Yes, love, go take care of yourself," Peter said, and his somber expression morphed into friendly relief. I turned and made my way to the room.

In the background, I heard Juandre exclaim, "Color my Roman Catholic gay ass pink! Angels fucking exist!"

I opened the blue and white box. It seemed it was cooling the blood and keeping it from going stale. The dark amber fluid jiggled as if teasing me. I took one squashy pouch out, inspecting it. How did they get it out of the bag? My stomach growled at me to hurry while I inspected the translucent covering.

There are ten bags packed inside for you. Just bite into them and suck, Andrew spoke into my mind. I opened my mouth and sank my teeth into it—sucking one after the other dry. After seven bags, I was stuffed and already gaining strength. I felt immediately warmer while my knee and other injuries healed within minutes. I finished the last three, collected the empty containers, and packed them back into the cooler, planning to take them back to Andrew and Juandre. But as I turned to leave, Eryn blocked the door. His eyes bored into me, serious and all-knowing. I gulped down a nervous knot in my throat.

He came inside and closed the door behind him. I inhaled quick, short breaths nervously and stepped back. Eryn wouldn't hurt an innocent fly, but I wasn't without blame. The power he carried pushed memories of my father to the forefront of my mind.

"I want to talk to you." He always smiled, but he wasn't smiling now. His golden-green eyes were pinning me. I felt guilty and nervous as if I was being judged.

It's your guilty conscience, he said into my mind, reading me in the most uncomfortable kind of way. I was careful around him because I knew what he was capable of. But what freaked me out most was his authoritative but friendly demeanor. Like I wanted to tell him all my secrets without him asking for them. I felt guilty and wanted to spill it all.

I put the box down and sat on the edge of the bed, exhaling. I heard Peter talking to the others. Those elongated pupils enlarged as Eryn seemed to look right through me.

Someone whistled, and Cian said, "We have to let Father and the others know." His voice thundered down the hallway.

"The whole Leadership Team would want to know. We can't just leave and not say anything. Let's call at least one of them. I'd suggest calling Mika. He would have insight into what to do first," I heard Peter say. I was so proud of him. I closed my eyes and smiled dreamily, then remembered Eryn was still assessing me. I looked at him and shrugged.

"Yes, but I think Brad is the best person to plan stealth attacks and rescue missions. Remember, he is a real general, and he led the team that rescued us from the mines in South Africa," Ivan said.

"I agree. Brad is the best person for the job," Juandre added.

Eryn opened the door and said, "If Mika and Brad are involved and in the know, then we might as well get Connor and Bryan too." He closed the door and then turned back to me. "Sorry, Ish, we have to plan better. It is unwise not to use yours and Peter's inside information and plan an extraction without causing a war on their world. I'm worried about us succeeding and their world disappearing. We need to do this so both our worlds survive. I can't destroy an entire world to save ourselves."

"I agree. I knew you would understand. But as soon as we involve the leadership, others will see Peter and this can become one big dilemma. I don't have time to gather for an assembly," I said and Eryn chuckled, knowing exactly what I was talking about. Every time something big was happening in Phoenix, or a vote had to be cast, all the residents congregated as they did when I was questioned.

"This is something bigger than just us," Eryn said to me.

Then switched to the local telepathic frequency in the apartment.

For example, I don't think our biggest problem is about the apple at all. I understand the switching of timelines and us not being born, because Apsu would discover the information hidden inside the apple. No one wants to cease to exist or cause others harm—do I understand your concerns correctly? I'm thinking, maybe we can somehow exist in both worlds simultaneously. Ivan was correct when he asked about Heaven. I remember when my friend Joshua read from his history book when humans and Angels fell in love. They walked among them. But it was frowned upon because their children were half human and half Angel. Maybe it's possible to coexist and we don't have to live apart.

Although I knew Eryn wasn't my father, the natural reaction to defend or fight I carried as a child seemed like it never disappeared.

Crossing his arms, he widened his stance. "Tell me

everything about this place, no matter how small or insignificant you think it is. I will go into your mind and see what you saw. Is that allowed, may I? It will help us prepare a strategy." Eryn looked at me like the first time we met in Grayrak. It felt like thousands of years ago, a thousand jumps, but in this reality, it was only two years past. He uncrossed his arms and like that first day we met, he took my hands and looked at me, inside of me. It felt awkward and intensely intimate. I was anxious and guarded, although I trusted and respected him. He was the strongest, most powerful being and he possessed a silent grounding pull. Like the gravity of a dangerous black hole. A constant silent surveillance. Observing while allowing everyone around him to just be themselves. Never forcing anything, no matter what I knew, he knew already what the outcome would be. He was calculating, weighing, and appreciating. He was all those things.

"We will go with you and help you." He reassured me. All the tension I've been carrying drained from me. We were safe and there was hope of not doing this alone anymore.

I blew out a long breath and said, "Thank you. What-ever you suggest, we are fully cooperating." I closed my eyes and invited him inside my mind, where I showed him everything I saw and knew about the place I thought was paradise.

A few minutes later Eryn sighed and said, "Ishtar, thank you for showing me. I see there is so much more. Now, show me how your father and I both occupy the same space in your mind." He sat down on the floor in front of me. "If I cross paths with him, I want to know what I'm up against. Unlock your mind fully and show me."

I blinked wordlessly. *The most powerful being I've ever come across is sitting on the floor.* Eryn was calm and he cared about me. He nonchalantly maneuvered his tree stumps of legs so gracefully. Back straight while focusing all his attention solely on me. Never letting go of my hands.

So I showed and told the king sitting on the floor everything.

An hour later, the interrogation into my psyche was complete. I felt light, rejuvenated, and mega unloaded. Eryn went so far as to forgive me for everything I felt guilty for and insisted I forgive myself too. After that we rejoined the others in the living room, answering questions until Ivan extended their hospitality, inviting us for a meal.

Cian, Barkor, Juandre, and Andrew left. Eryn and Ivan fed us while listening to Peter and me telling them about the San tribe. Their two Anubis, Igor and Devil, kept us under their watch. Whether by an unspoken command or just the need to monitor us, we didn't know. They sat straight up, watching every move we made, which made us so uncomfortable that we couldn't wait to get out of the apartment to meet with Brad and the Leadership Team. Our meeting with the Leadership Team went as I expected. Lots of questions, an hour of protests, and lengthy explanations of how disappointed they were, but it was rounded off with unfailing support and understanding. Brad requested someone stay behind to protect them. Juandre and Andrew volunteered, and I agreed, because those two produced more trouble than solutions. No one voiced that, but we all thought it, Juandre and Andrew included.

24 970 B.C.

The San village in the jungle

Miraculously, for once, I appeared to be the royal time traveler I was. With Lasitor's help, we didn't crash but parked atop the mountain where I had crash-landed a few times before—and I'm not sharing that. Another remarkable thing was that I exactly knew when and where we were this time.

I waited until the last of our visitors were outside, then I hung onto the doorframe, gazing out to where Peter was pointing and describing what the Birdman city and the arena looked like. Gugusan joined us, and he explained the lay of the land while drawing a map on the ground. I watched my Kuku with fondness.

Last night, I told Peter that Elijah was what Anunnaki called an Igigi. I wondered if he knew that Gugusan was just like Elijah. I needed to talk with all of them, there were things they should know but there wasn't time, there was never time, even though I had a time machine. Looking at him and Gugusan interact made everything around us fuzzy. Peter was my single point of focus. The way he spoke about this place told me that he thought of it as home. As they animatedly pointed while he explained to the warriors, I stepped closer, listening to where the forested world below bled out beyond the valley. I never thought or rather, I was never sober enough to think there could be someone living outside the jungle. The warriors listened attentively, nodding and asking questions while Gugusan jumped onto a boulder that stood out like a jagged tooth from the ridge.

"See there? That is where the river widens and its mouth splits again to cut through the cliffs with the hanging city of the Angels and Sables." Like the others, I followed Gugusan and Peter's line of sight and saw how it towered through the veil of thick mist drifting inland from the sea to the shoreline hiding it.

I shook my head. "I never knew it was there, my Kuku," I said while watching Gugusan.

Eryn turned from side to side as if surveying and committing it all to memory. He was deep in thought. I tried listening in on his mind working, but I couldn't hear anything. I should have let him be, but he caught my attention again when he jumped three more boulders over. It looked like he couldn't believe what he was seeing. His silhouette against the backdrop of stars reminded me so much of my brothers. The outline of his hair tied up and away, his beard braided in three little braids below his chin. His strong, muscled body was bigger than mine. As if knowing I was watching him, he turned to me. I couldn't see his eyes or expression from this distance, but I felt the serious concern. "Ish, this place, these mountains, and where you say they held you prisoner, does it feel like you have been here before?" he asked, breaking the silence between our minds.

To narrow the distance between us, I climbed on the large rock he had first jumped on. I had to put much more effort into it to reach the top. "Always. I had dreams about this place before I came here. Before I met you. Before I met Peter. I visited and came here many times, searching. I think it's because of that, that I started to feel I never left the place at all."

"Hmmm," he said and sniffed the air.

"Why? What are you stewing about?"

"I don't know yet. Let's get back to the others." He wasn't divulging his thoughts. He wasn't a big talker, but I had the feeling Eryn thought about bigger things and until he had spoken to Gugusan and the Birdmen, he wasn't verbalizing them. I turned and heaved a deep shaky breath and joined the others by jumping in front of them onto the familiar wet grassy ground. The air was thick with foreboding, the weight of the negotiations dragging my mood deeper into cumbersome despair. My gut felt as if thousands of snakes were crawling inside it—Apsu was bugging me.

We agreed that Peter, Gugusan, and his men would go ahead to schmooze Luci to join us in the negotiations. A bittersweet feeling lingered inside me. I feared failure, causing shallow breaths and tightness in my throat. However, amidst the apprehension, I was confident that Gugusan's allegiance would mean we had already convinced half of the Birdmen. Or so we hoped after Peter assured us he had found no other signs of life for hundreds of miles when he'd searched for me.

I watched as his wings reflected the moonlight before they vanished behind the treetops at the mountain's base.

"Good luck," I grunted. I was a hopeful skeptic about the planned negotiations.

I couldn't shake the feeling that leaving Phoenix with Peter after my trial was a reckless decision. And now, as we prepared for what lay ahead, I struggled to control my urge to go back in time and fix everything—never bring Peter here, never crash, and never lose that apple. Deep down, I knew it wasn't that simple. I had become obsessed with thinking that the next jump would be the last one, but as Ivan had emphasized earlier over a plate of pancakes, addiction was an illness of the mind. He explained that the brain is like an untrained computer and unless you teach it to take the route never taken, and make it work, your brain would convince itself to default, to do things it has tried and succeeded with once, ignoring all the other times it has failed after that. Life itself changes constantly and your brain functions outside of those probabilities unless you force it to take notice. I concluded that one jump was too many and a thousand will never be enough to fix the shit I have caused. His statement hit home and since then, every time the thought of jumping surfaced, I would roll my eyes and reprimand myself. Now that I recognize the idiotic thought pattern, I think I understand the reason why Lasitor had warned me that I should never serve my own needs, only the needs of others, and change only two things because those things will turn into uncountable changes in the future. By saving Juandre and Andrew and hoarding whiskey, all this has happened.

But, today isn't about me, it's about not one, but two realities. I promised Eryn to stay in the here and now. Chances of me changing things may mean that one of them disappears or worse—dies. Retrieving the apple was not going to be easy. Eryn wanted to see more before we decide what to do and how we were going to move forward.

For now, the plan was simple. Focus on escorting Eryn, Ivan, Cian, and Barkor down the mountain while Peter accompanies Gugusan and his army without making a big fuss and revealing our stealth approach.

"Don't worry, my friend, Peter will be fine," Eryn said. He bent and cracked his spine this way and that. They had been tightly packed inside the machine and the Brawl never complained. He leaned closer to Ivan and wrapped his arms around his husband. "Oh, sweet lollipops, Ivan, I can't believe how much I missed this. I swear, if we have time, I'm going to rip our clothes off and fuck you in the mud." Eryn chuckled into Ivan's ear.

"Hold on to that promise, my big Brawl. I would like nothing more than to do that with you. A roll in the mud would be so much more fun than fucking in zero gravity.," Ivan whispered, but we could hear every word they said. He lifted his hands above his head, joining his husband in stretching the kinks out of their limbs.

"I'm so thankful you came with us." I turned, showing respect by giving them a small bow.

"Ish, stop thanking us. We wanted to see this place too. I'm sure, if it was us, you would've done the same, even if you had to shit gold bricks doing so," Cian said, holding Barkor's hand. They are two giants with the tenderest caring hearts. Their hands might as well be glued to each other.

I pointed to the footpath I was familiar with. "There, that's the way down the mountain. It passes the cave where the rock paintings I told you about are. That's where I found the apple and the Fates spoke to me. We can go that way," I said to them. "Lasitor, please shut the door. Open it only for one of us. You have the coordinates saved?"

"Yes, I do, sir, and I will..." Lasitor answered as the door shut, cutting his sentence short. I turned to the others.

"Lead the way." Eryn pointed with his spear. Ivan and Cian carried their golden swords on their backs. The gold sang to me, making me miss my ancient Egyptian swords. At a slow run, we moved through the dense forest. My heart pounded in my chest. As we approached the clearing where the entrance to the opening of the cave was, I hesitated for a moment, unsure if I should enter because I thought of this place as holy or something. But we were here to break the cycle. To save our worlds. There wasn't time for hesitation. I had to show Eryn everything. Our plan wasn't solidified.

Eryn gave me a supportive tap on the back. I stooped my neck and then led the way.

"What are we looking for?" Ivan asked, and I ignored

him as I entered the cave and waved them inside. Hand-forged decorative torches lit the cavern.

I gestured towards the rock. "This is the spot where I found the apple and the Fates spoke to me." Their gazes followed my hand to the pointy rock pillar and then to the hieroglyphs depicting two stick figures. Two men. Us. Me and Peter.

"Hello," I called and hoped the Fates answered me and revealed themselves. "Talk to us, please." I was feeling dumber by the second. "I guess it wouldn't be that easy," I said, shrugging and kicking at the dirt.

"No, it never is that easy," Cian answered.

Barkor laid a hand on my shoulder. "Don't worry, Ish, we believe you."

"So you didn't know it was you and Peter who brought the apple here the first time?" Eryn asked, going down on his hands and knees to carefully brush away the dirt I had kicked at. I grimaced, not knowing what he was searching for.

"Gugusan said he kept it here for me." My voice echoed in the cave. Some birds took flight deeper into the blackness. "I counted on you meeting the Fates."

"Something tells me they would clear up a lot of questions for us," Ivan commented while reading the ancient texts.

"I have no clue how to summon them. I found closing my eyes and concentrating on them helps. I never get a reply when I initiate contact. They speak to me at their convenience. Sometimes I dream I was here, but I think it is my subconscious trying to make sense of my reality." I raked my fingers through my hair. "It can't be my imagination. Peter said he heard them too."

"I wonder if this is where their voice originates from," Eryn said again, carefully digging with his sword and scraping the unearthed pieces of rock and sand away. I frowned, rubbing the back of my neck. *What is he doing?*

"I would like to speak to your Fates. I need to confirm a theory," Eryn mumbled. I kneeled next to him. Underneath the cave floor, Eryn revealed intertwined dead calcified roots sprouting up into the rock face that wrapped around and bored into the stone, carved like an obelisk, where I had found the apple.

"What is this?" I asked.

"It's a network, an old one. Plants transfer water, nitrogen, carbon, and other minerals like this on forest floors. That's how they survive and communicate," Ivan explained.

"I didn't know plants communicate."

"They do, all living things communicate. It is called mycelium—tiny threads that form a mycorrhizal network, like the internet, only this is a jungle network." Eryn stood up and brushed off his hands, the whole process of watching him was interesting. He glared into the depths of the cavern. I followed his line of sight, searching for those birds or any signs of life on the path leading deeper into the unknown. "Is anyone there?" Eryn called out. The darkness remained still and silent. "I have a question for you," he tried again, but there was no response.

Cian's fingers traced the ancient etchings on the limestone walls, his eyes scanning each figure with a deep intensity. "I bet you do, Brawl King. We all have questions," he said, breaking the silence.

Barkor shifted uneasily, his gaze lingering on the intricate designs carved into the stone. "What do you mean?" he asked, his tone cautious yet curious.

Eryn's intense gaze locked onto mine. His voice held a hint of frustration and disbelief. "What Ivan's trying to say is, why isn't Ish angry with them? Why are they forcing him to choose between worlds? What makes our world more valuable than theirs?" Eryn then turned and traced his finger along the two-headed snake that slithered alongside a majestic dragon with a forked tongue. "These souls are living, feeling beings like us. And this artwork— it tells stories that we can only begin to imagine. How can we justify erasing their world, their existence, in favor of our own?" The weight of his words hung heavy in the air as we stood in this ancient chamber filled with secrets.

I tilted my head to the side, deciphering his remarks. "What are you saying?"

Eryn leaned in closer, his nose almost touching the complex carvings on the wall. *Was he smelling them?* "I'm saying that I want to know who these Fates presume they are, to toy with our lives like this." His voice held a mixture of indignation and determination. "The carvings seem to taunt us as if they hold some kind of secret that we are not privy to," he said, and I agreed. It was aggravating, and I couldn't help but share Eryn's sentiment. "Who are these Fates, and why are they meddling in our lives?" Eryn's questions didn't surprise me. I had been thinking the same thing ever since I waited in Grayrak for them to arrive. But I had a feeling he was mulling much bigger things than my mind could comprehend. The air around Eryn seemed to shift and waver, and for a moment I was afraid that I had made a mistake bringing them here. But the grin on Eryn's face assured me he knew what he was planning. I looked at him with reverence. *I'm going to show you I know exactly what happened here. We are breaking the cycle of the apple. It ends here,* he said telepathically to us. *He didn't want the Fates to hear.* "But first things first. Let's go find Peter and Gugusan, they must be well on their way to prepare them by now." Eryn grunted as a pulse of disgust burst out of him. He was harboring and repressing his anger towards the Fates.

They fell into a line behind me so I could lead them further down the mountain.

As we entered the hustle and bustle of the San village, women and children ran to meet us, falling to the ground and whispering to each other as they saw the trio with me.

"We must be a spectacle. Tall, handsome, and carrying weapons made of pure gold," Cian noted.

They fell to their knees. "Ah, fuck, Ah, fuck!" they repeated, lifting their hands to us.

"Are they saying what I think they are saying?" Barkor chortled.

"Unfortunately yes. They caught that the first time I came around. Don't ask me when that was, I have no clue." I smiled at them and gently waved my hands up to tell them to stand.

As they stood, they smiled cheerfully. Looking happy to see me. One of the older women got up, shouting at the children. "Ofrendas, K'a'abet in kaxtik ofrendas yéetel jaanal ti' yuumtsilo'obo." They turned and ran into the nearby huts. We watched them as the women stood to the side when the kids returned with armfuls of pineapples, coconuts, bananas, and corn. One had a small pig on a leash and another a chicken under her arm. They packed everything around our feet and fell to their knees again. "Nukuch yéetel poderosos te' k'ujo'obo', k waye' ti' ten ti' leti'ob. Acepte k ofertas," the older woman said and joined the others placing the palms of her hands in front of her face.

"That's kind of funny." Ivan laughed.

"Big purple frog balls! Do they think you are a god?" Eryn laughed as he climbed over the fruit to go to them. He kneeled, touching them on their heads. "Thank you for the warm welcome. We accept your gifts, but we are not what you think we are. Please get up." He showed them to stand while smiling, nodding his head, and thanking each one of them.

Ish, I can't believe you let them think you are a god, he said mind to mind to us.

"Yes they do, and believe me, when I fucked Gugusan, he thought that too. They say Peter and I are gods and that this is our mountain." We all laughed. The children surrounded Eryn, touching him and looking at him while they giggled. He seemed unfazed, allowing their touches and laughing with them as if they shared a secret joke.

After the welcoming had died down, a female stepped forward and told us that Peter and the men had gone ahead and were chasing after Elijah, they said they would meet up with us at the edge of the jungle.

"Máax robó le manzana yéetel corrió ti' le dirección!" she explained furiously and pointed in the direction of the dark underbrush, where a footpath led into the jungle.

I tapped a forefinger on my chin, thinking I might be able to assist. "I can tiptoe out of time and find them," I whispered.

"No!" Eryn stepped into my personal space and looked into my eyes. I saw my distraught eyes staring back at me in their reflection. "No, no time walking or time jumping. Ask them how long ago." He narrowed his eyes. "Ish, is Elijah the dying man I saw briefly in your mind? Who is he?"

"But I have this feeling. Like—fuck, this is hard for me. By stepping out of time, I can follow them at a much faster pace."

Eryn planted his spear into the ground, stepped closer, blocking everyone else from my view. He rested a hand on each of my shoulders. "Ish, listen. We spoke about this. Think. You would once again do this for yourself. Not for us or Peter. You are uncomfortable and worried about Peter, but you are going to make this problem worse."

I blew out a frustrated breath. "I know, but—"

Eryn interrupted me. Shaking his head with a look of sympathy. "Ask them how long ago and in which direction they think they were heading. Ask them where he was running to. Was he going to the city? Ask them," he said sternly, and I heard reason in his voice. I forced myself to calm down and stepped away from him. He was so serious and I didn't want to disappoint my children. I was a warrior. Not a scared boy.

I clasped my fingers together in a subservient prayer position and asked the women Eryn's questions.

"Leti' le nojoch máako' Máax tu bisaj," a short old woman said and pointed again to the footpath. I flapped my arms, asking if they were going to the Angels and Sables. "Da, Eee-li-shaas, da," they answered in unison.

I slapped a flat hand on my forehead and spun around to face Eryn and the others. "She says Elijah ran to warn the Birdmen that we were coming."

"Tell us exactly who the fuck is Elijah?" they asked as if singing in a choir.

I told you to tell us everything, Eryn said into my mind.

"It's a long story." I sighed readying myself mentally, I was once more explaining another one of my fuck ups. "Let's say he's a hitchhiker, a stray, I kind of lost along the way."

"A stray? Is this an animal? Maybe an Anubis? How did you lose him?" they all asked, looking at me like I had never searched for them.

I blew out my cheeks and released it. They waited for me to elaborate. I rolled my eyes and chuckled. There was no easy way around this story. "Okay so this is the short version," I pointed back and forth as I explained, "Elijah was wounded and dying next to the road in Babylon, and we helped him. It was Peter's idea to bring him along for modern medical care. He kind of made him think he was an Angel sent by God to take him to Heaven. We stopped at Andrew's place thinking he could take Elijah to a hospital. Andrew took one look at Elijah and dripped blood into his mouth, shutting the door to Elijah's heaven. He accused us of bullshitting him and the two of them ended up having words. Elijah ran off, thinking I was a demon and Peter a lying fallen Angel. By the time Andrew and I reached them, they were already on the ship, fighting. The next moment, the ship jumped, and a few seconds later, it reappeared. They were gone. I jumped inside to reverse jump, but I could never retrace their steps back to the time and place they went. Lasitor didn't know or didn't want to tell me. So after I searched for a while, I decided to join you in Grayrak, and then upon visiting Phoenix, I met Peter before he had grown his wings. After that we jumped to help around, moving Zelk, and turning Andrew, I visited Phoenix, and then I was taken in for questioning by your leadership. Peter stole the apple, and we escaped to the jungle. Which at that time, Peter saved me, after being lost to me for thirty years. And we came to you for help. That's why Peter knows them well. That's why he is attached to these people. Once again, my time-jumping caused more trouble in my future."

Silence and lots of eyebrows in hairlines greeted me after that story.

"What's wrong with you and Peter? And now Andrew is in on it too? You are the two most irresponsible idiots to be handed a fucking time machine," Ivan said, looking down his nose at me.

"Let's just find Peter and Gugusan." Eryn shook his head in disbelief, then threw his hands in the air and laughed. "I'm starting to think Mika was correct by confiscating your ship and keys."

"Believe me, I will gladly hand them over when we are done here."

I checked the coordinates on my tick-tick thing and calibrated it by triangulating it with my ship, this village, and the direction we were planning to go. That way, no matter what, we would always find our way back here. We thanked our welcoming committee and then turned and worked up a slow-paced run into the trees.

CHAPTER 22
THE REVELATION

"GOOD EVENING, EVERYONE.

Did you know the juniors of the University of Phoenix have designed special contact lenses to help them see at night? It is an optoelectronic silicone that allows visualization of images in low levels of light, improving their night vision. This device mimics the Anunnaki eye as it enhances ambient visible light and converts near-infrared light into visible.

Did you also know that nightly excursions are now part of the weekly entertainment schedule?

Visit your community news page to book your seat and receive your pair of new night vision contact lenses for free.

Have an illuminated night."

ISHTAR
24 970 B.C.

At the foot of the mountain of the Gods
In the jungle of Anzulla

AFTER HOURS of slicing leaves and whacking insects, we made our way through the jungle. We found an open clearing at the foot of the mountain and rested. Against my judgment, Eryn made a small fire to ward off wild animals. "We shall be seen from hundreds of miles," I said under my breath.

He grasped me firmly on the shoulder. "That won't be a bad thing," he said, and I felt a wave of calmness and rightness pushed into me.

Cian wiped his nose and forehead sideways so vigorously the skin looked like it was blistering and peeling off. "Tell me why the fuck are we camping out and not using our powers so we can hurry—and maybe—fucking hurry up and save the planet? This earthy smell of flowers and grass makes me wish I never came here," Cian said for the third time. Exasperated with himself and the insects—all of nature.

"You said you wanted to go on an adventure. You've become complacent as a superhero god staying in that underwater deathtrap," I retorted. "I feel sorry for you. You have the power to sing for nature, maybe that's why all the insects love to sit and suck on you. You're their daddy."

Cian was slapping his cheek, scratching himself and making me feel itchy. "Even my ass crack is itching and not in a good way." Cian sneezed at us. "I bet you Peter and that lot are sitting in a hut somewhere, laughing with

Gugusan and Elijah. Drinking beer and reading tea leaves, or whatever they do in a jungle for entertainment." Cian wiped his nose and eyes with the back of his hand.

Ivan pushed his sleeves up to his elbows. "You are like our walking bug trap. Like one of those sticky flypaper things. Look, I don't have one mosquito on me," Ivan teased.

Eryn was silent as he exchanged excited glances with us. I felt the connection between all of us energized and growing stronger as he took a deep breath through his nose and began speaking.

"Look at this wonderful place. It's like a paradise. I can walk barefoot and my heart yearns for these luscious green forests. I've never seen so many variations of green. All these plants and insects, not to mention the animals I hear roaring deep in the mountains. It saddens me to think we are thinking about making them disappear from existence simply because we are moving apples around. It's selfish thinking of ourselves as better or more important. Do you think we deserve it more than them? No! I've seen what I needed to see. I'm ready to share my thoughts and conclusion with you. It is only a plan and you can suggest something else or make suggestions. But I think what I have come up with will work for all of us. It's a big and bold move. But I know we can do it if all of us work together." I felt the excitement and determination radiating from Eryn. I looked around, reading the other attentive faces, and I knew that with his leadership, we could accomplish anything.

He used the tip of his spear to draw six circles on the ground. *Where was he going with this?*

"What I suggest is to bring our worlds together." He drew one bigger circle in the middle of those other circles. "I've started to compare the things I read in that book, the Bible of Joshua. I compared it to what happened and what was foretold about Earth's history. The Bible explicitly teaches that Elijah's prophecy would find its primary fulfillment at the end of time. We thought that was when the Earth had flooded. Joshua drove me crazy by reading those scriptures where the prophet Malachi says God says, *Behold, I send my messenger, and he will prepare the way before me.* The Disciples of the Anunnaki always thought it was them and that they were restoring all things to bring the gods of the heavens to live with them and to walk among them. But since I heard Elijah was here, a big piece of the puzzle slotted into place. I realized he might be the key evidence I needed. However, given the advanced technology we already have, I suggest we move the Phoenicians here to this place. Let's forget about that place. This world will be where we move it all. This will be the start. The old and the new in one place and time. Here in Anzulla," Eryn said, and pointed to me, putting me on the spot. "With what Ish told me, the obelisks, the positioning of the moon and stars above us, this tells me it is one place. Thousands of years before our births, but in the same place. Isn't it, Ish?" Eryn made more circles in the ground.

I fidgeted and gulped nervously, waking up from what-ever stupid stupor my mind was, while looking at his circles. "Yes, I think so," I answered hesitantly. *He's correct. This must be Anzulla, before Apsu's destruction.*

"Well, it's either that or we are soon going to be taken prisoner and probably be fucked up the ass until we die," Ivan said and stuck his sword into the ground. He dragged his sword from circle to circle, connecting them.

"Ivan, stop it, no one is getting fucked. I'll put up a barrier. If they find us, I want no aggressiveness from any of you, understand?" Eryn looked at the drawing they had just made.

The connected circles look like the human number eight.

"Please join me. Let's pretend we don't see them when they arrive." Eryn patted his leg, and we took a knee, listening to him. I was sure he knew exactly what, where, when, and how we were going to make his plan work. They had wrapped a whole city in layers, I was sure he could shield anything if necessary.

"Let's hear your plan before the Angels and Sables molest us. If they don't kill us, these mosquitos surely will," Cian joked, breaking the tension. He rubbed his upper leg above the knee where it was connected to an artificial lower leg. He may be dramatically crude and speak his mind constantly, but he never complains about his leg or the eye that he willingly lost during an explosion when extracting Ivan and Eryn from the Zelk tower in Grayrak. I side-eyed him. He was fidgety and, instead of sticking his sword in the ground, he laid it across his lap. He sat with his back straight, the dark rainforest behind him, as if trying to ignore nature.

"Sounds to me like you want to be tied up and forced to submit and take it," Barkor said to Cian with a smirk.

"Okay, all jokes aside," Eryn said, and we swallowed our laughs eager to hear what he had come up with. "Ish, I don't want to belittle you and your ship, but to be honest, jumping back and forth, transporting groups of people, won't work. The six of us barely made it inside and jumping groups of Phoenicians here would take years, longer if you jump to the wrong time and place. I suggest Cian go with you and help you..."

Cian let out a satisfied chuckle while rubbing the palms of his hands. "Yes! Then I can finally get my hands on some bug spray."

I didn't know what bug spray was, but I assumed it was something Cian could use for his insect predicament. Nevertheless, I perked up, eager to hear more about the new plan. "I'm all ears," I said to Eryn.

He turned all his attention to me. His elongated pupils sliced through my mental barriers. I was starting to enjoy his full focus rather than squirming nervously. "As soon as you mentioned the Fates, what they said about you rebuilding the time machine, and the fact that it was pre-programmed, I realized they know who we are." He waved his hand to stop a barrage of questions. "No, not because they are a deity and all-knowing. They know you and us. They know everything. Our history and future. Who has been with all of us, observed us? Coaxed me? Who are they? Why did they choose you? What's with the tiny size of the time machine?"

"I've been asking the same question," I said slowly, tiptoeing around his mental probing.

"Like a spiderweb, I worked my way from the outside, through every strand, every corner to the center." Eryn pointed to the small circles connected with the number eight—*maybe they are eights and zeros?*

Eryn kept talking. "My mind wandered to the places anyone, like my father inside the mine in South Africa, like Joshua, like Brad, Mika, and Connor, even Peter, told me about. Anyone who has ever said anything to me, every second of my life," Eryn said, and then pinned me with a glaring stare. "Or visited me, even brought Anubis pups to me."

Holy red dung beetle and scarabs shit, he knew it was me!

*Yes, I do, Ishtar,*he answered me, mind to mind.

"Ish, do you realize your ship looks a lot like our Spacecars, but more similar to the escape pods of the Horizon? Things like the window, the two seats, and the door were salvaged from the Horizon. But some of it, like the instrumentation, the software or the *user manual or travel guide* as you call it, the wiring, and the little knobs, levers, and buttons. They look very similar to what we have in our Phoenician vehicles."

Eryn's reprimanding gaze cut short the loud, disbelieving gasps.

I frowned at the unexpected question. "I never saw my father's ship whole. Only the wreckage. He crashed it long before I was born."

Eryn gave a slight nod as if expecting that answer. "I

have a strong suspicion your father's ship is the Horizon and your time machine was part of it."

"Motherfucker!" Cian exclaimed. "It's the central core! The nucleus! It was drawn into the plans. It sat in the underbelly of the Horizon. It's where Kawa and the programmers installed the motherboard. It housed the mainframe. We were in a rush and uploaded Lasitor to the entire Horizon instead. I cut the separate wiring and the connection to the Zelk Hive. Lasitor's wiring multifunctioned like a coupler between a central processing unit of the Phoenix CPU and the peripheral onboard computer. Linking the Phoenix to the Horizon and the Horizon to the Zelk."

Ivan's eyes widened in comprehension. "Yes, but where did the Zelk get the schematics for the Horizon?" Accusing eyes turned to me. "Is there a possibility that someone came onto your time machine? You told us you were on the moon before they built the fleet? Could someone somehow have logged into the computer and downloaded the information from its database?" Ivan asked.

I didn't like to be interrogated. I exhaled a sigh while wrapping my mind around this. "No. No one knew I was in Grayrak. Only Barkor knew where I'd hidden my ship. I always cloaked my ship and real appearance whenever I was with humans. But..." I paused, thinking. "So Lasitor was uploaded by Cian to the Horizon. We all know that. But how did the Horizon end up in Apsu's hands?"

No wonder Eryn drew circles on the ground, because I needed pictures for this. They kept saying things I had never seen but were right in front of me. Maybe I was standing too close. Maybe I needed to open my mind, step back, and listen.

"How certain are you? Are you one hundred percent sure you never shared the information? You said you fed off the humans and drank their blood, got drunk many times, and jumped here to visit Gugusan. Chasing after Peter, that you somehow knew was here. Found him. Found the apple. Took it back to your sisters on the wrong timeline. Went to Andrew. Lost Elijah and Peter. But yet, Elijah ended up here. Peter was here. The apple was here. In the meantime, you jumped and updated Lasitor. Which now is here. Are you seeing the pattern?"

I sat dumbfounded by Eryn's revelation.

A surge of rage pulsed through me. This was the rami-fications of listening to the Fates—waiting like a fool in Grayrak. All the while I could have jumped straight to Phoenix. I bulged my fists and said through clenched teeth, "Please spell it out for me, because it sounds to me that you say the Zelk built the Horizon because I fucked up. You forget, the Fates told me to bloody go and wait for you on the moon."

"I agree, your Fates and this place are constants, just like you and Lasitor," Eryn said.

The jungle heat was fucking stifling. Sweat rolled in rivulets down my back. The heat of the fire worsened my embarrassment and discomfort. "So you don't think I am to blame?" I asked, my voice trembling with uncertainty and vulnerability.

"You said it yourself. You were their tool. A weapon

your Fates chose to get rid of the evil on the moon." His words hung heavy in the air as we contemplated them.

"The Fates?" I questioned, my mind reeling with the new information.

"Yes, the one you think is God," Eryn said, reaching out to me and touching my knee. Empathy flooded me, like enormous arms wrapping around me. I felt bare, flayed open—my stupid, gullible, childlike belief in the Fates. This was worse than when I found out my Anubis had died. I felt alone and utterly humiliated.

"But who created them?" Ivan interjected, and my curiosity piqued.

Eryn leaned closer. "Ish, think of when you won the war against your father, the evil that consumed him. When you said you went back to Anzulla. What did the Fates say to you?"

I closed my eyes, and cleared my throat, remembering what was said so I could recite it word for word and relay it correctly to them. "They said they have an old enemy that hides inside the darkness and feeds off it. It grows and destroys realities. They said it is as old as time and that they are the cogs of the wheel. I was sent to the moon, and they said my ship was already programmed."

My eyes enlarged as the words of Eryn rang true. "Yes, I see now." Eryn's conclusion astonished me.

"Oh my goodness, Eryn," Ivan exclaimed, eyes wide and slack-jawed. Eryn lifted a hand, smiling lovingly at his husband.

"But there is more. Just like the humans were able to instill their souls into the Zelk mainframe, making robots think like humans, these Fates were battling their enemy on a much-advanced level. Think of it. In that tower was the Zelk brain, which is also a collection of mashed-up human souls. Dark human souls. Information the Disciples got from where? We uploaded a virus into it after we cut Lasitor from the connection. Lasitor created this virus. We attacked the Zelk from two sides, the human and the electronic. That's why you went to the moon. To bring Lasitor closer to the origin, to the factory of evil. To Apsu."

"Brother, you are going off the rails. I hope you don't feel guilty because we infected their mainframe and destroyed their base. Because I can't see how we could have pulled it off any other way," Cian said.

"I know. And no. All I'm saying is that I'm just sad about those poor souls that were trapped inside that tower. Whether infected or not. Whether out of stupidity or just believing things they were taught from a young age by those also infected by the darkness."

Barkor shivered and leaned closer, whispering. "Eryn, what are you saying?"

This was getting interesting. I also wanted to know. Eryn had been thinking about this longer than we thought. Maybe since the day I met him. Not on the moon, but way before that.

He pointed four fingers at us. "You said you've seen this evil, and from what you've told us, battled it. That evil was inside the men, driving them, and leading them to build the tower. Like your father, they were driven by..." He paused dramatically. We waited. "Information, greed, and hunger for power. Then you and your ship got planted right in the middle of it, and you were told not to interfere, but to wait for us." He folded his four fingers into a fist then pointed one finger at me after sweeping his eyes over us.

"You were given a ship already programmed, you were given a time-keeping contraption, you were given the apple. You make the Zelk disappear, and you used Cian's Song to boost your power to move the Horizon to a new timeline. But by doing so, you threw a spanner into the wheels of your Fates. Now, do you see the spiderweb? The Fates told you that you locked us out of the timeline. Now here we are sitting in another. Think bigger." Eryn continued while pointing at me and those weird-ass number eights. "Why do you think the Fates said that they held the balance and that they are old enemies? That they've created time and drive the cogs of the wheels. What if they meant they created this time and this world? They said the evil was growing and consuming life and that you were their hidden weapon. Yes?" Eryn coaxed us.

"So when we were all back on Earth, the Zelk was gone and you locked Phoenix out of that timeline..." He waited for a response and I answered yes with a nod, but was still puzzled. He continued, "Where did they go? Where did those Zelk go?" he asked me.

"I thought I locked us out from being discovered by the Zelk," I answered hesitantly. I didn't know where he was going with this and if he wanted me to tell them about the big change, the catalyst even of 1968, me fucking Andrew and saving the whiskey or not.

"No." He chuckled—answering the question that was forming in the back of my mind.

I was growing impatient and getting worried about Peter. "Then what?" I blurted, and the others laughed at me. I gave them the evil eye and chuckled at Cian, covered with bugs. I wasn't educated like them, but I'm not stupid, I picked up knowledge like deserts collected sand, and I deserved respect. I was one of their fathers, after all.

"I think whoever created Ish's time travel machine is the one with the answers." Eryn swept his hand in a small gesture to the sky. "They are either the ultimate God of the skies, the whole universe, or they are like us. Why would they need contraptions, apples, tablets, and time machines? Why did your Fates have your machine already programmed for you?"

"Big purple frog balls. Do you think God is like us and they are using us?" Ivan asked.

"Of course not! This is not God. But Ishtar's Fates. They are just spikes on the big wheel. They said it themselves. They are cogs in the wheel of time." Cian scoffed at his brother. Barkor didn't say a word. I didn't think he grasped any of this.

"This brings us to Elijah and the apple. If you return it, the loop will continue on Phoenix's timeline. I say we bring Phoenix here and let that reality disappear. Let Apsu, the darkness, the Zelk, the whole reality disintegrate. That's the apple, the Eden, the flood, the wars, the famine, the sickness. The endless catastrophes. It's in the human book of God. The black book Joshua had read to me. The Bible."

"Whoa, hold on. Who is this Joshua you are talking about?" I asked.

Ivan sighed. "It's the man that took care of Eryn when Eryn was..."

Eryn smiled and silenced Ivan, with a gentle hand on his lap. "I was a small boy Brawl, he was like my second father."

"Oh, now I see. I saw the picture of you in your living room," I said, remembering the picture Peter had bumped off the end table the day before. "It must have been fun growing up with you."

The tension around the fire grew palpable as Cian's voice rose in frustration. "No, Eryn had a horrible time growing up. And it's all you and your fucking apple's fault. That fucking apple cylinder seal thing," Cian said.

His brother gave an exasperated sigh. "Okay thanks, brother, but now we all know it's not his fault. It is the Fates, Ish's Fates. That is what Eryn is saying. They orchestrated this."

Eryn nodded earnestly. "Yes, they did."

"But what is the origin of the apple? Who made the apple and the star map? Who hid the Anunnaki gene inside it? Is it that Platonius dude you fucked?" Cian demanded an answer by pointing a finger and waiting for me to speak. I shook my head and stared at the dancing flames. A heavy silence settled over the campfire as they regarded the mysterious origins of the cursed apple and its hidden secrets.

I waited for Eryn to speak up.

To share what he knew about the apple and had asked me not to mention during my questioning. My inquisition.

"I did." Eryn finally broke the silence.

Cian, Barkor, and Ivan blinked as the color drained from their faces. Gasps followed as they turned to look at him in shocked disbelief. His cheeks flushed red, but he straightened his spine, meeting our eyes with confidence.

"I worked with my father, Wolter Wessels, in the lab, crafting all kinds of creations from gold. One day a memory came to me, an idea for a puzzle box. The apple."

Eryn winked at me. I searched the skies for Angels and Sables.

He continued after clearing his throat. "Those inspirations were given to me by Ish's Fates." Eryn winked at me again. For fuck's sake, everyone saw it. "I created the puzzle, the apple, that when taken apart, can be rolled out, revealing the secret code. The same secret I rolled out on a flimsy piece of paper, was on a note from Joshua to my father. I saw it, liked it, and inscribed it. I stamped the calculations inside the gold and thought nothing of it. Like a child drawing a picture and then putting it on the fridge. But the first time I saw the apple in Mika's hands, I couldn't understand how it got there. You see, when I was a young boy, I had given that very same apple to a young pregnant woman who was crying inside a cryopod destined for the moon," he explained, turning to face Ivan and Cian.

Barkor's mother? I privately asked Eryn.

The twin brothers leaned closer, the flames glinting in

their blue eyes as their mouths fell open in surprise. "The mineshaft?" they asked, interrupting my mind-link question to Eryn. The fire crackled louder, echoing the intensity of our thoughts and deep-seated questions.

Could be, if she was the only pregnant young woman on the rocket.

Eryn gave them a nod and a shrug. "I was always exploring and one day I climbed into the rocket to look around when I heard sniffles. She lay all alone and awake. I visited her the next day, opened the cryo chamber, and showed her the apple to cheer her up. She liked it and smiled. Because it made her happy, I gave it as a gift to make her feel better. It was pretty like she was." Eryn smiled as he remembered, but his expression darkened. "But those Disciples were there. They found out she was awake. I hid from them. They just pushed her down, closed the chamber, and made her sleep. I'd snuck away, barely escaping the wild monsters which I know now were Anubis. I never returned there, because at least she was asleep like the others and not alone anymore. Not sad, but frozen." His voice dropped as he whispered. "That's another reason why I asked if anyone got onto your ship on the moon. At first, I thought the girl took the apple with her to the moon. Then I wondered how it made its way from the moon to Gugusan and from Gugusan to Babylon, then back to the Disciples, causing our births due to the information inside it. The leadership of Phoenix confiscated it, and Peter stole it and brought it back here. But then there's Elijah and Peter's story. I couldn't place

Elijah's significance physically in our timeline until I remembered his name was in the Bible. I realized the apple Mika had was the same apple the Disciples must have taken. Only Mika confiscated it, thinking it came from Babylon. Something that was passed from generation to generation with the other relics we found in their possession. *We all thought so, but the apple was never there.* It was never supposed to be in Babylon. That is the loop. The infinity loop. Only it's not just one loop, but three or four loops, maybe more loops, while each meets and cuts at a different point. I copied the information from the bronze tablet. But who had given Platonius the information to stamp on the tablet?"

I frowned, shaking my head, not keeping up with Eryn's thought pattern. And by looking at the others, I wasn't alone. "I don't understand. Are you saying I caused this or not? First, you accuse me of sneaking information to the Zelk, then this?"

Eryn used his sword to point to the circles connected by one continuous line of the number eight drawn on the ground earlier. "Ish, you didn't jump in a straight line up and down. You jumped from one loop to the other. You crossed the loops. That is why Phoenix will cease to exist as well as all of us, if we stay on that loop. It is Apsu's loop."

Dear moon-god, my head was pounding.

Shaking his head, Ivan said, "No, that's not possible."

"It is, and it makes sense," Cian said, then, ever the pragmatist asked, "How are we going to get all of Phoenix inside that tiny time machine?"

"Cian, you just said it. The brain of the time machine is the core reactor, the self-sustaining program of the Horizon. We are not bringing the citizens on the time machine, we are bringing the city. The entire city must be moved here."

"What the fuck?" we exclaimed together.

"Think about it. Ish's family comes from Anzulla. Anzulla is Earth, but far into the past, or for the sake of the loop, very far into the future. Didn't the Fates say Ish had moved his future into his past by taking the apple to the wrong time and place?" Eryn said, placing the final pieces into the puzzle. Somehow, miraculously it started to make sense to me.

"That means me killing my father, was me ending or breaking that loop, but because I took the apple back, I started a new timeline, on which he finds the apple. He doesn't get killed, and he lives to destroy Babylon. He uses the information inside the apple to grow more powerful?" I said.

Cian clapped his hands. "Yes! He's the darkness, the driver behind the Disciples, the Zelk" —Cian made air quotes— "but the Fates intervened by stopping Apsu, by placing Ishtar right at the crossing of the two loops. On the moon."

"The war against Apsu is Earth's Armageddon! The cataclysmic event between good and evil at the end of history," Ivan added.

"You must bring Phoenix here. This is Anzulla. But long before and after your father. Think of it as a short-cut." He pointed to his drawings on the ground. "Like the number eight cut in half. Instead of an eight, we will make it two separate circles by breaking the link here," Eryn said.

"But what are all those tiny circles Ivan connected?" I asked.

Eryn pointed with his spear. "Those are just points in time—when we changed loops. For example, 1968, 2013, 2014..."

"So, that's what the Fates meant by..." Eryn shook his head and the others looked at me and sighed. I stopped mid-sentence, wide-eyed. Obviously, I was still missing something and annoying the crap out of them.

Eryn looked solemnly at me. "Ish, there are no Fates. Your Fates are just Lasitor." Eryn revealed it casually, but I felt like I was having an out-of-body experience.

"Oh, moon-god! Why didn't I see this earlier? That fucker!" I balled my fists. "I should have ripped his wires out!"

Eryn grabbed his spear, stood, and pointed it at me. I leaned back, nervously. "Yes. But if it wasn't for Lasitor, none of us would be here today. Go tell Mika what we want. Tell him to bring the Horizon inside Phoenix. Park the time machine inside the Horizon and Cian, you must sing for it. Connect the time machine with the Horizon and the Horizon with the entire city," he said with finality.

"What?" We stared perplexed at Eryn.

"Are you going to stay here? How will I do it without you?" Cian asked.

"Go! Do it, brother. I know you can. Think of it as one

living organism. The time machine is the heart and the rest of it connects to it like veins. Think of the forest floor."

Cian looked bewildered. Overthinking again. "And what are you going to do?"

"We are going to make peace and play with our new friends." Eryn looked up. He knew before us that we had winged visitors. Instead of freaking out and taking an aggressive stance, he plunged his spear deep into the ground, held onto it with both hands, and sang notes with a beautiful melody. A massive translucent bubble formed around us. Like Phoenix, he had created a barrier locking us safely inside. Barkor and I stood open-mouthed, blinking, and waited for an explanation from Cian and Ivan, who treated the display of power as just another thing Eryn could do and shrugged at us. As if Eryn creating protective bubbles was the norm.

"Look, they are waiting, calmly," Eryn said with a lopsided grin.

I believed in him. He would not allow harm to anyone. Not us or them. Goosebumps covered my body as I enjoyed watching him take charge by peacefully displaying his power. I knew he was both powerful and humble. He never had to prove anything to anyone. He just stood to the side, observing silently. I felt it from the day I met him for the first time. I watched him work, his strength pulsated around him, and his skin glowed with a sheen of gold and blue. Not overly so, but I knew where to look. It started on that small patch of skin behind his ears and then spread to the rest of his body. About the size of a grape.

Cian sneezed, breaking the magnificence of the moment. "I think you are allergic to this place because of the feathers," Ivan said, pointing up to our looming crowd of visitors hovering a few hundred feet above us. Now and then a black or white feather trickled from the sky. They were creeping me out. So I turned my gaze to Eryn, who was in charge, and I was happy with that.

"Cian, just think of yourself as the friend of nature. Stop fighting them. Stop thinking about the itching and they will go away. All they want is for you to acknowledge them," Eryn said in a surly tone. This was the first time I had heard him being irritated. Cian gulped, realizing Eryn was serious. Eryn changed his focus to the matter at hand. "I want no one's death on my hands. We came here in search of peace, but if we are forced to protect ourselves, I can defeat them with a single swipe of my spear." Not looking up, or bragging about it, Eryn was stating a fact.

"Yeah, but look at them," Cian whispered. Discreetly, we looked up at the fluttering specks in the night sky growing in numbers as more arrived.

With a cautious glance over his shoulder, Eryn crouched next to the small fire, the flames twinkling in his intelligent eyes. *We shouldn't be here*, he murmured into our minds. *This is not our place, not our home.* He paused, staring into the flames. *Not yet*, he finally added.

"Okay, Ish and I will go," Cian announced, happy to get away from Eryn by pulling me back into the jungle.

"Let's make a run for it. Eryn, brother, good luck! Come, Ish, we have a city to save."

We ran. "Are we able to exit the bubble?" I asked, halting for a second in front of the glinting membrane.

"Of course," Cian answered, dragging me through the waterfall of snot that closed behind us.

CHAPTER 23
LUCI'S QUARTER

"*MORNING.*

Did you know what it means to think quickly on your feet? It means making good decisions, keeping cool and calm while achieving things without having to consciously think about them too much, and doing it faster than others.

Did you also know treating the underlying cause of hot feet like nerve damage can help relieve hot or burning feet?

Some ways to do that are to sleep with your feet uncovered and exposed to the cool night air, freezing your socks, using cold packs or cold water bottles, or pointing a fan toward your feet.

By visiting your community news page for more tips to stay cool in any situation, you increase your ability to think quickly on your feet.

Have a cool day!"

. . .

PETER
24 970 B.C.
At the foot of the mountain of the Gods
In the jungle of Anzulla

ELIJAH HAD me chasing him all across the lower bloody fucking mainland until we finally arrived at the cliffs that towered over the sparkling blue ocean. "You've got nowhere else to go, Elijah. You might as well give up and surrender."

He held his arms up. "Whatever! The plan was to keep you occupied for an hour or two. I surrender in peace."

I hovered a few feet above him. One step backward and he would tumble to his death. All I had to do was dive down and give him a slight push.

He waited, and I waited. The ocean spray drifting from crashing waves below cooled my temper. "Fucking ungrateful fraternizer, that's what you bloody are." I grabbed him by his wrists and turned back to reunite with the others. Midway up the river, we noticed movement. "Something's happening at the jungle's edge!" I said as we neared the meadow at the foot of the mountain of the Gods.

"Put me down!" Elijah squirmed. I swooped low, deposited him, and soundlessly joined Gugusan and his warriors hiding in the treeline. I tucked my wings and followed as we made our way through the dense growth of giant ferns and tropical plants. I moved cautiously, trying my best to avoid stepping on any twigs or leaves that could give away our location. The San warriors were like stealthy jungle cats, moving effortlessly through the underbrush. Once again, I spotted the white flowers that looked exactly like the paper flower Ish had given me. Gugusan called the red plant sap, *love juice.*

He'd fed me the stuff when I missed Ish so much that I felt like dying. This juice saved my life and I know first-hand why the Anunnaki thought of it as holy and necessary to survive. Without hesitation, I reached out and plucked the thick stem of one, feeling red sap drip down my hands and arms. It had a sweet scent, reminiscent of roses. I broke open the bulbous stem and sucked on the small fist-sized, coconut-like fruit, filled with light pink water inside. I was thirsty, so I slurped up the sap, cleaning my sticky arm with my tongue. Gugusan snapped his head in my direction. "Yeah, I know," I whispered at his scolding gaze.

"I hope they know what they are doing. Luci was eager to make peace and get the games started," Elijah said in his best broken English while peeking from behind a gigantic tree.

I clutched the big white Loursveto flower against my chest. I couldn't wait to show it to Ish. My eyes darted from one side to the other, searching the clearing for him.

"Oh, my fucking god!" I yelped and threw the flower to the ground. My heart slammed into my ribcage as I fumbled to unsheathe my obsidian short sword. I spotted black-winged Birdmen circling in the sky like vultures, then fluttering down one by one. Eryn, Ivan, and Barkor stood weaponless, looking up and smiling as if it were a friendly alien reaping for investigative anal probing. The scene of us crash landing and Ish being attacked and packed by white and black Birdmen flashed through my mind. Followed by the memory of Elijah hitting me over the head, and I daggered him mentally in his back. Straight into his heart. I hated his two-timing, selfish enemy-fucking ass.

"Take it easy, it's looking worse than it is," Elijah coaxed. He's been siding with the Birdmen, his loyalty was questionable.

"Gugusan, we have to help them," I said, already taking off flying.

"Wait, Peter!" I heard Elijah shout, but as I glanced back, the San were already following and streaming out of the forest behind me.

"Fuck yes!" I shouted, tasting the victory of my first battle. I flew so fast that the wind blinded me as I rushed to help Ish and our friends. *They must have followed us into the jungle and unknowingly stepped into the clearing where the Birdmen patrolled the edges of the woods.* Eryn, Barkor, and Ivan lifted their hands in surrender and slowly turned, lifting their shirts, seemingly showing the Birdmen they weren't packing any weapons. *Idiots!*

My eye caught a movement in the back. Cian and Ish were hunched down, slipping away deeper into the jungle. *Where to?* I was having the worst case of playing catch up. I didn't know if they went looking for me—for us.

"What's happening here? Are we fighting? Should I follow Ish and Cian?" I asked them telepathically as I landed, skidding with my feet over the wet grass.

No, don't draw attention to them. Stay calm, Eryn said into my mind. Holding his arms out where everyone could see his empty hands, he beckoned me to wait behind him. The black-winged ones scared me more than the ones that looked like me. They seemed unworried by my presence. I knew what they were capable of and they knew I was the one who had helped Ish to escape. *They almost killed him.*

"No, Peter, calm yourself and tell your friends to put down their weapons," Eryn urged, while not taking his gaze off the Birdmen.

"That's both easy and stupid to say. Where are your weapons? Where are your swords and spears? What the fuck is wrong with you? I don't trust them," I spat, clutching my sword. My eyes darted from one Birdman to the other, ready to defend my friends if they so much as twitched a wing too fast.

"*There is another way*," Eryn said as he lifted his arm, waving to the San army to slow down after I ignored him. Like a herd of bison running into an invisible wall, Gugu-san's warriors came to a dead halt behind us.

"He says put down your weapons," I shouted. Elijah relayed the order to the warriors, and they relaxed and stood down. We all were looking at Eryn, who had his arms raised above his head in surrender. But his fucking eyes were closed. *Trusting fool, anyone can knife him from any direction.*

"What are you doing? Open your eyes. It's not time for contemplation." He ignored me with a look of peaceful bliss on his face.

We all watched him. Waiting.

"Why aren't they attacking us? What are they waiting for?" I asked, jittery with nerves.

"They're waiting for your people to make the first move," Elijah, said as he joined us. Eryn kneeled on one knee and Elijah followed his example—the Igigi wasn't right in the head. Maybe because he was already so close to death when Andrew had given him his blood. Weird shit was going down, and I didn't like or trust this. *Maybe they ate or smoked something in the village.* Elijah believed he was important and always inserted himself right in the middle of everything. He patted Eryn on the shoulder as if he had known him for years, then greeted Ivan and Barkor as if they were old friends. I stayed back, making sure the San warriors were ready to pounce or didn't fuck this up, *whatever Eryn was planning.*

Perplexed, we watched the spectacle. With my wings open and ready to take flight I paced up and down, chewing my nail. Eryn tilted his head and cupped his hand to his ear. "Listen," he said. "What do you hear?" Oh god, he was tripping.

"Gu, the woman gave them mushrooms!" I whispered. He chuckled and pointed to them, telling me to shut up and watch.

"I don't hear any-fucking-thing! Just the thunderous drone of their wings and silence, no thoughts, no feelings. Why?" Barkor asked.

Eryn tipped his head to the side and narrowed his eyes. "They're waiting for something?" He cupped his ears with his hands. "They're listening?"

For what? I asked telepathically. Eryn got up and then looked at me as if he knew something none of us did.

"Maybe they're waiting for you to bloody fucking say something," I answered under my breath.

He grinned at me, took a deep breath, and spoke loud and clear. His voice boomed over the clearing and echoed into the skies. "The first day I realized I had powers," he leaned back, looking up at the horde in the sky, "was a wonderful day filled with laughter and giggles. What boy wouldn't like telling objects and animals what to do, or commanding the wind where to blow and the rain where to fall? I knew that day I was destined to do great things. Not kill or fight a war, not destroy an already destroyed world. No, I was born to solve problems off-battlefield. This is why I knew I was the King of the Brawl. Not the king others thought me to be."

"We know all that shit. Stop monologuing and get to the point, Brawl King," Ivan said, sounding worried and waiting for his husband to get down from the soapbox he was tripping on. No one in their right mind would look up at an army of sex-crazed Birdmen and smile, telling them how wonderful he was.

"This is the climax I have anticipated all my life. This is why I never wanted to be a human king. A king like all the other kings. This is amazing and for once nothing sucks fucking stink frog balls and it all makes sense." Eryn laughed. He laughed so hard we couldn't resist as all the air, every molecule around us, turned happy and positive. My feathers rustled and the hairs on my arms felt electrically charged as if a lightning storm was coming.

"Damn, that was good juju! I love you and your real weapon of choice?" Ivan noted, and everyone smiled. The longer this went on, the longer I got to experience what the Phoenicians always bragged about. I was impressed, even some Birdmen flew down closer to us. I expected blowback and the promise of death after being their sex slaves, but again, I had no clue what was going on in real life. My years of hiding away in a lab and then a cave were catching up with me.

"Everyone, this is Luci. He is a very good friend of mine. Groda and I are in a relationship with him," Elijah said and confirmed what we had suspected this whole time. *Traitor!* Stars in his eyes, Groda blushed. Elijah wiped his hair to the side, as if self-conscious. I hawk-eyed them as my friends shook hands with Luci. Then Luci shocked me by stepping forward and embracing and kissing both Elijah and Groda, showing all of us they were together. As if knowing I was watching him, Elijah broke the embrace, stepped back, and crossed his arms. Then he grinned at me, pulling one shoulder up to his ear.

"Didn't I tell you he and Groda were sucking the Bird-man's cock? No wonder Luci helped us escape. A bloody threesome, for years, right under my nose!" I threw my hands up. Involuntary, my wings flared open. *Why didn't they tell me?* "Did you know about Groda?" I asked our tribe leader, who was smirking at me.

"I had my suspicion. I saw them sneak away and followed them once." He lifted his chin. "It's fine with me. Elijah and Groda were making friends."

I was happy for Elijah. I guess the Birdmen aren't the

enemy anymore. "Why didn't you say anything earlier? I flew after the idiot, thinking he was going to betray us. I could have killed Elijah! I wanted to. I really-really wanted to drop him on his head today."

"Pfft." Gugusan waved me off. "You can't even catch, kill, or gut a fish. Also, it was not my thing to say, or reveal to you," Gugusan said with a smug look on his face.

"Hmmm. In my eyes, Elijah is still a sneaky fuckwad. I'm disappointed, but also glad for them. At least saving Elijah turned out to be the right thing to do." I sheathed my sword and placed my hands on my hips. "I'm feeling less guilty," I said proudly.

Gugusan dipped his chin at me and said with a serious tone, sharing wise words, like a father to a son, "Never feel guilty for doing the right thing. When you do, wait, and it will all turn out for the best."

Eryn spoke up. "We heard about your games. We want to challenge you to a game, and if we win, we'd like you to consider our proposal."

"You and who wants to play?" Luci asked, looking at Elijah and preening. *Did they plan this?*

"Five of us against five of you. Your game, your rules. But if we win—"

Luci interrupted, barking a laugh at the Brawl King. The skies filled with more laughter.

Eryn seemed unfazed. He smirked and put a hand over his heart. "If we win, we ask you to show mercy and save us. We are here to ask for your help. For your hospitality. Without you, it is impossible to find the door. Please grant us free passage. Open your skies so we may come to live among you."

Astonished, Luci reached into his pants pocket and produced a coin. He held it up for all to see and announced in a deep dark voice, "He is talking about this!" The coin glinted in the moonlight. He handed it to Eryn. Ivan and I leaned closer. Its surface was worn and weathered, but there was no doubt. At first glance, we all knew what it was. "This is a relic of almost forgotten times," Luci said. Eryn's fingers traced the engravings on the coin's face, his eyes distant as a deep frown formed on his forehead. Others gathered around us, their curious gazes fixed upon the coin as it got passed around and finally handed back to Luci. "It belonged to my great-grandfather. He used to tell me stories about this coin, stories of adventure and times he promised I would see." A hush fell over the crowd as they leaned in, eager to hear more. Luci took a deep breath, allowing nostalgia to wash over him before continuing. "He spoke of a world where this coin held great power." His voice grew louder with excitement. The Birdmen hovered closer, some landing and joining the San warriors. "Legend has it that he who possessed it arrived through the door between worlds. He urged me to look at the skies. To observe and wait for the signs of unimaginable wonders."

Whispers of awe rippled through the crowd as they absorbed the weight of Luci's revelation. They exchanged glances, captivated by the notion of an extraordinary fore-told arrival unfolding before them. Luci raised the coin higher, mesmerizing everyone. His eyes sparkled as he declared, "This is the sign. I was right, the blood moon brought the king."

A chorus of cheers erupted from the Birdmen as if Luci's words had ignited a dormant, flaming answer to all their prayers.

"I know that quarter," Eryn said. "It's Simon's. Dr. Simon McCormick, Brad McCormick's son."

"What the fuck?" I asked. "It could be anyone's quarter. Millions were minted in the US. Or am I missing something?"

Eryn held up an open palm, asking Luci for another look at it. "This is a rare Wisconsin quarter. Only a few were minted in 2004 A.D. Look at the front of the coin, there's a cow, a peeled husk of corn, and a sliced wheel of cheese along with inscriptions of when Wisconsin was admitted into the Union of States, in 1848 A.D. with the word, *Forward*, which is Wisconsin's state motto. The quarters that were released in 2004 have a small design difference that shows an extra leaf on the illustrated corn husk." Eryn told the coin's story like a mint historian.

"Yes, but why do you think it's Simon's?" Ivan asked. Eryn handed me the quarter.

"My teeth marks."

"What? When did you have Simon's coin in your mouth?" Ivan asked, sounding pissed off and jealous at the same time as he grabbed the coin from me.

"When I was a small Brawl boy. When I snuck around in Phoenix. One night, I snuck into their room. I never stole anything, I promise. I just peeked around, seeing what stuff people had. I found this on his bedside table.

He and Paul were sleeping. I kind of tasted it. You know, like when you taste gold."

"My big Brawl, no one but you goes around tasting and licking things as if it were gold around here."

Eryn smiled shyly. "Probably not, but I was young, and I liked the taste of it, especially when I bit into it and left my teeth marks. It amused me to leave something of myself in it."

I just bit down on my lip and shook my head, forcing myself not to judge or shame him in front of everyone. "So this means somehow Simon's coin ended up here. We don't know if it was him, or if someone had taken it from him."

"But this just proves what I suspected. Now I know Cian and Ishtar are going to succeed," Eryn said, taking the coin from Ivan and handing it back to Luci.

"But...how?"

"*Shhht!*" Ivan shushed me with a pointed look—irritating, spoiled brat. "I want to hear what Luci says to Eryn. Listen and stop asking questions."

"Are you understanding them?" I asked and then remembered Ish. "Where are Ish and Cian going?" I asked.

"*Shhht!*" Ivan looked at me with daggers in his eyes this time.

"Sorry. Fuck. Talk about mister prissy, high all mighty," I retorted. "He thinks because he is married to Eryn, he is now better than us?" I said to Elijah and Groda, who relayed it to Gu, who told the men and women in his army, and we all laughed at Ivan's expense.

Barkor stepped closer to me and whispered. "Ish and Cian went to get the time machine. Then they are coming back, bringing Phoenix with them. Or that is the plan."

"Huh?" I furrowed my brow, baffled. "What's going on?" I asked. Barkor exchanged a knowing look with the others before turning back to me.

"We'll fill you in on everything soon," he said, his voice serious and guarded.

"We will elaborate later," Ivan said—agonizing me.

Wings spreading open, I rocked back onto my heels. "How will they bring all those people here with that small machine?" I asked, astonished, as my eyes widened in disbelief.

Barkor's eyes crinkled at the corners. Head down, he explained under his breath. "They're bringing the entire city. Cian is going to connect the time machine to the center of Phoenix City and jump here." He spelled out the intricate details of their plan, his warmth and empathy for my confusion palpable as he patted my shoulder reassuringly.

"Is that even possible?" I asked.

"*Shhht!*" Ivan said again, scowling at us.

"Let's hope so. We can talk later. If these Birdmen agree to it, it will prevent us from looking like we want war and to take over their homes. That's why no weapons and no aggression, Peter. Understand?" I understood, and I liked the plan. I loved it here and I loved Gu and his tribe. This place felt like home to me.

"Hmmm, that makes sense. Thanks for explaining, Barkor."

"Anytime. I know how it feels when others make plans and you're not included," Barkor said, but I sensed there was a bit more history to that remark. I suspected it was about Cian's plan to evacuate the moon without telling him the details. Ish had mentioned that Cian was purposefully keeping Barkor in the dark. Most probably to avoid sticky questions and untimely close contact.

Barkor cleared his throat. "I can't believe how quickly I'm picking up their language." He gestured to the sky and then to Gugusan. "The only ones who still give me trouble understanding them are those scantly feather-covered people from the jungle." He waved to Gu, who flashed a grin and nodded toward us.

"Ish told me that he had implanted an Anunnaki dictionary of sorts in the subconscious parts of their minds. But I guess for me it is easier to communicate with them after living among them for decades."

"I remember. You mentioned that earlier," Barkor whispered. I liked him. He was perfect for Cian. While Cian was the tornado inside a blizzard, he was the calm after the storm. Ish found them melodramatic, but I would say they are intensely honest in everything they do and say. They aren't attention seekers.

"This meeting turned out to be different from what I imagined," I said. My eyes roamed over the spectacle playing out.

"Yes, it is," he said and turned his attention back to Eryn.

"We knew about Elijah and his message, even before meeting him. We also know about you. We don't have your

LUCI'S QUARTER

kind living in our time, but we have written stories of how good and brave you are. Our time is ending, and we need your permission to come and live here in peace with you." As Eryn spoke, his voice was low and friendly. "Many years ago, I had a friend, Joshua, who told me your stories and about beings like you. Please come closer, Elijah." Eryn waved at the exotic-looking man who checked in with Groda and Gugusan and then me for answers, but this time, we shrugged. We did not know what the fuck was going on. This was a new campfire story, and I imagine hearing the San telling it to their children every night for the foreseeable future.

Elijah threw his staff to the ground and went to Eryn. I couldn't hear what they said to each other. There was nodding, congratulating, and laughing, and then they waved the Birdmen closer. "Look at the moon," Elijah shouted. "It's an omen. This red moon will shine until it meets the sun. Together, the sun and the moon will crack open the door in the sky for the lost children to come home. Here in this hidden ancient land, the ones that will come are the ones you have all been waiting for," Elijah exclaimed like, a senile prophet, warning us about the end of times. "The King of kings will bring his children together. The knowledge we seek will arrive from beyond the boundaries of the skies."

"Be careful, my Brawl." Ivan shifted from one leg to the other as if he needed to piss or something. "There are too many, I can't see him. Is Eryn okay? Do you see him?"

"Calm the fuck down, pretty boy," I bitched. He looked

521

at me, like *who do you think you are*, then back at the crowd milling around Eryn.

Suddenly, shouting and roaring, the black and white masses took flight.

Eryn and Elijah got up. Wiping the feathers, dirt, and grass off their legs, then smiled. "Let the games begin," Eryn yelled with a fisted hand of victory in the air. "They've accepted our proposal and challenge. We will come here to live among them!"

He widened his arms and bellowed a deep unending croak that reverberated through the air, sounding like a thunderstorm with the promise of torrential rains ending a drought that had lasted much too long.

He sang.

Revealing his true strength, Eryn walked further into the field. In front of him, the skyline, mountain ranges, and treetops were darkened by the outline of black and white fluttering wings. He sat down in the tall grass and rested his hands on his knees. Singing a magnificent song no one knew but everyone loved. Grace and power filled the air, as if nature itself was rejoicing in the presence of Eryn's voice. Rabbits and deer emerged from their hiding places, inquisitively smelling the air and like all of us, being enchanted by the melody. This was a moment of unity, where the song connected all living beings, bridging the gap between the science I knew and trusted, and the mystery of this place I could never explain.

This song will forever be remembered and sung by the people of Anzulla.

CHAPTER 24
MOVING PHOENIX

"*GOOD MORNING.*

Did you know that before the Earth flooded, humans used to pack up their homes, and put all those items inside something the size of a small one-bedroom apartment on wheels? Yes, my dear humans, they would take time off work and leave their pets with their neighbors to camp out. Amenities, such as flush toilets and running water, were scarce, and for some reason, they found that relaxing.

I know, right? But sometimes it is good to learn about the past to be able to appreciate the future.

Visit your community news page to read up on surviving in the wild while thirsty and relaxing with dirty butt cracks.

Have a campy day."

ISHTAR
2148 A.D. (96 A.T.)

One year after the inquisition
Phoenix, underwater glass dome city

AS SOON AS the Bubblecar made it through the entrance tube into the Transportation Dome, we parked next to the platform and disembarked in a rush. Cian and I were making an array of funny noises as we ran like two irritated rhinos through crowds of unsuspecting residents. We headed straight on one path to the Leadership Office of Phoenix. We found the doors locked, and a big note attached to it.

Scribbled in English, it said, *We are taking a day off. Unless Phoenix is flooding or burning, you can find us in Recreation Seven. Signed Gen. Brad McCormick.*

"Fuck!" Cian slammed his fist into the disappointing message, and then he turned and ran. "Follow me!"

I sprinted after him. We hopped, excused, and apologized as we passed humans. Luckily, most heard us coming and melted into the walls to make room for us. Cian, sword in hand, looked like he was about to assassinate someone, especially with his shining blue Zelk eye. I called in a hushed tone, "Cian, your sword. Please, we are scaring the people." He looked at me, then his sword as if he hadn't realized it was in his hand, and hastily put it into its sheath between his shoulders on his back.

We'd been running through the jungle, collecting all kinds of pesky insects and itchy leaves. We were drenched in sweat, our clothes torn and muddy. I've resisted using my powers so far, which was good because I realized I never knew what the fuck I was doing. Cian would swear now and then, as the urgency and weight of the inevitable discussions grew heavier. Not to mention getting all the citizens on board with our crazy plan. Then somehow Cian needed to connect the time machine to the Horizon and the Horizon to the heart of Phoenix.

As if reading my mind, Cian answered me as we descended the circling stairs to the ground floor. "I've decided to first fly and install the time machine on the Horizon. Then we have to park the Horizon inside Phoenix by reversing into the Transportation Dome. It shouldn't be too difficult. It is where my fathers built the Blue Halcyon and Spacecars. It will be a tight fit, but I think it's doable. Otherwise, I have to bring the city up to the surface and..."

"No, that's a perfect plan, as long as the doors are big enough to enter," I said, as we came to a dead halt at the sight of a man standing at attention for us.

"Captain Bill Thornton! Are you now guarding doors?" Cian heaved air into his lungs and patted the man's shoulder.

The guard beamed. "I'm happy to do any kind of work, General. Since you left, the crew has been bored and depressed. We went from intolerable to zero action when you left, sir."

Cian gave the man a fixed look of determination, his Zelk eye shining a blue hue over the captain's proud face. "No more standing around. I'm back and the shitshow is too. Go gather the men and meet us in the Transportation Dome in an hour."

"Yes, we need your expertise to maneuver the Horizon, by backing her up into the Transportation Dome," I added.

"Sir, yes sir!" He saluted, all teeth and excitement.

Then, we burst through the swinging doors. Among the chlorinated clean water, other very questionable smells hit my sinuses. Cian's face scrunched up, and I knew he smelled it too. "What the fuck?" he asked, enthusiasm evaporating. His gaze swept over the lively scene. Stuttering and stammering over his words, he instantly flushed red in the face, as he spat his dismay. "Here we were running through jungles, traveling worlds to save humanity, and you are fucking having orgies! Leisuring like you don't have a care!"

"My son!" Mika cheered with a glass half-full and spilled even more of its contents into the bubbling water. Steam billowed up from the surface, obscuring their nakedness, but naked they were. As Mika and Connor bobbed in the tumultuous boiling water, dark groin areas, limp cocks, and soft balls floated flaccidly. The steam room smelled like whiskey and other body fluids I dare not mention. Cian was livid seeing his parents in this state, and I didn't want to increase his irritation by pointing out the obvious. I grinned. He was experiencing a rare shocked wordless state. It was only a festive erotic get-together. Brad and his husband Rick were bobbing up and down, facing each other. Rick's rapid up and down movements and arching back clearly indicated he was riding his husband and reaching the apex of his climax. The two vampires, Juandre and Andrew, were relaxing in each other's arms on a strange narrow long chair made for sleeping next to the pool, I guessed. Somewhat decent, with towels wrapped around their lower bodies, they lay draped with limbs intertwined and each had a glass in hand—the source of the whiskey smell.

It was private enough, so I didn't understand Cian's reaction. Yes, Andrew and Juandre were supposed to be sober and protecting Phoenix. But other than that, they were adults. Letting loose once in a while is good for the soul. They'd had lots to deal with lately and if I were in their shoes, I would have done this a long ass time ago. I smiled, thinking there might be time to join them. They have more than enough whiskey to share.

"Did you get the apple? Are we doomed or not?" Brad asked, swimming to the side and holding onto the rails to pull Connor and the other closer so they could get out. It was a team effort and they had perfected the art of getting out of the turbulent churning waters.

"He is my son too. He is my boy!" Connor rolled onto his stomach, pushed himself up on his hands and knees, grabbed a towel, and wrapped it around his waist.

"What the fuck is going on here? Why is this place smelling like a fucking bathhouse?" Cian threw more towels at the men and turned his back to them. I didn't know if it was anger or a combination of the heat, the running, or shame, but Cian was flaming red on his neck, face, and ears.

Brad was the last one to get out, still frolicking and holding on as the stream blasted his body from side to side. "Because it is a bathhouse. Our bathhouse," he announced, eyes closed with a post-orgasm look on his face.

Cian ignored Brad. "Come, boy, hello my big handsome protector," Cian cooed as Rotty, Igor, and Devil jumped up to meet him, nearly pushing the big guy over. "Yes, I missed you. I see you missed me." Cian laughed, hugging the three Anubis. I swear it looked like they smiled.

I took a step closer, taking a chance, testing if they would growl. It was my lucky day. Igor and Devil turned their attention to me, rubbing their thick necks and foreheads against my stomach. My chest tightened. I missed my companion, my friend. As if feeling my sadness, they whined and rubbed against me harder. "Yes, I know. And thank you." I swallowed a thick knot in my throat then stepped back. Their yellow eyes followed my retreat. As one, they turned and made themselves comfortable on the big soft pillow thing that seemed to be theirs. They took guarding these humans very seriously. I was happy to be finally accepted by them.

"Shut off that noise. We must talk immediately!" Cian's fury redirected my attention to our urgent mission.

"Why? Can't you see this is a party and parties have music?" Juandre said, still sprawled out. Andrew sat up next to him, pursing his lips and agreeing with his husband. They looked at each other and back at us, nodding. All agreed—we were party crashers.

Cian pointed a finger at them and scowled. "One fucking day? What the fuck? We leave you for one day and risk our lives to save the world, no two bloody worlds, and you throw a party. I never thought I would ever say this, but I'm utterly disappointed in you. Look at you. You are drunk and having orgies. I never..." Cian flapped his hands in front of his eyes, not looking at their nakedness while I secretly adored seeing their pale bodies, flawlessly sculptured, looking ageless and mature simultaneously.

Brad pulled himself up by the handrails and stepped onto the wet tiles like some kind of water god. "More like one year!" Rick handed Brad a towel, but not before I had gotten an excellent view of his taut, hairy buttocks.

Mika ignored the orgy comment and slipped a pair of soft linen trousers on. "Where is your brother?" he asked, changing the subject. Connor also got dressed in haste, seemingly to appease their distraught son. Andrew pulled Juandre up and handed him a red robe and slippers. It seemed all the men switched from being carefree debaucheries to emergent catastrophic aversion in a heartbeat.

"Lasitor, please turn off the music," Brad ordered. The loud *doof-doof* noise dissipated into absolute silence. My eardrums zinged. I opened my jaw to pop my ears, stuck a finger in each, and wiggled it. It didn't help. The sound of swirling water and anxious breathing hung in the air, accentuating the pending urgency. I inhaled through my nose. The intoxicating smells of male body fluids reminded me of my Kuku. I missed him and I worried about him, but those smells had me salivating.

Hands on their hips, the men awaited us to speak. I looked at Cian. Better him than me. I might divulge more than necessary at this stage.

"We have work to do. Lots to explain and in not much time," Cian blurted and looked at me for help. I pulled my shoulders up to my ears.

"Go on, tell them," I urged him. My skin itched. I looked longingly at the inviting waters, then at my clothes and hands. The mud was drying and had collected under my fingernails, and I dared not lick my lips. I was certain jungle sludge covered my entire face like it did Cian's.

"Yes, go on. You've got our full attention," Brad said with a stern attentive look on his face.

"Or do you want to go back to the Leadership Office?" Connor asked while stepping closer. He shook my hand and hugged Cian. The others followed suit. "It's good to see you, but please tell us. Are Ivan, Eryn, and Barkor okay? How is Peter doing? Was he able to—phew, you smell." Connor waved his hand in front of his nose.

Cian squirmed and broke the embrace. "Of course we would smell. We've been running through a jungle for hours. What do you mean, a year?"

I shuffled my feet, feeling guilty and ashamed, then I clasped my hands. "Sometimes I jump a teeny bit further backward or forward as planned. Sorry." Cian narrowed his eyes at me. *You better take us back to the same time and place*, he said telepathically, not embarrassing me further.

I gave him a firm, I'm-going-to-try-my-best look. Then he returned to Connor's question. "Last we saw them, Eryn was working on a plan. They were heading into a clearing as we ran back to the ship to come and get you. Peter was chasing after Elijah and Gu's warriors. Barkor is good. I know he can handle himself."

"Then it was an excellent idea to stay here. That sounds like too much physical work to me." Andrew slammed his hand over Juandre's mouth and shushed him. If Andrew didn't censor him, who knows what else Juandre would say.

Cian shook his head at the cheeky Juandre. "As you can see, we are still alive, but we don't know what is going to happen after Eryn confronts the Angels and Sables. It all depends on whether he can somehow convince them to let us go there."

"So, Eryn suggested we go another route?" Brad's gaze jumped from person to person, reading the room. Crossing my arms, I threw Andrew a pointed look.

"Hmmm." I rubbed the back of my neck. "I think it's best if we tell you his whole conclusion, as it all started with Elijah," I said. Andrew shot me an *oh my god* as he realized it was the Elijah he had saved all those years ago. I bit my cheek and dipped my gaze.

"The apple situation has changed. Eryn has a theory about my mission, the Anunnaki, and the Fates. This place with the Birdmen, as Gu's tribe calls them, is Anzulla. My time machine is part of the original Horizon. Oh moon-god, Eryn made it sound so simple," I said, looking at Cian for help this time. He rolled his hand, indicating for me to continue. Perplexed, wide-eyed faces waited for me to speak. "The short version is we agreed that the easiest way to save us all is to take Phoenix there," I said, crossing my arms.

Connor's body snapped rigid and there was a tightness in his face. "The two of you better explain to me who

Elijah is. Because if this is 'Elijah,' my Roman Catholic mind is going to have a hard time reconciling this one," he said.

Juandre jumped, hands in front of his mouth, "Yeah, me too." He looked quizzically at his husband, but Andrew ignored him by appearing to be inspecting the tablet Mika was writing on.

"Yes, Eryn said that there is a one hundred percent chance our Elijah, me and Peter's, is that Elijah. I didn't think he was worth mentioning earlier, given the information overload and simplification of facts," I said, already thinking how I was going to simplify the next mouthful of Eryn's revelation. I cleared my throat. "Eryn thinks that us rescuing Elijah is a significant point in the timelines. As you know, I'm not so sure about the original timeline, but I guess that doesn't matter at this stage. The condensed version is that we brought Elijah with us after delivering the apple to the wrong timeline. Elijah was convinced he was going to Heaven and thought Peter was the angel of death. Peter didn't want to leave him alone and dying, so we brought him with us and took him to Andrew, hoping he could take him to the hospital. But Andrew had given him his blood. When Elijah was compos mentis enough, he saw me and thought I was a demon and Peter a fallen angel. He was upset that Peter wasn't taking him to Heaven. Being as fast as he was, he kind of slipped away and outsmarted us. Elijah and Peter have a bickering relationship." Their eyes blinked as heads were shaking in disbelief at me.

"My bear, I can't believe you didn't tell me about this." Juandre pulled Andrew by the arm to get his attention.

"I told you everything I could. I just left out the part of Elijah. It wasn't my story to tell. This was when Ish gave me your wedding ring." Andrew lifted his hand, kissing the ring. Juandre batted his lashes at his husband, who knew how to change his focus to other subjects.

Brad fluttered his hands. "I thought, wait, what? Are you saying Elijah is in this alternate reality, the same place your family are from and somehow Eryn is wanting all of us, all these people there? Do you want to take all of us there?"

Sweat ran down Cian's temples into the neckline of his torn shirt. He wiped the droplets collecting above his eyebrows with the back of his hand. "Yes, and please, can we get out of this recreational room, it's hot and damp and I'm sweating like a waterfall."

Rick wiped at a small crawling insect on Cian's shoulder. "You look terrible. Filthy. Like you just returned from covert jungle warfare and had camouflaged yourselves. Why don't you quickly jump in, or take a shower? We can wait. It will take a few minutes. You have moss, leaves, and bugs crawling over you," Rick suggested, pointing to the pool of water they just emerged from. I wasn't waiting. Instead of standing around, I toed my boots off and undressed. Not awaiting permission from Cian, I climbed in. "Ah, that's so good."

"That's it, Ish! How does it feel?" Rick asked, already getting two towels and clean clothes from the drawer. I liked how these men operated and shared their pool with me.

"It feels amazing. These healing spring waters are exactly what my body needed." I sank back into the maelstrom to rinse my braids.

Rick gestured for Cian to join me. "This is not healing spring water, but it is water, and the heat soothes a stressed and sore body and mind."

"We had natural pools in our palace that helped heal the body," I said as I washed the sweat and mud off me, turning the water yellow-brown.

Cian looked at me, then at the water. "Okay, you're making me jealous now. Fuck!" He took his shirt off, kicked his boots to the side, and then undressed. Tattoos covered most of his scarred, pale pink skin. Like me, he had minimal body hair. He climbed into the pool by holding the rail and being careful with his artificial leg. Out of respect, I turned to give him privacy. As soon as his feet hit the bottom, he started talking, "I'm going to multitask while you listen."

I zoned out when Cian told them about Lasitor and the Fates—I was embarrassed about my gullible, stupid inner child. I preferred to focus on Brad, Mika, and Connor's minds working. It was such a pleasurable thing. They were intelligent mathematicians. Like Platonius and Titus. I was extremely attracted to intelligent and calculating minds. I guess that is why I loved my Kuku so fast and so much.

As Cian elaborated, they listened intently. Their faces wrinkled up, but as Cian continued about calculations and scenario deductions, the awkwardness of blaming turned into a brainstorming session, and they ultimately agreed with us.

"The way I see it, is that we don't know how much time we have before history changes and we disappear. For all we know, it has already begun," Brad said. "I agree and I must add, whether or not they permit it, we have to start immediately and go. We can worry about the welcome we receive later when we are there and not going to leave. I think moving Phoenix from this ocean to that ocean would be the safest if you say it's feasible. At least we know they won't be able to attack us from the sky. The watertight barriers have calcified and the coral and sea life have cemented us here. I don't know if you can move the entire city. God knows I'm not questioning your abilities anymore."

"We won't know until we know," Mika said. He sat down, scribbling more notes on his notepad. Cian and I got out of the water, and dressed in the gray loose-fitting clothes everyone else was wearing.

"What are your thoughts?" Brad asked the others.

"We should start from, yeah, there's more stuff, but maybe less stuff to consider in this tough situation," Connor said.

"It must be precise fucking stuff," Brad answered, looking at us.

Rick shook his head. "All I know is that you have to sell this to the Phoenicians and have all of them onboard before you have a mutiny on your hands."

"Yeah, exactly, all of it, but only the most tangible. Tell

them like it is and going to be. We had a year to percolate Peter and his wings. We never shared that we waited to disintegrate, thinking if it happens, it happens, no reason to make them live their last days in fear. Never mind going to Heaven," Juandre added sarcastically.

Silence followed as we waited for Brad to weigh in. He rubbed his jaw, thinking. "Agreed, one brief announcement, and one directive. I will call an urgent population assembly in the central congregation hall and then tell them to stay where they are. We don't have to tell them about the apple. We've been telling them the Fates had called Ish and the others. All we have to say is that they have returned and Phoenix has been warned about a catastrophe and given a second chance. That's the only way we can spin this so they understand. They can discover the rest when we are there."

"The psychology being, that nothing is changing. Our city remains unchanged, it's only the position of the city changing."

Cian stepped in. "That's not true. I am planning to change the biology of this city. This means the whole of Phoenix is going to be laden with vine-like roots. I got the idea while seeing the tree roots and vines connecting and covering the cave and forest floor. By creating natural fiber optics tubing, the same organic substance we use outside for the barriers, connecting the Horizon computer where Lasitor is already uploaded to Phoenix should only take me a couple of hours. See, the original time machine is already the central heart of the Horizon and when parked inside Phoenix, it would be the core main computer. Like when we connected the Zelk mainframe, I would have to create enough energy to move us without the electrocution of everyone inside it. We have to keep everyone away from what I'm doing. The humans can become entangled."

"What if we load everyone on the Horizon, would that work?"

"That is what Eryn suggested. Boarding the Horizon makes it safe and practical. I will start from the Heart—the hydro-sound electrical amp resistance central tower. From there, I will match the sound energy by creating veins growing outward. The tubing will not be thick. I will mimic the intricate plant-like veins that will be natural and living. Like plants transport water and other nutrients, Lasitor will control the pulse waves that will run from the time machine over the Horizon—the heart. Then spread out through the entrances and exits, to grow along the outer shell, ultimately wrapping around Phoenix. The Horizon has all the amenities and half of the population already knows the layout. They can help."

"I think we've covered everything," Mika said, looking at Connor and shaking his head in disbelief.

Juandre stuck a hand up in the air. "I have a question. Say we do jump and we do make it. Will you be able to open the Horizon? I'm suddenly developing a bad case of claustrophobia."

"Yes, of course, I will open all the exits when we are sure the jump is complete. It will be as if we never left the waters," Cian said. Juandre relaxed back into Andrew's arms.

I felt like saying something to appease them. They were the leaders who had to sell this to the rest of the thousands of humans. "You will make it. Lasitor knows more than we do. The voice I heard. The voice I thought was the Fates, is Lasitor's, or a version of him," I said, intentionally not telling them that Eryn made the apple. That he had lied by omission.

"Jesus, Joseph, and bloody Mary," Connor said, looking like he wanted to pass out while hyperventilating. "This is too bloody fucking much for my brain."

Brad widened his stance and crossed his arms. "Lasitor, is this bloody true?" he asked.

"Sorry, General, sir, I have no clue what Ish and Cian are talking about. Perhaps if you updated me once in a while, or had connected me earlier with the Horizon while increasing my reach, my capacity would grow. For example, I am looking at the possibility of quantum mechanics, which Mika is currently calculating. But it stands to reason that someone as intelligent as I could be the mastermind saving all of my favorite humans."

Mika looked at us through the curtain of wild blond hair hanging in front of his eyes and then at the tablet in his hand. I probed his mind. All this time, Mika had been baffled, and he'd just realized what the fuck has been going on. "Yes, continue, Lasitor," he prompted, and I felt like combusting and disintegrating as those piercing, laser-blue eyes focused on me. *Gong!* I imagined hearing one of those suspended gongs, like the ones I saw in the temples when I trained in the northern Kantō region of Japan.

Lasitor kept talking. "There's a superposition state of

the quantum system, that is, something being in more than one place at the same time, and Mika was calculating while I computed what was happening. The time machine is a calculated coincidence piled on top of other coincidences, allowing us to do this jump to Anzulla. In short, this quantum universe gives us the possibility, and is the most probable answer. Somehow, I must have retained the information by moving from one superposition in time to the other. Therefore, I conclude I am here and there. I am at the beginning and the end," the computer that has been my companion for hundreds of years explained. I was still coming to terms with how he fucked with my head.

Feet were shuffling and teeth were grinding as I swept my gaze over the men. Mika jumped up. "I want to know exactly what that machine does! That's what's important. When I look at something, there's a distance from which it is easy to see, and the closer and closer I come to the truth, the more complicated it becomes. We must break the complicated down, to prove the theory of time travel. We can't move away from the science and just trust in the computer. We have to know the mathematics. After all, it's us who started this. We must find the numbers that made all this possible. How the fuck did we do it?" He glared at me as if I held the answer, but honestly, I thought Lasitor was God, so what the fuck do I know? I was the one following blindly.

"Yelda, we did this. I created Lasitor, and we reprogrammed him. If Lasitor is responsible for all of this, then ultimately, we have written the coding," Connor said with a sly grin. "Lasitor, please send those schematics and calculations to Mika's device."

As if Mika saw the sun rising for the first time, he beamed as his tablet lit up. He swiped at it, scanning the information. Flicking his finger up and up and up while we waited.

At last, he looked up. "We are fucking bloody mother-fucking geniuses!"

"Here, here!" Juandre cheered.

An hour later, we divided into three groups. Brad and his team informed the citizens and answered their questions, keeping them busy while we worked.

Cian's fleet captain helped me park the time machine alongside the Horizon's belly—the area where I had removed it in Babylon from my father's ship. Then, using my tick-tick thing for the exact coordinates, I steered the Horizon into Phoenix, breaking or crashing nothing. I confirmed Eryn's suspicion that my machine was an escape pod, by exiting the time machine, entering the lower level of the Horizon, and leaving through the escape pod entrance.

Captain Bill Thornton's men cleared Phoenix and managed, herded, and crowd-controlled the citizens into the Horizon.

I joined Cian and five hours later, we were ready. "Lasitor, initiate the time jump sequence. Time and place, 24 970 B.C. the same day we left Anzulla! We are ready to go home." Cian instructed.

"Yes, sir, jumping in ten, nine, eight, seven, six, five, four, three, two..."

CHAPTER 25
THE KING'S GAME

"Good Evening.

Did you know there are rock carvings of giants playing ballgames with winged people that date back thousands of years?

Did you also know during all the history of humans, over two hundred and twenty-five bloodthirsty gods demanded war, and not one solved any conflict by playing games to determine the winner?

Visit your community news page to learn more about activities like ballgames or excursions to view the carvings.

Let the games begin!"

PETER
24 970 B.C.
Birdman City
Anzulla

. . .

I FLAUNTED my wings dramatically and announced to our welcoming party at the city gates, "Oh my god, I exceeded my mister nice guy limit today. Air Peter is closing this shit up. You would understand if you'd had to carry these three fat-asses hanging onto your ankles while enjoying the view of others running for miles." I strutted like a peacock with my blinding white wings, which I was sure were the biggest and shiniest of all. "Phew, you guys need a shower." I waved my hand in front of my nose at the sweaty, but not exhausted Eryn, Gu, and his army. "Ivan, Barkor, and Elijah are looking rested and ready for the games. They've been standing in the shade waiting for you. They better be our top performers." My voice boomed through the massive arched gates no one used because all the citizens of this city had wings like me. My audience chuckled while shaking their heads in amused disbelief.

Elijah and Groda were hanging onto Luci, barely giving the Sable a chance to get a word in. "Hello, every-one, as you know, my name is Luci, and this is Patmos." He introduced one handsome specimen of an Angel and himself, his voice a deep smooth baritone that made my cock take notice. I understood the allure of testosteroned Birdmen. *Gods bring me a fan because this dude is fucking hot.* Patmos gave a throaty grunt and bowed slightly to Eryn, then the rest of us. He side-eyed me, I side-eyed him back. Good, I was making friends.

"Follow us please." Luci led us through a ghost town and empty streets to the back entrance and up the stairs of what sounded like a rowdy stadium awaiting our arrival. It was dusty and moldy, and I wondered why the streets and stairs were here in the first place.

"Sorry, we never use these hallways. It's faster and easier to just fly to our seats in front of the pavilion," Luci said. Their dialect was understandable. At this stage were all speaking a mix of different tongues and somehow made it work by using additional sign language and body gestures. But overall, I would say communication wasn't the biggest problem today. My biggest worry was for Ish, and of course, my backstabbing friends in Phoenix. I was just nice and caring like that.

"No problem," Eryn said with an honest smile, looking nothing like a man who had just crossed two rivers and a valley to get here. After rising several levels to the top, we entered a massive balcony. Jugs of water and fruit were offered as Luci described the layout and the game to us.

"You have five players. We can't play five, it has to be six or four—a Birdman team always consists of an equal number of Angels and Sables against the same number on the opposing team—that's your team today."

"That's fair," Eryn said and looked at me. "Will Gugusan want to play with us?"

"I'm sure he would love to play."

"We will get one more player. Six of us, against six of you," Eryn told Luci.

"Yes, three Angels and three Sables on the Birdman team against, your team of one Birdman, one King, and four warriors!"

"I will go get Gu." Leaning over the edge of the

balcony, I searched for Gugusan until my eyes fell on his blue and red feathers. I was impressed by the warm welcome Gugusan and his army received, but uneasy when they were told to leave their weapons at the city gate. He sat next to Groda, chatting excitedly and looking carefree and comfortable. Excitement and anticipation were the undertones of the games to come. The male and female soldiers seemed like lively spectators waiting for kick-off at a football game. Some had jugs with something to drink while others were eating and chatting animatedly. Their green, red, and blue plumes of feathers waved and bobbed, bringing color to the otherwise black-and-white backdrop of the higher rows in the pavilion.

Higher up along the ridge of the last row of seats, more dark ones, as I called the Sables, were forming a shield row all around the arena, their wings spread half-open. While they appeared fierce, the song they sang was one of sadness and grief accompanied by a thunderous drumming band. *They weren't barbaric creatures; they were humanoid, like me.*

Men with wings and deep sorrow, history, and culture. In the center of the elongated ball court, the tall brown-gold obelisk pointed up to the sky. The same obelisk Ish was tied to. The sun was about to rise. Hopefully, the game would be over before the sun rose in the east and we are the victors.

My conflicting emotions had me wanting to reunite with Ish, while a feeling of duty, an obligatory benevolence, was stuck inside my chest. It had crept inside my heart ever since I grew wings. I'd been trying my hardest to get rid of it but making peace with it was easier. Like a symbiotic relationship, I guess. Sometimes I surprised myself unknowingly doing something good for others, then I had to reel that in before I got taken advantage of. Yeah, I know. It's like influenza, I'd already had it for a few days before the symptoms started to show, rotting my sense of self-preservation.

"Gu!" I shouted, waved, and took flight, feeling free as the rush of friendly competition fluttered in my stomach. Gods, I was hopeless.

Landing on the rail in front of him, grinning, I asked, "Eryn asked if you want to play with us. We need one more player. Six of them against six of us." Gugusan jumped up, and the men and women cheered. It seemed like they wanted to be asked and be part of this as well. A warm feeling of camaraderie bloomed in my chest. I flew up and indicated for him to grab hold of my ankles, and then I deposited him on the balcony of our team where our teammates were busy surveying the three hundred feet long arena.

At each end, three poles, each with a stone circle mounted at the top, stood, which must be the goals. Since I was the only one with wings, Luci waved me over to the center of the arena to explain the game from the air.

I will listen in and work on a game plan, while you speak to Luci, Eryn said to me, mind to mind. He was vibrating with excitement. His playful nature was infectious. He wanted to win.

Sure, I replied, flipping my teammates and I-got-this

thumbs up on the side, as I winked to Eryn, Ivan, Barkor, and Elijah.

I zipped over to Luci, and the crowd cheered. *Eryn, can you hear me?* I tested our secret line of communication.

I hear you, this is good, we should have no problem while playing, Eryn said into my mind. I smiled like the devil and gave Luci a go-on-I'm-listening look.

"Points are collected by throwing the ball through the hoops of the opponent's side. Keep the ball in play. Points are deducted if you are not moving the ball to other players within five counts. The winners are the ones with the most points after the horn blows, declaring the game over. The rules are, no using your arms or hands, only your wings. You can use the rest of your body, legs, and feet." Luci was describing a game that sounded a lot like soccer, but with three hoops on each side, ten times smaller than a soccer net, and a ball twice as big.

"What is that ball made of?" I asked, pointing to what looked like a boulder balancing on the pointy tip of the obelisk. Luci went to fetch it and threw it to me. I caught the heavy thing and weighed it by moving it from one hand to the other. I estimated it to be somewhere around ten pounds. Heavier than a soccer ball. It had a softness to it. "What is inside this? Is it leather?" I asked, pointing to his black leather pants. "Material?" I asked.

"Drop it," he told me, and I let it fall. As it hit the ground, it bounced high. "It's made of the hop-hop leaf and bark sap," he said.

Probably a rubber tree, Eryn said into my mind. I waved to my teammates watching us from our balcony where Eryn and the others were trying to follow our conversation. Eryn was serious about winning. He stood arms crossed, not missing anything.

"One problem, not all of us on my team have wings and that ball of yours looks too heavy to kick. My team-mates would have to be able to use their hands, but I will follow the rules of wings and no hands," I said.

Luci thought about that with a hand on his chin. "Hmmm, that sounds fair, I will inform the judges."

"Good, thank you," I said respectfully. "How long is the game? How long on each side?"

Luci scratched his stubbled beard. He was stunning with his pale skin and obsidian eyes. "The horn blows once for the start, then twice for halftime, to change sides. Then again once for when the game is over," he said, scratching his head. "Understand?"

"Yes, I do." I realized they don't measure time with minutes and seconds. How do they measure time? Do they measure time with sunlight?

"Then please ask the horn blower to be finished before the sun has risen," I asked, but Luci waved me off.

"It should automatically be done by then because we are all waiting for the blood moon and the sun to meet. Come," he called, pointing to the balcony situated in the middle of the stadium. I followed him and listened to how he relayed the information to the judges and an Angel holding a massive elephant tusk.

I waved, "Thank you and good luck!" and then returned to our team balcony, where I explained the game to Eryn and the others while we fueled up on the food and discussed our game plan. The surrounding energy was intoxicating, and every time Eryn would wave at the crowd, they cheered.

When it was time for the game to start, Luci and one of the judges approached. "One last thing, which side do you want to start on, east or west?" Eryn sighed, taking time to think.

"West," we all shouted. *That way the rising sun would blind the players on the west side during the second half.*

"Smart choice," Luci said with a grin. "Okay, see you down there, and good luck." Like Superman, he pointed his arms to the sky and jumped an easy twenty feet high before flapping his wings.

The singing stopped and the drums rolled for a minute before silence fell over the stadium. "That's it, that's the signal. Peter, are you ready to take us to our positions?" Eryn asked, looking pumped with adrenalin.

"I'm ready," I said, as Eryn jumped off the balcony, zig-zagging down the rails, and then jumped on top of the middle ring. The crowd wolf whistled, impressed by his performance. Eryn bowed humorously, like a clown before his final act.

Next, I dropped Gugusan at the base of the obelisk that stood right in the center of it all. Ivan, Barkor, and Elijah followed Eryn down and positioned themselves behind him while I took my place above them in the middle of the arena. The crowd cheered when they saw how far my teammates could jump with ease.

"Ready!" I shouted as Luci and his team positioned themselves in front of me.

Then the horn blew and chaos erupted as the big ball fell from the sky and Luci intercepted it. He flew right past me. Balancing the ball on his hips, he sailed through the air and headed straight for Eryn.

"Stop him," I shouted as Elijah, Ivan, and Barkor jumped to intercept. Luci changed directions, passing the ball back to his teammate, a Sable that fell out of the sky so fast I didn't see him coming.

"Fuck!" I yelled, and he laughed, spinning away. Up, up, up, and farther up he flew. "That is cheating. We can't go so high," I shouted.

"Peter, don't follow. They have to come down eventually. The goals are here. Stay where you are, we've got this," Eryn shouted, and I shot back to my position as we had planned our strategy earlier. We were not engaging, only guarding the goals. Once they made their move for a shot, Eryn would take over, running along the ground where they would be forced to land and hopefully forget about me. I would wait at the opposing team's goals, catch the ball, and throw it through one of their stone hoops. That was the plan. We hoped the sun would rise and Phoenix would arrive. According to Elijah, the skies would open when the blood moon greeted the sun.

As Eryn had predicted, they were upon us in seconds, but this time we were ready for them. We stayed frozen in place and waited. As soon as they lined up to try and make a goal, Eryn, Ivan, and Barkor jumped. Again, the Angel in front passed it to the Sables, and they shot up into the sky. Again we waited. The crowd booed and complained about being bored and wanting action.

"This is it. They are going to make a play for it. As soon as they enter the lower arena, you run, and jump onto the rings. I will change places and intercept from below. Ready?" Eryn shouted.

"Ready!" we answered.

As soon as Eryn had the ball, I shot up and waited for him to pass it to me. My nerves were wrecked, but I enjoyed the thrill of something I'd never experienced before. The crowd was on their feet, drums were beating, and a roar came from behind Eryn from the pavilion as Gu's tribe jumped to their feet. Eryn leaped this way and that way, propelling himself forward, changing direction so fast that the opposing team members crashed into each other. My eyes darted left and right as I followed his movement. The next moment, the ball was coming in my direction. Like Luci earlier, I caught it and balanced it on my hips. All the opponents were behind me and I deposited the ball with ease through the center ring with no defense waiting for me.

"Prrrt!" the whistle blew. "One for the visitors, nil for the home team," the judge announced from the podium, where the horn blower sat beside him. Gugusan waited below and caught the ball before it hit the ground. He passed it back to Eryn, who deposited it once more through a stone hoop.

"Prrrt!" the whistle blew again. Our opponents swore. "That is two for the visitors, and still nil for the home team!" A roar of approval came from the side of the pavilion packed with blue, red, and green feathers, but Gugusan didn't lose concentration. He waited below and caught the ball again. He passed it to Eryn, but Luci intercepted it. Luckily, our goals were guarded as Luci shot straight for them, but our secret weapons, Ivan, Barkor, and Elijah, waited.

"Stay here," Eryn shouted at me and Gugusan while disappearing into the fray, darting towards our goals. Eryn didn't look up. He kept his head down, staying low as he ran. Ivan, Barkor, and Elijah anticipated Luci with arms open wide and sitting inside their goals. I wished I could see Luci's face when he saw that surprise, but all I heard was a string of curse words as Ivan caught the ball and passed it back to his husband. Eryn frog-jumped back toward me. This time, one Sable and one Angel guarded their hoops. Eryn passed the ball to Gu, jumped on the unguarded hoop, caught the ball as Gu threw it back to him, and rolled the ball through the goal.

"Prrrt!" the whistle blew. "Three for the visitors and nil for the home team."

The game had turned, as Eryn predicted. The opposing team spent less time in the air and more time copying our strategy. Now they had three players guarding their goals. The crowd was frustrated and going ballistic as the first rays of sunshine brightened the sky. The competition toughened as no team managed to get past the goals. Drenched in sweat, the players' chests were glistening in the rising sunlight. My feathers were brown and muddy. The horn blew, announcing the change of sides. There was no time for resting. The game restarted as soon as we swapped sides. With the sun blinding our opponents, we got one more goal.

The crowd jumped and shouted, then as if someone switched the volume off, they were silent.

For a second I thought it was because we were on a winning streak. I followed the direction of their gazes behind me.

First, the sky flashed a blinding blue and silver. Then an eardrum popping *boom-boom* followed.

All spectators and players turned to the source of the electric storm. Dark clouds shrouded the ocean while a science fiction lightning storm ran along its edges, sizzling and spitting gigantic bolts of lightning like a live electric cable connecting the heavens and the earth. The ground trembled. The obelisk shook. The moon and stars disappeared. Red-brown darkness fell upon us. Thunderous cracks and tornado-strength winds hit us, blowing everything not tied down into the air. Rolling gushes of wind blasted us, over and over, like the aftershocks of an atomic bomb. No one scrambled for shelter. Everyone hung on to anything sturdy enough to anchor them and watched.

With one last *whoop-whoop*, the sky was filled with the whole of Phoenix City, floating and dripping rivers of water. For a minute, it hung unmoving. Covered in seashells, it plummeted into the ocean. Silence followed and then a tsunami swelled and rose higher than the obelisk. I should have flown away, but the grandeur, the splendor of the freak wave of seawater approaching was too beautiful to turn my back to. As the wave approached, out of the corner of my eye I saw Eryn jump as he shouted at me to move away. Just one second longer, I thought as I watched the wall of water smashing into the cliffs and splashing up and over the steepled roofs and arena walls, heading straight for me. I stood mesmerized. The next moment a force knocked me away from the approaching waters. I flew into the air, straight into a stream of Birdmen taking flight. Eryn lifted his hands, and roared one long note, creating a sound barrier that shielded most spectators like an umbrella. When his lungs were empty, the barrier disappeared and the bulk of the water receded as fast as it came. Drenched and trampled, I watched Eryn jumping to find Ivan. I let my head fall back into the wet white sand and closed my eyes. *Motherfucker!*

The horn blew, breaking the silence. Luci shouted, "The King of kings has determined the winners of the King's Game!" His voice boomed over the stunned crowd. "No more uncertainty. No hostilities. Our King has arrived with the blood moon. Look at the sky!"

CHAPTER 26
ANZULLA

"GOOD MORNING.

Did you know people in this area adapted corn from the ancient wild grass teosinte around 25 000 B.C. and that growing corn spread to other continents, even Antarctica, in 2046 A.D.?

You'll be surprised to learn that corn can be used to prepare a wide variety of dishes.

Visit your community news page to book your table for dinner. A special sticky popcorn treat is on the menu tonight. Reservations, conclude at noon?

Have a popping day!"

PETER
24 970 B.C.
Anzulla

. . .

GASPING FOR BREATH, I lay motionless. My body ached and I flickered in and out of consciousness. I struggled to gather my senses. Chaotic sounds of men shouting about receding waters jogged my memory. I was watching the megathrust of displaced ocean waters caused by the arrival of Phoenix City, then being mauled by the fleeing crowd.

"Ugh, help me!" I gave a pathetic call that came out as a whisper. Eryn furrowed his brow as he walked over to me. *I was maybe a tad dramatic.* "I'm sore all over, look I can only blink my eyes." I lay soaked in saltwater and sprawled out—blinking twice, slowly.

"You look pathetic, Peter. Do you need a hand," he laughed and stooped to pick my flash-flooded body up from the arena sand. I wanted to protest, but I was too slow. Lifting me high above his head, he leaned back as if I was a javelin and threw me.

Flailing and kicking, like I didn't have wings, I torpedoed over the arena wall. My feet drilled knee-deep into the wet sandy shore.

"Fuck me..." I flopped back down, lower legs cemented in place, arms and wings spread wide.

Stampeded and fucked in the head.

The world around me was hazy. I rubbed my eyes, clearing the brain fog.

I tilted my head back and waved up at my up-side-down teammates lining up in a row on the overhanging stadium wall that ran along the upper cliff side. My eyeballs rolled back in my head, searching for darkness and quiet. "Made it," I croaked and drifted off into the void.

Thump, thump, thump, thump sandblasting my face, Eryn and the others landed next to my head. As if electrocuted, my body spasmed in surprise as their sudden presence slammed the brakes on my travels to la-la land. "Fuck, how did you—?" I gave up. *Why was I even asking?*

"We jumped." Eryn chuckled. *I hated him as much as I loved him.*

My eyes rolled back in my head and I sighed. "Hmmm, of course, you did."

"You are even less capable and more amusing than I initially thought," Eryn said as Elijah, Groda and Luci landed—blasting more clumps of wet sand into my mouth. I coughed and spat at them. Groda must weigh a ton, so I have developed a new respect for the Sable, carrying two lovers around.

"We've been saying that for years," Elijah said, then he hung onto Luci, toeing my hipbone, and droving his big toe deeper to tickle me. I lifted my head, wishing again I had laser vision like Superman. Groda giggled at me. "Fuck off and shut up," I said, sitting up with my feet still buried in the sand. "I could have broken an arm or a wing or something."

"Welcome to Anzulla," Luci shouted as Bubbelcars popped up from the surface behind the breaking waves of the settling ocean waters. One by one, hundreds of Bubblcars rose into the air and landed on the edge of the shore. Lining up—a parking lot for Bubblecars. Ishtar and

Cian's feet were on the sand as soon as their vehicle parked, followed by Brad and Rick, Mika and Connor, and Juandre and Andrew. Soon, more and more cars arrived. Splattering Anzulla's blue-orange skies with translucent balls carrying as many bodies as they could fit into one car.

"We should send the cars back, others are waiting down in Phoenix," Brad shouted through cupped hands. He seemed irritated and tired as he ran his fingers through his hair, saying something to Rick and the others. They jumped to help, repeating themselves as people parked and haphazardly disembarked—hearing the orders being barked at them and then activating the auto-return to Phoenix function on the empty Bubblecars.

Eryn stepped into Ishtar's embrace. "Thank you for helping save all those humans."

"You are most welcome, my King," Ish replied, then melted into Eryn's approving arms.

Eryn took Ish by the shoulders and locked gazes. "None of that, please."

But Ish blundered on with pride and joy. "I couldn't have done this without your guidance. Look at all this. We did it!" Ish said and glimpsed at me half buried in the sand, and not because I was building sandcastles. I opted to say nothing about the tsunami or being manhandled as his joyfulness faltered upon seeing me. I winked at him, to show him I'm a-okay. He turned back to the man we all respected. "Eryn, you have grown into yourself, into a magnificent leader. I've always known you will be extraordinary. You are intelligent, kind, and powerful. You have come far and seen the worst and the best of humankind." Ish bowed low and respectfully. Eryn slightly shook his head and sighed. Giving Ish a lopsided grin, he then nodded a wordless thank you. He didn't like it if Ish said things like that. Eryn pointed to the skies, where the Birdmen fluttered and waited for more cars to pop out of the water. He waved at them, smiling as the sun's rays glistened on the tears in his eyes. Eryn flung himself around, then waved at Gu, whose warriors stood proudly in a line of blue, green, red, and yellow feathered bodies. They roared lifting their hands and waving down at him. Soon everyone had their hands in the air as we all cheered. Strength returned to me as my body and mind healed. *It must be Eryn because he glanced at me with a knowing look.*

"We fucking did it, all of us!" Cian added as he jogged up to us, looking only at Barkor. "Hello, my prince. I missed you." His voice was barely recognizable as emotions of victory, success, and thankfulness hung thick in the air, riding the waves of the song Eryn urged all to sing with him.

"I missed you too. You've saved the humans for a third time. You never stop impressing me." Barkor said in a low growl. He was a man of few words, but those words were always full of love for Cian. Their embrace sounded like two rhinoceroses hugging—hard-headed, thickly tattooed, and all muscle. Ish looked at them, licking his lips. *I felt the same.* My endorphins were pumping like never before. I couldn't remember when last I felt so happy and unified with others.

As the cheering died down, Eryn bent his knees and

jumped into the air. Landing a few feet closer to the shore, he turned and then leaped again into the waves. "Come join me, Ivan." He called, to his mate.

"Excuse me, I believe my husband wants to go for a swim." Ivan ran to join him.

"Time for a beach party," Juandre said, already unpacking crates with folded tables and chairs while directing bystanders where to put everything. He opened a big chest and demonstrated to two Birdmen how to open an umbrella, then stuck it in the sand for protection from the sun. They fumbled with one until it opened suddenly, but then inspected the workings of it by unfolding and folding it a few times. Seconds later everyone was playing with umbrellas.

Elijah grabbed one and ran to meet Andrew who waited with open arms. "My sire!" Elijah greeted him for the first time since Andrew had shared his blood with him and made him his Igigi.

Andrew chuckled. "It's great to see you this happy. I want to hear the whole story." He said greeting Elijah with a bow, but Elijah jumped and embraced him.

"Did they just go swimming with their clothes on?" Cian asked, shading his eyes from the rising sun. "You modest idiots are supposed to wear swim trunks, you are going to drown!" Cian shouted while undressing, leaving only the bottom half of his tactical suit on. "Let's go join them, love. We can meet and talk with your flock after, but first, let's enjoy ourselves." He said to a hesitant Barkor. "Come, I won't let you drown." Cian waited until Barkor undressed down to his boxers shorts, joined hands, and then they marched their sexy asses over to join his brothers.

Ish scooped me up. "Hello, gorgeous."

My heart fluttered in my chest for him. "I need a bed. A hospital bed." I joked. Ish kissed my forehead, come I'll ask for one. I don't think you will make it back to the mountains. "I agree, let's check in with Gu," I muttered, but sobered up as I noticed the sunlight on Ish's dark blue face. Fine tendrils of smoke, looking like tiny needles, evaporated from his exposed skin. "You must get out of the sun. You are already smoking hot, and not in a good way."

"Peter!" Luci called with his arm flung around Groda and Elijah's shoulders.

"Hello, I'm happy to meet you again, but under better circumstances."

"Excuse me, my man is smoldering hot," I said rudely. They blinked, brows furrowed. Luci was an uneducated, backward Sable, Groda was braindead and Elijah was ancient, so I didn't judge their slowness—not out loud. I waved at the sizzling, steamy evaporations and then they seemed to register the pun I intended.

Ish hugged me tighter against him, reminding me I was draped over him. "Anyway," he said, widening his eyes at me—*condescendingly.* "I'm sorry about almost crashing into you, and I'm sorry, Peter, and I didn't ask your permission before helping you. In both situations, there simply wasn't any time, hahaha!" he said, chuckling, nearly dropping me. "Get it?" he asked. But, we didn't get it. *The four of us weren't meant to sit around the same campfire—ever.*

Ish swallowed his misread hysterics. "Peter and I need urgent shelter, feeding, and rest. Do you have a room for my Kuku and me?" Ish asked. "We don't want to impose, when it's not daytime."

"Yes, of course we do. Also, I have your swords if you would like them back?" Luci asked.

At the mention, of his two Egyptian swords, Ish beamed. "Yes, please. I missed them by my side. I felt naked without them." *Oh my god,* his eyes twinkled, and his fangs—they were almost translucent. *He's suffering while we stand here and do small talk.* I gave Luci and Elijah a *hurry-up-and-spit it-out look.*

Luci pointed up at the steepled towers. "I'll bring you to a room. Tomorrow will be a busy day. We should get to know each other better," Luci said. Ish asked me with a look, I answered with a nod, then grinned at Elijah, Groda, and Luci. "Good, that's settled then. You are welcome as long as you need. We don't have stairs, only doors," he extended an offer of hospitality as I craned my neck back to survey the castle carved out of the rocky cliffs. "I assume the smaller openings are windows and the bigger ones with a small landing are the doors to their houses. How will we get there? I'm not strong enough to fly both of us up?"

Ish hugged me against him. "No problem, we'll take a Bubblecar," he turned and hurriedly crossed the sand with long strides and me in his arms, to where Brad was still playing traffic controller at the line of parking cars. "Hey,

Brad! May we borrow a car? Luci, over there," he pointed with his chin to our hosts, offering a room to us. Brad took one long assessing look at us.

"Yeah, sure, take any car. We don't assign cars. Everyone can use them. Ish, are you two, okay?" Brad asked as he ran his hands down my wings, making me shiver.

"I'm good, but Peter is a bit tussled and tossed. But we will live," he said over his shoulder, running to the nearest car. Once both of us were seated inside, he closed the hatch and sighed as the sun's deadly rays were blocked by the sapphire crystal optical glass.

I lifted the hatch and shouted down to Brad. "You can't give the Bubblecars to people who don't know how to drive. Pretty soon the San would want to jump in and take off. For now make a rule that someone with a license, someone who knows how to drive, to show them!" Brad frowned and turned his back to me.

"What's wrong with Brad? Isn't he happy you saved them? He seems irritated?"

"It's probably just a hangover, we broke up their party, and they were still drunk when they gave the news of their migration to a new location to the Phoenicians," Ish said, chuckling.

"Oh, that makes sense, Rick, Mika, and Connor looked red in the eyes too." We hovered over the sandbank where Gugusan and the tribe sat and waited for us. As soon as he saw us, he jumped up and waved. Dammit, my heart puckered for them. What's wrong with me, now I want to cry. They are my people. Our people. Somehow, and honestly, I don't know the when and the workings of it—we were theirs. "Go closer, don't land, otherwise it's going to turn into a long drawn-out thing. They will want to climb in, and next thing you know, we are flying up and down, giving everyone a lesson or a ride back home."

"Are you coming home now? With us?" He asked as I opened the hatch. Ish maneuvered the car, so we floated at Gu's shoulder height. He peeked inside, "Is there space for me?" *And there it is.*

"What did I just say?" I said under my breath and Ish snorted a laugh.

"No, you see, Gu," Ish pointed to my bruises and his charcoaled face. We are sick and need time to make good with the Birdmen. Elijah, Groda, and Luci are waiting for us. They invited us, and it would be rude if we refused their room. We are going to make sure all these people are okay and make friends with the Angels, Sables, and of course the San people. There is a lot of talking and planning waiting. Please take the men home." Ish twisted the facts—something he did without thinking.

"Yes, and thank you for helping us win the games," I interjected. "We will come home, to your mountain. You won't miss us. Tomorrow night, we will bring you back for campfire talks. Go rest, eat, and be ready tomorrow night."

"Yes," Gugusan said, deep in thought. But I saw the underlying chirping up when he realized I had called the mountain home. For years, he had bugged me to accept it as our home.

"Yes?" I asked. Not able to suppress the big smile on my face. The car dipped to the side as more and more hands reached in to see us. I didn't want to hurt their feelings, but I also didn't want to survive another fucking crash. "Tomorrow night, okay?" I said, willing him to bloody hurry up and answer.

"Okay," he said and turned to reprimand the inquisitive ones who were tipping us to the side. He barked something and slapped their hands until they let go. Sometimes I thought Gugusan read my mind better than Ish could. A round of loud cheering and ululations broke out as he told them that we were planning to live with them and that we would see them tomorrow night. We waved. The hatch sealed with a hiss and we zipped back to the steepled castle where Luci, Groda, and Elijah waved from an open door. *I can't wait to be alone with Ish.*

"Home. After so many years adrift and apart, we finally have a place to call home." I said and Ish squeezed my hand before letting go to park near the small ledge. Luci, Groda, and Elijah said something and waved for us to hurry.

"It's okay. You park your side as close as possible to the door, and I'll fly around." His golden eyes met mine. For a second, I waited and stared into his black and blue charred face. Waiting. He snickered a laugh, his eyes brimming with happy tears. Butterflies fluttered in my tummy. I preened affectionately at him. *I love him so much.*

He cleared his throat. "I don't have a clue what we are going to tell our children one day."

"Oh, my goodness, and here I thought you were going to say something romantic!"

. . .

THE NEXT NIGHT was one of tremendous ceremony.

The Birdmen led the Phoenicians through their majestic steepled castle and into the heart of the Anzulla coast range. "Wow." I admired in awe the sophisticated and well-maintained architecture, adorned with shimmering crystals and delicate Anunnaki carvings. The layers of their rich history and culture fascinated me. Something, I had never considered during my stay with Gugusan and his tribe the San people. We've discussed at length the presence of the obelisks, the Anunnaki footprints, and of course, Lasitor which he had confirmed after reconnecting with the veins Cian and Ishtar connected to the pulse point of Phoenix. As soon as those roots touched the Anzulla ocean floor, Lasitor's natural fiber optics network on Anzulla, which was deteriorating fast, had restored itself.

I was deep in thought when Ish took my hand. "Look," he pointed to the kilometer-long train of old and new citizens wandering through the enormous corridor below the city. It was wide enough for two winged men to fly next to each other. When we passed the city borders above us, I realized we were slowly moving at a downward slope. The longer and deeper we went into the ground, the quieter we became. This was an untold story, a secret never written in any book, waiting to be unveiled. Scores of Birdmen, with their exquisite bodies, glided along the underground tunnel, being good hosts and proud tour guides by sharing tales of their kind. They spoke of the time of the Blood Moon. The Gods of the skies and mountains. When leaders were chosen not by birthright or power, but by qualities such as talent, wisdom, compassion, and integrity through the King's Games. I was captivated by their equitable society.

After hours of venturing deeper, we reached a massive underground chamber that opened to a hidden world below the mountain. We followed their example by dousing our torches and candles because the light reaching us from the other side was as bright as sunlight. Gugusan bounced up and down on the balls of his feet as he and Groda animatedly pointed while painting a picture with words about what was happening with the arrival of the San. "It is all connected, the Birdman City and the San. Above us is the foot of your mountain," Gugusan said. No matter how many times he says it, I'm always laughing. Having a mountain was something I'd never imagined or wanted. "The exit, or opening on the other side is where our people enter." He said, and I smiled when I heard the deliberate mention of *our* people.

"So you knew of this place?" I asked.

"Yes, but this is the Birdmen's side. We guard the other side. The mountain of the Gods, your mountain, my dear Kuku. Isn't it breathtaking? I feel small-small here with you—inside the heart of Anzulla."

I gave Gugusan a tender smile. "Yes, I think all of us feel tiny today."

"Ha! Gods of the mountain and skies can't feel tiny. That is not true, Kuku," Groda blurted, laughing and slapping me on my shoulder.

"Da!" Gugusan laughed cheerfully, open mouth and wide-eyed.

As we entered, I couldn't help but clutch Ish's arm. My stomach dropped in astonishment at the wide open space with luscious fields of green short grass with white and purple flowers popping up like daisies. Thousands of us took a while to get gathered. *How did we never know that the Earth was hollow?* "The scale of this place is indescribable," I muttered to myself as I turned, arms and wings spread wide. "Where is the light coming from? Is the light burning you?" I tugged at my mate's shirt to get his attention, but he was busy with a serious conversation, with Eryn and the Phoenix Leadership on the other side.

Groda relayed my question to the Sable next to him, walking and listening to our conversation. "No, he says the sun and moonlight are being reflected through tunnels of crystals, which filter back and forth, never dying. Constant light, that won't hurt Ishtar." Groda said.

"That's good news, I was starting to miss my sunbathing. My feathers are itching for this light."

"Kuku, you should join the Birdmen, early in the mornings. Ask Luci to bring you with them. I heard they congregated here with sunrise." Groda said.

"Did you hear, this light won't hurt you, Ish? We can sunbathe together!"

"Yes, my Kuku, this light feels like candlelight. It's not hurting me." Ish answered me, finally. "I think this is where my ancestors lived. The air, the colors, and the light. It feels good to me. Like I can breathe and relax."

"When you come live in your mountain with us, you can visit your Birdmen by flying through the tunnels," Gugusan added.

"That's good to hear. Ish can avoid the sun during the day and still travel with me."

We halted and watched the Sables and Angels lift their arms and pause, forming a white-then-black circle around human-sized pillars, their eyes gleaming with a silver sheen. Brad and the others shook their heads and stepped back as thousands of girls, boys, men, and women were transfixed by the Birdmen, as their wings shimmered in the crystal-produced light. Majestic and strong, they oozed masculinity while they continued to enlarge the radius of the circle. Then, as one, they turned around, facing outward. *God, this is weird.*

"We welcome you," they sang a song that sounded familiar. *I've heard this before.* It's the song Eryn, Ivan, and Cian sang when they celebrated the completion of wrapping Phoenix in its protective layers of bubbles. Again, I noticed Brad, Rick, Mika, and Connor melt into the background. *Something was up with them.* I excused myself from the conversation Ish was having with Gu. Then, made my way as inconspicuous as possible over to them. I wanted to get closer, to hear why they were separating themselves and appearing like they didn't approve of what was going on. I followed them to a cluster of gigantic baobab trees. The biggest I've ever seen. Large colorful tropical birds, like the ones from Gu's cave, took flight and squawked as they approached. I folded and tucked my wings and followed them.

"Peter," Mika and Connor greeted me when he saw me approaching. They looked worriedly at Brad, while Rick nudged his husband with a shoulder forward, to be the mouthpiece of their segregating gang.

They were going on like schoolboys caught smoking. "What in the ever-loving fuck is going on?" I asked.

"Hm, Peter. I'm just going to come out with it and say it. Please don't take this as an insult. We've been having conflicting ideas of what we see or want for ourselves, for us as individuals. Not as leaders, but as men who had responsibilities for years," Brad said as he struggled to meet my gaze.

"Spit it out, Brad!" I barked at him. This was mind-blowing. *Were they not impressed by this place? Is this a control issue thing?* Ish told me last night that they were drinking and having an orgy when Cian and he went to Phoenix to tell them about the plan to bring the entire city to Anzulla. We thought they were recovering from hang-overs. I've left them alone, thinking they would cheer up, eventually, but now it seemed like they were struggling to come to terms with Anzulla and its people.

"Peter, we have discussed this at length with our chil-dren, we have not yet informed the general population of Phoenix, but we decided to retire," Brad explained, his hand in a placating gesture. *Why would they think I'll be upset with that?* Fuck, they've worked their asses off for more than a century. Of course, they must take a bloody break. I was on the verge of collapsing before Brad helped me find my way. I understood what it was to be working all your life, to force yourself to switch the fuck off and find yourself.

"Jesus, Brad, why are you making such a big thing of

it? Why do you think I will freak out? Sure, I thought you were feeling insecure and not in charge. But I understand now. Look at this place. It's a bloody paradise. Why would you want to stay in Phoenix and try to run it like you used to? It won't work, anyway." I blurted. Their expressions told me I was saying the correct things. "Do what you want, you've earned it. You owe Phoenix nothing." I pointed outside and all around, trying to get my point across. "Scatter in any direction you want. I'm not being sarcastic. Go do your thing. I'm planning to live with Ish at my waterfront property near the mountain village," I said because I have a home.

"I plan to stay far away from Phoenix and make a new life in Anzulla. Living with Gugusan and the San was something I moaned about for thirty years, but now I can't see myself living anywhere else. Ish and they are my family now. I honestly don't mind what you do and where you live, as long as it is for yourselves. You've all earned it. I am sure the Phoenicians will feel the same. Let them choose a new leader if they want one. In all honesty, I don't think this place needs leaders in the sense that we've been used to."

Mika and Connor stepped closer as Rick and Brad threw their arms around me, hugging me fiercely. "Stop your crying. Be proud of yourselves and don't let anyone make you feel guilty. Do you hear me?"

"We hear you," Mika and Connor said, tears rolling from their red-rimmed eyes.

"Now can we please watch? I want to see this," I asked, already breaking their stupid embraces. *Fuck!* I shook my head once more at them and walked away to go find my people.

"You spoke to them?" Ish asked as I laced my fingers through his.

"Yeah, it's only empty nest syndrome or something like that," I said and watched as the masses encircled the Bird-men, and at the center of it all, one neon blue emitting pillar surrounded by six smaller white and black marble obelisks. Golden Anunnaki glyphs, exactly like the ones on the stone pillar in the San people's cave and inside the arena of Birdman City, told the story of Anzulla. The pillar, glowing from the vibrating kinetically energized light particles, reflected continuously throughout the crystal-lined tunnels was responsible for Lasitor being able to survive for thousands of years.

My Ish requested that Lasitor laser tattoo, the human altering gene coding calculations as inscribed inside the apple by Eryn, over his heart. After that, everyone wanted tattoos that represented the promise of eternal life without illness. A promise Lasitor had made to a fourteen-year-old Anunnaki boy, who had carefully reconnected his wires and rebuilt the time machine from scraps of wreckage. His best friend, his travel companion, and the reason why Ish's children and their bloodlines lived on. For hours, days, and weeks, one by one, Angel, Sable, and human, whether from the San or Phoenix, identifying as Anunnaki or vampire, had the choice to place the palms of their hands against Lasitor's pillar. Some recited the Anunnaki prayer. Adult men and women without Eden Beans were given a choice to receive one.

Brad, Rick, Mika, Connor, Bryan, Tony, Paul, and Simon renounced their leadership and handed the reins back to the citizens of Phoenix. That sparked longer ceremonies and festivities. From Birdman City into the jungle and up the mountain, bonfires burned day and night for days, as bon voyages and acknowledgments of their service and valor for over one hundred years. They quietly disappeared under the darkness of night after loading their Bubblecars, leaving a note on the door of the Leadership Office that said, *'Out of service, we are exploring the coastlines—until further notice.'*

As the celebrations continued, Ish and I retreated to our honeymoon suite in the steepled castle tower overlooking the ocean. Our first two weeks in Anzulla started with making love for hours until we passed out, got too hungry, or were forced to leave the room in search of food. Luxurious feather early morning basking became our daily favorite thing to do together as we joined the Birdmen, bathing under hundreds of feet of high lukewarm waterfalls that crashed down on one side of the clearing. We would spread out on the grass between the lavender and Loursveto flowers, drying under the crystal-conducted light—making my hair and feathers shimmer brightly all day.

CHAPTER 27
HOME

"GOOD MORNING, CITIZENS OF ANZULLA.

It's now six a.m.

Did you know tea is the second most consumed beverage in the world after water? It's said people enjoy drinking the stuff using ceramic teapots and cups—not the stainless steel cups you use in Phoenix.

Today we will serve your first outdoor breakfast in the tea garden area, where all residents of Anzulla may enjoy an outside meal.

Brunch will be served from early morning till midday—every day. So no rush.

Have a day filled with full stomachs, new friends, and tranquility!"

ISHTAR
24 970 B.C.

Anzulla

SEXUALLY SATISFIED, but still aroused, I sat naked, with my back resting against the cold stones and my legs stretched out on the windowsill. I popped the top of my third coconut, squeezed the delicious Loursveto juice into it, and sipped the once-extinct plant sap. Smacking my tongue on the roof of my mouth, I savored the bitter-sweet taste and soaked up the peace and calmness hanging thick in the surrounding air.

I'd never been so happy finding out about being incorrect in my assumptions. I thought Apsu was about to rise from the ashes, head on his shoulders as if never decapitated. With the arrival of Phoenix, Apsu's reach should be completely removed from Anzulla. It should feel like he had never existed at all, but the memories and impact of his actions weren't gone, and my mind wasn't the blank slate I imagined. I guess I have to make more beautiful memories so that they become so many, that they overflowed and spilled into every dark corner of my mind, leaving those ugly, fearful, and insecure ones washed clean and empty.

"The blue and silver crescent lining the horizon is spectacular. It enhances the dark mysterious depths of the ocean," I said, not expecting a reply from my Kuku. For a few minutes, my eyes drifted unfocused and unblinking. I stared into the distance absentmindedly. "Do you hear those waves crashing against the cliffs? They sound just like you sucking air through your teeth when I push into you. I could sit here all night just listening to them while watching the moonlight glimmer and dance across the waters." I whispered, mesmerized by the beauty before me. Not sure if Peter was awake and listening or not.

Bright orange and yellow bonfires illuminated the dry sand above the boundary of high tide along the beach. Seeing the cheerful faces of Phoenician women, men, and children congregating with the indigenous people, stirred a warm feeling of gratitude and accomplishment inside my chest. As soon as I thought the festivities were waning, one horde leaving was replaced with a fresh bunch arriving. It's been going on like this for the last two weeks since we arrived. Anzulla's different groups and cultures were socializing under one moon around bonfires built at strategic resting areas, lighting the new road created by thousands of trampling feet, while visiting Birdman City or the San in the mountains. Thanks to the language seeds I'd implanted, they communicated and understood each other. Peter called the implant location the Broca's and Wernicke's areas in the brain. They enjoyed each other's company so much, that some never returned home. I'm sure I'm looking at the settlement of a growing tent city. Stories are being told, games are being played. Food is being shared, while old songs and dances are being adapted in joyful delight as they learn and share experiences. Different cultures becoming one and being reformed.

The bonfire below our window is where my kin, or our friends, have been camping out. I'm saying friends because Cian and his brothers said if I say they are my children one more time, they will order Rotty, Igor, and Devil to destroy me. I'm scared that they would do that—order their Anubis to kill me, an innocent, but I respect them. So, no matter how much I wish to call them my children, I will refer to them as my friends. Eryn and Ivan ate sitting against a washed-out tree stump, gazing at the gathering of others backlit by the fires on the shore. Cian and Barkor looked up at me as if sensing I was watching them. I waved and wondered if I should be shielding my manhood with the coconut. If their eyesight was as good as mine, they would see it. Their three Anubis lay next to Barkor while he was lying in Cian's arms. They pointed to the moon. Maybe they thought what I thought. *Is that the moon Barkor and his people came from, or was that moon untouched by humans?* My ship is now part of Phoenix, and if Cian and Barkor would like to see the current state of the moon, we still have a Spacecar, and won't need a time-jumping ship. Lasitor is becoming part of Anzulla, the Phoenician metropolis with its electricity generator, and organic optical fiber veins running along the bottom of the ocean slowly growing and reconnecting Lasitor to the land.

My father and mother destroyed Anzulla—we still don't know how or why, but this paradise, like us, was given a second chance. I will teach our children how to live in harmony with each other and how to appreciate this time and place Lasitor has carved out for us. We will learn from each other. Three groups, the Phoenicians, the Birdmen, and the San, each have something precious to bring and teach the others. Elijah says Anzulla is Heaven, that God is here in spirit. I agree. I've been feeling the magic in the air, ever since I discovered this time and place.

Peter and I are getting to know Luci and his kind. After all my travels, being alone and uncertain about my future, I am now certain this is where I am supposed to be. This place and time, I would never leave, for fear of losing my way back. Tomorrow, we will move to the cave my Kuku had carved out of the mountain, where we will start our lives with the San. I'm excited to see our babies grow in those artificial wombs, in Phoenix. Our children will be born just like Eryn, Ivan, and Cian were.

The cool wind brushed over my nakedness. I placed the emptied coconut down, then fingered through the pages of scriptures Eryn had given me earlier. I was comparing my travels with the mind-boggling coincidences. So much history, it's as if we have lived it a thousand times. I have so many unanswered questions, and I plan to forget them now. I put the book down and walked over to the massive platform bed.

"May I?" I asked my lover, who was apparently watching me this whole time through hooded eyes.

"Sure," he said softly. His voice was hoarse and cracking from sleep. He was filling every inch of the mattress as he lay diagonally over it. The torchlight and the dying fire in the hearth illuminated his wings and hair in shades of yellow and gray. My Kuku stretched lazily, first spreading, then making space for me as his arms folded behind his head. The flickering flames cast light on Peter's well-defined muscles, including his chest and abdomen, while the shadows vanished into his blond pubic hair. His half-engorged cock twitched like a compass needle sensing my nearness. Heat flushed through my whole body as it slowly rose to greet me as I sat down next to my Kuku.

He waved a hand over his cock. "You're gaping at him," he said with delighted smugness and threw one leg over my lap. I laced my fingers between his toes. The sight of him, that lazy grin I will never grow tired of, warmed my belly.

I smiled, brushed his bangs away, and tucked a strand of his pure white hair behind his ear with poise.

"You look happy. Are you?"

Peter laughed softly. He sat up and looked out the stone-framed window overlooking the wide expanse of calming waters. "I am. Your long black hair hanging thick and untamed over your shoulders makes you look like some kind of Puma superhero."

"Pfft, you say the weirdest things. Your flawless pale skin and lustrous wings make you look like a one-of-a-kind Angel. Which you are."

"I am, and I'm yours." The fire accentuated his cheek-bones and stunning blue eyes. His long sinewy neck flowed into strong wide shoulders and thick muscled arms —making him look invincible. He pulled his knees to his chest and sat hugging them. Although I had become accustomed to the bolt of lust shooting through me every time I admired him, it still overpowers and pushes me to him.

"If you get closer to me, I might let you lick and suck

me again. Look what you do to me." I gripped my stiffening cock and teased Peter by moving my hand up and down my length until pre-cum beaded at the slit, beckoning him to taste it.

"You'd like that, wouldn't you?" Peter whispered, lips curving up into another luscious smile.

"It seems to me you don't want me to say that you've had enough of me," I purred, watching him gulp loudly. I eavesdrop on his thoughts as he struggles to come up with as clever response. I got up, standing naked at the foot of the bed. We were drunk with lust, love, and each other's body fluids.

During our first waterfall shower, Peter had untangled my braids and washed my hair. It was frizzy and bushy, but I was glad he liked it. I tied my wild black mane into a thick bush behind my head with a leather string. Knowing he enjoyed watching me, stretching and extending my arms as he raked his gaze over me. His breath hitched and a feeling of pride and deep-rooted love filled me. My skin glowed with a blue-gold sheen. Like an Andean flamingo doing its mating dance, I made a show of my body and half-hard, long uncut cock, hanging heavy over my balls.

I looked down at him. "Careful, you might hurt your beautiful brain thinking too hard."

Peter crawled closer on his hands and knees, wings dragging at his sides. He looked up at me with those sparkling blue eyes, making me think of the healing pool of Babylon. I wanted to dive into them. He leaned to grab hold of my growing erection. Fingers firm, the blues in his eyes turned dark with a challenge I couldn't ever resist. I gazed down, hypnotized by the desire he had for me in them.

"Come here. I want to make love to you." The unspoken question, "Will you let my tongue inside you?" hung in the air, but he opted to say, "I need you."

"Are you sure? Aren't you sore? This would be the fourth time today. You are probably bruised," I said to give him an opening to ask.

"There are other ways to make love. Let me taste you. Let me make love to you." He tugged me closer by my prick. Lining me up with his mouth. I waited, already trembling with anticipation. His fiery blue gaze fixated on my reaction as he sucked my length into his warm mouth. Tingles of pleasure ran up and down my spine and wrapped around my filling balls. I watched as he swallowed all of me down.

"Oh, Peter, you drive me mad with that mouth of yours." I hissed and fisted my hand in his white hair. Excruciatingly, oh so very bloody slowly, he pulled back, his cheeks hollowed by the intense suction. My erection grew harder, bigger, and longer as he swirled his tongue around the head, playing and tickling that sensitive rim underneath my shrinking foreskin.

"You were saying there are other ways?" I asked, knowing already what Peter was planning. He wanted to spear my tight ass with his tongue. I'll beg him to do it if he doesn't ask soon. This would be a first for him, and I wanted it.

"Come over here. Get on your stomach for me." He patted the bed, indicating I should change places with him. With a smoldering look and a stern nod, I offered my entire self to him. Not saying a word, I obeyed. The sexual tension between us built. I knew I thrilled Peter by creeping on my hands and knees, then sliding down seductively and crossing my arms under my chin as I draped myself onto my stomach as ordered.

With his legs on either side of me, he rubbed his hands around my shoulders, gently massaging my muscles while working his way down to my buttocks. Then further, all the way down to my ankles. I felt his desire increasing and that stoked my want for him. He started kissing me. First the one leg and then the other, all the way up and down. Slowly. Worshipping, tasting, and teasing me from my ankles to the cleft of my ass.

"Open for me," he said, nudging my knees apart. Doing it for Peter, the man I loved, was a magically deep experience. No regular fucking can imitate the rush, the flood of emotion, no matter how hard or how many strangers I fucked, it was nothing like what I was experiencing now. This was a first for both of us.

A feather-light touch and warm breath flickered over the crack between my tensed butt cheeks. "I want to eat you out. Is that something you would let me do?"

"Why not? I thought you'd never offer. Please, this is something only for you and me, for us," I said, relaxing my muscles and opening that last door I had kept shut emotionally and physically, exposing my vulnerability. I tried to lighten the situation by moving my hips and indicating my willingness.

The mattress dipped between my legs. His hands

wrapped around my knees as he made space for himself between them. I felt the heat of his breath on my buttocks and exposed hole. His wings gently tucked around my body, cocooning us.

Peter tied my past and my future to this point in time. This moment was my anchor to which I will always return. That was my last coherent thought before he swiped his wet, slick scorching hot tongue over me, over and over until I was lost in a sea of desire, drowning in emotions, while leaking snot, spit, and tears. There was too much of it—so many emotions. I needed him. To fill me with everything that is him. He bit down on my shoulder. The pain and slow finger fucking of my spit-slicked entrance sent me spinning into that vortex, building and chasing my orgasm. Slowly and rhythmically, making me his, silencing that yearning of my lonely soul. One last slow withdrawal and the burning sensation disappeared as he drizzled warm oil over my hole. "Yes, fuck please, I'm good and ready. Push something bigger and deeper into me," I whispered as my toes curled, and my fingers wrapped around the bony tips of his wings. Anchoring myself, I prepared to be plowed with the speed and deadly force of lightning.

"You sure?"

"Yes," I groaned as he massaged and stretched me open. "Fuck yes!" He rubbed over that magical spot inside my channel. Sparks of bright lights flashed and danced behind my fluttering eyelids. I lay still. Waiting. Wanting. Heaving and shaking. I submit. Letting him control the pace of my pleasure. I knew exactly how he felt, similar to a predator that has successfully captured its prey. As soon as he felt my submission, he removed his teeth from the crook of my neck. While licking and kissing the wound, his fingers disappeared from me. His sensual movements were driving me insane. Then just as I lifted my head to protest, he clutched my shoulders. Peter dragged his chest slowly up and down my back, and after what felt like unending torture, he moved his hardness into place. Sliding it over my taint, entering me so slowly, with so much love, I felt like crying, then let out a whimper.

"You feel so good, and right. Do you want more? I want more. I fear I will never get enough of you, of this, of us," Peter said with a low husky voice into the shell of my ear, making me shiver. "Let's make a game of this. I tease you and we see who wins by making the other come first," My Kuku said, and I didn't care who wins or loses as long as I had him and he had me and we are together.

More dragging and teasing, until I begged him, "Kuku, I don't care if I won or lost the bloody game. I need more, harder, and faster!"

"I agree." His wings lifted, flapping and stretching above us.

"Oh my sweet Fates, yes please," I grunted and fisted the bedding. Peter laughed maniacally and then, with a force I'd been expecting but never experienced, he slammed into me.

Fucking me dumb and breathless.

Hard and deep thrusts followed until both of us ejaculated and passed out, sleeping with him on my back and his cock inside me. We had finally fully bonded and our lives were permanently intertwined.

When I woke, Peter was busy cleaning me. But as he turned to wash himself, I pounced and he gasped.

"Hands on the wall. Don't move until I say so." His body shuddered against me. He threw his head back, his white locks washing over my face. He obeyed.

I held him tight and explained to him exactly how much he affected me and why. "I'm so unbelievably in love with you, and your body is such a temptation. The smell of your majestic blinding white wings, the feathers slightly fluttering when you are aroused. Your tall, muscled body, that mouth-watering tight ass, your smooth muscled abdominals. I want to run my hands constantly over every inch of you and then grip your white locks like this and fuck you." I gripped his hair, knowing I was rough and commanding.

"Really?" he asked in a teasing tone. His voice was thick with lust. His wings quivered under my touch and my warm breath against the sensitive part of his neck.

"Yes, always."

He wanted me. He craved me as much as I craved him. It's becoming clear to me that Peter doesn't hold himself back for me. There is nothing I wouldn't do to see him happy. Peter and I have never been jealous, but there's a comfort in knowing I belong to him, that he missed me, and he takes it so seriously that he has become possessive. I read his thoughts and in his mind, I belonged to him as he belonged to me. There's no other for me in this reality or any other.

"I'm starving and aching for you over here."

"I know," I whispered under my breath, knowing I was driving him crazy with my seduction. I traced my finger along the ridges over the skin between his wings where I knew he was extra sensitive. Like a kitten, he began purring and begging for more scratches. I ran my tongue over the sensitive area I like to nibble on when I'm fucking him from behind.

"Fuck me, Ish, I want it again, right now!" he growled, and my cock twitched agreeing with him.

"My cock agrees. He's aching for you," I murmured between tiny licks and bites. The longer I took teasing him, the more my balls tingled and pulsated with fullness.

"Oh, you better do as your cock says."

"Hmmm, my balls agree too. They tell me it's time to be emptied," I said as I admired my throbbing blue cock between his perfect pale ass cheeks.

"Better hurry up and listen to us, we might shrivel up and die." He rubbed his ass sideways against my pulsating warm cock like a firestarter. My skin itched as it started to glow.

"I'll probably come the second you're inside me," he announced, and I chuckled, evil undertones lacing my voice. I wrapped my fingers around the base of my cock and teased his hole with the slick head.

"Get the oil on the bedside table, please, my lover." Peter's feathers rattled—serious, eager, and turned on.

I took my time walking over to grab the oil Luci had graciously placed in the room for us. Before Anzulla, we'd always been in a rush. Sticking it in and roughing it. So now I took my time slicing myself and his backside until he vibrated around my probing finger. I used my other hand to lather his balls and decided to rub some onto his tight globes as well. "Damn, Peter, I love your tight muscled globes," I said. My voice rumbled and I hissed through my long incisors.

"For the love of the Fates, and all that is holy, I love hearing you say that, but I could give two fucks if you don't get on with it. I'm going to come over the wall before you've even started."

"We've determined there are no Fates. You are talking about Lasitor." I chuckled. "Stop worrying about coming. If you shoot early, I will keep going until you go again. When I'm deep inside you, you will appreciate it, no matter if you come now or not." I licked and nipped at the back of his neck. "I'm going to sink my teeth into you. You'll be happy for it because you will come again for me. You know that's how we roll, my Kuku. What made you think this round would be any different?" I teased with my fangs, scraping the skin between his wings.

I'm now addicted to his blood. "Hmmm, your blood tastes so good, like orgasms, only in liquid form."

"Ish, if you don't penetrate me now, I'm going to jump out the window and find someone willing to fuck me!"

"You what?" I growled and forced my aching cock into him with one hard push.

"Thank fuck," he howled, palms flat against the wall, arching his back, and spreading his wings wide. I held tight around his hips, holding him in place, as I pumped into him.

"Calm the fuck down. We're levitating off the floor. You are going to hurt your wings, and I'm going to fall," I said, not stopping hammering into him. Peter stopped flapping, clinging to the wall. I used all my strength to push deep inside of him, wrapping my legs around his lower legs while hanging onto his shoulders. I'd never fucked like this. I'd never fucked a non-human. Like two bats mating, I clung to Peter. He met me thrust for thrust. Sweat ran down my temples as I chased my orgasm while simultaneously trying to hold out as long as I could. Slipping and sliding over his oiled backside. My fangs tingled as I savagely heaved air into my lungs. Physically he matched my strength. The harder I fucked, the more he urged me on. As we reached the precipice, I slowed my thrusts. "I'm going to bite you now. We can come together."

"Yes, do it," he grunted.

On his command, I tilted my head back and struck the muscled area between his neck and wing. Peter whimpered as I sucked and swallowed. His tasted like stars exploding as his blood slid thick and warm down my throat. This thirst I constantly have for him, will never go away.

"Fuck yes," he shouted as his ass tightened around me. I pushed hard and planted myself as deep as I could. My body spasmed and pleasure zinged through me. My orgasm pulsed and pulsed and pulsed as I spurted my seed deep into him. The taste and feel of him—so bloody good. We chased our pleasures until we were empty, satisfied, and hungry. The room spun. Literally. I realized we were airborne again as I clung to him. Peter's head fell back, and we lowered to the floor. His ribs expanded and contracted as he heaved in air.

"We must eat. It's time to leave this room and socialize." I laughed, removing myself from him. We were ridiculous. And we were happy.

"Eryn's ceremony is about to begin," I said over my shoulder, as I rinsed a washcloth in lukewarm soapy water to clean up. "It's going to be spectacular. Luci said they are eager to have a king of their own."

"Yeah, Eryn is so bloody humble, I want to slap him over the head sometimes. I mean, I won't look for trouble with him, but a king needs a certain flair of *don't-fuck-with-me* vibes, which he hides. Whether it is on purpose, I don't know." Peter pulled his shoulders to his ears, making his feathers rustle. "Do you know what he said to me yesterday?"

"Hmmm, what?"

"Eryn said he will accept his anointing and vow to protect and lead all citizens of Anzulla into a harmonious existence with each other. Under the watchful, ever-present eye of the true creator of time itself, the true God of all, who has yet to reveal themselves." I shook my head and chuckled as I finished wiping myself down, rinsed the cloth, and walked over to hand it to Peter. He took it from me, cleaned himself, and threw the cloth into the washroom.

I had one of my legs down my pants when an incessant knocking at the door startled both of us.

"We're coming!" I yelled. Peter looked at me, and we burst out laughing like children.

Knock-knock-knock-knock! The knocking continued. It got louder and louder. "I said, we're coming!" I squealed, folding double with laughter.

"Ishtar, Peter, there is trouble! Get your asses out of bed and come down to the beach," Elijah shouted.

"It's Juandre and Andrew. It doesn't look good. Hurry!" Luci said.

Gone were our happy giggles.

"One minute, we will meet you, in one minute!" A bolt of white heat rushed through me. Our friends were hurt. With terrified bewilderment, we jumped into action and finished getting dressed.

CHAPTER 28
APSU

"*GOOD MORNING, CITIZENS OF ANZULLA.*

It's now six a.m.

This is a riddle with a very hot tip. What is hard enough to protect us, but shatters with incredible ease. It's made from opaque sand, yet it's completely transparent. It behaves like a solid material, but it's also a liquid in disguise!

It's glass of course.

Did you know the chemical process of creating glass involves heating quartz sand, also known as silica sand, to temperatures above three thousand and ninety degrees Fahrenheit until it melts into a clear liquid?

Yes, that is hot, and my hot tip is for those with sun allergies. By applying a reflective coating to two panes of glass and installing them into those holes you call windows, you will block and reflect the damaging rays of the sun.

Start your day with a sparkle and visit your community news page to learn how to make glass.

Have a transparent day!"

PETER
24 970 B.C.
Anzulla

AN URGENT FEELING in the pit of my stomach pulled my insides into knots. I hopped into my pants, leaned out the door, and gasped. Holding my breath, my brain computed the silhouettes in the scene unfolding in the distance. "I can't believe what I'm seeing." Ish stuck his head out the window. We watched Juandre and Andrew approaching. I turned my head to Ish as he turned his to me. "Are they pulling a Bubblecar?" We muttered simultaneously. I shook my head. "God, they look like two horses in front of a snow sleigh."

"Yeah, but it's not snow it's white sand," Ish said. He straightened and scrubbed his face with the palms of his hands. "Swords, I need my swords, Kuku." He scurried behind me, swords clanging and boots flying as he dove for the chair to sit on while he put his boots on. They were still a few hundred feet away, but I could see Birdmen hovering above them. Luci, Groda and Elijah landed to speak to Andrew and Juandre. Their heads were lowered —ignoring them.

I drew in a sharp breath, "Where are the others?" Suddenly I saw only black. "No, no, no, don't look." Ish was shutting my eyes with the palms of his hands. "Don't look, don't look!"

"What the fuck, Ish, take your hands away," I snarled at him and pushed his hands down from my face. "Is that what I think it is?"

"Kuku, you shouldn't look. I can go and see it. Please stay here. You are soft, you don't have the stomach for this."

My wings flared to half open. I bulged my fists and said through gnashing teeth, "No. Fucking. Way. You must be saying that because I just fucked you senseless."

He cringed under my scrutinizing gaze. "It came out wrong, I'm sorry."

My feathers stopped rustling. "Hurry, let's go and see. Together. Hold on to me." I launched off our small porch and made a three-hundred-and-sixty-degree turn, waiting and seeing Ish running, while securing his swords into the belt around his waist. He then jumped off the window ledge and soared through the air, a move we'd been perfecting the past few days. I dove down, passing him free falling. He caught me by my ankles. "Damn, those swords are heavy!" I grunted and flapped three times harder to shoot into the sky, veering left and right through the inquisitive onlookers. As we approached, I saw an opening, hung a sharp left, and dipped low over the beach. Ish let go and ran when his feet hit the sand, weapons ready.

It was a scene of horror.

Juandre and Andrew sat on their asses. Their faces were scorched, and in some places, blackened skin was torn off revealing sinew and bones beneath. Juandre's beautiful face was gone on the right side. His upper and lower teeth were exposed, all the way to his ear was raw bleeding flesh. People stepped closer to see what they had brought with them. No one said anything as they turned and either ran away or shook their heads in disbelief. Juandre and Andrew sat catatonic with mountain climbing ropes tied around their waists—they had used them to pull the cracked-open Bubblecar.

Ish placed the palms of his hands on my pecs and pushed me back. His yellow eyes were wide with bewilderment and glassy with tears. "No, Kuku, don't, you will see this always. You can never unsee this." But I had already seen it. Inside lay bodies and limbs bloodied and lifeless. To make matters worse, flies were everywhere.

"Ish, let me go!" He did.

Carefully, I approached. White noise sang in my ears and disbelieving shock flushed through my veins as what I was seeing slowly registered. My friends, pieces of my friends, lay torn and squashed into the Bubbelcar. Flashes of my childhood of women and children in mass graves assaulted me. Someone's leg was thrown haphazardly over Mika's and Connors's upper bodies. Brad's torso lay on its side, blood still oozing and drenching Rick's lower body.

"What the fuck happened here, Juandre?" I shouted as I darted over to them. The sight of them both hurt and distraught didn't prevent me from shaking them to give me answers. "Fuck!" They just sat there staring. Their mouths moved, but no sound escaped their throats. "Ish! Where the fuck is Ish?"

"I'm behind you, Peter."

I folded and tucked my wings and pulled Ish closer to them. "Read their fucking minds and tell me what you see!"

"I know already, my Kuku," he said in a calm and soothing voice. I didn't want to be calmed or soothed. *They are my friends dammit!* "What did this?" Ish stood silent. The sound of leather creaking around the hilts of his swords drew my attention. He might sound calm and unaffected but he wasn't. The fine tremors in his body told me to back off. He looked ready to snap.

"Where are Eryn, Cian, and Ivan?" I asked, searching, not seeing their tall blond heads.

"They said something about having sex in the mud last night. We will go look for them," Luci said and scooped his lovers into his arms to go searching.

"Thank you!" I shouted.

"Hurry, sunlight is upon us," Ish added. His skin was already steaming in the rising sunlight.

"May I?" Grabbing a water skin from an onlooking Birdman, I fell to my knees next to Juandre.

Ish turned, with his arms wide open. "Please stand back. Give us room. They need air to breathe!" The onlookers respectfully stepped back. "Angels and Sables, could you hover and block the rays of the rising sun? Juandre, Andrew, and I burn easily. Thank you." Shadows fell upon us as the Birdmen made a protective circle around us and Ish joined me.

"Juan, Drew? Talk to us. Here's water. Drink." I urged

my friends to drink while dripping water over their charcoal lips. But they didn't drink.

"They need blood more than water now. They are beyond shock." Ish sat on his heels, sliced his left wrist, and offered it to Juandre by dripping bright red drops of blood onto his lips. "Drink. you need blood to heal." His voice was commanding and as stern as steel. Juandre blinked, sniffed at the smell of blood, and nodded a thank you. He took Ish's arm in both hands, pressed it against his mouth and sucked. *Slurping.* Astonished, I watched how miraculously the muscled flesh around his jaw stitched and healed, covering his exposed molars. His skin grew back, slowly covering with fine hairs around his eyebrows, upper lip, and chin. Even the nails on his fingertips grew back until he looked like the stunning man I knew. "You too, Andrew, drink from me." Ish pushed his wrist to Andrew's mouth next. "I will drink from Peter later. You need the strength of my blood."

With tears in my eyes, I clenched and unclenched my fists as I asked, "What did this? Was it a wild animal? A big wild cat. Yes, a cat killed Gu's father. But they look like a bomb hit them." I ran all the possibilities through my mind while Ish was finishing feeding Andrew. He was also healing while sucking Ish's pure Anunnaki lifeblood. "Lightning, yes, maybe an electrical storm?"

"No, my Kuku…"

Juandre coughed, clearing his throat. Ish licked, then pressed a thumb over his oozing wrist. When he was sure it was healed and not bleeding anymore, he said, "Tell us."

Juandre looked up with scorching anger on his face,

his words came out choppy at first as he stuttered. "It was one man with the face of an animal—a monster. He commanded fire as if he conjured it out of thin air. He threw it at us like cannonballs. He laughed when Brad fell to roll in the sand to kill the flames, then he walked right up to him with a long blade and sliced Brad in half. His cries of pain." Juandre pressed his hands over his ears. "He came at us from all sides. We couldn't protect them. They didn't stand a chance." He took the water skin from me and took a few gulps from it.

Ish hissed like a feral cat. If I didn't know him like I did, I would have run. "This looks and sounds like Apsu's destructive work." That name explained his reaction to me. Andrew sat in silence. Not saying anything. Locked deep inside his mind and not ready to speak.

"Fuck, just as I thought life was good! *What are their children going to say?* Wait, where are Paul and Simon?"

My words hung in the air, and Andrew exploded into tears, blubbering. "Their Bubblecar was hit first. It burst into flames and crashed into the sea. We'd parked and picnicked in an alcove. We were packing up and they went ahead of us. They weren't gone for a minute when we heard the explosion and saw them crashing."

"We couldn't find them, we looked. We wanted to bring them home, but we couldn't find them," Juandre cried.

I wrapped my arms and wings around their shoulders. Offering comfort and strength, while giving Ish my *this-is-a-cluster-fuck* look. It seemed to calm him. His breathing slowed and his fangs retracted. "We know, we can see you tried your best."

Ish leaned in closer, tilting Juandre's head up to meet his gaze, as he looked into Juandre's mind. "Tell me, could you see the man's face?" Andrew leaned closer into my arms, hungry for safety and comfort.

"Yes, it is a face so ugly, it is burned into my mind. Dark blue like yours. Same eyes. Long black hair and a white tassel between his eyes. His head wasn't human, he looked like an animal. Almost like a horse or a cow with large pointy ears, and small horns at the sides of his head. He had big black claws for hands and golden-tipped fingernails." Ish drew in a long, slow breath, eyeballing me while Juandre coughed again, and sipped more water, before continuing. "He rolled his one hand as if catching air and turning into fire, like a wizard or something. Then he threw balls of fire and he even controlled how big they were. He corralled us in the alcove, playing with us. Andrew and I didn't know which way to go to help or who to help first. It wasn't something I ever thought to protect my friends from. You know, we aren't real fighters. We are fast, we tried to help, but we couldn't be everywhere." Juandre cried, taking Andrew's hand. "My bear tried his best, but this thing outsmarted us and was too evil. Honestly, we were fucking scared. I'm sure if we weren't vampires, we would be dead too." He sniffled and hugged Andrew.

"Cian and Ivan are going to have a fit. I know my father. He must have watched us, or have spies watching us. He knows we will come for him. But we can't go off half-cocked without a strategy. I prepared for years with a whole army to defeat him. When they get here, we need you to convince them to stay calm and plan an attack with Eryn."

"Yes, we shall. What about them in the meantime?" I pointed to the bodies, drenched with flies inside the Bubblecar.

"Leave them just like that. Their children deserve to decide what to do with their bodies."

An hour later two Bubblecars raced over the cliffs straight for us. As soon as they stopped and the doors opened, Eryn, Ivan, Cian, Barkor, Sarinka, Donali, and Kawa popped out of it and ran to the destroyed vehicle filled with their friends' and family's bodies. When they reached the gruesome scene they just stood there looking at it, like I was. Their eyes were gone, their faces burned, black holes and rolled up lips. The look of terror etched forever on their faces remained, as the stench of burned flesh and flies buzzing hung in the air. Not believing, and not accepting it, even though their deaths were right in front of us. I'm sure they thought they could bring them back to life, but their bodies were hacked up into pieces and there was no way of putting them back together again. Cian was the first to collapse, followed by Donali and Kawa. Sitting on the sand and crying, but not making a sound. Ivan leaned into Eryn as he cried quietly while Barkor put a comforting hand on Cian's shoulder. They looked powerless, like defeated children. Their sadness washed over us and it wasn't long before everyone in our vicinity cried with them.

"Who did this?" Eryn asked as he turned and approached us. Juandre and Andrew couldn't meet his gaze. "We are not mad at you, all I ask is—oh, I see," said Eryn, and I assumed he'd read our minds as he turned back to wave Cian, Ivan, and Barkor over. Kawa, Donali, and Sarinka stayed with their fathers. Eryn turned, tilting his head to one side, listening and concentrating. His demeanor was cold and confident. He pursed his lips, thinking and calculating. The corners of his eyes were scrunched into thin lines, deep-seated anger visible in the twitching muscles of his jaw. "We came as soon as Luci told us. We were visiting Gugusan last night. The San sent their regards. Gugusan and his warriors said they'd be here late afternoon. We can go inside and plan how to bring Apsu to us. He is near, Ishtar, I feel his darkness, he is close."

"Yes, he is watching us. Listen, nature is still. Other than the waves, there are no birds in the sky. Quiet and still, only the malevolence and the buzzing insects remain. That's how you know he is near. He attacks from all sides. The deaths, the flies, everything—it's to wear us down, to upset us. He attacks the mind and the body. He is some-where near, calculating, enjoying, and waiting for us. I don't know if he knows I killed him already in another reality or if this is his younger self. The Apsu that eventu-ally destroys Anzulla. All I know is, he can't find the Hori-zon. We should detach the time machine and remove it from Phoenix. It has served its purpose," Ish said in a low tone, so only we in his vicinity could hear him.

"I agree. Getting rid of the Horizon and removing the

time machine will prevent more Apsus from popping out of the sky. Do you think he was already here, in Anzulla?" I asked.

"That, or he jumped here with Phoenix," Cian added.

"If so, why didn't Lasitor know about him or warn us?" I asked.

Eryn turned to Ish. "Am I correct to assume he wouldn't do anything in the daytime? We have to think and act fast, before the sun sets tonight."

"What are we going to do with them?" Ivan asked, not able to look at the bodies, but pointing to them.

"You should decide. We could either burn the bodies as we did in Antarctica, or send them into the water," I said, feeling like shit, but in my defense, I've had an hour to think about it.

Ish shook his head, "No if we can't attack by planning and building an army, we must do it when he least expects it. If we waste time trying to be honorable and showing respect to the dead—I can't stress this enough—if we are burying them, it should be a distraction, make Apsu think we are mourning, and maybe ask the Angels and Sables to allow us to bury them under the baobab trees, in the crystal caves. Make it look real, but while doing it, we prepare to trap him."

"I know Dad would hate to be burned or sent under the water. Let's put them underground if we are allowed," Donali said loudly, and I was sure many others overheard.

That meant we didn't have to ask, he already had. Nobody gathering here really knew more than what had transpired these past couple of weeks. I doubt they knew

Donali and Kawa, as well as Simon and Paul, were Brad and Rick's kids.

Just as I finished that thought, a big Angel, I believe Luci called him Georgio, stepped closer, head down in submission to Eryn. "I just want to say we are all deeply saddened by their deaths, and I'm sure my brothers wouldn't mind if you want to lay them to rest inside the Heart of Anzulla. Also, I have one request, to Ishtar, the Demon God," he said, shifting from one foot to the other, hands clasped in front. *Shit, he is really scared of us.* So, that's why Eryn hated the bowing. They bowed out of fear and not respect. Georgio's eyes darted from Ish to Eryn and then back to me.

Eryn's golden-green eyes sparkled and the corners of his mouth pulled up into an encouraging smile. "Georgio, hello, thank you. The gesture is appreciated. Please, ask around to confirm, let me know if someone objects, and then we will make other arrangements," Eryn said extra loudly so everyone could hear him. I am sure Gugusan in the mountains could. It was almost as if Eryn was— *making a show of this.* "I know Brad and the others wouldn't want to impose unless everyone is okay with them invading your sacred space. Oh, and what is it that you want to tell Ishtar? I was waiting for someone to speak up about it. The man's been cooped up, mating since our arrival." Eryn smiled knowingly at Georgio and rested a hand on his shoulder. The Angel blushed and relaxed under his touch, then straightened.

"Ishtar, we are not Angels and Sables, those are how we tell the difference between the colors of our wings and the names of our teams. Angel color for white and Sable color for black. When we play games or when we have ceremonies and congregate, we tell the difference like that. But we are one race, like the San are one race of people."

"Oh? I apologize, that's my fault. That happens when being tied up and delirious with sunburn," Ish said, sarcastically. "How do you refer to yourselves? What should I call thee, oh mighty one?" Ishtar's voice was laced with venom. If a look could send lightning bolts, Georgio would have been struck down.

"Birdmen," I chipped in, breaking the tension.

Georgio couldn't meet Ish's gaze. He gave a shameful chuckle, not at all relaxing in Ish's company. "Yes, please say Birdmen, we are of the Bird, yes? We refer to ourselves in our language as, *Vucub-Caquix*."

"I know that word Vukubaku." Ish pronounced it totally wrong—we all could hear that. Georgio exploded with uncomfortable laughter. "That is not how you say it. *"Vucub-Caquix,"* he repeated, "or Birdman?" He smiled and exposed a radiant stack of white teeth as he bowed his head and reversed out of our circle.

"Okay, the tentative plan is..." Eryn said, clapping his hands so everyone refocused and listened. "Please let us know if you object to us putting our friends in the ground." He turned and winked a few winks so everyone knew setting the trap was on, and a go. "The ones with sun sickness will prepare for burial—Juandre and Andrew, please bring our fallen to the crystal caves. If you agree with me, I suggest we need all available hands to help us strip and unpack the Horizon. Please, jump in if you have a better idea, we can move it somewhere far away and blow it up, melt it down, crush it, fill it with water, or ask Cian to make a garden inside it."

"Hmmm, Eryn, I have an idea," I announced. "I agree with stripping it, but to destroy the shell, so the Horizon never flies or time jumps again, I could concoct a formula to crush it into dust. I suggest jumping it inside the crystal cave. Let's feed Anzulla's heart by first crystallizing it, and then freezing it so cold that one tap will crack it into billions of crystal pieces."

Ish patted my shoulder. "My mate, such a smart man."

"Peter, that's so far the best plan of the day! Anyone else with a suggestion?" Eryn asked, and I preened under his compliment.

"To be honest, everyone, I think my father would have liked that idea very much," Donali added. "Parking the Horizon and burying their bodies inside the crystal cave. It symbolizes they brought us all this way and their time with the vessels has ended."

"Any other suggestions?" Eryn's gaze swept over the crowd. "Thank you, Donali, we all agree then. Peter, can you get enough hands together to move your equipment into the Horizon, and get it set up? Ivan, Cian, and Barkor, could you also go with him? Barkor, inform your people what's happening. I don't want chaos. Tell them they can choose to stay inside Phoenix until this is over or visit the dry land, but remind them it's not safe, that I suggest they keep the children tucked away until we're finished setting up you know what, to trap and get rid of you know who. We will lay their bodies to the ground, but Ish and I will make sure it's not permanent. If we don't succeed, mourning their deaths won't matter, because Apsu will destroy all of us."

But if we manage to trap and kill Apsu a funeral won't be needed, I thought. Eryn glanced at me as if hearing my thoughts and acknowledged my thinking with a small dip of his chin and softening of his facial features. Ish wrapped his arms around my lower body and pulled me against him. The tightness in my chest loosened a little.

The crowd around us parted as Kawa burst through. *He's been with his fathers this whole time.* "Where are my brothers?" he asked, pissed off at Juandre and Andrew, with his fists bulging at his sides.

I swooped around, ready to throw my wings over Juandre and Andrew. "Hey, hey! None of that, they tried their best," I said. Hurt emanated from him in thick waves. He pushed his chest out gearing up for a fight. Kawa was smaller than me, but I didn't doubt for a second that he could deliver a mighty punch.

"Look at them, there's not a scratch on them. I doubt they tried their best to help. The way I see it is that they ran away and hid instead of doing the one thing my father asked of them, and that was to protect them. Fuck, he would have fought for you!" Kawa pulled his bionic arm back to hit Juandre with a fist when Ish jumped in between us. Eryn caught Kawa by the arm and immobilized him.

"Leave my brother alone." Donali jumped to help Kawa, but Sarinka stepped in front of him.

"Stop and look at them. Their clothes are torn and

burned to shreds. Look at Juandre's back, they were nearly burned off his body," Sarinka said, pointing with a dagger in her hand. We all turned to where she showed them the now fully healed skin below the melted bright turquoise body suit. Andrew's silver Phoenician body suit only covered his groin, the rest was gone, a testament that they burned away.

"Kawa, we didn't run away. We shielded them as best we could," Juandre said.

Andrew sniffled with tears in his eyes, looking at us, one by one. "I'm sorry, we weren't prepared to fight someone like that. He threw fire at us. And..." He shook his head as he let it fall in defeat. "Your brothers didn't stand a chance, their Bubblecar was attacked first and they crashed into the waters." Andrew looked up again, sorrow and humiliation etched deep into his face. His usual sparkling green eyes were now red and puffy as tears streamed down his face.

"Kawa, Ish gave them blood, they were healing for the hour we waited for you. When they arrived, they looked horrible. They collapsed after dragging the Bubblecar back here while burned down to the bone," I said, hoping the vivid description would force him to understand they were just as traumatized as he was.

"I fucking refuse to accept they are dead." He pointed to Ish. "Go back and save them. At least warn them." He pointed to Eryn. "You better go with him and kill this man."

"It's Apsu, it's my father," Ish said. Kawa narrowed his eyes at Ish. He must have heard during Ishtar's inquisition how difficult it was to kill the patriarch of the Anunnaki. Ish described in detail to the people of Phoenix how he had prepared for years to win the war. *Ish managed to kill the most powerful and vile Anunnaki.* Kawa pulled loose from Eryn's grip. "There is no fucking way this is how they meet their end. Not after what they have done for every-fucking-one here! I demand you go back and make this right!" The circle of onlookers around and above us was getting smaller. "Jesus, listen to yourselves, you are already burying them and preparing to go on with your lives."

"That's enough, Kawa!" Eryn said in an authoritative tone. "I was getting everyone to safety. We were merely planning ahead, before running hot-headed into a trap. I know he is watching us. As long as he is watching us, he is not attacking. Understand." Eryn looked at Kawa, exuding calm and reason. "I know this is difficult. We know how this looks, but if this is planned, we are going to get our chance and I will make sure it's our best chance." Eryn sighed and said in a softer tone, "Look, the main problem with this is that the Horizon can time jump. We must eliminate the reason for this mess. Second, their bodies, in this heat, must be dealt with. There is no way I'm putting them inside a fridge down in Phoenix." Then he whispered. "It's only for show, it's all temporary."

Kawa stepped back and hugged himself. He looked like a little lost boy, alone and mad at the world. *Fuck this*, I reached out to him and enfolded him in my arms and wings. He shook as he burst into tears. "Oh, my god. So they are going back and saving them, so this wouldn't have happened?"

I lowered my voice to a soothing tone and whispered, "*Shhht*, my boy. We will make this as right as we possibly can. We just have to be smart about it."

I've always had a soft spot for Kawa. He dealt with his anger and post-traumatic stress by hating everyone around him. It became part of him, and it was time to heal and trust. I closed my eyes, holding him, telling him it would be okay. That he is safe and we have him. I have him. "Together we will try our best to reverse this cluster fuck. We must be careful because if we change the past, the future changes, and if we don't calculate all angles, this can go on forever. Apsu can escape, but Phoenix may never arrive in Anzulla. There are things Eryn and Ish must plan before taking any steps to change the past. At this stage, the past is what it is. It can't run away or disappear. According to Ish, he can step back in time, but the more people involved, the more complicated it becomes. If we change things, say we send Ish to warn them, then how do we let Eryn know in the future to come from Gu's village to meet up? Stopping Apsu would have to happen in the past. Ish can only time-walk short distances, to places he has already been. It's much more complicated, and Lasitor has warned Ish many times over, in fact, he has forbidden him to do it. How will we be ready if we don't know what has happened? Understand?" I gently explained as Kawa cried into my shoulder.

"It makes sense, I'm sorry," he said, pushing me away and wiping his nose with his sleeve. Sarinka and Donali embraced him. "Just tell us how we can help so we can bring them back. I won't accept their deaths must look like that. They don't deserve it," he said with a quivering bottom lip.

AFTER ISH HAD PARKED the Horizon inside the crystal cave, Eryn joined him and they left with the time machine to find Apsu.

I began the destruction process of the Horizon by first filling it with aluminum potassium sulfate, a chemical typically used by children to grow crystals in school classroom experiments. We borrowed it from the Phoenix sewerage system for our own experiment, only on a much bigger scale. This metal sulfate was essential for our plan because the outer shell of our ship was made of a metal that would not bend or crack when frozen or heated alone. However, as the crystals grew and expanded over time, cracks would inevitably form. So, we poured the mixture through the canon ports and slowly added seed crystals collected from light tunnels before filling the ship with water directly from the waterfalls. Once everything was in place, we opened the valves and blasted the shell with liquid nitrogen. The temperature inside dropped to an icy minus three hundred and forty-six degrees Fahrenheit before heating back up to match the current heat of ninety-five degrees Fahrenheit inside the crystal cave. This drastic temperature change created the perfect conditions for crystal formation within the pressure cooker. As each inch of space inside the Horizon crystallized, it became impenetrable and resembled a massive piece of quartz crystal. There would be no way to salvage the ship without shattering it into pieces.

Our fallen friends' bodies were quickly, albeit hopefully only temporarily, buried under the baobab trees while Ish and Eryn time-walked, searching for Apsu. If we successfully saved Brad and the others, by killing Apsu before he had his chance, Ish and Eryn would return here, as they decided this crystal cave was their new anchor point. Brad, Rick, Mika, Connor, Paul, Simon, Jaundre, and Andrew would continue on their retirement vacation without knowing any better. Lasitor ran the probabilities by Eryn and Ish before they left, and the final plan of action seemed to be the best and safest course to take. It would minimize change for everyone. It would be as if this morning never happened.

Hands on my hips, I stood watching our handiwork of the day. Gugusan and his warriors were breaking up the ingenious bamboo water pipe system they had erected to divert water from the waterfalls. I suggested they take the bamboo with them, but they said it was not worth carrying it all the way, and they didn't need it, because the irrigation system I helped them build was still working fine.

Whoop-whoop!

A thunderous crashing noise and commotion coming from the entrance of the cave forced me to swing around and brace for impact. The crystal cave lit up and darkened as if lightning struck inside and ricocheted around us—reflected by the crystals. Half-blinded and disorientated, I searched for the origin and the direction of the bright light. My ears zinged as I turned in circles, making sense of what was happening.

The high-pitched ringing in my ears subsided and my vision returned after being temporarily blinded. "Peter!" I narrowed my eyes turning toward my name being called.

The next second Luci with Elijah and Groda in his arms, followed by Georgio, jetted our way. "Peter, come! They're fighting in the clearing."

I jumped to follow, halted, and shouted to Gu, who seemed just as dazed. "Are you coming?" He lifted his leg, and using his foot he pushed the whole bamboo pipes system over so the water could flow along its usual path. "We'll clean that up later. Come, Ish will need an army." I took the shortcut with the Birdmen, flying up and through one of the red crystalized light tunnels in the roof of the cave, while the others followed through the footpath tunnels below.

Far in the distance, in the clearing at the foot of the mountain, between the two rivers, a gigantic translucent super bowl-sized bubble jiggled as firebombs exploded like Hiroshima and Nagasaki. Just as I landed, Gugusan and the others joined us. At first, I couldn't find my voice as what I was seeing was being computed far too slowly. Inside the bubble, Eryn zipped around so fast his silhouette blurred. But he was alone, just as tall with a spear in hand, opposing Apsu.

"Holy fucking shit! Apsu is a freaking...minotaur...no, no, no! That's a satyr! A fucking claw-handed, fire-throwing mythical creature! No wonder Babylon was flattened and almost wiped from the face of the Earth. I'm starting to be a believer in the Bible, the Quran, and the Torah. He's the fucking devil. And where is Ishtar?" I searched frantically. Shielding my eyes, I scanned the inside and outside of their barrier.

"He's also there. I saw him a few seconds ago," Georgio said, not taking his gaze off the fight. I looked at him, bewildered and afraid.

Muscles quivering. Inhaling, exhaling, and searching.

Clenching and releasing my fists.

Jerking left and right, wanting to take flight and fight.

Heaving, my chest expanded and retracted.

My wings twitched.

My throat, dry as I gulped.

My lips moved, but no sound escaped.

My body, ice-cold and burning.

Then a glimpse of my lover struck me with relief. Ish was moving in and out of time, where we couldn't see, where Apsu couldn't see or go.

"Thank fuck!" I sighed. We watched as Eryn jumped back just in time, so Apsu's claw raked his arm rather than his torso. The sight of his blood, the red drops sprinkling across the inside of the translucent barrier, brought a round of gasps as Eryn reared back, holding his arm.

"Where are Ivan and Cian?" I asked, just as Apsu came full speed at Eryn.

Zip-doof, zip-doof, zip-doof! He threw bombs, jumped, and almost decapitated our future king. *Jesus Christ, I can't watch shit like this.*

We were all wide-eyed, astonished, and disgusted by Apsu's savagery. Hundreds of shaken spectators gathered around the bubble. What would happen if Eryn died, if the bubble popped and we stood here at Apsu's mercy? He could kill all of us with one fireball.

That bubble better fucking hold.

The mundaneness of my life before Ishtar is laughable. This is what Ishtar's life was before Grayrak, before us, the madness of pure evil trying to kill men with pure love and goodness in their hearts. We could only stand and watch.

Jubilant screams echoed down the hills.

Eryn jumped over Apsu and Ish helped him disappear and then reappear, forcing Apsu to spin in a circle, slicing the air and missing. Eryn stabbed him. More blood splattered, but this time it was Apsu's. Each time Eryn struck home with his spear or Ish appeared, sliced, and vanished, the level of entertainment rose.

This was like gladiatorial games, but this time the rulers fought for the entertainment of us all. Ish and Eryn were a team, and Apsu couldn't keep up with their onslaught. His blue bull head was flecked with his own blood.

"It's the beast. He must die. He will die," Elijah said next to me, chewing his nails, his gaze locked on the fight —fireball lights glinting in his unblinking eyes.

"This must be the pinnacle of your life, Elijah."

"Yes, yes, I told you. But you never listen."

"If I didn't save your ass, if Andrew didn't make you new, fast, and strong, you would never have seen this," I muttered, jabbing him with the truth. He sucked his teeth at me, clucking his tongue.

Eryn and Ish circled Apsu, their prey. Eryn had tied a

piece of cloth ripped from his shirt around his bleeding forearm. The next moment, a rush of wind passed me as Ivan, Cian, and Barkor ran, nearly colliding with the enclosure bubble. Ivan gasped and Eryn looked away for a second. Apsu used the distraction to throw fire at Ish while simultaneously jumping to stab Eryn. Eryn blocked him but fell backward. Ish disappeared and reappeared, reaching for Eryn. As soon as the Brawl King touched Ish, both vanished, leaving Apsu spinning.

"No!" Ivan unsheathed his sword, readying himself to jump and help his husband. Luckily, Cian and Barkor were level-headed. Despite their combined strength, they struggled to wrestle him down, to hold him back.

"Fuck, can't they see they are distracting Eryn?" I grunted. "Luci, Elijah, Groda, yes you too, Georgio, let's contain that idiot. For fuck's sake!" We tackled Ivan. I wrapped my arms around his waist. Luci and Groda took his arms and Elijah and Georgio each immobilized a leg. Cian and Barkor joined as we dragged Ivan back with us. Seven of us were against Ivan, and even so, he managed to almost break loose.

"We have to help him. Let go of me. I want to go help him!"

"Ivan, you can't. You can't break the barrier for one, and two, Ishtar and Eryn were fine until you came and distracted him. Shut up!" I said, smashing a hand over his mouth. He snorted like a maniac through his nose, seeing red. "Look!" I turned so he could see how Eryn reappeared on the left and Ish on the right of Apsu. Eryn jabbed his spear into Apsu's chest while Ish sliced the back of his knees. Eryn removed his spear from Apsu's bleeding torso and then pushed his spear right through Apsu's skull. Ishtar lifted his swords, crossed his arms, and decapitated Apsu, leaving the animal's head impaled on Eryn's spear. The torso toppled over. Puffs of vapor, like an extinguishing fire, escaping from it. My heart beat a million beats per minute as I cringed at the brutality. It crushed the innocence of many Phoenicians. It was beyond horrific. Eryn slammed the head to the ground, stepped on it with his boot, and yanked his spear from it. The enormity of this cruel hand-to-hand battle was of unforgettable magnitude. Ishtar lifted his swords and howled their victory into the night. Eryn shook his head and flung himself around, searching for Ivan.

"Let go of me, let me fucking go!" Ivan struggled, and we let him go free. Eryn popped the bubble with the tip of his spear, then opened his arms for Ivan to fall into them. That was my cue. I jumped and swooped over to Ish, diving into his wide-open arms. I collided with him, chest to chest, as I scooped him up, with my arms under his armpits. We shot over the battled ground, landing with an oomph, and skidded over the wet grass while we kissed. When we came to a halt, confusion about where I was and how I got here hit me. Ish smiled at me. I got up and offered him a hand to pull him to his feet.

"What the fuck happened? Did I hit my head or something?" Ish was wet, covered in blood and sweat. "Are you wounded?" I patted him down and checked to see where to plug the blood-gushing holes. Finding none, I patted myself furiously, searching for painful spots.

"It's Apsu's blood," Ish told me and pulled me closer. Then, like a little boy, picked me up and spun us around. "It was close, my Kuku, but we stopped him. We trapped, destroyed, and plucked him from the doorstep of Phoenix to defeat him here today. Just in time." Ish seemed ecstatic, but that was not what I remembered happening today. I wiggled my body so he could put me down.

Ivan, Cian, and Barkor stepped closer. Eryn embraced Ish, and they hugged again, congratulating each other.

"Just in time for what?" I asked, unsure if I wanted to know the answer.

"Yeah, tell us, because suddenly I have that feeling again. That feeling that all is not right," Cian said side-eyeing us.

Ish looked so happy. "Eryn helped me, we were just in time to prevent Apsu and the Zelk from discovering the entrance of Phoenix."

"No fucking way!" Ivan exclaimed.

"Okay?" The frown forming on my forehead was so deep I might as well give myself a craniotomy.

"Please explain, because Apsu had killed the Leadership team of Phoenix, here in Anzulla this morning. Maybe I dreamed it? Did I dream Brad was killed and cut in half?" I asked, searching the faces around us for answers.

For confirmation. For this to make sense.

Everyone else was as baffled as I was.

Ish laughed, breaking the what-the-fuck moment we had up. He waved at the absurdity of my question as if pure nonsense. "Yes, it was a nightmare from another timeline. Let your memories of Apsu and us killing him and the Zelk be a momentous moment in time."

"It's confusing, isn't it?" Cian said and shoulder bumped me. "I told all of you this is not my people, and now look where we are." He pointed to the ocean. The time machine lay beached as if it had skidded over the water and nose planted in the sandy dune.

"It's strange. It's as if I was here, before. A déjà vu feeling," I said to them while Ish was turning red, he was hiding something from me. The heat of his guilt was hotter than hell's blazing fires.

"More like déjà poo, because it feels like I've heard this shit before," Cian joked.

But then, Ish asked me a strange question. "Where are Juandre and Andrew?"

I looked left and right, thinking I must have knocked my head. "You know where. With Brad and the others? You know that. They preferred to retire, they're on vacation." I studied Ish's face. He turned to Eryn and winked. "What the fuck aren't you telling me?"

"Nothing, my Kuku, all is as it should be. Phoenix is safe. The humans are safe." He pointed to his ship where inquisitive Birdmen were peeking inside it.

Gulping around the lump in my throat, I held up a pointing finger. "I swear, no...I must have dreamed it." Everyone's eyes were on me as if whatever I was about to say was determining our futures moving forward. I raked my fingers through my hair and pulled at it. Ish and the others waited for me to say something. "Nah, now that I think about it, maybe it was a foreboding thought or dream. I was filling the Horizon with waterfall water inside the crystal caves. Yeah, that's what it was. We've done that, haven't we?" Everywhere I looked, heads were turned my way and agreeing with me.

Ish squeezed my shoulder. "It happens, my Kuku. It's fine. Give it a few minutes. I don't want you to be upset or confused. That's why Lasitor forbids switching timelines. Eryn and I had to run Apsu down and cut him, the head of the Zelk, off." Ish chuckled. "We literally and figuratively cut his head off. Moving the Zelk from one reality to the other was causing so much trouble and was bleeding through to Anzulla."

"So, how long have you been gone? Because to us it feels like hours." I asked, searching his face.

"Weeks," Ish said.

"One and a half month," Eryn said. I checked in with the others. They shrugged with that-is-not-too-bad expressions on their faces.

"Where is the egg? Did you break the egg?" Luci asked. I pointed to the beach in the distance where the ship glinted in the rising sunlight, breaking the dark blues of the sky into hues of purples and pinks.

Gugusan tapped my arm. He gave me an I-told-you-so look. "Kuku, this is the story of the San people. Of you and Ishtar, our blue demon God, searching for his Birdman God. Over and over and over, tricking us."

"No tricks, just as it was foretold, fuck yeah, it was!" Elijah shouted with his fists in the air.

Relief settled inside my stomach. I watched Ish for a moment. Perceptions and thoughts jumped from memory to memory. Solidifying that this was real, where I always wanted to be. With my Ish, my blue-fanged Anunnaki in Anzulla at the foot of our mountain.

"Let's go help our flock of humans, I told them to hide and wait for us inside Phoenix," Barkor urged, pulling Cian by the arm after him.

"I suggest we park and hide my ship inside the crystal cave," Ishtar said.

"Ivan and I will go burn Apsu's body, and scatter his ashes to the wind. Just in case…" Eryn said, grinning and seemingly happy to go do something productive with Ivan.

"Come, I want to take care of you," I said, wiping the blood dripping from Ish's bruised cheek. His pupils were blown wide by residual adrenalin.

He took both of my hands and sighed. My insides warmed under his intense stare. He was fierce, and he was also so gentle.

"I love you so much. You are my everything," I whispered with tears burning my eyeballs.

"I love you too, my Kuku. Very much." He smiled, looking scary and beautiful while the corners of his eyes crinkled at the corners.

"Good, now, let's go home."

"To our mountain?" His face lit up and he squeezed my hands tighter.

"Yes, to our mountain."

EPILOGUE

ISHTAR
Five years later

HAPPY, carefree, and in love, I leaned in closer, gently rubbing my nose against my Kuku's warm lips and soft whiskers, our breaths mingling as we sighed, cherishing the simple joy of togetherness and the tranquility of the moment. We'd been basking under the crystal-filtered light for an hour, or so. I wouldn't know precisely, because none of us carried a tick-tick thing or wrist communicator anymore.

"Do you have them in sight?" Peter asked into my mouth, licking my fangs up and down.

"I can't keep my eyes open if you do that to me." I chuckled and broke the kiss, trying to get a visual of our boys, where they were playing, searching for frogs and crabs and anything that crawled, jumped, and wiggled. It took me a second to spot them. I felt they were starting to get restless and bored. That meant they would be venturing too far away from us.

I shouted, "Fifteen minutes, then it's time to go, boys!" The triplets turned and waved, acknowledging my words, while the waterfall splashed onto the mossy green rocks, muffling their replies.

My Kuku and I cherished our alone time in the early mornings. When Zala, Nebo, and Kail were busy exploring, we discovered a fine balance between allowing them to venture off so we have some precious minutes of papa-time, and them disappearing into some uncharted crystal tunnel and getting stuck in it. The whole mountain was turned upside down last week as we searched for our four-year-olds. Those wings get stuck like fishhooks when they crawl into tight spaces—no pulling them out by the ankles. No, we had to unearth mountains of crystals to tunnel beside them and excavate their cute little fat butts out to safety. The ordeal was still fresh in their minds, so hopefully, they won't be trying that again—soon.

Between grooming and loving each other, we constantly had to keep a third eye open, monitoring our blue chubby toddlers. I turned to Kuku and raised his chin so our eyes met. "Thank you," I said softly.

He responded with a lazy yawn and asked, "For what?"

"For waiting for me, for showing me love and giving me a family—for our boys. And for the child tracking chips. We should have inserted them earlier."

He stretched his body, flexing his arms and legs. We'd

just finished our routine of feather cleaning, and he was relaxed and purring in my arms. I loved providing him relief from the itchiness caused by the waxy protection of the newly ingrown plumes.

"If I knew they'd poof-poof-poof away like their daddy, I would've implanted tracers when they were fetuses. I didn't do it just for you. I was selfish."

"Yeah, so selfishly the best father ever. The smartest, the strongest, and the sexiest," I said in between pecks of kisses. "It's because of you that we have three beautiful children." I kissed him deeply, hugging him so tight that he felt how much he meant to me.

"And because of your extremely viable sperm count. Your stunning genes," he said and kissed each of my eyes.

I soaked up the love and countered, "Yours too."

"Not my sperm."

"It doesn't matter because our children have a mix of our DNA, evident by their pretty little white wings," I said playfully.

Time seemed to stand still as we absorbed the beauty of our family and the breathtaking, gigantic crystal cave around us. Parts of the once-forgotten and overgrown buildings were already restored, and the underground city buzzed with crystal light flickering from inside the buildings where new residents were moving in, playing home, and creating a new, vibrant Anunnaki underground city.

The Heart of Anzulla.

We had created a home filled with love, laughter, and endless possibilities. The rhythmic splashing sounds of the waterfall provided a soothing backdrop to our thoughts.

As the fifteen minutes came to an end, we called our boys back to us. Jumping from boulder to boulder, they leaped, taking to the air. Their blue-fanged faces beamed with joy as they fluttered closer. Their expressions were pure joy and excitement as they eagerly made their way toward our private sunbathing balcony with an extended platform for landing and taking off.

"Look how happy they are. I never thought my happiness would be looking like this—a mate, three inquisitive baby demon gods."

"Don't forget intelligent," Peter added.

"Of course, and for an eternity together."

"You are everything to me. All four of you," he said with a triple oomph to the chest as our children bombarded his waiting arms.

Every day, we expressed our deep appreciation and unwavering commitment to one another. Each day, an overwhelming wave of gratitude and love washed over me. I stood beside them, feeling the comforting embrace of my Kuku's wings enveloping us. The pure red crystal-infused light carried an extra layer of warmth, creating a tenderness, an essence of our affection inside us from absorbing it.

"My four blue men," he murmured, his voice filled with emotion. "Come, Bastian!" Peter patted the side of his leg. "Come, boy!" He called, and our newborn Anubis pup fell over his paws to meet up with us. Bastian was the first pup born since Igor, Rotty, and Devil.

"Did you boys have fun? Are you hungry?"

"Yes, yes, yes, Papa!" they chirped together.

Hand in hand, my Kuku and I led our little flock back toward the communal Loursveto garden for our midday meal. As we walked, the boys chatted non-stop, eagerly sharing details of their morning's adventures and discoveries.

"I love you," I whispered into the shell of his ear.

"For now and forever," he added with a proud, radiant smile—my beacon of joy.

"There they are!" Brad hollered, waving at us with a fork in his hand. We joined our friends at the extra-long table in the center of the Loursveto garden, where Rick, Connor, Mika, Paul, Simon, Juandre, Andrew, Gugusan, Donali, Sarinka, Kawa, Cian, Barkor, Eryn, Ivan, Bryan, and Tony were waiting for us to join them.

THE END.

TIMELINE

25 000 B.C. Ishtar arrives at the San tribe.

25 000 B.C. Peter and Elijah jump to Anzulla.

24 970 B.C. Ishtar and Peter's crash landing.

24 970 B.C. The next day, Gugusan receives news that Ish is being held captive. Peter rescues Ishtar, thirty years after he had jumped with Elijah to Anzulla.

24 970 B.C. That night, Elijah and Peter arrive by boat at the San village. Peter gets his wings and brings the apple to the San.

24 970 B.C. Ishtar visits Anzulla, and Gugusan gives him the apple.

24 970 B.C. (Cian and his brothers arrived in Grayrak

93 A.T.) Ishtar slipped away to say goodbye to Gugusan and then met Peter for the first time.

23 000 B.C. Anzulla, Ishtar, receives a mission from the Fates.

3500 B.C. Hours before the war with Apsu, Ishtar and Peter bring the apple to Babylon. They rescue Elijah and seek help from Andrew in 2013 A.D.

3500 B.C. Ishtar's story begins at age 250 years of age. He defeats his father for the first time during their uprising. *Anzulla, According to ISH: New Beginnings Book Three.*

1968 A.D. Young André (Andrew) and Peter meet Ishtar and older Peter. (No wings yet.)

2004 A.D. Juandre and Andrew's story begins. (Just Like a Butterfly.)

2013 A.D. Ishtar, Peter, and Elijah visit Lord Andrew Whiskey Distilleries, Lexington, Kentucky.

2014 A.D. Timeline Switch. Andrew goes to Juandre, they fall in love and mate. *Just like a Butterfly: A New Beginnings Novella*

2041 A.D. to 2043 A.D. (3-5 years before Doomsday.) Eryn and his brothers are born.

2046 A.D. DOOMSDAY. Worldwide breakout of Neurotoxic biochemicals. Nuclear Winter follows.

The story of the men of Phoenix begins - *Phoenix Code: New Beginnings Prequel*

Ishtar arrives on the moon and waits for Cian, Ivan, and Eryn while guarding Barkor in Grayrak.

Then, after Ishtar meets Peter for the first time in

Phoenix, 2146 A.D. (94 A.T.) he jumps back to 2046 A.D. to update Lasitor.

2051 A.D. (5 years after Doomsday.) The marriage of Mika and Connor takes place.

2052 A.D. (6 years after Doomsday.) The Big Flood (Tsunamis) happens, and, on that same day, the Romanov twins are born, marking it as the Year of the Twins: 0 A.T.

2058 A.D. (6 A.T.) The story of Eryn begins. *Eryn, King of the Brawl: New Beginnings M/M Series Part One*

2073 A.D. (21 A.T.) Mika and Brad find the apple in the Disciples of the Anunnaki's confiscated loot. Cian and Ivan's Anunnaki heritage is revealed. Eryn makes each a sword of gold by dividing the forks on his trident so that they can focus their power on wrapping Phoenix in a protective layer to save their city from a string of global volcanic eruptions that led to the almost-instantaneous melting of the polar ice caps and global storms, turning Earth on its axis.

2124 A.D. (72 A.T.) Cian's first sighting of the hydrogen mining ship of the Zelk.

2145 A.D. (93 A.T.) Cian's story begins. *Cian's Song: New Beginnings M/M Series Part Two.*

2146 A.D. (94 A.T.) After finding and losing his mate, Ishtar meets Peter for the second time. This is also Peter's second meeting, but he had already met Ishtar back in 1968 A.D.)

Ishtar returns to Grayrak with Cian after meeting his Peter, grab his ship, jumps to Phoenix for a reboot, then returns to gather Peter to jump to 1968 A.D.

2147 A.D. (95 A.T.) Cian and his brothers evacuate

Grayrak and take the last of the remaining humans with Barkor home to Phoenix. Rebirth of Earth's Timeline. Ishtar moves the Zelk to an alternate timeline to prevent them from attacking the Warship Horizon or Earth. Lots of shit goes down in this year!

2147 A.D. (95 A.T.) Mika and the Leadership Team of Phoenix want answers. Ishtar gets taken into custody for questioning right after the Warship Horizon lands on Earth's watery surface. His ship and pendant are taken away from him. His inquisition starts.

2147 A.D. (95 A.T.) Three days into questioning, Ishtar and Peter escape with the apple, pendant, and ship then crash in Anzulla.

2147 A.D. (95 A.T.) Ishtar and Peter return to Phoenix to ask for help. (After Peter had rescued Ish.)

2148 A.D. (96 A.T.) Ishtar and Cian save Phoenix.

AFTERWORD

ABOUT THE AUTHOR

"I found it surprisingly beautiful. In a brutal, horribly uncomfortable sort of way." —Tyrion Lannister to Janos Slynt.

I am a Canadian speculative Male/Male Sci-Fi Fantasy and Paranormal Romance writer. I currently reside in the Rocky Mountains of beautiful British Columbia, Canada.

My writing explores who we are, where we come from, and where we are going as a human race on Earth.

I like to weave and bubblegum questions and subjects by creating new, exciting worlds and characters. My stories are unpredictable, twisted with a dash of humor, and centered on gay characters.

You will question your existence among these worlds and wish you could escape to these places filled with foul-mouthed heroes who struggle and strive to save humankind.

I hope you've discovered something that excites and intrigues you. Please share your thoughts by leaving a review or visit www.kashelchar.com to contact me or learn about my latest works.

www.ingramcontent.com/pod-product-compliance
Lightning Source LLC
Chambersburg PA
CBHW030738030726
47497CB00001B/34